T0282827

ST. LOUIS SAM
AND THE DESPERADOS

ST. LOUIS SAM AND THE DESPERADOS

PINKIE PARANYA

THORNDIKE PRESS
A part of Gale, a Cengage Company

LIBRARY OF CONGRESS CIP DATA ON FILE.
CATALOGUING IN PUBLICATION FOR THIS BOOK
IS AVAILABLE FROM THE LIBRARY OF CONGRESS.

ISBN-13: 978-1-4328-7110-9 (softcover alk. paper)

Published in 2021 by arrangement with Pinkie Paranya

Printed in the United States of America
1 2 3 4 5   25 24 23 22 21

St. Louis Sam
and the Desperados

CHAPTER 1

Arizona Territory, 1874

"Sam! Grab this pistol and hit the floor," Garth shouted when masked men armed with rifles and guns galloped after their stagecoach.

Samantha watched her brother reach into his canvas bag and draw out two pistols, handing her one. She grabbed the gun and peered out her window while the stage rocked and chattered along the dusty trail. She heard the driver holler, "Whoa," but the horses had their own idea about when to stop. In the other window Garth must have scored a few hits, judging from the curses and the shrill neigh of a horse. The stage guard's rifle boomed, the sound echoing across the desert floor above the noise of galloping horses and shouts from the outlaws.

Sam spared a look down at the other two passengers, a couple in their sixties, lying flat on the floor with their hands covering their heads. The attack had happened so quickly, Sam hadn't had time to be scared. She reached under the seat for the small case she always kept at her side, removed her pad and pencil, and started to scribble hurriedly.

"Sam!" Garth shouted. "What in the Hades are you doing?"

He sounded breathless, not to mention irritated, but didn't take time to look at her again. She made one last entry in her notebook and tossed it aside. Picking up the pistol, she closed one eye and aimed the weapon out of her window at a horse and rider barreling so close, she could see the man's narrowed ugly eyes and his long, stringy beard. At the last moment she couldn't aim to kill another human being and shot into the air above him. His hat flew off, spinning into the air, frightening his horse, and he jerked the reins away from the coach.

Only a week ago Garth had made her practice holding and firing the heavy revolver. She had to give him credit for thinking ahead. The roar of the rifle from the top of the stage ceased and the sounds of pounding hooves receded across the desert. The stage came to an abrupt stop. Sam struggled with her long skirt and petticoat, trying to get up off her knees where she had hunkered down by the window. Her corset must have turned sideways, and she wondered how she would get it back where it belonged so she could breathe again.

Garth reached to open the stage door and jumped out, grinning, his sandy hair awry, his once immaculate waistcoat smudged and wrinkled. He had lost his new flat-brimmed Stetson when he stuck his head an alarming way out of the window to take aim, but the loss didn't bother him.

"Good shooting, Sam. Haven't we come to a grand place? Imagine this happening back in St. Louis." He laughed and she wanted to slap him. Thankfully he didn't notice the scattered notebook, and she shoved it underneath the seat.

Her thoughts retreated briefly to the quiet veranda of their elegant home back in St. Louis. They had come so far since the death of their father and had both grown in so many ways.

She bent to help the elderly couple upright. They appeared quite shaken but unharmed.

"Gracious," the frail-looking woman sighed. "Does this sort of thing occur often?" She straightened her bonnet with trembling fingers and glared at her husband as if the recent ruckus were entirely his fault.

Garth shrugged with what he probably considered world-weary nonchalance. "Just about every day you can expect something like this happening out here. This *is* the West, you know."

Samantha looked out the window to let the couple assimilate what she hoped was Garth's flagrant exaggeration. A lot *he* knew about the subject, except for those dime novels he devoured about gunslingers and wild men of the West. She turned to glare at her brother and scolded.

"I'm sure you overstate things. These poor folks are shaken enough without your prattling on."

His expression was unrepentant. "I hoped you'd quit acting like my mother, just because you're three years older than me, Sam. This is a new life we're starting."

By then the guard jumped down and opened the door. "Everyone all right in here?"

The elderly couple glared at him. Clearly, the whole episode reflected mismanagement on his part.

The guard's glance slid past the couple and landed on Garth. "Say, young fella, that was mighty fine shootin', 'specially for an

Easterner."

Garth puffed up with the man-to-man praise until Sam was sure the buttons on his vest would pop off, one by one. She hid a smile behind her glove and gingerly laid her gun on the stage floor.

The driver climbed down from his perch and looked at them each in turn as they descended from the coach. "Reckon you'll have to walk to the relay station. It ain't more'n a mile. Ben will walk with you to be sure you're safe." He stared down the outraged look the guard shot him. "Axle's broke, or leastwise bent bad. If we can make it to the station, they'll fix it for us so we can go on."

The couple looked startled at the notion of walking a mile in the desert with the warm breeze blowing dust. "Surely those ruffians will not return to plague us whilst we walk, will they?" The lady straightened her skirt and smoothed out a wrinkle that seemed to annoy her more than the threat of returning ruffians.

"No, ma'am, I doubt they'll be back. From here on it's just rattlesnakes, Gila monsters, jumping cactus, and prairie dog holes you might step in along the way. Ben can watch out for you all."

"Wait up a second," Sam said, opening

the stage door and retrieving her writing equipment.

"I thought you were going back for your parasol or something," Garth said, pointing to the elderly lady who had hers held firmly aloft. "I should have known. Was that why you didn't start shooting right away? Some help." He sniffed in disgust.

Sam scribbled in the notepad while they walked along. "I've decided to write a western romance. They are very popular now. But I need to record our adventures in case I forget anything important."

"Well, I hope that is the last of that kind of adventure," Garth said, laughing.

Garth and Sam both preferred walking in the heat of the desert to sitting any longer in the bouncing stagecoach anyway. Sam lifted her skirts as high as she dared, careful not to go above the top button of her boots, matching Garth stride for stride as they walked along.

"Where did you lose your new hat?" She felt grateful for the bonnet she'd retrieved from the coach and worried about Garth's bare head.

"I guess it blew away while I was busy shooting." Garth kicked stones out of his way. He'd mentioned that his new boots needed to look more "lived in." If they'd found his hat, it probably would have served that purpose too.

Plodding along gave Sam time to rethink this past month. Moving from solid and proper St. Louis, Missouri, to Arizona was akin to traveling down the Amazon in Brazil.

"If only Uncle Millard hadn't been such an unmitigated bastard." Sam spoke out loud without realizing it and saw the amused look Garth shot her.

"Not ladylike, dear sister." He shook his finger at her in mock rebuke.

It had always been hard for her to draw the line between the unladylike language and behavior she used on necessary occasions, and the prim, genteel appearance she'd been brought up with when their aunt took over after their mother died. Many people who saw her were shocked at her riding their horses astride instead of with a sidesaddle. But how else could she help with their training?

Sam found it hard to believe Uncle Millard could have been so corrupt. Her mother's brother and their father had been partners in business for many years, long before the births of Samantha and Garth.

"He never wanted his beloved sister to marry George Kirkland," Sam mused. "Even though Father was a self-made millionaire, Uncle Millard always felt him beneath Mother, socially." The two families prospered through the years, branching out into banking, investments, stock market, and insurance companies. It was a shame her mother never lived to see it, but died giving birth to Garth. Uncle Millard hated baby Garth and the whole family after she died.

As if Garth read her thoughts, he broke into her reverie. "Our dear uncle must have started siphoning funds from the corporations soon after I was born. He ended up with his own private empire, leaving us with nothing."

"Well, not quite nothing, but Father shouldn't have named him our guardian. When he died, I think that's when our uncle went wild with our money."

Garth grimaced. "I'm sure not making excuses, but it couldn't have been easy living all those years with Aunt Grace." They called her Old Prune Face behind her back, and that was generous.

"A bony, mean-tempered harridan — they deserve each other," Sam said.

Uncle Millard covered his devious dealings so well that when there finally came an accounting with the companies and stockholders, he blamed his partner, their father.

Facing disgrace, maybe prison, losing his family and in a financial disaster, their father had to know what his own brother-in-law had done to him. One night he sat at his desk and put a gun to his head.

Garth and Sam were devastated when their father left them, both certain he wouldn't have, without all the provocation brought on by their uncle. It wasn't until after their father's funeral that she and Garth had begun to suspect Uncle Millard of doing the damage he had done. They knew their father would never have embezzled any money, which left only their uncle.

Samantha shuddered at the memory and tripped on a rock in her path.

"You all right, Sam?" Garth took hold of her arm. "It's a long, hot walk in all those draggy skirts, isn't it? Too bad you can't wear trousers."

She turned to him, shocked. Trousers indeed. Who ever thought of such a thing? Even for comfort, wearing trousers would not be done. When she rode the horses, her aunt had devised a split skirt and even then her legs didn't show. But in this July heat she'd sure like to get rid of her corsets. Maybe she could dump them out here where no one knew her. She would need to suffer along in her thick dresses until she could find a seamstress to make her one or two of lighter material. Back home, it was probably snowing. At least she'd swept up her long, heavy hair off her neck, and knotted it high on her head, under her bonnet. That was some comfort, even though springs of chestnut curls clung stubbornly to her sweaty cheeks.

"Will it be much farther, do you suppose?"

Garth pointed ahead. "Beyond that rise. That's the way the stagecoach disappeared at any rate. Do you want me to ask the guard?"

The huge fellow walking some feet in back of them with the old couple had slung his rifle carelessly across his shoulder.

Sam shook her head, wiping dust grains from the corner of her eyes. "Never mind. It takes too much energy to talk. Just keep walking." They continued on in silence with only the sighing of the hot wind through gnarled mesquite and palo verde trees along the road.

Sam let her thoughts go back to the night she went to Garth's room to ask him something and, after knocking and getting no answer, she pushed open the door. He wasn't there. They usually let each other know when they were going out. She sat down to wait by the fireplace in her bedroom with the door open. He bounded in about midnight, dressed all in black with a dark stocking cap pulled over his light hair. He admitted then that he'd been using the keys in their father's desk to delve into files and records at their uncle's various offices and enterprises around town. He paced the room, excited.

"He did it, Sam. I know it. Dad swore to me he didn't have anything to do with the pilfering of funds and we believed him. Even if his suicide does put a bad light on it. I've found things in Uncle Millard's desks and safes that could tell the story if I could piece it all together."

"You broke into his offices and safes?" Sam worked at keeping her voice from rising to the ceiling in disbelief.

His usual grin was gone and his lips tightened in frustrated anger. "Many times. I'm looking for evidence. What I've found so far might not hold up in court, but it makes a believer out of me. Look."

He spread papers out across her bed and went to his room, coming back with a fistful of documents. He brought out more papers hidden beneath his clothing.

They sat and looked at the pages, one by

17

one. Love letters from someone in a strange place in Arizona. Sam read a few lines and put the letter down quickly, blushing to the roots of her hair. She had a problem imagining her pudgy, pompous uncle receiving mail like that, much less answering in kind. Her glance collided with Garth's and, in spite of their bitterness against their uncle, they couldn't stop laughing.

"Look at this one," Garth said. *"My Handsome Man,"* he began in a high falsetto. *"I can hardly wait until I see your manly physique in person. I do so look forward to it.* Peachykins signed them all."

At the time, they hadn't known where to go from there. Accusing such a pillar in the community of conspiracy and murder coming from a twenty-eight-year-old woman and a twenty-five-year-old man wouldn't carry very much weight. They might even be laughed at, and where would that get them?

The very thought of Uncle Millard causing the ruination and death of their father sickened Sam. Even if their father had committed suicide, their uncle might as well have pulled the trigger on the gun. Now it was as if he hovered over their shoulders like a malignant shadow.

When her uncle entered a room, his scent

preceded him. He must have used thick pomade on his hair to keep the part precisely in the center of his head. Did he use the same pomade on his mustache and sideburns? The perfumed smell combined with the odor of cigar always let her and Garth know when he was near. But what about Aunt Grace? Did she know about his lust for power? She surely benefited by it.

That was when they made their decision to go to Arizona and take down their uncle's secret empire.

CHAPTER 2

They trudged, hot, tired, and dusty, into the relay station. At first glance it looked like nothing more than a shack stuck out in the middle of nowhere. The smells of fresh baked bread and some kind of soup or stew coming from the kitchen welcomed them. A long wooden table monopolized the center of the room, leaving barely space for chairs. An Indian woman muttered to herself in a grumpy voice while she stirred what looked like batter in a large bowl nestled in the crook of her arm. A bearded man greeted them.

"Y'all kin git washed up over there in the corner." He gestured toward the back wall. "Stage'll be fixed up afore you know it."

The driver, lounging in a chair against the opposite wall, rose to greet them with a grin. "Wasn't such a bad walk, was it?"

"Cabbagehead!" Sam whispered to Garth as she dusted off her skirts the best she could and tried to rearrange her corset without a room full of people becoming aware of her actions.

After they had taken turns at the community washbasin, they ate the stew set in front of them.

"Not bad," Garth said, using a biscuit to sop up the last of the liquid at the bottom of his bowl.

Sam decided to ignore the newfound manners he was acquiring from watching the other men who ate at the table. She excused herself to use the privy in back of the building. Looking out over the brown desert, interrupted only by a few cacti and scrawny trees, she couldn't help feeling sorry for herself. Did she attend finishing school and make her society debut for this? Well, the society debut didn't turn out spectacular. All the young men were either seeking fortunes in their prospective wives or wanted someone delicately beautiful. Sam figured she had neither accomplishment. Her Aunt Twila had told her many times she was passably pretty, with her even features and long chestnut hair. But her jawline was a mite too strong and her speech maybe a tad too forceful for a young lady. And she was tall.

If she had to stay a spinster all her life,

that wasn't a problem. She'd read the Brontë novels over and over and wanted her own Heathcliff. A strong, brooding man who would treasure her. She wanted a marriage like her mother and father had. Not likely to find that out here, but she'd determined never to settle for less.

Garth came to join her on the rough wooden bench in the backyard.

"Do you think Uncle Millard will suspect us of coming here?" Sam asked.

"I don't see how he could. You wrote him a letter your friend in New York will forward. We explained that we were taking a European tour."

"Mother was such a dear, leaving us all that money without any strings. If she'd tied it to the business like Father did, we wouldn't have a dime to call our own. We'd be at his mercy."

Garth bent, picking up a smooth rock and throwing it across the desert floor. "Eventually he'll grab that monstrosity of a house we never called home. I hope he and Aunt Grace will enjoy it while they can." His voice hardened.

"What will happen to Aunt Twila? She didn't want us to leave, even though we weren't exactly honest about where we were going. Will he kick her out?"

"His taking over the house won't happen that fast. He has to go through channels."

"Can't figure out why Father bought the house in the first place. He didn't care for it either."

"I reckon he wanted it for Mother and you, especially, to look good 'coming out.' The stables were perfect for raising and training show horses."

"Humph! Did you say 'reckon'?" Sam turned to look at him, a big grin on her face.

Garth gave a sheepish laugh. "I have to practice speaking 'western,' don't I? In the books I've read, they kind of talk that way. Speaking of books, how is ours coming along? You sure have plenty of fodder if you intend to write a western. Where the romance comes in, I'm not sure you are experienced enough for that." He snickered. "But I would think that falls in a man's province — the western part, I mean."

Sam nudged him with her elbow. "I think we have read too many books, that's why I need to write one, from firsthand information and a female point of view." She had already described the stage house and the inhabitants in her notes so far.

"Speaking of books, we never talked of it much." Garth darted a look around to see if anyone was near. "My plan is to break into his offices, banks and places he owns near Powder Keg. I'll take pages from his book-keeping journals; steal documents and maybe stock certificates, and bearer bonds — things that will make him have to re-imburse his customers. That should take a bite out of his fortune."

Sam knew Garth had learned lock picking at military school. Not something to brag about, surely. "We decided to stay in Powder Keg, didn't we? You said that Wyatt Earp is a famous lawman and presides over Tomb-stone. That should put us far enough away so he might not notice us. That is, if you don't overdo your forays," she said.

"I was hoping you wouldn't keep pulling that 'big sister' stuff on me, Sam. I'm as much an adult as you are."

She laughed. "Phooey. I'm twice as mature as you and you know it, little brother."

"That makes you a really ancient old spinster on the shelf at twenty-eight then, doesn't it?" He laughed and ran inside to avoid the stone she picked up to throw at him.

The stagecoach traveled through the night, rocking along as if trying to make up for lost time. The older couple who had started out with them, suffering through the robbery attempt and walking across the desert to the stage stop, slept leaning against each other, snoring gently.

Garth tried a tentative whisper, encouraged by the fact that the couple didn't awaken. "We'll be in Powder Keg before you know it. Nervous?"

The moon was rising from behind a background of rugged mountains, throwing an eerie film of silver across the desert. Sam's face looked almost ghostly above her dark dress. She had a slight tan from working outside with horses and a definite set to her jaw at times, which he supposed wasn't what the young bucks wanted in a prospective wife. He hoped she was up to what they had set out to do. He was sure his sister had a backbone of steel hidden beneath her sometimes prissy behavior. For certain, she hated Millard Tremayne as much as he did. He moved his gaze from her to stare out at the flat desert with dry sagebrush strewn across the landscape, all in ghostly shadows. When he turned back, his jaw felt tight in an effort to speak low.

"We have to clear Father's name. I doubt we'll ever find out for sure how he died though. It's only right that Uncle Millard gets his comeuppance and we get back the money that rightfully belongs to us. He's spending a fortune setting up this dynasty out here. I'd bet my last dollar that he intends to flee St. Louis and Aunt Grace, and at the right time, disappear as far as he can get — away from the scandal of Father's death and the embezzlement talk."

"You're right, of course. We can't let him get away with it." Samantha refused to think of her uncle coming out victorious.

She had closed her eyes, and the reddish crescents of her lashes lay against her cheeks. Garth felt as if they'd both grown up in a heck of a hurry. He was now the head of the family, but was he up to it? All he'd ever done in his short years was to play at being the son of a wealthy businessman, without a care in the world. The same with Samantha. After finishing school, she took up working with horses at the jumping ring near their home. She'd never liked to stay indoors if she could help it. They'd always had nannies and servants.

He tried to see her from a stranger's point of view. She was almost as tall as he, and slender, which might have driven some of her would-be suitors away. She could have been called pretty, but that description was too simple. She was more than pretty, if he had to be honest. As a whole, her features were interesting, in an engaging arrangement that fell just short of being striking. He grimaced, thinking he'd better toughen up if he wanted to survive out here.

Sam opened her eyes, searching his face as if for answers. "What we'll be doing is criminal and outside the law," she reminded him.

He combed fingers through his hair as he always did when agitated. The gesture postponed an immediate answer, giving him time to think. "I know. And if we are caught, we face serious consequences. But Sis, we *have* to right this wrong." He tried to keep a grin from his expression. That would set her off. But he intended to *enjoy* this adventure.

CHAPTER 3

They arrived in Powder Keg at midnight, but it might as well have been noon. The saloons up and down the dusty street were ablaze with lights, and raucous music filled the air from at least a half-dozen out-of-tune pianos.

As the coachman dumped their luggage to the ground, Garth and Samantha flinched on hearing a smashing of furniture and breaking glass in a nearby saloon. The driver grinned.

"You two tenderfeet, you'd best hightail it to Crazy Kate's boardinghouse. It ain't much — reckon it's nowhere near what you're used to — but she's a good old gal, no harm to her. Unless you got someone meeting you?" His bushy eyebrows rose in a question mark.

"Nope," Garth answered for both of them. "Point out the direction of the rooming house. About anything will look good to us as long as it doesn't have wheels under it. I swear, I've been bounced on every square inch of my body." He looked at Samantha. "Lucky for you to have all those, ah — petticoats and wrappings to protect you."

"Garth!" Imagine discussing her underwear in front of the stagecoach men!

The boardinghouse wasn't far. The driver and his partner helped them carry their luggage to the porch. Garth knocked while they stood waiting for at least ten minutes before they roused the woman. She thumped loudly down the stairs and when she flung open the door, she looked ready to bite nails. Wide as she was tall, she smelled suspiciously of demon rum, at almost one o'clock in the morning. Sam held back the nervous giggle that threatened to burst from her throat.

"Good God! Can't a body sleep around here?" She pushed the door open wider with a scruffy slipper, peering at them standing on the porch with their trunks and luggage strewn around them.

Even in her semiconscious state of disrepair, Sam figured the woman could smell quality and money. She pulled her wrapper together with a pudgy hand and smeared her greasy-looking gray hair back with the other.

"Well? What are you waiting for? Come on in." She heaved herself down the steps to help bring in the luggage.

"Here, let me do that. It's too heavy for you, ma'am," Garth said.

"Oh my, a gentleman," Kate purred. Sam hoped Garth would be on his best behavior and not tease the old lady. But he seemed not to notice anything out of the ordinary in the situation.

Garth asked for two separate rooms, but adjoining if possible. At the woman's leering smile, Sam started to tell her they were siblings but Garth frowned and shook his head.

When they finally settled in their rooms, Garth explained.

"We can't come in here as brother and sister in case Uncle Millard ever hears of us. And we can't very well use the last name of Kirkland either. We can both use Aunt Twila's last name of Brody and tell folks we're cousins."

"Aren't you a bit concerned about my reputation?" Sam asked.

He smacked his forehead with his palm. "Oh hell, that didn't even occur to me."

"Pshaw. It will work out. We shouldn't be seen together in town often. And by the time we return to St. Louis, who will know?"

"Good girl. In the morning I'll go out and check a few things, especially Peaches and the saloon. You stay put until I figure it out. I don't want you walking the streets unescorted."

There he was, mothering her again, but they did it to each other, so she needed to accept his care for the good he intended.

Odd smells of burned bacon and strong coffee wafted up the staircase, awakening them the next morning. When they dressed and went downstairs, they almost lost their appetite. Something smelled charred and the odor of grease hung in the air. A motley group of codgers sat morosely around the long wooden table next to the kitchen. When Sam and Garth entered, they barely looked up, indifferent to strangers. The one female of the group stared at them, eyes bright and curious.

Crazy Kate appeared at the kitchen doorway bearing a tray of burnt meat and eggs already congealing in their grease. She plunked the tray down on the table as if offering food of the gods and beamed at them all.

"These are our new boarders. Ain't we glad for a breath of fresh air such as the likes of them?" She didn't appear to notice the lack of enthusiasm surrounding the table. "That old fart over there in the corner is Seth. He's a prospector. The one next to him is an ornery old cuss name of Jasper. Last but not least by any means, our school-marm, Mrs. Danvers."

Only the middle-aged schoolteacher ac-knowledged their introductions with a smile and a friendly tilt to her head. She looked very prim and proper in a beige skirt with a narrow trim and a no-nonsense white blouse buttoned up to her neck, even as the morn-ing was turning hot. She mentioned she wouldn't be staying long, since her mother wanted her to return to Chicago. Summer here without a school in operation was a good time to leave.

After breakfast, Samantha went back up to her room to finish unpacking and make more notes in her book. Garth went to town. Sam sat on the bed and thought of Aunt Twila back in St. Louis. She missed her so much, and she knew Garth did too, but they refused to talk about their aunt. Their father's widowed sister had come often to visit after their mother died. Sam smiled, thinking of the times Aunt Twila had tried to give her a "marriage talk" about what was expected of a young lady when she took a husband. She never went so far as to shock Sam, but the chats were uncomfortable. So far Sam hadn't seen any reason to contemplate marriage. No man back in St. Louis had appealed to her since Jeffery. It must be those novels she'd always read. She had decided to stay a spinster until she met someone she couldn't possibly live without.

Sam heard Garth's footsteps on the stairs, taking them three at a time, probably. The boy never could do things slowly, and patience was not one of his virtues. He went into his own room and came through the adjoining door, to stand and watch her mend her stockings. She looked up at him and noticed that he had a more certain air about him, as if coming West had developed an innate leadership within him. He was tall and slender with a shock of sandy hair that curled slightly around the bottom of his neck. In spite of needing a haircut, or maybe because of it, he had a clean-cut handsomeness she hadn't paid any attention to before.

"I've never seen you with a needle, Sam. Aunt Twila tried to teach you embroidery. I've heard her lectures often enough."

Sam grimaced. "Ouch! Damnation!" She brought her pricked finger to her lips.

"Tsk, tsk. Not a very ladylike way to talk." He laughed.

"Don't smirk. You know I would rather be training horses than sewing any day. But I don't know what the Powder Keg mercantile might sell, and I have to have stockings."

"One thing I found out. The locals call this place Powder. Only Eastern dudes call it Powder Keg."

"I stand corrected. I wish Aunt Twila was here. I don't know how many more meals I can stomach like the ones Crazy Kate puts out."

Garth sat on a chair and stretched out his legs. "I miss Aunt Twila too, Sis. She was like a mother to us."

"I'm so sorry. I didn't mean to be insensitive. Of course you miss her even more than I do. You always were the apple of her eye." Sam changed the subject. "What did you find out?"

He shrugged. "Not a lot. I had a few ideas before we got here, but they're fast going up in smoke."

"What do you mean?" Sam asked. Garth looked worried, which was unusual for him.

"The town of Tombstone isn't far away from Powder. Wyatt Earp and his brother are famous gunmen and own that town. They are the law. That kind of puts a kibosh on my plans, and now I don't know how to get started."

Sam threw the mending on the bed and walked to the window to look out. She turned back to Garth. "Why don't we buy out Crazy Kate and take over the boarding-house? I bet she'd sell in a minute. Then we'd have a — a cover? Is that what you'd call it?"

Garth stared at her with amazement in his expression, his eyes lit with new interest. "By gosh, that's what we need, a cover and a place to begin our plans. Think the old woman will sell?"

"I'd bet anything on it. When I went downstairs for a drink of water, she looked me up and down, sized me up, and told me she'd like to leave Powder in the worst way. She's a terrible cook and housekeeper, and the teacher said the poor soul is drinking herself to death."

Garth rubbed his newly emerging mustache. Suddenly, he jumped up and smacked his fist into his palm. "I've got it! Let's do buy this old place, and send for Aunt Twila. If she comes, she'll soon whip it into shape and we won't starve. There's a back door going into the alley, and we can come and go without the town knowing a thing. It's my thought to round up a gang, nothing violent." He held up his palms toward Sam in a placating gesture. "We need to harass, annoy, and cause Uncle Millard's enterprises as much harm as we can. I can't see us doing it alone."

"But what if Aunt Twila won't come? And if she agrees, it will take time to get her here. Meanwhile, how will it look for a lady to run a boardinghouse all alone? What if young men want rooms?" She paced the floor in front of the bed, her thoughts in a whirl.

"We need to change our last names," Garth said.

"Why don't we use Aunt Twila's last name, Brody, as we already planned to do? That way if she comes here, it won't get too complicated. If we need to explain ourselves, we could be cousins. We do look a bit alike, you know."

Garth nodded and walked to the trunk in his room. He bent over and buried himself in clothing he began tossing out on the floor. At last he grunted in satisfaction and held out a dress to Sam.

"Here, try this on. I'll shut my door for a minute."

Puzzled, she took the dress, the heady feeling of excitement transferring from him to her.

"All right, open the door." They both laughed while Sam looked in the mirror over the dresser. The dress was old-fashioned, buttoned up to the neck with long sleeves, and it fit like a flour sack on her slender body. It must have been their grandmother's, since she'd been about Sam's height only rounder, according to their father's description when they asked him about her.

"The question on my mind is why you have a dress in your trunk?" she asked her brother.

He looked uncomfortable, his face flushed. "I'm not sure myself. I saw it in Mother's room and guess I wanted something I thought belonged to her."

He motioned for Sam to sit. Golden brown eyes met blue eyes in the mirror.

"You're a good-looking girl, Sam, almost a beauty."

"My, that's a kind thing for you to say. I don't recall you ever mentioning it before."

Garth cleared his throat as if embarrassed. "The only reason I'm mentioning it now is that I don't want you compromised if I'm not always here to protect you. If you look like a middle-aged maidenly spinster, there won't be a whole lot of interest in you. Do you mind that?"

"Gracious no. I wouldn't welcome a lot of attention from your wild West cowboys, that's for certain."

"I didn't think so. Do you have some powder?" At her questioning look, he continued. "You know, that rice powder none of you females admit to using to hide the freckles across your nose."

Of course she had powder — and she had freckles, too. She brought the box out and set it on the dresser. She was touched that he'd wanted something of their mother's to bring with them and a bit chagrined that she hadn't thought of it.

"Hold your nose and close your eyes," he warned. He held the long sweep of chestnut hair that hung down her shoulders almost to her hips. After he had dusted it with the rice powder and it settled in the air, he deftly twisted her hair into a tight knot at the base of her neck and pinned it with the hairpins on the dresser.

"Sit still one more minute." He went into his room and came back with a pair of gold-framed spectacles.

"Oh, no! That's too much," she protested.

"Wait. Hear me out, Sam. They are only clear glass. I had them made for me when I was trying to court Adele Harrington. She preferred 'older men.' If I recall, I also grew a rather neat mustache and beard for that lady."

"Like that scrawny thing you are trying to grow again? Whatever happened to Adele, by the way? I considered her to be quite attractive, if a bit stiff. Actually I always thought of her as Addled Harrington, because she talked so much and said nothing." Sam giggled.

Garth scowled at her. "You did not!"

Sam nodded. "You bet I did." She remembered a tall, elegant young woman with a haughty air who wouldn't have suited Garth. Luckily he found that out before Sam decided to do some sabotaging.

"I'll always blame Aunt Twila for that debacle, even though I dare not accuse her since I haven't any proof. I brought the lady flowers one afternoon and a half-dozen baby frogs leaped out of the rolled up paper she held in her pretty hands." At Sam's amazed look, he continued.

"That's not even all of it. Later we went horseback riding and Aunt Twila must have spiked the iced tea. Since everyone knows I detest tea, poor Adele drank the lot of it and got soused to the gills."

When Sam and Garth quit laughing, he said, "That's not all yet. Adele made quite a fool of herself half falling off her horse every so often since she insisted on riding sidesaddle. Like some heroine from one of your novels, probably."

Sam knew he referred to her riding her horses astride, sometimes without saddles, but her reputation stayed safe since that was her job as a horse trainer. "I can't wait to hear the end of Adele."

"Well, she, of course, blamed me for the whole debacle when she sobered up. I listened to her temper tantrum for ten minutes and then bowed out of her life. I shaved my beard and mustache and had almost forgotten about her."

"Poor baby." Sam balled a fist and hit him lightly on the arm. "Aunt Twila, as well as anyone else with a grain of sense, knew you two weren't suited. You'd have made each other miserable."

"At least I've tried to find someone — more so than some people. I can't believe you aren't interested in any of the men who called on you, Samantha. That's why I thought you'd be more comfortable disguised. You'd have all the cowpokes and barflies over here standing in line otherwise."

"Lordy me." She batted her eyelashes. "I do believe you paid me another compliment, kind sir."

Garth rolled his eyes and snorted. "Don't take it too seriously. There's a definite shortage of women out here, is all I'm saying."

He picked up the glasses and, setting them on Sam's nose, stepped back to survey his handiwork. They were both amazed at her transformation. The rice powder on her hair turned the bright rich chestnut glow to a drab indeterminate color. With the spectacles firmly on her nose, she had gained about twenty years in minutes. The dress hung on her, giving her at least twenty extra pounds.

"Ugh!" She stuck her tongue out at her face in the mirror.

Garth smiled with smug satisfaction. "Now do you think you'll be safe without my protection?"

"That is a certainty. Not even poor old Seth or Jasper would notice me now." She shook her head in mock remorse. "I'm not sure I want to go around the rest of my life looking like Aunt Twila's sister though."

"Oh, come on, it's temporary till I figure out how to settle Uncle Millard's hash. How long can that take? Besides, you said you weren't interested in being courted. You only have to dress this way until Aunt Twila comes to chaperone."

She raised her eyebrows. "I didn't mean *never* courted. But then, perhaps once was enough."

41

"Aw, kiddo, don't let Jeffery close you off. He was a colossal jerk. As soon as he thought we'd lost the mansion and were left penniless, he skedaddled. I'm glad he showed his true stripes before it was too late."

"I am too, but it hurts to know he was marrying into the company and not me."

"When we accomplish what we need to, we can go back home and buy another place, not quite so fancy. You can train horses again if you want to. You were getting a reputation for your ability. Some didn't approve of a woman handling horses, but you changed that in St. Louis. Unless, of course, you become famous with your western novel."

"Oh, you!" Sam laughed and pushed him out of her room.

As soon as the bank draft came in, Crazy Kate hugged them both, relief plain on her face. She packed up and moved out the same day they paid her off. She left so quickly, both Sam and Garth wondered if they'd been too hasty in buying the boardinghouse and sending for Aunt Twila. If their aunt didn't come, the whole plan would fizzle because Sam was a worse cook than Crazy Kate. They would be stuck with a boardinghouse neither of them knew what to do with.

Another positive note with Crazy Kate leaving, she apparently was more than a very close friend of the stable owner who gave Garth and Sam the pick of his stable before he pulled out of town with Kate.

Sam tried her best, but either burned their food to a blackened crisp or brought it to the table half cooked. The last straw was the morning she almost set the kitchen on fire. The schoolteacher suddenly decided to return to civilization, and the three old boarders pitched in and began cooking their own meals along with Sam and Garth's. It was only promises that help was on its way that saved the boardinghouse from a mass exodus.

CHAPTER 4

One miraculous day Aunt Twila arrived. She gave a quick look around, her thin lips becoming straight lines of disapproval of all she saw, hugged Sam and Garth to her bony frame, and took over. She almost didn't recognize Sam. When they explained the disguise, she approved, or at least they thought she did. Hard to tell with their aunt, since she never had been much of a talker.

"I guess you two helpless babes have missed your old aunt, haven't you?" She folded her arms across her chest and looked much too smug for Sam's comfort.

"You know we have." Garth kissed her cheek.

She thrust him away gently, but they could tell she was pleased.

"I think you should know first off that we aren't acting as brother and sister," Garth said. "We are cousins and using your last name. Hope you don't mind."

"Now what are you two up to?"

Sam's relief to be done with kitchen chores and out of her onerous disguise almost overwhelmed her. She wanted to kiss her aunt too, but knew the old woman would only tolerate so much outright affection from them before she shooed them away. They'd always felt the love and caring in her eyes, and it had been enough.

"Time for explanations later." Garth brought in her trunk from the front steps. "Let's get you settled and see if you can find us something edible to eat. I'm about starved." He ducked when Sam threw a sofa pillow at him.

During the next weeks, Garth spent the days riding out, scouting around for his "gang." No one would take him seriously. One glance at his baby face and blue eyes, and men turned back to their drinks in disgust. Even Garth's burgeoning mustache failed to impress. Plus, it did look peculiar since it had become singed around the edges when he tried to help Sam light a clogged lamp.

One night Sam and Garth sat in the living room alone. Aunt Twila busied herself in the kitchen, and the boarders had retired for the night. Garth stared moodily into the fireplace when Sam leaped to her feet.

"Sit. Stay." She commanded. "You're so great at disguises. I want you to see something." She dashed up the stairs. When she returned a few minutes later, Garth stood in surprise. Sam posed before him, legs encased in denim britches, one of his long-sleeved shirts hidden beneath a thoroughly disreputable baggy leather vest that fastened loosely across her chest. She'd tucked her hair up into a flat-brimmed hat tied firmly beneath her chin. He hadn't noticed before, but her work in the flower and vegetable garden since they arrived had given her the start of a golden tan.

She grinned. "Close your mouth. You look like a fish out of water." When he failed to answer, she came into the room and sprawled on a chair much as she thought a man might do, slinging her leg over the arm. "I'm the beginning of your desperados," she announced. "We have to start things now. Time is going by and nothing's been accomplished. Not that you haven't been trying real hard," she hastened to say at his darkened glare.

"I have to agree, you do look the part of a man — well, a boy anyway. But I can't let you get involved. It could get dangerous."

"Piffle! It's the only way. If we can pull a

46

few jobs, maybe some nefarious gangster will decide to join us. That should pave the way for others."

"Where are you coming up with this stuff? You been reading my novels I hid under the bed? 'Pull a job' and 'nefarious gangsters' . . . I don't think they refer to rustlers and stagecoach robbers as gangsters out here, Sis. Maybe *banditos.*"

"Doesn't matter," Sam said. "We agreed to avoid violence. How can it be so dangerous? To steal stocks, any incriminating papers, and money enough to pay off our gang members . . . things like that," she finished lamely.

"The danger won't come from us, but you can't expect others to surrender property without some kind of a fight. I can't do all the jobs I have in mind at night after the banks close, and there will have to be stage robberies as soon as I find out which stages our dear uncle brings his payroll in on."

"Don't some stages actually belong to him? I've been seeing some kind of a crest he uses on the back similar to the one on his stationery." Sam sighed at the freedom that came with slinging her denim-clad leg over the chair as she'd seen Garth do. "Why should you begrudge my participation?" Who was older anyway?

"In the first place, you'd never fool anyone with that getup."

She leaped to her feet, fists balled on her hips. "Is that so, Mr. Bossy-Know-it-all? I'll make you a deal."

"What kind of a deal?"

"The toughest will be Aunt Twila, of course, but if I go through an entire dinner tomorrow evening with no one guessing my identity, will you consider me at least?"

He laughed. "That's ridiculous. You could never fool Auntie for a minute, and I doubt you could even fool Seth, who is sharp as a tack for his advanced years." He patted her on the back, raising a cloud of moldy-smelling fine dust from the leather vest.

"Where the hell did you resurrect that monstrosity from?" He wiped his hands on his trousers.

Sam smiled. "You came close. Resurrect it I did. I saw a dog burying something in the alley and I thought it a poor creature to rescue from harm's way. Turned out to be this. Lends a certain credibility to my gangster . . . er . . . bandit's outfit, don't you think?"

When Garth finished laughing, he finally agreed to her deal, as he knew it to be useless to argue.

The next evening when everyone sat down

to supper, only Sam was missing, but sometimes she came down later.

A loud knock sounded at the back door and Aunt Twila, grumbling, set down the tray of pork chops and went to answer. There came a moment or two when her voice rose querulously and Garth feared trouble. He scooted his chair back and hurried to join his aunt, just as she bustled through the hallway leading a most scruffy individual.

Sam refused to meet Garth's eyes, probably for fear she'd burst out laughing. She kept her head lowered and the brim of her hat pulled down.

"This poor lad was begging at the door. I usually don't hold with suchlike. Everybody should be able to find some kind of work, but he does look puny." She turned toward Garth as if asking his opinion, but as usual, didn't ask for it. "Should I feed him out in the kitchen? Poor lad can't talk — makes a sign language I can't understand, but I get the part about him refusing to wash his dirty face or remove his hat." She sniffed and tried to hide her obvious soft streak.

Garth shook his head. "Why not bring him to the table with the others? Give them something to talk about. Maybe he isn't exactly right upstairs." He tapped the side

49

of his head with a finger, ignoring Sam's frown. "I wouldn't worry about his hat or his dirty face."

And so it was that Sam passed the acid test, and Garth reluctantly agreed to let her ride with him. Aunt Twila was fit to be tied when she discovered how Sam had flummoxed her. The sight of her niece in trousers was enough to keep her silent the whole evening until they finally dredged up the nerve to let her in on a part of their plans.

Aunt Twila appeared unimpressed, disapproving of the whole idea. But her morbid hatred of Millard Tremayne finally outweighed her misgivings. Garth and Sam knew they could count on her loyalty, no matter what.

CHAPTER 5

Their first job! Garth pretended a nonchalance Sam was certain he did not truly feel. For herself, she had gooseflesh up and down from her neck to her back with a strange mixture of fear, excitement, and worry.

A stage shipment due with Millard's payroll for one of his mines would be their target. Garth had listened at the post office and heard the gossipy clerk confiding to a friend.

He and Sam saddled up the horses from the stables behind the boardinghouse and crept stealthily out into the dark streets. Gas lamps lit the main part of town as usual. Loud, raucous music and laughter emanated from the saloons and bawdy houses lining the street. Sam imagined they would have done as well to saunter down the middle of all that commotion. If they'd both sprouted two heads each, no one would have paid them any mind.

Making their bedrolls that night near the trail, they hoped to catch the stage at the crack of dawn when reflexes would be slow and light would be poor. Garth worried that someone might recognize Sam as a woman. They didn't get much sleep though. Neither of them prepared for the myriad sounds of the desert at night. Coyotes howled and yipped, owls swooped down, and rabbits squealed in their death throes. Once a small snake or lizard crawled into Sam's bedroll and her ensuing dance almost convinced Garth Indians had discovered their camp and were leaping around his body.

But the stage was late and must have taken a shortcut to make up the time. Garth wouldn't have noticed if Sam hadn't pointed out the dust rising between them and Tombstone.

"Damn! I'll bet that's the stagecoach. For some reason it's off the road. Come on, Sam, let's go."

They'd packed up long ago and loaded their bedrolls on the horses so it didn't take long. But this wasn't to be their day. First Sam's horse threw a shoe and then stepped into a prairie dog hole, nearly breaking both their necks. For a moment it seemed Garth might go off alone, but he turned back to help Sam.

They could do nothing except face the ignominy of failure and go home.

Days later, when Garth was on one of his scouting trips, Sam heard a terrific din coming from the street. For the most part, noises sifted inside from the street without undue notice, but the grunts and crashing sounds of flesh against flesh heralded a vicious fight.

"What is that ungodly racket out there, Sam?" Aunt Twila asked as she turned a pancake over in the pan.

Sam sniffed, her chin in the air. "Garth said it's always the Indian." She looked at her aunt's puzzled expression.

"He used to be a prizefighter, back East somewhere — a pretty good one, or so I've been told. People are always buying him drinks and drink's got the best of him. The government doesn't allow Indians to purchase liquor. I don't know about that law where he's from. Maybe he developed a mighty thirst since he's come here. Anyway, he's fallen quite low." She grimaced, and her hand trembled as she pulled the curtain aside to look out. "Looks like someone has gouged out his eye."

Aunt Twila jumped up and ran to the window. "Put the fellow's eye out? Barbarians! What place have you brought me to?"

She turned to look at her niece as if she was to blame for it all.

Sam shook her head and smiled gently. "It didn't happen here. Garth said he lost his eye at a boxing ring in New York City."

If this knowledge impressed her aunt, she failed to give Sam the satisfaction. "Then why do they permit him to brawl openly in the streets?" She didn't sound as if she expected a sensible answer.

"He's a saloon swamper. Cleans up after everyone goes home for the night, if they ever do. For the promise of a bottle, he will fight all comers and I suspect men make bets on the outcome."

"Oh, my. That is just awful! He is only a savage, but . . . oh dear, look! No! Never mind child, don't look." Aunt Twila turned away from the window, clutching the front of her apron as if needing something to hold her together.

Sam peered out into the street again, aghast. From her elevated position at the window, she could look over the heads of the ring of men to the center. At first sign of the altercation, she'd brought out her pad and pencil. She scribbled furiously at first, immersed in the palpable excitement of the crowd. When she looked up, her mouth turned down in distaste and her fists clenched in impotent anger. Two bloodied men faced each other. The Indian was huge and formidable looking. His muscled arms bulged powerfully beneath the tattered shirt he wore, and his wide chest heaved with exertion.

The Indian was tiring and what appeared to be a slender mountain man, though smaller, was light on his feet and faster moving. He wore dingy buckskins and scuffed boots, his beard long and tangled. The Indian outweighed him by about fifty pounds, but the mountain man fought mean and dirty. He must have known every trick in the book, for soon the Indian began to lose ground and couldn't lay a hand on him.

Sam threw down her pad and rushed outside. Ignoring the shriek of protest from her aunt, she pushed into the circle as the watchers cheerfully made way for her, probably sensing more drama.

She found herself at the inside edge of the yelling crowd. The mountain man left no openings in his defenses. The Indian must have known he couldn't hold out much longer, and led with a powerful left hook that would have split the lean mountain man in two if it had connected. Before it even came close, the mountain man leaped into the air and landed square on the

Indian's chin with his booted feet.

It happened quickly and the Indian hit the ground like a huge felled tree. The man twisted his arm up behind his shoulder blades when he kicked him over on his side.

Sam swallowed against a dry throat when she saw the pain in the Indian's one eye as his body writhed on the ground beneath his opponent's straddling legs. A bleeding cut on his forehead blinded his good eye.

Without warning the man gave the fallen Indian a chop on the side of his head below his ear. It must have been very painful, for the first near-moan she'd heard came from the big man. The mountain man grinned in triumph and straightened his back to glare at the crowd, which was yelling and shouting by now. The man leaned down and placed his thumb close to the comatose Indian's remaining eye.

"Maybe I should gouge out this damn fool Indian's other eye?" He looked around again at the crowd in smug satisfaction, basking in their full attention.

The watchers appeared divided. Some mumbled and walked away. A few cheered him on. By now it was apparent the blood-lust had begun to simmer down in the mountain man and it looked as if he'd gotten himself into a corner, had lost his stomach for blood and gore, and was ready to get back to his serious drinking. But he couldn't back down and lose face. He hesitated for a fraction of a moment; his thumb poised, and suddenly found himself rescued from his dilemma.

"You . . . you monster! Let that man be!" Sam rushed in, flapping her apron at the astonished man's head and wishing she'd brought her rifle.

"Hey, wait lady, don't take on so." The man batted away her flapping apron.

One look into his grizzled face and Sam could see he was embarrassed, but relieved.

"You ruffian! Can't you see he's had enough? Leave him be." Sam forgot her usual ladylike decorum and barely noticed the men around her moving away, looking chagrined and surprised.

She had so diligently thrown herself into her disguise as a middle-aged, mousy spinster before Aunt Twila came, that if they had noticed her at all, they obviously didn't expect this sort of behavior from her.

The men in the crowd shuffled their feet self-consciously and began to melt away back to the saloons.

"Suit yoreself, ma'am. I wouldn't put myself out none worrying about this here heathen though. What's an Injun need two eyes for anyways?"

With that statement, he shrugged back into his grimy jacket and made for the bars. From somewhere in the dispersing crowd someone threw a full bottle of liquor down beside the fallen man.

Sam knelt by his side and felt for the Indian's pulse. It was still beating strong. The last blow must have knocked him unconscious. She bullied and shamed two men standing by to help her drag him up the porch steps and into the kitchen, laying him on the floor.

"You sure of this, ma'am? He's probably never been inside a house before." The two men guffawed and backed toward the door when they looked at Sam's glowering expression.

"Thank you for helping me," she said and turned her back on them.

Grimly disapproving, her aunt brought out hot water and towels and handed them to Sam, who knelt on the floor and cleaned off the battered man the best she could.

"Can you give me something to put under his head, please?" she asked her aunt. When Twila brought a pillow from the settee in the parlor, Sam lifted the fellow's head and tucked the pillow beneath him. Eventually he struggled to awaken, his face reflecting shock at seeing Sam sitting by his side. Her being there seemed to bother him more than his injuries. He especially tried to divert the side of his face with the empty socket. Sam had to admit it was ghastly: red, puckered, and ugly.

"Aunt Twila, could you make him a patch for his eye? I believe it bothers him for us to look upon his face."

No one in the family had ever seen an Indian before. Sam pretended to take this sudden introduction in stride, but her aunt wasn't able to assimilate the idea of what she considered a wild savage lying in her kitchen.

She ran upstairs, and Sam heard the treadle sewing machine. While her aunt was busy, Sam took the Indian's arm and beckoned him to follow her into the parlor, pointing to the strongest chair in the room. He looked dazed, more because of where he'd found himself than from his wounds.

When Aunt Twila came down the stairs and saw him in the parlor, she drew in her breath, her long narrow nose twitching. The man sat straight in a chair as if hoping he might become invisible.

Sam recognized the scrap of material her aunt clutched in her hand as coming from the inside lining of one of the jackets she

59

had decided to wear in her male disguise.

"Now that the rascal's awake, let him go back to his saloon," Aunt Twila demanded, handing the patch to Sam, but being careful not to come too close.

Sam fitted the eyepatch over his head, minding the twitch he made when she touched his cheek. She tied the string behind his head that held the patch in place. He promptly showed his trust and gratitude by drifting off into a tired sleep, his head lolling forward on his thick neck.

Sam stood and brushed her skirts briskly. "We can't send him back out there. He's got no one to care for him."

"Why should that be our responsibility? He's none of our business. Why, the heathen will probably murder us in our sleep. I couldn't close my eyes a wink with him in the house. Besides, Garth won't like it."

"Ah, you know your nephew better than that, Auntie. He used to bring in every stray he could find when we were children. Anyway, he's neither a heathen nor a savage. I've heard he's been to New York City, Boston, and Chicago and maybe even to Europe. He's been more places than we'll ever go."

"Be that as it may, he doesn't look like anyone I'd care to have in my parlor. But then, this is your house. You take care of him, missy. I want nothing to do with him." She flounced away, skirts swishing in reproof.

A few minutes later Sam answered a loud knocking on the front door.

She looked at the small, wizened man standing on the porch, holding a large camera under one arm and his hat in his other hand.

"Yes? Can I help you?" He didn't look like a prospective boarder.

"Yes, ma'am, at least I hope so. I'm Stanley Johnson, owner of the *Powder Keg Daily.*"

She was puzzled.

He chuckled. "The daily newspaper in Powder," he said, as if that explained everything.

"I didn't know we had a newspaper." She smiled to encourage him. For a newspaper man he seemed extremely timid. "Please come inside."

He slid underneath her arm as she held the screen door open for him. She motioned to a chair in the parlor. He stopped abruptly, Sam running into his back. She grabbed him to keep him from falling in front of her. He was staring at the Indian, who had awakened and stared back.

She motioned him to be seated, and he sat gingerly on the edge of the sofa. He seemed uncomfortable in the presence of the Indian, but then he turned his back on the man and addressed Sam.

"I do all the reporting, and I couldn't help but notice you stepping in so bravely to rescue this . . . this poor savage. I thought it might make a good story. Powder isn't exactly a beehive of interest, as you might have guessed."

"First off, it is rude of you to refer to him as a savage, especially where he can hear you. I don't know if he speaks English, but he might understand. Secondly, I am a writer myself and if I think there might be a story here, I will write it."

"Oh, you are a writer. Are you published? Have you written for a newspaper?" He sounded hopeful. It was apparent he didn't enjoy his reporting duties.

She bypassed the published question. "Do you have your own printing press?"

He nodded. "Certainly. I brought it with me in a covered wagon from Missouri. Would you care to show me some of your writing? I may be able to use a part-time reporter."

She might have misjudged him because he was old enough to have reported on

Noah's Ark and probably a stiff wind would have blown him away, but he perked up at her answer.

"That sounds like something I might like to try," Sam said. "But it will have to wait until we get settled." She thought of their idea for a gang to raid their uncle's property and it didn't strike her as sensible to encourage any kind of reporting now. But she had accumulated batches of notes on bits and pieces of interesting information she'd like to expand upon. Someday.

The Indian looked as if he might bolt any time. She stood and held out her hand. "Thank you for stopping by, Mr. Johnson, and you will hear from me in the near future. But meanwhile, I don't think it would be a good idea to write about what happened today. I don't see any way to present the fight so that the town people don't come across as barbarians. They might not care to read about themselves in that light."

"You're probably right, Miss. I'll let myself out; don't bother showing me to the door." He looked in the Indian's direction as if he didn't trust him not to leap on him.

Aunt Twila was upstairs making beds, or she would have been right there to see who knocked on the door. Sam peeked into the kitchen to look for her, and out of the corner of her eye saw the Indian about to sneak out the back door.

"Where are you going?" She ran to the door and stood in front of it. He towered over her, his face a mass of bruised flesh, but he wore the eyepatch.

"Out," he said simply.

Sam shook her head and took hold of his arm. She felt the flinch of his muscles when she touched him. "Oh, no. You aren't going anywhere right now. You'll stay here awhile with us, out of trouble until all this dies down."

His one eye was unreadable, black as his hair, but she felt no fear.

"Are you leaving to find a bottle?" She released his arm and crossed the room to pick up the unopened one the crowd had thrown at him.

She handed it to him, her expression not showing rebuke or judgment.

He wrapped his big hand around the bottle and followed her meekly to a room behind the kitchen.

After that, the Indian stayed without complaint, as if the decision was out of his hands.

"You don't have to stay in that room," Sam told him after he didn't come out for two days. She brought him his meals and had seen him go to the backyard privy, wash up at the pump house, and then go back into his room. She was aware he was scared to death of her aunt.

"What are you called?"

He looked puzzled. So far he'd only spoken in grunts and monosyllables, but he had taken up a hammer and fixed the sagging porch and the outhouse door without anyone asking him to do so. He had started to repair the once-white picket fence around the place.

"What is your name?" He didn't seem comfortable with her in the small room so when he went outside to the garden, she followed.

"White man don't like my name. Hard to say Indian name." He frowned as if in concentration and looked down at the bravely struggling grass Aunt Twila had planted when she first came with flower and grass seeds in her trunks.

In changing his bedding, Sam hadn't missed the unopened bottle of whiskey sitting on the floor near the cot.

"But what does your family call you?" Sam persisted

"No family. My name is Umetewah. White man no like."

"I think 'tis an admirable name. Does it

have a special meaning? What tribe are you with?"

He grimaced. "Shoshone. Too long gone. No go back." He hadn't removed the patch since they gave it to him. In the meantime, Aunt Twila had made him several more, each time improving on the pattern.

The last time she'd brought one and laid it near his plate, he pushed back his chair and stood, acknowledging the gift with a solemn bow, which surprised her.

At first he refused to eat inside at the table with them, but gradually he lost some of his fear and shyness. They'd noticed he had manners as respectable as any of their boarders.

"Does your name have a meaning?" She persisted.

He scuffed his moccasins and looked down at his feet. "It means 'Great Bear Who Runs From Nothing.' " He looked up to watch her face, as if to see if she laughed.

"Why, that's even more interesting and lovely," Sam said.

"When I fight they ask me my name. I tell them Big Bear. Close enough." He took a deep breath and rushed on as if she might lose interest in talking to him.

"Everyone know me. Know my name Big Bear. Important person in big cities. Not here." The mammoth shoulders that had begun to straighten with pride drooped again with a weary resignation. "Now I nobody. Nothing. Dirt." He spoke matter-of-factly, but Sam could detect no self-pity. His craggy features reflected pain for a moment before they changed into the usual mask of passive acceptance.

She reached to take his big rough hand in hers. He tried to pull away, his eye wide with apprehension.

"You don't have to fear me. You are not dirt. Not unless you think of yourself in that way. You are the same man as you ever were. It's just that you've fallen on some hard times. Wait until you meet my brother. He might have a job for you. Please don't go back to the saloon."

"Skinny lady don't like me."

Sam hid her grin. That was an understatement. "Nonsense. Aunt Twila's bark is worse than her bite. She's never seen an Indian up close. I expect she is waiting to see how you'll turn out."

"Turn out?" He looked puzzled.

"Yes, well, I mean if you are going to start drinking again and fighting."

He thumped his chest with his fist. "Life better now. Quiet. Too old to fight. Don't want hurt anybody, even white man."

"Good. Then we only have to wait for Garth." She noticed he didn't mention giving up drinking, but when she tidied up his room, the bottle remained unopened on the floor beside his bed.

CHAPTER 6

Unfortunately Garth didn't see matters her way when he returned.

Sam introduced him to Big Bear and they shook hands, both eyeing the other up and down.

"Aunt Twila tells me you've been helpful around here while I've been gone," Garth said guardedly.

Sam snorted. "Piffle. Even with you here, you wouldn't have known how to mend the roof on the storeroom or level the outhouse that's been tilted since we bought the place or build a hayloft to store extra hay where we keep the horses."

Garth tried not to show the jealous streak he didn't realize he had. He lifted his chin in disdain. "Where would I ever have had a reason to learn all those things? Really, Sam."

"Oh, my," she put her hands to her cheeks in mock horror. "Did I forget our station in life? In case you forgot, dear brother, we don't have that luxury anymore."

Garth looked properly chastised and turned to Big Bear to thank him.

Big Bear looked uncomfortable, as if he'd found himself in the midst of a family squabble.

They heard his hammer ring throughout the afternoon after a late lunch.

Later, Garth sounded his exasperation. "Of all the ridiculous ideas, this one takes the cake. Why in the hell — pardon my expression — would we want a punch-drunk, one-eyed, over-the-hill giant Indian in our gang? How could we disguise him, for one thing?"

They were sitting in Sam's bedroom with Aunt Twila nearby, knitting up a storm, but not missing a word.

"Fine. Tell me, how many gang members do we have lined up to join us?"

"Don't be sarcastic, Sam. It isn't becoming," Aunt Twila put in.

"Don't get me wrong. It was very courageous of you to rescue him and bring him here. He's already proven very useful in helping around while I'm gone. But turn him loose, for God's sake, and let him go back to the saloon."

"No! He doesn't want that life anymore.

That bottle of whiskey has been sitting by his bed unopened since he arrived. He needs us, and believe it or not, we need him."

Minutes before their argument Garth had been bemoaning the lack of available outlaw material. All the outlaws he ran into were either too ornery or vicious, and he realized he could never control them. He was getting nowhere.

"Maybe I'm going about this all wrong. Should I put an ad in the *Tombstone Epitaph*? Something like, 'Wanted, personable bandit-type, nonviolent outlaw. Only those experienced need apply.' " He smiled wryly at Sam and Aunt Twila's laughter.

"You might put an ad in the *Powder Keg Daily.*" Sam smiled at the secret she'd held close.

"What? Does this dinky town have a daily newspaper?" Garth's tone was of disbelief.

Sam grinned. "It surely does, and I've been invited to contribute as a reporter." She struggled to keep the crowing from her voice but that proved impossible.

"What?"

"Yep. Mr. Johnson is the owner and publisher. When I told him I was a writer, he said he could use a reporter. It was obvious he hated the job of talking to all sorts of people."

"What did you tell him?"

"I said maybe when we get settled. Don't worry. I could see it wouldn't be prudent to get involved with a newspaper at this stage of our plans."

Garth looked relieved. "That's for sure."

"I think eventually, if — and that's a big word — if things work out for you two, this reporting job is what Samantha needs. She's never had anyone look at her work. Never shown it to anyone." A note of reproach entered Aunt Twila's voice.

Sam reached to take her aunt's hand. "I'll show everyone one day, Auntie, but right now they are a jumble of notes I've jotted down over the years."

A bit mollified, her aunt went back to her knitting.

"I didn't get to finish about where I've been," Garth said. "I found the perfect hideout." He leaped to his feet and began to pace. "It's safe and foolproof. Exactly the right place. I want you to ride out with me to look it over. Something else I want you to see," he added mysteriously.

"What sort of location have you found?" Aunt Twila obviously tried to hide her anxiety. She laid her knitting down on her lap, her faded blue eyes troubled. "I know you get impatient when I worry, but I wish there was another way to get even with Millard. What will it profit us if something bad happens to either of you? If you're caught, you could go to prison."

Garth reached down to pat her shoulder. "I don't see how they can catch up with us, Auntie. We need to hurt him where it will do the most good, in his pocketbook, and then his pride. Thinking of what hell he caused our father keeps me up nights."

"Well, come on now, where is this wonderful place?" Sam felt a tingle of hope for the first time since they came out West.

"You would have to see it to believe it, Sam. I don't know how I was lucky enough to stumble on it. You ride through this long stretch of desert, then rise to a sort of meadow with giant cottonwood trees, wildflowers, and a creek running through it. A low ridge of mountains surrounds it on three sides. When you ride out of the valley, you see mountains, honeycombed with holes and caves. Most are natural, but some look as if they'd been mined. The cave I found is big enough to bring in our horses and it flares out in back, opening to an area full of sun and grass. Only thing missing is water."

"It sounds marvelous," Sam exclaimed.

She clapped her hands together, excitement welling up inside and bursting out. "With Big Bear and me, at least you'd have a start at getting back at Uncle Millard."

"You sure can belabor a point. Just won't let up, will you? Have you asked him if he wants to do this? Have you thought about how we'd disguise him? I'm hoping we won't have to pull any jobs close to home, but if anyone recognizes him, they could track him back here to us. They'd probably hang him."

Sam made a face. "They won't recognize him. Aunt Twila can make him a mask. We can find different clothing and maybe boots instead of moccasins." Sam sensed capitulation on Garth's part.

"One last thing. He'll know about your part in our gang. I only permitted you to carry on with your silly posing as a male when no one knew your identity."

Sam couldn't decide which made her madder. His notion of silly or him *permitting* her to do something. She held her anger inside for a long moment, knowing it wouldn't do any of them any good to let go. Silly posing? Permit her? Her temper flared, and she wanted to shake him.

Before she had a chance to react, help came from an unforeseen source. Aunt

Twila broke the silence between them.

"The way I see it, Garth, you don't have a choice. Either abandon this crazy scheme, forget about Millard Tremayne and return home, make a new start for yourselves out here — or begin your so-called gang with Samantha and Big Bear. In a way, it might work to your advantage because Big Bear obviously worships Sam. He can watch over her. I shudder to think what might happen if one of those bloodthirsty riffraff you plan to gather around you should learn of her disguise." The old lady sat rocking as if waiting for her words to sink in.

And so it was that Big Bear joined them.

CHAPTER 7

Sam rode on her mare, trailing along with Garth and Big Bear as they roamed the countryside. Garth suggested that they familiarize themselves with the surrounding terrain. Both Sam and Big Bear had a lot to learn about shooting, and Garth spent many hours patiently showing them. Luckily there was empty space to practice in because Garth wasn't sure who the worst shot was. Sam closed her eyes when she pulled the trigger and the Indian ducked when he pulled his trigger.

When they passed through the rowdy town of Woebegone, about ten miles from Tombstone, they watched as a stagecoach rumbled past.

"That coach is probably carrying a ton more payroll and supply money than Uncle Millard's," Garth said wistfully.

"Never mind. We're only interested in our uncle's property," Sam reminded him. "We aren't thieves. We're only taking back what should be rightfully ours."

Garth held up a hand to shush her. "I know, I know. I'm only making an observation."

The trio stopped at Antelope Springs and later, Soldier's Hole, to water their horses and rest in the quiet shade of a cluster of cottonwood trees.

Garth's face lit with a huge smile. "I want to show you a surprise. Follow me."

They rode through flat, monotonous land filled with mesquite and greasewood bushes. Prairie dogs sat up and looked inquisitively at their passing, and sometimes a long-eared jackrabbit took off from a shady bush as if begging to race. Once a roadrunner ran alongside them. Even Big Bear laughed at that spectacle.

Sam hadn't seen Garth so happy in a long time. She almost wished they could leave off getting even with their uncle but knew that was impossible.

They gradually moved out of the arid area after crossing a small rise of mountains that had looked purple in the distance. Big Bear never spoke, but they could tell he was content to ride with them.

They gradually descended a deep path that then sloped upward to look down on a long, narrow valley.

"Oh! How lovely!" Sam stopped the mare and stared at the sight in front of them.

Accustomed as her eyes had become to the sere grays and browns of the desert, the sight of the verdantly lush valley was almost unbelievable. On either side of them, rugged ridges of mountains protruded into the cloudless sky. A spring burbled in the center of a grove of huge cottonwoods and gracefully swaying willows. Wildflowers blossomed abundantly near a rambling creek.

Garth grinned proudly, as if he'd discovered a treasure. "It's something, isn't it? I've been saving this to show you, but I was afraid you wouldn't be properly impressed."

"How could I not be impressed?" Sam reached out and touched his shoulder. "Let's water the horses at the creek and look around. My legs feel numb." *Not to mention my buns,* but she wouldn't say that out loud. It had been a while since she'd ridden a horse.

They sat under the shade while Big Bear walked around, searching the ground intently, as if looking for something.

"I think BB is discovering how it is to be an Indian again." Sam spoke into the silence.

Garth nodded at her shortening of the

Indian's name. Between them they'd called him BB for some time now. He leaned back against a tree trunk. "I think so too. I guess he spent most of his life tagging around with white folks, living in crowded cities, not belonging to either world. It may take him a while. He's as green about this country as we are, but soon he'll be right at home."

"I hope he's not recognized when we start our jobs. It will go bad for him." That worried Sam.

"With a mask from Aunt Twila and other clothes, it should hide most everything that could be familiar, and there are a lot of big people out here. From what I've seen, more than back home."

Not that big, Sam thought, but let it pass. "When we first came out here, I just about hated everything," she admitted. "But now . . ." Sam left the sentence unfinished, unable to explain that for the first time in her life, she felt really alive and was looking forward to the future.

Garth's smile lit up his sober demeanor. He had become so serious since he took on the idea of outsmarting their uncle. Seriousness was unlike him, but Sam understood.

"That's why I wanted you to come out here to see this. I can close my eyes and visualize a ranch house sitting right about there." He made a circle with his two hands, fingers together, and looked through the middle.

"But doesn't someone own this land? It must belong to someone."

"I'm sure not, Sam. There's so much land going to waste out here. Back home every square inch is accounted for. This land is probably up for homesteading."

What an unusual expression, *land going to waste.* Although she understood if the land sat there with no one caring about it — it might be considered wasteful. But that only made it all more interesting and beautiful.

"No ranches out this far yet. I think it's only a matter of filing a homestead claim. Or maybe a mining claim and then a home-stead. But hey, no use to get your hopes up. We haven't even started on Uncle Millard, and everything else has to take a back seat. You do realize that, don't you?"

There he was, being serious again.

"Sure I do. We both agreed that even if we couldn't clear Father's name, we couldn't let that devil get away with what he did. We might not be more than a couple of flies on the rump of a horse, but that can drive a thousand-pound animal crazy." She took a swig from her canteen and savored the clean, cold water. "If and when we finish, we'll probably head back home anyway. That's where we belong, isn't it?"

She looked at Garth, but he had turned his face up to look into the sky, and she wasn't sure what he was thinking.

That night, the full moon caught their moving shadows as they rode across the desert toward the tiny town of Woebegone. Two scraggly-looking businesses huddled together on the dry, dusty main street. One of the storefronts happened to be Millard Tremayne's office for the Peaches Mine.

"He probably wants to keep everything low-key so no one will think of robbing him," Garth said.

They entered the dark alley. In no time Garth had the padlock jimmied, the door wide open and inviting. The safe was a bit more trouble but finally proved no match for Garth's trained ear and determined fingers. Sam recalled the many hours he spent practicing on locks and tumblers from the time they had headed west from St. Louis. All that effort was beginning to pay off now.

Only the sharp clink of the last tumbler falling into place broke the heavy stillness of the night. The safe opened with a whisper.

Sam had been concentrating on watching the door, but looked over Garth's shoulder to see the contents, neat stacks of green-backs and bags of silver spilling out on the safe floor.

Garth ignored the money this time while Big Bear stood, unimpressed by the wealth he saw before him.

Garth was more interested in the stacks of paper, which would probably be stock certificates and mortgages. The account book was a wonderful find, and he handed that off to Sam.

They heard a footfall outside on the rickety wooden sidewalk, and stopped to hold their breaths. The three crouched in the shadows while Garth quickly turned off the kerosene lamp they had lit. They hesitated to walk across the squeaky floor to get to the back door.

The front door rattled and then, wonder of wonders, the footsteps moved on. "A night watchman, probably." Garth managed a relieved whisper. "I checked it out, and this town doesn't have a sheriff." With that, they lifted their sacks and let themselves out the back door. Fortunately no one had come around the alley to notice their waiting horses.

Sam spoke when they were well on their way home. "Maybe next time we should leave someone outside to move the horses if they hear a noise."

"Good idea." Garth grinned. "We're all new at this, but we're learning fast."

That night, safe in their parlor, Garth and Sam examined the contents of their pouches. They could have taken bags of silver meant for payroll, but their goal was not to steal money. The stock certificates and meticulously kept books of the Peaches Mine would be invaluable. Maybe their uncle couldn't replace them.

"Oh, this will hurt bad!" Garth rubbed his hands together, gloating. "For him to lose bearer bonds and negotiable certificates! I wish to God I could be there to see his face."

"But I don't understand. What's so great about these papers? He can replace them, can't he?" Sam was plainly puzzled, and so was Aunt Twila who, until now, had sat silently watching them.

"That's the absolute beauty of it! He will *have* to replace them. But out of the bank's resources, which means his own pocket.

"You see, these were issued to stockholders and were trusted to his safekeeping. Each one is in an envelope with the person's name written on it. But the bonds themselves are like cash, and anyone who finds them can cash them."

"Does that simply mean we have more money here than we thought?"

"Not exactly. You're missing the point. It's not the money we care so much about. But for pure, unadulterated nuisance value, this is the greatest. He will have to reissue all of these bonds and certificates to the rightful owners and then, not knowing for sure where the originals are, he will be on pins and needles waiting for them to turn up again sometime — somewhere. And without these books to back him up, it will be years before he even knows for sure what he's lost. We don't need to steal actual money from him. We'll hold on to these and see what happens. If he doesn't make good, he could go to prison. Or maybe the good folks will get together and string him up to the highest tree."

Both Aunt Twila and Sam looked shocked and speechless.

Garth relented and shrugged. "Well, even *I* don't want that for the old buzzard, but we'll see what happens down the road."

CHAPTER 8

Garth disappeared for hours at a time in the next days, and Sam couldn't figure what to make of his absence. She was certain he wouldn't dare try "recruiting" so close to home. Yet he was usually eager to head out of town toward Dry Gulch or Woebegone to look for men for the rest of their gang.

Finally, her curiosity got the better of her and one morning she followed him, staying well back so he wouldn't notice. She had pulled her hat down so far, she almost lost him when he paused in a doorway, glanced around, and then pushed through the swinging doors.

Sam stopped in amazement and looked up. The Silver Buckle Saloon and Gambling Emporium, the gaudy painted sign read. She leaned back against the building, her thoughts awhirl. Why would Garth spend time here of all places — in Uncle Millard's stronghold with his infamous Peaches managing it? It only took a moment before she thought of the answer. He must be infiltrating the heart of their uncle's stronghold.

When Garth returned to the house that night, she accosted him before he had a chance to close the connecting door between their rooms. It was never her way to sidestep an issue or tread lightly, as her father and aunt had troubled to point out often. Not a very ladylike trait, according to them. Garth looked sheepish and uncomfortable until his usual bravado asserted itself.

"I've discovered I can learn a lot by becoming friendly with Uncle Millard's hired hands," he said defensively.

"That's all very well and good, but I saw you go inside that place in broad daylight. I'm not even sure it was open for business yet." She waited for his explanation, hands on her hips.

He flushed, his mouth tightened. "I don't have to explain anything to you, Miss Nosy. But since you insist on trailing after me, I might as well tell you that my plan is to get acquainted with Peaches . . . er . . . Miss Peaches. I think she's the center of the dynasty he's trying to set up out here. Actually, she seems like a very fine person. I'm puzzled how she got mixed up with that old rhinoceros."

Sam's raised eyebrows made him continue without pausing to take a breath.

"What I mean is, she gets letters from the old goat. I need to establish some link or connection between us so that I know what he's going to do next. Forewarned is forearmed," he added virtuously.

Sam wanted to smack him for his pompous words, or should she laugh? She wasn't sure which, so she nodded as if she believed every word. "If he writes the sort of drivel we read in his letters, I don't see how she can help. Don't you feel the slightest bit guilty about spying on Miss Peaches like that if you think she's such a fine person?" She turned away to look out the window at the darkened night. "Anyway, do what you think best. Only don't let Aunt Twila know you frequent such places."

Neither one of them wished to stir up the old lady's ire since the boardinghouse was running like a well-oiled machine. Sam found herself with less and less to do as her aunt took over, so she began gardening, which was a challenge. Unlike the rich soil of St. Louis, here every blade of grass or speck of a live plant had to be cajoled and babied to spring out of the dry alkaloid desert soil. Everything else she found growing had thorns, spines, or poisonous leaves.

The idea of gardening in fact had begun to pall. On the other hand, she disliked being indoors, and loathed needlework of any kind and most other ladylike pursuits.

Her next idea was to work with the horses. They had purchased two mares, a gelding, and a stallion from the horse stables of the man who had probably run off with Crazy Kate. The stallion was not biddable enough to ride as of yet, and neither she nor Garth had been able to bring a saddle near him. Someone had mistreated him horribly, to judge by the scars on his rump. But he was a beautiful animal, and she had persuaded Garth she could eventually train him. What might tame him more than anything was the mare she put next to him. A colt would be nice to have, too. She missed Garth and Big Bear since they rode out of town a lot lately.

It was on a look-see trip with Garth and Big Bear they found their next gang member, although a more unlikely one none of them could have imagined. Their second day away from Powder, they rode through the desert, soaking up the quiet warmth of the afternoon.

"Sam found out at the bank that there's

to be a payroll shipment coming in this weekend on the stage," Garth mentioned casually to Big Bear. "I guess we could check out a likely place to lie low and wait for them."

Never one to waste words, the Indian nodded. They continued.

"Say, do you smell smoke?" Garth twisted around in his saddle, nose in the air, trying to discern the direction.

"There." Big Bear pointed. Off in the distance they saw a tiny wisp of smoke barely visible in the bright sunlight.

Garth turned to grin at Big Bear. "Hey, you are sure getting your Indian senses back in a hurry. I could barely make out that smoke so far away."

"Waugh!" the Indian grunted. "It's only natural," he conceded.

Garth put his hand over his mouth to cover a smile. From the very first, this appeared to be Big Bear's favorite expression and covered a multitude of circumstances, however minor or important. Both Garth and Sam suspected Big Bear was conning them, until he knew them better. They were sure he was as well spoken as anyone, because of the life he led before coming back out West.

When they topped the last rise, they

paused for a moment on the lip of the plateau. "Oh, my Lord!" Garth exclaimed.

Big Bear turned his head aside and then back to look stoically ahead. A blackened, still smoking wagon lay turned over on its side like a dying beast. Whoever had burned it had cut the horses loose from their traces and taken them away. As far as their eyes could see, mounds of white lay scattered across the landscape. Sheep! Garth and Big Bear spurred their horses down the incline, drawing their guns in readiness.

Garth shivered in spite of the sweltering hot day. They both heard a mumbled voice and turned to do battle. Near a large rock outcropping, a figure sat huddled, bent over with his hands covering his face. Tentatively, they drew closer and then dismounted.

"What happened here?" Garth asked.

A jumble of words, none of which Garth understood, spouted hysterically from the brown-skinned, weathered man. He reached to touch the man's shoulder gently, not knowing what else to do.

Big Bear knelt in front of the man, and they spoke together for some minutes. Big Bear then turned to Garth, pausing as if to catch his breath, an expression of anger on his face.

"Well?" Garth urged with impatience.

"What did he say?"

"White men do this. He say cowboys, men with cattle. Kill sheep, burn wagon, tell him to leave."

"But how did he get here in the first place? I've never heard of any sheepherders in this part of Arizona."

Big Bear asked in slow, careful English, and the man answered in Spanish. It was a strange conversation, but it worked.

"He come from Escondido in Sonora, Mexico, heading for California. Says he's not Mexican but Basque. Has people in California." This was a lot of words for Big Bear, and plainly he felt uncomfortable in the role of a go-between.

The man reached over and patted a dead lamb nearby. Tears rolled down his seamed cheeks, and he rubbed them away with his ragged coat sleeve.

"He had to kill the lambs himself, because the mothers were all dead," Big Bear explained, shaking his head.

"We'll have to take him with us, of course," Garth said.

The Indian shrugged his massive shoulders, and a near grin touched his mouth. Garth knew he wanted to say, "It's only natural," but he refrained.

And so Esteban Enrique Pasqual Hernandez Sandoval joined their group.

CHAPTER 9

If Garth wondered what Sam would have to say about the sheepherder, he didn't have to wait long to find out. As soon as he took Big Bear and the man up to their mountain hideaway, he hurried back to Powder to get Sam and some supplies. It wouldn't do for anyone to see the sheepherder until the incident was almost forgotten. There was no way to bring the guilty to justice. Garth, Sam, and the man would only get into serious trouble trying to buck the cattlemen.

The sheepherder wanted to bury his sheep, but that was impossible due to the numbers and the hard, rocky desert. They all knew it wouldn't take long for the coyotes, wolves, and vultures to take care of the carcasses.

"Come on, Sam. Change your clothes and let's go." Garth greeted her when she bounded down the front steps. "I want to show you our hideout, and I've got to talk to Aunt Twila about gathering more supplies."

While Garth loaded up provisions, Sam donned her male disguise. Then they headed out of town.

"Why are you bringing an extra horse?" she asked.

Garth smiled with irritating smugness. "You'll see."

She knew better than to keep asking so she gave up and enjoyed the ride. When they reached the rocky mountain slope to get to the hideout, Sam looked impressed. Garth couldn't help preening. After all, he'd discovered the cave himself.

Big Bear met them at the entrance, and they tied their mounts to nearby palo verde trees. There was no need to hide the horses inside as yet.

Sam automatically ducked her head to enter the cave, although it was wide and tall enough that she hadn't needed to. When her eyes adjusted to the inside gloom, she stopped short to stare at the sheepherder sitting next to the fire, stirring the embers.

She turned to Garth, her eyes questioning.

Garth smiled. He loved surprising her, seeing her brown eyes widen and her mouth forming an O. "Let me introduce you to . . .

oh hell, I forgot his name, there's so much of it."

"But who is he? How'd he get here?"

"He's a sheepherder, at present without sheep," Garth said. He told her how they'd found him after the cattlemen had done their work.

Sam ran forward and knelt next to the fellow, putting her arms around his shoulders. "Oh, you poor man — and having to kill the lambs! Can't we do something about those horrible men?" She looked up at Garth and Big Bear.

Both men shook their heads. "Cattlemen are kings out here, Sam. We can't solve his problems by adding to ours. We have to stay out of the limelight and keep quiet so we're not noticed."

The sheepherder let loose a barrage of speech and touched his hand to Sam's cheek.

Much to Garth's surprise, the two spoke back and forth. Her words were halting at first, not nearly as fluent as his, but they understood each other.

"Hey, I didn't know you could talk the lingo," Garth said, impressed.

"Lingo?" Sam smiled and stood. "I had to learn something at that expensive finishing school, didn't I? My best friend was from

Barcelona, Spain, and we exchanged languages. I don't understand every word when he lapses into Basque, but he's apparently been in Mexico long enough to learn Spanish." Suddenly she broke into laughter, and even Big Bear smiled.

"Well, what did he say?" Garth demanded.

"He says I'm too young and *delicado* for this place and you two mavericks. He said I reminded him of a girl, and I should be home with my mama."

"Humph!" Garth answered with a cynical eyebrow raised. "He sure doesn't know you yet then, does he?" He regarded Sam and the Basque sheepherder for a moment. "How do you suppose he's guessed you're a girl? It's enough that Big Bear knows about you. I don't want the whole gang knowing."

Whole gang? She turned away before she could laugh. Some whole gang: a feminine boy, a traumatized sheepherder with no English, and a giant Indian who would be hard to hide. And yet they had made some progress with what they took from the bank in Woebegone.

"I'm sure he doesn't know anything about me for sure, Garth. He probably has sons of his own and feels as if he should say something like that. Don't be a worrywart." She looked down at the sheepherder, who was intent on not looking at her.

"I don't know how he would help in our gang," Sam said. "He looks as if a good wind would blow him away. I wonder how old he is."

"Don't let his looks fool you. He's not frail, in spite of his size. I don't think he's nearly as old as he appears. We need someone to hold the horses don't we? He'd be perfect."

"Yes! That's a good idea. But I'm afraid by the time we finished calling him Señor Esteban Enrique Pasqual Hernandez Sandoval, we would be past the need for our horses," Sam said ruefully. "But my school chum had a brother named Pasqual and they called him Pancho. I wonder if he'd mind."

"I dunno. I can't see myself calling him Pancho. That is undignified at best. Look at him, Sam. Even in those dirty rags he's wearing, he has this reserve and dignity about him."

Sam bent close and spoke to the sheepherder, and his face split in a dazzling smile. She stood and brushed off her jeans as if to say, it's settled then. She turned to Big Bear and Garth.

"I asked him if we could call him Don Pancho, and he said he would be honored.

Is that okay with you two?"

"It's only natural," Sam and Garth chorused before the Indian had time to open his mouth, and even he joined in their laughter.

Sam looked around the cave in wonder, now that the situation with Don Pancho had come to a satisfactory end. She had never expected to find such a place in the barren-looking mountains. It was perfect. Far enough away from Tombstone and, hopefully, the Earp brothers' notice, yet close enough to the stage route and the Tremayne mines. Their main problem was to stay clear of Curly Bill's outlaw gang, a fierce and fearless group of rogues and murderers who would not tolerate any competition.

So they worked out the details as Big Bear and Don Pancho sat silently by. The three men would live in the cave for the most part, but nearby Dry Gulch would be fine for supplies or when they felt the need for some livelier company. Sam would continue living at the boardinghouse, bringing them supplies, and Big Bear or Garth would come for her when a job was ready. She was not to cross the desert alone, they cautioned. At first Sam chafed at the idea, but after thinking about it, the restriction made sense.

The next few days passed quickly for Sam. Almost before she was prepared for it, Big Bear came for her one dark night. This time the job went like clockwork. Don Pancho held the horses and served as a lookout. No one on the stage they stopped gave them any back talk. They didn't rob the passengers, but only demanded the leather bag and safe box lying between the stage driver and his helper. One look at the looming, majestic hulk of Big Bear, head covered with an ominous black mask, was enough to keep even the bravest in line. At one time the driver made a half-hearted attempt to kick up a spare rifle lying near his feet, but Garth promptly retrieved it. They tied the guard and driver securely, and also tied the stage doors. By the time the passengers had worked the many knots loose and untied the men, they hoped to be as far away as possible.

Back at the cave, with the contents of the bag and safe box spread on the ground before them, Garth, Sam, and the other two men sipped coffee that had been warming on hot coals and sifted through everything. The money was obviously meant to be the payroll for the Peaches Mine. Sam wondered fleetingly if copies had been made of the payroll sheets as Garth blithely consigned them to the campfire. A smile touched her lips, thinking of the problems Millard Tremayne might have replacing everything they'd taken.

They split the money four ways. At first Garth had a hard time convincing Big Bear and Don Pancho to take their share. Uncle Millard had been pilfering the corporation for years, apparently, and was now stealing from their inheritance. They had no qualms about taking some of his money. Soon it was settled, if somewhat reluctantly, and between Don Pancho and Sam, they put together an almost edible supper.

When Sam returned to Powder, she found Aunt Twila and the boardinghouse much the same as she had left it, with the exception of a new boarder.

"A deputy! Aunt Twila, how could you? You should have told him we were full and there were no more vacancies," Sam said. Her mouth felt dry and she tried to keep from frowning. Their aunt was very sensitive to criticism.

Aunt Twila shook her head stubbornly. "He's quite harmless, child. Just a big, overgrown lad. Besides, frankly I'm afraid, being here alone at night with only those two old fogies. They lock themselves in their rooms as soon as the chickens go to roost, and with you and Garth being gone half the time — I'm all alone."

"Oh, love, we *are* being thoughtless, aren't we?" Their aunt had seldom complained about anything and when she did, it was time to listen. "This country and people are all so strange to you. But a *deputy*? What if he observes that Garth and I leave periodically and return without notice?"

"Nonsense. I said he was harmless. You'll see. He's a sometimes boarder. Besides, I didn't know he was a deputy. He came in and asked for a room, and he looked so clean-cut and gentlemanly. Garth said we weren't supposed to ask personal questions of people out here."

"Right, that was one of the first things we learned. For some reason these folks are very tight-fisted with their past and present. Back home, gossip bared everyone's life. But if we asked for references, for example, we'd never get any customers."

Aunt Twila appeared appeased by Sam's explanation, and if she thought these strangers were odder than ever, she didn't say so. "He claims he will be out of town a lot. Sometimes he might have to sleep at the jailhouse if he gets a lot of weekend guests, is the way he put it. He mostly wanted somewhere safe to leave his belongings and get a decent meal now and again."

That sounded reasonable to Sam, and she hoped Garth would agree. It would be embarrassing, not to mention suspicious, to toss the man out after he'd made arrangements to stay with them.

That night at the supper table Sam met Deputy Wade. It was easy to understand why her aunt had invited him to join them. He did appear to be completely harmless. He was almost as tall as Big Bear, but lean and wiry and not exactly handsome, with his square-cut jawline and deep-set gray eyes. He didn't talk much, but Sam couldn't help but notice he watched her when he thought she wasn't paying attention. This gave Sam pause. Normally she would have been flattered; since giving up her disguise as a middle-aged woman, it felt good to have a man notice her. But the hairs on the back of her neck warned her that she shouldn't awaken his interest.

"How in the world did you come to be a deputy in this particular town?" Aunt Twila wanted to know. "Isn't it awfully dangerous? I've heard tell even Wyatt Earp can't take control of some towns."

Before Sam could protest her inquisitiveness, Wade grinned at her aunt, which flustered Twila. Sam looked away to hide a smile. It wasn't often anyone could muddle Aunt Twila.

"No, ma'am, I don't rightly think it's so dangerous. Leastways not for me. The Earps are old friends of my father. They promised to help me anytime I needed help, but I don't hanker after any outside interference, even if it's well intentioned. So far I've only had to mess with a bunch of drunks and them mostly on weekends."

Sam set her glass down before her suddenly twitching hand spilled water on the tablecloth. Garth would be upset about this turn of events. But then again, at least they would be able to keep an eye on the deputy. Plus, it was obvious this man didn't want the Earps around. Fine with them.

He sounded like a country bumpkin for sure, and Aunt Twila's face wore that smug "I told you so" look.

Deputy Wade ate with enjoyment as if he savored every bite. The others at the table watched him. They had grown used to Aunt Twila's cooking and didn't feel obliged to shovel it in so fast. After he had eaten, he thanked everyone and presumably went back to the sheriff's office.

The next morning when Sam walked past the mercantile store, she paused upon seeing Eugene Wilder, their uncle's attorney, and the bank president talking nearby. Sam stopped and pretended to peer into the grimy window of the storefront. Garth had pointed out the attorney to her on one of their walks around town, and had told her the attorney's name when he found it on papers they'd confiscated.

The two men didn't appear to be concerned about anyone hearing their conversation.

A new bank was holding a grand opening in Charleston.

Sam figured since Mr. Wilder was not only Uncle Millard's attorney but his front man for all his western dealings, the bank opening would have to have something to do with their uncle and the tentacles he'd spread out here.

She couldn't wait to talk to Garth. If they could somehow thwart or hinder the bank opening, wouldn't that singe old Millard's buns?

Sam had reckoned without Aunt Twila. The older woman put her foot down and promptly forbade Sam to venture out in the desert alone, especially at night. Deep down, Sam knew she was right, so she waited and fretted impatiently for the arrival of Big Bear or Garth.

One late afternoon Big Bear showed up,

entering stealthily through the hidden doorway in the alley. Garth wanted her to come. Sam could hardly wait until dark to put on her "outlaw duds," as Garth called her trousers and loose-fitting plaid shirt. After a short argument with Aunt Twila during which Sam assured her Big Bear would watch over her, they headed out toward the cave.

While they made their way across the dark, silent desert, a rush of gratitude toward her aunt surged through Sam for restraining her enthusiasm. She might have been able to find the hideout in the moonless night alone, but it could have been a risky task. Each time she and Garth had journeyed across the desert, it had been moonlight and the landscape stood out clean and clear.

She wasn't prepared when suddenly Big Bear's horse bumped hers rudely. Before she could voice a complaint, he turned and slashed his arm down in a gesture that meant silence. They both stopped, got off their horses, and muzzled their mounts to keep them quiet. It wasn't long before she heard the clip-clop of horses passing nearby and voices lowered in earnest conversation.

How had Big Bear heard them coming from so far off? Was it part of his heritage

— a special instinct?

"Come on, Curly Bill. I'd ruther go to Dora's place. I'm a hungering fer some female companionship." The whine ripped loudly through the quiet night.

"Aw, quit yer bellyaching," came the terse reply. "I got business to tend to first. We'll see to Dora's girls after. Come on, get the lead out. We got to move on." With that, the sound of more horses clopped by, within a stone's throwing distance from where Sam and Big Bear stood silently beside their mounts.

Sam's heart did flip-flops until she was sure the outlaws could hear it as they passed by. What a terrible thing if they had been discovered. Surely they were all armed, and how many were they?

"Ten riders," Big Bear whispered as if he'd heard her speak.

She swallowed past a dry throat. Curly Bill's gang was well known for its ruthlessness and senseless violence, especially toward Mexicans, Indians, and women. Sam shuddered. It had been a close call. They made their way directly forward when they could be certain they were out of hearing distance.

Sam decided not to tell Garth of their close encounter and hoped Big Bear would remain silent about it. It wouldn't take much for Garth to decide she was safer staying home with Aunt Twila. She'd never let him get away with that, but it would cause trouble between them.

When they reached the hideout and Sam told Garth about the new bank, he paced back and forth with renewed enthusiasm.

"That's perfect. If we can interrupt the opening or somehow disturb it, that should twist his tail. I want him to gradually suspect something, but not be sure about it until we progress more with our tormenting."

They left at dawn and went back to town.

CHAPTER 10

The next day Sam and Garth arose before dawn to sit in the back patio, away from Aunt Twila's curiosity, contemplating their next moves.

"We need to harass him good, but not so's he'll suspect any out-and-out adversary," Garth was quick to point out. "If he becomes suspicious, he might hire gunmen to watch his property."

Sam agreed, and they talked about how they would begin the siege. They didn't have a lot of time, since the celebration for the new bank would take place the next afternoon.

Big Bear and Don Pancho had joined Sam and Garth when they arrived at the scene of the bank opening. Crowds were beginning to mill around the board sidewalks and spill out into the dusty street. The raucous sounds of revelry rose into the air, mixed with the braying of mules tethered to the hitching posts and cowboys on horseback yelling at people blocking their way as they galloped down the street toward the saloons.

Just the distraction they needed to begin their work. Sam noticed Big Bear lurking near the edge of the crowd, if you could call standing head and shoulders above the crowd actually lurking. Don Pancho had steadfastly refused to come near the noisy crowd, and they figured he was back with the horses, waiting.

Volunteers had hurriedly constructed a rickety platform in front of the new bank building. A hush fell over the waiting populace as the corpulent, pompous-looking bank manager and his twittering assistant gazed down over the town from the top of the platform. He was about to begin a speech.

With a barely perceptible nod from Garth toward Big Bear standing close to the flimsy two-by-fours holding up one side of the platform, they passed by casually and darted a swift booted kick to the portion of the board they had previously sawed partway through the night before. After accomplishing their mission, they nonchalantly moved on, back into the crowd.

Shrieks of horror rent the air and then, for a moment, complete silence reigned.

The superstructure had caved in. Painfully, slowly, it very nearly disintegrated before their eyes. The sight of the portly, prim bank manager descending, stiff-legged, eyes closed and hands clutching the pages of his speech like a Bible in front of him as protection, and the skinny assistant flapping his arms as if he might fly, was too much for one cowboy in the crowd.

He emitted a low guffaw, slapping his hat against his leather chaps loudly. Soon the crowd joined him in riotous laughter. Everyone talked at once, slapping each other on the back, tears running down some cheeks. It was the funniest sight they had ever seen, many vowed. Three ladies frowned at the men nearby and ran forward to help the banker while he tried vainly to recover his dignity. He crushed his speech and stuffed it into his back pocket. Someone pulled up a wooden box to enable him to stand on the threshold of his bank and drag out his key. With as much ceremony as he could muster, he fitted the key into the padlock on the front door.

Nothing happened.

Futilely, he twisted and turned the key, but it didn't fit. Impossible. Sweat beaded on his forehead and across his bare scalp. Someone within the crowd began to titter.

He turned to glare in the direction of the offender before turning back to the door. He shook, pried, and tugged, but the key would not open the door. Garth had changed the lock.

"Looks like our money might be safe in there. No one can get inside."

Sam recognized Garth's raised voice and grinned.

"Hellfire, no," someone else answered. "Who could get in there to steal anything?" There were many answering catcalls.

"Here, let me take care of that for you." A cowboy strode forward, spurs jingling on the boardwalk. Before anyone could speak, he whipped out his pistol and shot off the offending lock. Then, without another word, he turned and disappeared into the crowd.

Garth and Sam's glances met over the crowd as it surged forward. Couldn't have planned that scene better themselves.

By now the bank officials were completely unnerved. They mustered their aplomb as best they could while the manager tried to stem the flow of the curious to some kind of normality.

Their sigh of relief at seeing everything in the bank in order was short lived.

The assistant knelt in front of the large safe and, with self-importance, turned the combination. When the heavy door swung open, the crowd rushed to get a glimpse of the stacks of gold and silver along with paper money inside. Suddenly shouts erupted, accompanied by a mass exodus of humanity when five rattlesnakes poured out with hisses and tails rattling, angered by their enforced confinement.

"Rattlers! Hundreds of them!" came the battle cry into the streets as people retreated as fast as they could. The manager and the assistant led the crowd. Waist-high wooden kegs of beer lined the sidewalk, intended for imbibing after the bank had opened. The populace collided with the barrels, knocking them over, and soon the sidewalk and street were awash with smelly, foamy brew.

Garth and Sam returned to the boarding-house, still laughing, while Big Bear and Don Pancho went back to the hiding place.

The next day the *Powder Keg Daily,* along with the *Tombstone Epitaph,* reported the debacle with snide humor, mentioning the fact that from opinions expressed by prospective customers, the bank drew bad luck like a magnet drew steel shavings, and it might be wise to avoid investing in the place.

So much for Uncle Millard's latest enterprise. When Sam and Garth told Aunt Twila what had happened, she bent over with laughter, but pretended to be miffed because she hadn't been there to join in all the fun.

By now Garth was almost resigned to having a "gang" of four. Even so, they were getting a good start at harassing the old devil. Sure, they were not mortally wounding Uncle Millard, but that wasn't their intention. The small nibbles and bites would eventually add up to his downfall — out here, at least. That was their goal anyway. If only he didn't discover that *he* was the sole target. If he did, he could put two and two together and begin to suspect them.

CHAPTER 11

The stage was late. Garth watched the setting sun, his expression grim.

"Don't fret so," Sam soothed. "We've robbed a stage once before in the dark. It wasn't all that hard."

He shook his head. "I don't like it, Sam. It's too risky. You can't tell how many shotguns they've got riding and who is on board. Recall the time we almost raided the stage carrying three majors and a captain from the army outpost? If Big Bear hadn't seen the insignia on the captain's coat as they flashed by . . ." He shuddered to think of it.

"All right. I agree it's risky. If it gets dark with no moon and the stage isn't here yet, let's give it up as a bad job this time. Wait! Do I hear something?" She looked up at Big Bear who watched from a vantage point high above them on a rocky crest. He gave a low whistle, the signal that someone approached. He scrambled downward, noisily rolling rocks and exclaiming as he stubbed a toe of his moccasined feet.

Garth grinned at Sam. "So much for the stealth and cautious cunning of the red-skin."

"Aw, boss, I'm learning. You've been reading too many novels. It isn't all that easy," Big Bear countered, breathing hard. "I had to slide halfway down the mountain." His vocabulary had continued to increase at a steady pace. This only confirmed Garth and Sam's earlier suspicions that he was enjoying his little inside joke.

"Sure, Garth. He's more Indian now than he was when we first met him." Sam patted Big Bear's arm fondly. He was coming out of his shell, his protective covering of lurking silence. They discovered he had a sense of humor all his own.

"Jefe. Jefe. El autobús!" Don Pancho whispered loudly. They had forgotten the stagecoach.

Garth insisted they all wear kerchiefs around the bottoms of their faces. He explained that no one would be able to recognize them, but Sam secretly thought his reasoning mostly came from his Wild West novel reading. She argued it would be better to have Aunt Twila make them all black masks. Garth nixed that right away as not being manly enough. He probably meant "authentic" enough. Only Big Bear was allowed a black hood to cover his entire face.

Big Bear was a sight to behold. For his size, Garth had to find a special horse, a huge black mustang they finally tamed and named Thunder. Big Bear reared his horse, front legs pawing the air, and shouted the command to halt. This ploy never failed. Even if the driver and guard had shotguns, they were too stunned to think of them.

As soon as Garth rode his horse in front of the stage, he and Big Bear removed the guard's and driver's weapons and Sam held them at gunpoint. Garth yanked the door open and demanded all the passengers step down out of the coach.

The passengers meekly obeyed and stood in a line. Two older women wearing widow's weeds simpered and sniffed into handkerchiefs, and one man, who looked like a banker or an accountant, leaned on an elegant cane, seeming anxious. The remaining man stepped out of the line, moving slowly toward Sam and Garth, refusing to hold up his hands as the others had automatically done.

"Get back there where you belong, mister," Garth growled in his most intimidating voice.

It was then the gang noticed the man's attire. If impersonating a cowboy was a crime, he would have been the guiltiest, Sam thought. His boots were narrow, pointed, and shiny black. His shirt was a bright plaid with pearl buttons down the front, and his Stetson was glaringly white, towering above his head. New and expensive, his outfit fairly shrieked.

"Major Chauncey Claybourne, lately retired from His Majesty's Service." He clicked his heels together and swept his hat off, uncovering a toupee resembling a small carnivorous animal trying to crawl over his forehead. He bowed low to Garth and the gang crowding around him. The hairpiece didn't even match the major's gray and black mustache.

"I say, a ripping good show, old boy." He looked at Garth, and when he cocked his head, the hairpiece tilted alarmingly. "But you could do with a bit more assistance." Paying no attention to Garth's waving pistol or Big Bear's growled warning, he proceeded to climb up on the boot of the stage and drag a trunk to its back. It looked heavy from the way he huffed and puffed to get it to the opposite side of the stage. But he was careful not to let it drop.

"What the hell are you doing?" Garth exploded. "Can't you see this is a holdup?" Before the situation got more out of hand, Garth motioned the passengers back into the coach. He unloaded the box beneath the driver's seat, shoved it into a bag, and attached it to his saddle. He then ordered the drivers to leave if they knew what was good for them. The stage took off with a mighty jerk, and in a moment all they could see was dust from the retreating vehicle.

Beckoning to Don Pancho and Sam, Garth leaped on his horse and turned to leave.

"What about *him*?" Sam asked. They all turned to stare at the apparition left behind on the opposite side of where the stage had parked.

The major, hat pulled firmly down around his ears to prevent it blowing off in the desert breeze, put what appeared to be the finishing touches to assembling an apparatus resembling nothing they had ever seen before.

He looked up with a big grin. "Lovely, isn't she? I found Annabel at a fair in New York when I first landed in America."

"What is it?" Sam asked.

"It is called a Steam-Cycle," he announced with shoulders pulled back as if he'd invented the contraption himself. "If you wish me to be technical, I can repeat what the inventor told me when I purchased the machine. I memorized his entire explanation."

Garth slid from his horse with an expectant look on his face. He loved anything mechanical. He didn't appear to be unduly alarmed about the stage leaving, but it was quite a ways into town before anyone on the stage could report the holdup.

Garth, Big Bear, and Don Pancho walked over to the major to look closer at the machine.

Sam thought it looked like a big ugly bicycle with thick tires and a cow's udder attached beneath the body.

"You see before you a marvel of modern ingenuity. A charcoal-fired two-cylinder engine powers Annabel by connecting rods directly driving a rear wheel crank. This produces steam to get her going." The major proclaimed this as if he read from a pamphlet. He'd obviously memorized the brochure.

"That is truly a marvelous invention. I wish you well. The nearest town is in the direction the stage headed." With that said, Garth mounted his horse again, motioned to the others, and they were off in a cloud of red dust.

When they were far away enough to feel safe, they reined up their mounts and rested in the shade of a small oasis created by a group of palo verde trees. A steady putt-putt sounded, coming their way and shattering the quiet of the desert. The horses began to pull nervously at their reins tied to the trees.

"Could it be?" Sam spoke in a hushed wonder.

With a cross between a snarl and a groan, Garth motioned for them to mount up and ride. They didn't stop until they had nearly reached their hideout. When they paused to let the horses blow, they heard the same noise fast approaching.

They turned their mounts up the narrow rocky trail leading to the cave. "Let's see that joker maneuver his contraption up here," Garth said. "And if he tries, I'll shoot his brainless head off as he tops the rise," he threatened.

By now, Sam feared he might do that. Garth was slow to anger, but when aroused, it took a lot to calm him down.

At the entrance to the cave, they pulled their mounts inside and to the back cave. Stretching their limbs as they headed toward the front, Big Bear sighed the loudest. None of them were used to riding horses for hours at a time.

No one mentioned the major, but they all listened. Don Pancho set about lighting a campfire so he could make coffee, and Sam put on a pan of bacon when the fire had died down. Eventually they were satisfied that no rude sound broke the stillness of the night.

While they ate in companionable silence, the fire crackled; the cave lost its musty, damp smell; and they felt secure and at peace with the world. Garth had retrieved the box he'd confiscated from the stage and promptly shot off the lock.

"That passenger who was on the stage struck me as nervous. I think he knew what was in this box."

"Hey, boss, why didn't we get the big box that usually holds money or gold?" Big Bear was speaking more complete sentences every day.

Garth shook his head. "Can't do that. If we take too much from the stage line, they'll be tracking us right away, sending a Pinkerton after us. This box has Uncle Millard's seal on top, and I want to foil my uncle. I think we have." He dumped the contents of the box on the floor of the cave.

Sam reached over and rifled through the papers. "Anything good here?"

Garth nodded. "You bet. Bearer bonds and some mortgage papers." He handed Sam a small bound stack of bills. "This is enough to give everyone something to get by on. All of us can stay at Aunt Twila's when we need to."

A swoosh of air caught them by surprise as the major entered the cave, removing his tall hat to get inside the opening. Before anyone could speak, he sniffed, his expression appreciative. "I say, dashed good smells in here. Mind if I join you? Haven't eaten all day." He looked plaintively from one to the other sitting around the campfire. Finally Garth threw up his hands in disgust and motioned toward the stewpot. Sam had already jumped up to dish some of the fragrant concoction into a bowl for the strange man.

They let him eat for a few minutes before Sam spoke, not trusting Garth to be rational. "How did you find us?"

The major smiled and his mustache danced a slight minuet. "Oh, lassie, t'was easy. Annabel and I, we've been through a lot together, and she's almost human. Like a bloody bird dog, she is. Pardon me, miss."

Sam figured *bloody* was a swear word to

him and nodded.

"But the real question is *why* did you find us?" Garth glared at the man and found himself barely able to restrain a grin in spite of the righteous anger he tried to maintain.

"Why?" The major's eyebrows rose in question, and his toupee was in danger of sliding forward from his wrinkling forehead. "But I told you, old chap. I am joining up with your outlaw gang." He looked at each of them. He had their complete attention.

Don Pancho couldn't take his huge brown eyes away from the wig perched so precariously on the Englishman's head.

The major polished off the remaining stew in the bottom of the bowl, smacking his lips in relish. "You see, that is precisely the reason I came to America. Ever since I read my first penny dreadful about the grand and glorious West, I dreamed of becoming an outlaw. A desert buccaneer, a dry-land pirate, if you will." He watched the campfire as if seeing his dreams float by in the fire. "When they cashiered me out of the army . . ." He broke off abruptly, as if he'd said too much.

"Cashiered you? At your age? What in the world for?" Sam asked.

For once the major looked ill at ease. He squirmed and frowned and then, seeing their combined looks of interest, he shrugged with resignation.

"Oh botheration. Might as well get it said once and for all so I can put it behind me. I am half Scot and half English. I served in His Majesty's Cavalry in India. But I took a sudden aversion to horses." He looked about to break down and sob, but sucked it in and continued. "I became allergic — to the blasted animals." He paused dramatically to let this statement soak in.

"Yes, I quite know what you are thinking. Twenty years a cavalryman and suddenly I couldn't bear to look at the silly beasts." He shuddered at the memory. "I broke out in great hives when I had to ride one." He felt on his head to make sure his hairpiece was there. "I eventually lost my hair, and the doctor said it was a result of the allergy. I refused to continue my service since they did not believe me about the horses, and they sent me back to England."

He took a deep breath after speaking nonstop, likely to get it over with. His expression cheered when he spoke again. "I wanted to come to America and have a bit of an adventure before I cock up my heels. When I arrived in New York, I saw the inventors of steam machines and knew machines would be my solution. I worked hard to learn how to take this beauty apart and reassemble her again." He looked fondly in the direction of the apparatus he'd brought up the hill and left at the cave entrance.

Garth groaned. "Why me? Why did you have to pick on us to join? There must be dozens — no, hundreds, of outlaw gangs roaming the West. Why me?"

The major must have been smiling behind his formidable mustache, as it shifted to a somewhat different elevation on his face.

"I like your style, old stick. A fair bunch of desperados, you are, but you never harm anyone." He seemed not in the least put off by Garth's lack of enthusiasm. "At first I thought I would search for a bloody awful gang of hoodlums and ruffians who shot everybody within sight. But after I thought that over, it's far better to start off easy-like." He noticed Big Bear and Don Pancho staring at him and hastened to explain.

"Dash it all, I do believe your gang is terribly dangerous. I do, most certainly. But I also noticed you are dreadfully nonviolent. Though p'haps you will improve once you get the hang of it, don't you know." He stood there, a knight of old, bestowing his largesse on his lowly subjects.

Garth tried to hide the grin tugging at the

corners of his mouth. He automatically reached a hand up to smooth the scraggly mustache he had been trying to grow and mentally compared it to the major's.

"Well . . . we might consider taking you on." He looked at the others, and they nodded in agreement. Sam giggled. "But we can't have that noisy contraption tagging along with us. You'll have to get rid of it and get a horse like the rest of us."

"A horse!" The major exploded in indignation. "Most certainly not. Have you not heard a thing I've said about the despicable animals?" He pulled off his hairpiece, showing a bald pate surrounded by a small skimpy band of white hair circling the bottom of his head. "I lost my hair because of horses. Allergic. Annabel will go anywhere those beasts will — within reason, of course. She won't have to stop and rest and eat and drink like your animals. With a couple of additional pieces of charcoal, she's raring to go. And once she gets going good and proper, most of the noise seems to be muffled."

Big Bear pulled away from the shadow he had immersed himself in and sliced a meaty hand across the air in front of his chest. "Much noise. Easy to track. No good." He jerked off his head mask and looked very formidable.

Sam knew he couldn't resist a bit of showmanship, but the major didn't appear to be even slightly intimidated.

"By Jove! An American Indian! How could I not have noticed the blighter? That seals it. You *must* accept me." He looked fondly toward his Annabel. "The old gal will not slow us down. I promise you that. As for tracking me, if you follow on your horses, it will be sure to wipe out Annabel's wheel tracks."

"*If* we can get the horses to tolerate your Annabel," Sam said.

"What you use make that go?" Big Bear asked.

"Come on, Big Bear, enough of that pigeon-Indian talk. The major has seen your face. He might as well know what you sound like." Sam punched the Indian lightly on his arm.

Big Bear grinned sheepishly. "Then allow me to rephrase the question. What is the principal mode of propulsion governing your motor bicycle?"

The major raised bushy eyebrows in surprise while Garth and Sam laughed at his expression.

"Now you go too far in the other direction, Big Bear. Can't you strike a happy medium?" Garth was still laughing.

"Steam, my dear boy, steam. All I need is to light charcoal in this burner below the apparatus and it makes steam. I bought the only one completed from the inventor at the fair. Had to pay a prodigious price, but he guaranteed it to work."

"And those are chunks of charcoal in your saddlebags?" Sam asked.

"Aye." The major nodded. "It is no use discussing it. I have quite made up my mind to join you. I am loath to threaten you, but I know your faces and I know your hideout. I believe you need all the help you can get." He looked around at the group staring back at him.

"Of course we welcome you," Sam exclaimed. She looked around at the others. "He's right. We need all the help we can scrounge up." She grinned at them to take the sarcasm from her voice.

And so Major Chauncey Claybourne joined the gang.

CHAPTER 12

As time passed, the group became a closely knit, smoothly running outfit. Sam and Garth were having the time of their lives. Although they suffered many close scrapes, none of them were hurt, nor did they have to harm anyone else. They finally knew for sure they were getting under Uncle Millard's skin.

The five of them sat relaxed, drinking coffee under the shade of a crazily leaning palo verde tree that pointed out the entrance to their cave.

Garth watched Sam as she poked at the campfire. He couldn't believe the difference between her now and the prim, hothouse flower that had embodied her only a few months ago. A smooth tan replaced her pale, delicate look, and her face had lost its roundness. Now her cheekbones and jawline showed strength and determination. Often he wondered how men, especially, could not recognize the woman behind her disguise. So far only Big Bear knew her secret, although sometimes he caught Don Pancho eyeing her with veiled curiosity.

Having her tag along continued to worry him, although she kept up her end. He knew Aunt Twila fretted a lot, but from the start, he could never talk his sister out of coming with them. Big Bear watched over her, much to Sam's ire, and he found the others gradually becoming protective toward his "kid brother."

Garth didn't like the idea of Deputy Wade staying even part-time at the boardinghouse, but they decided it would look suspicious to turn him away when there was obviously room for him there.

The deputy made Sam uncomfortable when she caught him looking at her in a way she thought speculative, but his expression showed no more than a casual interest.

One late afternoon Garth and the major sat at a table in a saloon in Dry Gulch. Garth and Sam hadn't told their gang any details, but they finally admitted they were carrying out a vendetta against the mine and bank owner and those were the only stages or banks they would ever touch. None of the men were inclined to pry even though they knew the major to be extremely curious about everything.

Garth looked around to discover, surrounding them, the wildest looking cutthroats outside of Curly Bill's band the Territory of Arizona had probably ever seen. In fact some of them could well be a part of Curly's gang. It was a good thing Don Pancho and BB had decided, as usual, to stay in the cave. He didn't imagine a lawman would be skulking within twenty miles of this saloon.

"Howdy. My name's Elvin. At least that's what I go by."

Garth and the major halted their conversation to stare up at the young man standing at their table. He couldn't have been any older than Garth but the worldly wise look in his wide blue eyes belied his handsome, baby-faced appearance.

"Sit. Buy you a beer?" Garth asked politely.

"Sure. I'm broke as usual." Elvin ruffled his too-long, curly hair at the nape of his neck in an abstracted way. He accepted the bottle of beer and tilted his head, his Adam's apple bumping up and down as he drank thirstily. Before anyone could speak, he gave a huge sigh.

"Bartender there says you been nosing around for someone to join up with you."

It was Garth's turn to sigh. Red, the bartender, was scared spitless of the men who came in to drink at his saloon. When Garth and the major showed up, he seemed relieved and became friendly. That was when Garth let him know they were doing things just under the law, and if he saw anyone who might be interested to please let him know.

But this dude didn't fit even the basics of what he needed. Garth regarded the young man's garish silk shirt and his skintight leather pants.

"I might have been looking around. But with the major here, I reckon I'm no longer looking."

Elvin appeared saddened, but resigned. "Well, heck, it was only an idea. I'm always a day late and a dollar short. Wish I was back in Yuma."

"Yuma?" Who in their right mind wanted to go to Yuma?

"Yeah, Yuma. The territorial prison, if that's what you're wondering. Just pulled a three-year stretch, my second," he said proudly. "Armed robbery. I was about getting the hang of it when they caught me again. Warden said they'd put me away forever if I went back. That would suit me fine." He took a healthy swig of beer. "The best friends I ever knowed in my life are back there behind them walls. A man couldn't want for better or truer. Not to mention three meals a day and a bunk to lie down in. What more could a man ask for?"

Garth and the major must have looked unconvinced.

"Sure you can't use another hand? Bartender didn't know what you all were up to, but it didn't seem important to him either way. I suppose I can rustle cattle if I have to."

Garth and the major exchanged glances. The major's bushy eyebrows crept up into his toupee, threatening to dislodge it.

"You could hang for cattle rustling. I reckon we could use your experience." Garth rubbed his would-be mustache thoughtfully. He chased away the image of the man dangling from a tree.

"You won't regret it! You'll never regret it!" Elvin jumped up from his chair, sending it crashing to the floor. No one in the saloon even looked their way.

"There are some rules," Garth said. "Have you ever shot anyone when you robbed them?" He didn't want a bloodthirsty gunman in their gang.

"Heck fire, I never had to use a pistol. I only robbed two mercantile stores, and both times the owners hid behind stacks of clothes until I left. Unfortunately they identified me."

And so the sixth member of their gang joined.

CHAPTER 13

At the boardinghouse, Sam knelt on her hands and knees in her so-called garden, oblivious to everything but urging the struggling, spindly plants to hold their own against the fierce heat and ever-present wind. She leaned back and remembered the feel of Missouri's dark, soft loam between her fingers. She had taken her beautiful rose garden for granted, but couldn't imagine any roses flourishing in this soil.

It had taken a while, but she gradually began to admire the harsh, dry desert, even while missing her thriving garden back East. She heard the steady clip-clop of boot steps across the porch. The walker was too slow to be Garth.

Looking up from her scrawny plants, Sam suddenly became very aware of her dusty skirts trailing in the dirt and her disheveled hair blowing around her face as it slipped out of her long braid. The man standing before her was the epitome of fastidiousness. He wore a tight cravat that, in spite of the heat, did not wilt or seem to bother him in the least. His shirt looked to be spotless underneath his vest; his trousers were creased to knife-edged perfection. He was dressed completely in blue. The color just matched the cool blueness of his eyes.

Sam struggled to her feet, catching her boot in her hem. He reached out a gloved hand to help her, but the pained expression in his eyes that said he would rather not touch her dusty hands made her push his arm away impatiently.

She straightened up to her full five feet, eight inches, but had to look up to meet his eyes in order to glare at him.

Ignoring her attempt to stare him down, the man shifted his wire-framed glasses and, gazing leisurely from the top of her head to her dirty boots, ordered decisively. "Kindly announce me to Miss Brody, your employer."

Sam stared a moment in stupefaction. He was taller than Garth but leaner and sinewy looking in spite of his clothing. She blushed at the idea of thinking about his clothing.

His jaw was square and suggested a stubborn streak, while his expression bespoke reserve. His lips were firm and somehow sensuous. She turned away to look at the toes of his shiny boots.

She recovered with a gleam of mischief in her eyes and made a polite curtsy. "Certainly, sir. If you would be so kind as to wait here."

In a moment Aunt Twila appeared on the steps, with Sam hiding behind the doorway so she could hear but not be seen.

"Yes, young man? Please state your business." Aunt Twila looked down her long, narrow nose in her best St. Louis society manner.

The man seemed a bit taken aback but trying hard not to show it — his mouth curved in what could have been the start of a smile.

"I have been staying at the Silver Buckle for a week now, and the food there is abominable. I have made inquiries, and your rooming house has been highly recommended. Perhaps I shall change lodgings." His glance took in the peeling paint on the front of the building and the warped boards here and there on the porch that neither Garth nor Big Bear had found a chance to remedy. The man seemed to have second thoughts about the idea of changing his residence. He brushed an imaginary speck of dust from his sleeve and finally noticed

Aunt Twila's patient scrutiny.

He deposited his briefcase reluctantly on the porch, first pulling a white handkerchief from his vest pocket and waving it over the boards to dislodge any dust. "Oh, yes. Here is my card."

Aunt Twila read out loud: "Clarence J. Westcott, Accountant, New York City, New York." She nodded and handed the card back to him. The sound of a whispered but emphatic "No!" coming from behind the door made the older woman put up her palm to hide her smile.

"I really can't say if we have any vacant rooms now. But if you would care to partake of your meals here, we could make that arrangement." Aunt Twila ignored the rude sounds coming from behind her.

"Splendid. I will begin this evening. What time is dinner served?"

When Aunt Twila told him, he picked up his briefcase and touched his fingers to his forehead in a gesture of farewell.

"What a prig!" Sam said when they closed the door. "I don't think I would have let him join us even for meals."

Aunt Twila lifted an eyebrow. "People aren't always how they appear. It takes a lifetime to figure that out, and by then, often it's too late." With that enigmatic maxim, she walked back into the kitchen, leaving Sam staring at her swishing skirts.

That evening Sam dressed with more care than usual. She refused to admit that the stranger had gotten under her skin. Weeks ago she had washed all of the offending powder from her hair and brushed until it gleamed with chestnut highlights. Aunt Twila had been after her since she arrived to abandon the spinster role and get back to her own self. With her aunt here, there was no need to worry about lacking a chaperone. Sam pulled the sunshine yellow muslin dress over her corset, letting the soft material sift down to cover her button-up boots. She fastened the row of pearl buttons in front of her dress. She wondered why, of all times, she'd decided to wear the dratted corset.

The shocked look on Mr. Clarence J. Westcott's face more than repaid Sam for his previous impertinence when she gracefully came down the stairs and took her place at the head of the table.

"My niece, Miss Samantha Brody," Aunt Twila began the round of introductions.

Mr. Westcott's eyes behind his spectacles showed a brief flash of what could have been appreciation at Sam's appearance, along with chagrin, but the expression was quickly gone. That only added to his firm profile and the confident set of his shoulders. Sam looked away before she could blush at the ideas rattling through her head.

Fortunately Deputy Wade didn't come to dinner that night. Two young men sitting together at the table might be more than she could handle at the moment, and she didn't bother to analyze why.

Later, after everyone had eaten the delicious pot roast and trimmings and left the table to go their own ways, the new man followed Sam outside on the porch.

He leaned casually against the railing. "Don't you think that a bit childish? Why didn't you introduce yourself when we first met?"

Sam sniffed. "I only allowed you to think what you wanted to think. Your preconceived narrow-mindedness did the rest."

He had the grace to look embarrassed. He took off his glasses and polished them vigorously on his blazing white handkerchief.

"Your aunt told you I have been staying at the Silver Buckle? I found tonight's meal surprisingly splendid. I wonder if —"

"I regret very much, Mr. Westcott, but we have no more vacant rooms to let at the moment." Sam heard her aunt clearing her throat and banging a kettle in the kitchen. They had plenty of rooms to let, but Mr. Westcott made her feel uncomfortable. His crestfallen look gave her a hitch of guilty pleasure.

A dark eyebrow shot up above his glasses. "Are you quite certain? I have heard in town that you only have a few boarders at the moment." His blue eyes gazed at her beneath spiky black lashes.

Sam nodded, arms crossed over her chest in her best no-nonsense pose.

"Well, then, I pray you will permit me to take my meals here. My indigestion quails at the thought of another meal at the Silver Buckle." He rubbed his flat stomach. "I shall fade completely away into the . . ." He turned and looked in distaste at the ground at the edge of the porch. ". . . fade away into the dust."

That did it. All he could think about was dust and looking down his patrician nose at everything. He was obviously even more of a greenhorn than Sam and her kin were. But in spite of his arrogant and condescending manner, there was something appealing about the man. A thought that Sam firmly denied. Yet how could she refuse his plea for eating privileges? The man did look sincere. And maybe on the slender side.

Aunt Twila would soon tackle that.

"We could probably find room for you at our table. It might prove expensive though," she warned. So there; maybe Aunt Twila wouldn't be so provoked with her. She was surprised to see a quirk of amusement playing at the corner of Mr. Westcott's mouth. She didn't want to think overmuch about his mouth.

When she and her aunt were alone later that night, Sam discovered her aunt was far from pleased at her actions.

"What in the world got into you, Samantha? I'm nearly at a loss for words. Such a genteel, refined young man, too."

Sam wrinkled her nose, knowing it made her freckles move around. She'd made faces in the mirror enough to realize that most young women didn't sport freckles.

"You? At a loss for words?" she countered, laughing to take any perceived bite from her voice. Her aunt could be overly sensitive. "I couldn't tolerate that pompous ass from the moment I saw him." That wasn't exactly true and Sam felt uneasy for telling a fib to her aunt. In spite of his stuffy ways, there was something appealing about the man. And that annoyed her.

"But we need all the boarders we can get. You struck a hard bargain with him for the privilege of dining here, and I hope we can live up to it. The new helper Garth hired could be useful if she ever shows up for work."

It had taken a bit of wheedling to get their aunt to agree to take on outside help, but Garth said Miss Peaches highly recommended the young woman. As if a recommendation from a pool hall floozy and their uncle's paramour was any basis for hiring anyone. Anyhow, the girl hadn't made her presence known yet.

"You looked very nice tonight. Like we had our old Samantha back. I'm glad you decided to get rid of your spinster disguise, dear."

"You forget. I *am* a spinster in real life, Auntie."

"Nonsense, child. Twenty-eight is just the beginning. Jeffery was a cad. I knew it all the time you and he were courting. Even if your poor, misguided father had the wool pulled over his eyes. Someday, someone will come along and wipe all the bad memories away. I wasn't married until I was thirty-two, if you recall." Her gray eyes misted as she thought of the long departed Stephen Brody.

"Of course. I remember Papa speaking about him. Your husband was a self-educated man, a Polish refugee without a cent to his name, and you two were madly in love. I thought it so romantic." Sam looked at her aunt fondly, wondering how it would be to grow old with everything exciting and wonderful behind and nothing much left to come. "You gave the Kirkland family a run for their money, didn't you, dear?"

Aunt Twila smiled, her eyes twinkling. "You bet I did. The whole family wanted to give up on me. That's precisely why I loved your mother so. She was the only one who understood and talked your father around to my way of thinking. Without all of you, I wouldn't have any family at all. After Stephen died, there was nothing left for me." She shook her head sadly, the iron gray hair struggling out in delicate wisps around her face, while the rest stayed in place in a tight bun at the nape of her neck. The lamplight softened her somewhat angular features. As she bent over her knitting, Sam could almost picture the girl she once was so long ago.

Several days later Garth dropped in to the boardinghouse, and Clarence J. Westcott was properly introduced. Later, alone in Sam's room, Garth made fun of him.

"Here is my card, sir," he mimicked. "Clarence J. Westcoot, at your service. Oops, I articulated your name incorrectly. I meant Westcott." They both laughed.

"He does look a popinjay, doesn't he?" Sam wiped the tears of laughter from her eyes.

"That's it, Sam! You know what he looks like more than anything in that ridiculous Lord Fauntleroy's blue suit and those glasses that keep sliding down his nose? A gen-u-wine blue jay. You know, like the bird."

Even though Sam joined her brother in laughter, she had to repress a slight sense of guilt about speaking of the man behind his back. True, they did grate on each other's nerves, but he was unfailingly courteous to her and respectful to Aunt Twila. Sam couldn't help but think his blue eyes hid something significant behind those spectacles.

While they talked, Garth spread out some papers and money the gang had stolen on their last robbery foray.

"But Garth, I thought you were going to send Big Bear for me so that I could join you. I want to be a part of this, too," Sam protested, ruffling through the papers distractedly.

"Yeah, I know, sis, but there was no time to spare. Besides, I've got four men and myself now, so we can handle it. There's no sense for you to be involved." He held up his hand when she opened her mouth to argue. "You're helping me more here in town than you can imagine. You got us the last three jobs we wouldn't have known about if you hadn't overheard the gossip. Especially since Deputy Wade has begun eating at the boardinghouse. No telling how much you'll be able to learn from him."

Sam shook her head. "He's very close-mouthed. I maybe could learn more from the blue jay if he ever got his head out of the sand. Anyway, I enjoyed the company of our desperados, they are all so interesting." She looked down at her hands clasped together. Some of her beaus back in St. Louis used to flatter her about her long fingers and pale hands. She turned her palms up to stare at them as if they belonged to someone else. Her hands were brown from the sun, her palms calloused from working in the garden and with the horses. She decided she liked them better this way.

"Tell me more about this Elvin character," Sam said.

"Oh, he's just your normal, average, good-natured stage robber." Garth barely repressed a smile. "I can hardly wait until you two meet. You'll either love him or hate him, and I won't lay odds on which it will be."

Even though it would test her patience, Sam decided to wait and see.

CHAPTER 14

On the fifth night out after Elvin had joined their gang, the major sidled up to Garth sitting alone at the campfire in their hideout.

"I say, young man, appears that everyone is asleep except us."

Garth nodded, waiting. The major had expressed dismay at the idea of bunking out in the cave, even though they all had thick bedrolls now. Garth considered letting him come into the boardinghouse, but how to disguise Annabel?

"The new man," the major said, and then paused hopefully, but Garth didn't speak. "I believe you Americans have a saying like 'odd duck,' maybe. He is, old chap, no getting around it."

Garth thought for a moment and then sighed. "Does it bother you?" He had suspected as much about Elvin, and his suspicions had been confirmed the second night out, when Elvin expounded about how much he enjoyed his prison companions and missed them. After that, Garth waited to hear from others in the gang. So far, the major was the only one to speak out on the subject, but then Garth recalled Don Pancho and Big Bear covertly watching Elvin with what seemed mild curiosity.

The major shifted from one foot to another, for once at a loss for words. "I can't really say. Seems to me it should be rather like one's religious preferences. One's own business, more or less. I thought you should be aware in the event it causes problems in the future."

Garth smiled in the darkness. "That's how I ended up figuring it, Major. I don't know how the other two men think about it." He groaned in exasperation. "I sure know how to pick a gang, don't I? A one-eyed Indian, a homeless Basque who doesn't know a word of English, an ex-cavalry officer with an allergy to horses, and now a leprechaun outlaw. If I didn't feel responsible for the lot of you, I sometimes feel like chucking the whole thing and going back to St. Louis."

"Now, now, my boyo, it never helps to wallow in self-pity. We are getting the job done, aren't we?" The major nudged Garth lightly on the shoulder. "But getting back to Elvin, he has never bothered any of us with any unseemly approaches. I believe he will do fine. He seems to have a bit more experience in the desperado line than the rest of us."

"I reckon you're right. We'll have to wait and see. He is a good cook and a fair guitar player and always loses at cards. That's in his favor."

The major nodded with a vigor, seriously endangering his toupee, but it stayed in place. "What about the young lad, your brother, when he returns? What will he think about the situation?"

"Sam?" The idea startled Garth. "He'll have to find out for himself, won't he? The kid needs a more worldly education anyway. He's far too naïve for a growing boy."

After their next stagecoach haul, Garth sent Big Bear to bring Sam to the hideout. She gave them the high sign when she entered the cave, at first wanting to hug them all, Then she thought that might be overmuch for a young man to want to do. Garth introduced her to the new member.

Elvin grinned at her, and she thought what a handsome young man. Garth had described him as a hardened outlaw used to being in prison, but he didn't appear that way to her.

Garth smiled, his teeth white in the gloom of the cave, and patted the blanket he sat on, motioning for her to sit beside him. The others gathered around. He dumped the big leather bags they'd taken from the stage.

"It was a pretty good haul, Sam." He held up papers in each hand. "We've got stock certificates from the Peaches Mine, the payroll — which we can split — and letters from Uncle Millard to his lawyer, Mr. Wilder, and — hold on here, what's this?" He had been casually glancing through the papers, reading a line here and there when he stopped and stood, quivering in anger.

"What's the matter, Garth?" Sam looked up at her brother, unused to seeing him so upset.

He held a letter in his shaking hand. "Sam, can you believe this? That damnable uncle of ours has ordered a spy sent in our midst."

"But surely he doesn't know about us."

"No, I don't think that's likely, but he's asked his lawyer to hire spies for the small surrounding towns, and Powder is one."

"Does it say who he hired?"

Their eyes locked and they both thought of the blue jay at the same time.

"But he's only an accountant, if you are thinking of the blue jay," Sam disagreed.

"Of course, he's only an accountant. Don't be dense. I'd bet my bottom dollar he's the spy in our midst. That means we're getting to the old coot if he's willing to put out money for a spy." His exasperation turned to glee and he sat down again, much calmer.

"You are sure he doesn't know about us, who we are and where we are?" Sam asked, amazed at Garth's sudden change.

The rest of the gang receded back to their beds, listening, but not understanding all that went on between the siblings.

"That's so great about the whole idea. For sure, Uncle Millard hasn't a clue we are involved. Why would he? By the same token, his spy would have no reason to connect the names Tremayne with Kirkland or Brody. The blue jay is Uncle Millard's toady and likely knows nothing about his personal life or his life back in St. Louis. Remember, our illustrious uncle wants to eventually shed that skin and move on."

"Sounds good," she commented.

"Are you remembering to send the old goat letters once in a while from your friend's address in New York? He has to think we are there."

Sam nodded. "Sure am. In fact, I sent one last week. It galls me to have to write to him, pretending that I don't know what he is and what he's done. What I wouldn't give to have a real confrontation with him and let him know for sure it's *us* doing this to him."

"We may do that one day." Garth grinned.

"We wouldn't dare, would we? I mean, he could have us sent away to prison."

"Uh-uh, I don't think so. He couldn't do that if we get enough evidence against him. He wouldn't dare. He can't go back to St. Louis, and he couldn't stay out here. But on the other hand, I wouldn't put it past him to try to remove us somehow. Like he did our dad. Even though Dad's death was a suicide, Uncle Millard caused it. In fact, he would almost be forced to kill us to protect his own hide."

Sam didn't hide her shocked expression as she watched him scoop up the certificates. "We'll burn these, save the letters that might incriminate him, and split the money."

Sam looked at the men sitting silently nearby. "Do they know why we are doing this?"

Before Garth could answer, the major spoke into the quiet. "Have no cares about concealing your personal campaign, laddie. I think I speak for all of us when I say we do not care. We are here for various reasons, and it is helpful to earn some money at the same time. Our lips are sealed, right?" He turned to the three sitting nearby. Don Pancho nodded, even though they knew he probably hadn't understood much of the conversation.

"Not to cast aspersions, but how do we know *he* is not the spy?" Sam pointed at Elvin.

A loud burst of laughter from the men greeted that idea. Elvin stood and approached Sam. Garth moved to stand in front of her, but she pushed him back, wanting to hear what Elvin had to say.

"You see this?" He pulled down the collar of his shirt, and they saw the tattoo of a snake that started with its head behind his ear and the rest trailing downward past his shirt collar. "I got me this in prison so that if I ever went back, they'd remember me. I ain't no squealer, that's for dang sure. Know what they do to squealers and spies in prison?" Elvin and Sam were both the same height when he leaned forward to look Sam in the eyes.

She shook her head but refused to back up.

"Well. It ain't for your young ears for me to say. But I swear I would never spy for anyone."

Sam leaned forward and offered her hand. "I'm sorry if I offended you, Elvin. It was a passing thought, and it won't come to mind again." They shook hands, and at the last minute Sam thought he wasn't going to let go. A puzzled look swept over his face before he abruptly went back to his bedroll and plopped down.

"Getting back to the real spy, isn't it dangerous to have him nearby? I wish to God I hadn't let him come to dinner every day." She felt strangely upset by the notion the innocuous blue jay might contribute to their downfall. She had secretly grown to look forward to his company at the dinner table. They argued and disagreed on every subject that had come up so far, but the elderly boarders hardly talked at all.

"No, it's a grand idea," Garth said. "We keep him in our sights and, at the same time, watch ourselves that we don't give anything away. Feed him faulty information that will get back to Uncle Millard. That way we can see how close the old buzzard is to getting wind of the idea that he's the sole victim. That's when we'll have to slack off and let him alone for a while. But until that happens, we need to warn Aunt Twila to stay on her toes, too."

155

"He could also be spying on Mr. Wilder. I wouldn't put it past our uncle not to trust his lawyer."

"You're right. He could be the 'in' we need."

Big Bear took Sam home that night to the boardinghouse. Even in her disguise, the hideout was no place for her at night. At least she and Garth agreed on that.

Back at the boardinghouse, Sam tried valiantly to ignore the blue jay when he came to dinner, but it became increasingly harder to do. He entertained everyone at the table with witty conversation and charmed her aunt, even though Sam had warned her they suspected him of being a spy for their uncle. Even at his most foppish, Sam thought she could see something beneath his cool, reserved exterior he didn't want them to see.

Seth and Jasper hung on his every word when he told them he'd seen Wild Bill and Calamity Jane perform at Madison Square Garden in New York. Deputy Wade regarded him as a freak of sorts and patently ignored him. Sam set aside her suspicions long enough to decide it would be in their best interests for her to gain his confidence.

That seemed easy enough. There were

times when Sam was bewildered by his measured study of her, even though he tried to hide his scrutiny behind hooded eyes and his spectacles. Aunt Twila even remarked how, when Sam sat down at the dinner table, he hardly took his attention from her.

Sam did notice he seemed jealous of Deputy Wade and tried to steer any conversation between the deputy and Sam back to him. But she reasoned this could be his obviously inflated conceit. He didn't want any male competition. Sam assured herself he was in no way attracted to her. She maintained her distance as best she could.

CHAPTER 15

One evening Sam sat alone on the porch swing, a knitted wrap thrown over her shoulders. In spite of the heated days, nights were refreshingly cool on the high desert. She wondered idly what winters would be like.

"You seem very thoughtful tonight, if I may say so, Miss Brody."

Sam looked up to see the blue jay standing in front of her, smoothing the razor sharp crease in his trouser leg — as if it needed it. He seated himself on the edge of the swing, first dusting off the seat with his ever-present white handkerchief.

Sam wrinkled her nose in annoyance. "Oh, for heaven's sake. My name is Samantha, and I already dusted the darned seat off before I sat down."

He looked at her, his glasses sliding down his straight nose. Up close, she saw how startlingly blue his eyes were, with curious white flakes in them that looked rather like miniature icebergs.

He shook his handkerchief, folded it carefully, and placed it exactly in the same place in his vest pocket. "Certainly, if that is your wish, I will be less formal. Samantha is an unusual name, isn't it? Don't your aunt and some of the boarders refer to you as Sam?"

"Maybe. People I *like* call me Sam," she added.

He continued to smile impassively at her, as if he didn't understand her barb.

Immediately she was ashamed of her bad manners. "Where are you employed, Mr. Westcott? You mentioned you are an accountant."

"Oh, ho, it's my turn now. You must call me Clarence J."

She couldn't help notice he sidestepped her question.

"I gave your aunt my card."

"But where do you account?" She thought she caught a speculative gleam in his eyes for a second, but then it disappeared into his usual bland expression.

He smiled at her choice of words. He could actually be attractive if he wasn't always so stuffy. A curve of straight dark hair fell over his forehead at times, almost making him appear boyish. She'd never seen even the beginning of whiskers, so he must shave often. In fact, with his dark hair and expressive eyebrows added to his starkly blue eyes and chiseled features, he might have been appealing, if good looks hadn't seemed shamefully wasted on Clarence J. because of his snooty attitude.

He failed to answer her question about his employment. Very suspicious in itself.

"Well . . ." He hesitated and then, as if having made a decision, he began to speak. She could almost hear the gears turning in his head.

"My employer wanted me to come here on the q.t. so I must ask you to honor my confidences." He pushed his glasses back up his nose.

When he fell to brooding, she spoke up. "Who is your employer, and why would he want your working for him to be a secret?" Sam tried to moderate her voice over the beating of her heart.

"Perhaps it is best that you know something of my background. I think you might be of some help to me, for you have been here much longer than I, and you know many of these people in this ridiculous town."

Sam raised her chin in defiance. At first she'd thought the same thing about Powder, but she'd slowly grown to recognize the good in some of the townspeople she met. She kept quiet, not wanting to alter his confiding mood.

"I am employed by a very generous and distinguished firm in St. Louis."

"St Louis!" she blurted. "Your card said you were from New York." Her heart raced at the certainty he was speaking about her uncle. She swallowed with a dry throat, struggling not to cough and call attention to her realization. She waited to see if he would continue. What kind of a spy would spill his guts like this, or was this a ploy to gain her confidence? If so, he might suspect something going on at the boardinghouse connected with her uncle. Something deep inside her wanted this not to be so.

"Yes, yes, I am — was — from New York, but my current employer is from St. Louis." It seemed as if he knew he might have gone too far sharing confidential information and didn't know how to stop.

"At any rate, my employer believes something peculiar is going on out here concerning his holdings and . . ."

"And *you* were sent out to investigate?" she asked, not trying to hide her scorn.

He flushed at her obvious derision. "Yes and no. I've had the desire to visit the West for as long as I can remember. Something about this place calls to me. But I'm merely here to check out the possibilities of a swindle, bookkeeping-wise. It might possibly have to do with Miss Peaches or Mr. Wilder." He paused, clearly dismayed. "Oh dear, surely you and Mr. Wilder aren't acquaintances, are you? I might be speaking out of turn."

"No, I don't know either of them personally," Sam assured him, taking pity on his apprehension even as she decided he didn't deserve her consideration. It was a relief to know he hadn't mentioned any robberies. At the same time, he'd made it clear he worked for their uncle.

He looked relieved for a moment, pushing his boots against the porch floor to get the swing moving. The loud, protesting squeal of the chains startled them, and they both laughed, breaking the tension.

But Sam had to ask, "How did you come from New York and end up working in St. Louis?"

He made a dismissive gesture with a wave of his hand. "I carry a discreet ad in the *New York Times* regarding my services. I surmise Mr. Tremayne saw the ad. He offered a bonus if I discovered chicanery with the books, and here I am."

"Have you discovered any skulduggery with Miss Peaches and Mr. Wilder yet?"

He shrugged. "Not really. It's tedious going, sifting through all the bookwork. Some of the books seem to be missing, and Mr. Tremayne cannot account for them. Mr. Wilder claims someone stole them, but why anyone would care to do that, I couldn't even guess. The most difficult part is that Mr. Wilder mustn't suspect he is under scrutiny. It is entirely possible he is innocent of any wrongdoing. Naturally he would be most indignant should he find out he is being investigated."

"Naturally," Sam said dryly. "And this person named Miss Peaches? Who is she, and where does she fit in?"

He raised a black eyebrow. "I don't think there is anything to justify my employer's mistrust as far as she is concerned. She keeps a perfect set of books, interestingly enough. She manages a local gambling house for Mr. Tremayne."

Sam felt an odd flash of jealousy. Did he know the woman personally? Garth certainly seemed to admire her. She had seen Peaches from across the street once when Garth pointed her out. She was a handsome woman, a bit too well rounded for polite society maybe. Her hair was a discreet

163

strawberry blond, and her coloring matched. Her name suited her. How a young woman her own age could fall under her uncle's so-called charm was beyond her. Yet Garth admitted he was quite taken with her, and now the exasperatingly sensible Clarence J. seemed to hold her in high esteem.

"Why are you telling me this?" Sam asked bluntly, smarting from her unwilling spark of jealousy.

The blue jay appeared uncomfortable. "Actually, I thought — presumed, rather — that you might be of some assistance to me. You are in a position to hear a bit of gossip or information that might prove useful. Not everyone is willing to converse with me, for some reason."

Well, that's a huge surprise. "I think you have a lot of nerve, trying to drag me into your furtive detectiving. I certainly am not in the habit of dashing around town listening to gossip and innuendos, much less repeating them. Do you suppose that's all I have to do in life? You admitted you can't find anything going on here in Powder to report to your employer. You're either a terrible accountant, or your employer is an unreasonably fearful idiot. Either way, *I* certainly am not planning on becoming involved." She was proud of her tirade and waited for his reaction.

It wasn't long in coming. He had the grace to flush. Then he closed his eyes for a moment, as if to hide his emotions. His expression hardened and he was about to open his mouth to retaliate, when Deputy Wade stomped up onto the porch.

"Oh, there you are, Miss Samantha. I thought I might take a meal with you today since my workload is light." He ignored Clarence J. as if he weren't present.

The blue jay stood hastily. "I was just leaving. Good day, Miss Samantha." He tipped his index finger to his forehead in a mock salute to Wade and left abruptly.

Deputy Wade crossed the porch and sat down beside Sam, laying his Stetson on the porch floor. The blue jay wouldn't be caught dead doing that, she thought.

"Do you reckon this thing will hold me?" he asked. "I'm a trifle heavier than our departing friend."

Sam looked at the man sitting next to her. He might be in his thirties, same as the blue jay, with wide shoulders, and his hands were big to match. It was obvious there was not one ounce of unused flesh on his large frame. He wore his light brown hair shorter than most men she'd seen in town. His cheekbones were high, and his jaw straight and uncompromising, in spite of his usual good-natured smile. She might not define him as actually handsome, but he did have an undeniable maleness about him that contrasted sharply with the blue jay's chiseled features. Odd and equally annoying was how she didn't get that sudden flash of anticipation when Deputy Wade appeared as she did with Clarence J.

"I saw you out here with the dude and almost didn't interrupt, but you looked so irritated, thought I'd best rescue a lady in distress."

Sam laughed. "Thanks a lot. That's exactly what you did. He *is* sort of hard to take in big doses, isn't he?"

They talked for a while about nothing in particular. She had never spent much time with the deputy, knowing she had to be careful with her words. Any officer of the law could be a danger to their mission. She wondered vaguely how it would feel to be courted by someone other than her ex-fiancé. Jeffery had been only interested in her money and position in St. Louis. Now she didn't even have a dowry, having spent so much of it on the trip out here and buying the boardinghouse. Didn't matter, she assured herself. She wouldn't be opposed to staying a spinster. Even so, the thought of a family and children intruded. She brushed the thoughts away.

That night as Sam lay in bed thinking over her conversation with the blue jay, she felt at a loss. She was sure something sinister hid behind his innocuous revelations, but what? Did he suspect her in any way? She hoped Garth would come for her soon so she could tell him about the conversation.

She awoke later that night to hear the familiar bird call of Big Bear. She leaped out of bed and ran to the closet for her riding clothes.

CHAPTER 16

The gang's next job turned out to be at a gambling house owned by their uncle in a town miles from Powder called Lodestar. According to some of the records Garth had intercepted, the Lodestar Saloon and Gambling Emporium made almost as much profit as the larger establishment in Powder.

Sam's excitement at being a part of the gang swelled with the satisfaction that Garth needed her. One quick pleased glimpse in the mirror before she left showed a scruffy street urchin, a budding juvenile delinquent. The streets of Arizona towns contained many such boys, some homeless, some orphans, but for the most part, all ignored. Garth was counting on this. He needed her for a lookout while Don Pancho held the horses.

The saloon never closed, but some hours were busier than others. Late night was the best time, the time he planned to break into the safe. The only way into the safe was through the back alley. The safe was in a room connected to the main saloon by a brick wall between them. Sam knew Garth had checked it out days before.

Sam leaned against the hitching post at the edge of the alley. If she strained her eyes, she could see the form of Don Pancho with the horses across the street and in back of the opposite alley. What was keeping them? They had been gone a long time. Edges of tension crept across her shoulders, and her stomach began to roil. But she dared not leave her post. She was to hoot like an owl if she saw anyone approach. Her heart lurched when she heard the jingle of spurs coming from across the street and heading her way. It was too late to give a signal. She pretended to doze against the side of the saloon. A rough hand shook her hard on the shoulder. She looked up to see a shiny badge on a man's chest. She hadn't even had a chance to warn the others. Holding her breath, she looked the sheriff in the eye. He released her shoulder abruptly.

"Time you was in bed, sonny. Yore folks know you're out this late?" His eyes held kindness, and she took advantage of it.

She nodded her head, her floppy hat bobbing, struggling to lower her voice and keep her heart working properly. "I'm waitin' for my pa. He said to stay right outside here." She motioned toward the front door of the saloon.

"Oh, yeah," the lawman snickered. "Reckon you are a mite better off out here than in there." With that, he turned and headed toward the other side of the street again. Would he see Don Pancho lurking in the shadows? She strained to look, but Don Pancho and the horses must have backed all the way into the alley. The sheriff passed on down the empty street.

She heaved a sigh of relief when Garth and the others walked cautiously forward. Together they hurried across the street to grab their horses and head back to the hideout.

It was too dark to make it safely to the cave, so they bedded down under the stars that night in a grove of cottonwood trees beside a stream. Early in the morning, they headed for the hideout — including Sam, against Garth's protests.

Once there, Garth split the money and put the documents in his saddlebags.

"I'll come to town soon," he told Sam, "and we can go over the papers then. Meanwhile, maybe you'd better go back with Big Bear."

170

Sam shook her head. "Not on your life. I need to take a look at our horses after that long night ride, and I want to stay one more night. I like looking out at the stars before I go to sleep."

The next morning Sam was worried and preoccupied. She barely spoke to anyone. After a while Garth missed her. She had not come to the breakfast call, which was unusual. Elvin was a great cook. Garth went looking for Sam and found her sitting alone in the shade of a large rock outcropping.

"What's up, Sam? You've been jittery all morning, and it's not like you to miss a meal. Did that brush with the lawman scare you?"

"You know better than that. It's something else. I might have to quit the gang." She looked as if she was fiercely holding back tears.

"Why? What are you talking about?"

She wriggled on the stone where she sat and wouldn't look at him directly. "I think the new man, Elvin, sees through my disguise. We agreed that if anyone guessed, I'd have to quit."

"How could he, when no one else has, Sam? That's ridiculous. Only Big Bear knows, and I'd stake my life on him not saying a word about it."

"Elvin tried to — he tried to get familiar with me," Sam blurted.

She might have said more, but Garth's laughter interrupted her speech. His face went red from laughing and he had to hold his sides.

Sam stood, hands on her hips, her brown eyes flashing exasperation. For a moment she was speechless, but that didn't last long.

"Some brother you are! You are supposed to champion me and uphold my honor." Tears came to her eyes. "You can forget about my honor if it means so little to you. I don't want to quit the gang. They are all so interesting, and they accept me. I can't hide in that boring boardinghouse the rest of my life."

Garth sighed. He understood her anxiety, but her worries were so ironic. Gently he took her arm and sat her back down again. He sat by her side so they wouldn't have to talk too loudly

"Now, ah . . . brother, I'm going to talk to you like a Dutch uncle. I don't know how much you've been told about the proverbial birds and bees, but it's time you realized people are different in many ways. There are men, and I suppose women too, who crave attention from their own sex as opposed to the opposite sex. Elvin happens to be one of those, and he took you for a young man. He was just checking you out. I suppose you put him in his place right quick."

"To be sure." Her eyes were wide with shock, and Garth wasn't sure if she truly believed his explanation.

"But what do they do about it? Together, I mean."

Garth shrugged. He couldn't remember ever being this uncomfortable. "Do you know what men and women do together?" he countered.

"No. Not exactly. I was too young when mother died. And as for Aunt Twila —" She smothered a giggle behind her palm.

"Well then, don't worry about it. Everything will come to you when you're ready." Garth wasn't about to give his big sister a lesson about sex. Not now. Not ever.

"I'll never be able to face him again," Sam said.

Garth pointed inside, where they could see beyond the opening of the cave and the men sitting around the campfire. "Look at Elvin helping Don Pancho fix that bridle strap. You have no idea how many times Elvin has volunteered to get Annabel going for the major when he needed to get away quickly. The kid is a wonder with mechanics. He's a great cook, too."

"He *is* a fine cook," Sam admitted. "And he keeps everyone laughing."

"That's it, Sam. You liked him yesterday. He's the same person today. I guarantee you, he won't try anything funny again once he's put in his place."

She shifted her weight on the rock and watched the men for a long moment. Garth could almost hear her thoughts. What he'd tried to tell her went way beyond a young lady's acceptable knowledge, but she wouldn't have settled for less of an explanation, and he didn't want her to quit the gang. They were having too much fun.

"I guess I may be able to come to grips with the idea in time. You sure he won't try any shenanigans again? I wouldn't be able to close my eyes at night."

"Nope. I'd lay odds he won't, but to be on the safe side, since you're such a tasty morsel, I'll have a talk with him. Okay?"

It was later afternoon before Garth worked out a chance to be alone with Elvin. Without ceremony, Garth began abruptly before he thought much about the awkwardness of the situation. He couldn't give away Sam's disguise.

"My kid brother tells me you . . . well, what I mean is . . ." They were sitting out by the horses.

174

"Shucks, pal. Don't beat around the bush. You ain't hurting my feelings." Elvin grinned, unabashed. He'd tied his longish brown hair with a string at the back of his neck. With his spare wiry body and his baby blue eyes showing his humor and good nature, he resembled nothing like the experienced outlaw he tried to portray.

When Garth proved at a loss for words, Elvin spoke. "So what about it? You got something to say to me? Seems like your brother is older than twenty. Not like I'm trying to rob the cradle or nothing."

"Did you try everyone in the gang?" Garth asked.

"Well, almost. I tried that there major fellow first. If he don't look like one of us, I don't know who does."

Garth could only imagine how horrified the major would have been to hear this description of himself.

"And?" Garth prompted.

Elvin grinned. "He damn sure ain't no kindred spirit, that's for sure. He let me know it right away. And the big Injun, I was half afraid of him, but you know how it goes. Nothing ventured, nothing gained. Shucks, he didn't even get riled up about it. Let me know he wasn't interested. As to the Mex. I know better than that, and he's a mite too long in the tooth anyway." Elvin shrugged. " 'Course I wouldn't have tried you in a New York minute. You're too damn mean." He slapped his knee and laughed.

He seemed not a bit put out by the various gang members' refusals, and apparently none of the others took serious offense since Garth could detect no changes in their behavior toward Elvin.

"Okay then. You've had your game, and it's all over now, isn't it? I mean, none of them seem to hold a grudge against you. It's important that we all get along, living so close together like we do. Do you want to keep on with us or not?" Garth kept his voice stern and uncompromising so Elvin wouldn't think he could joke around about the matter.

Elvin looked up from smoking his cigarette in astonishment. "Keep on with you and the fellows? 'Course I do. What's that supposed to mean? Your pitiful gang is the only friends I've got out here. Pert near as good a bunch as the ones back in Yuma Prison." He drew a deep breath and exhaled a ring of smoke. "I ain't gonna mess with no one. Just had to check them out. Period. Finished. Now let's get down to Dry Gulch soon. I'm feeling a raging thirst coming on."

CHAPTER 17

Big Bear escorted Sam home and then joined the group in a cantina across the border in Mexico, the only place that allowed the Indian to sit at a table with them while they had their beers. He never touched a drop of liquor. Garth believed they shouldn't all hang together and get in a habit of going to the same places. So far the robberies had gone well with them using the head masks Aunt Twila made for them. Don Pancho stayed hidden with the horses and the major had to be the watch because of Annabel. Sometimes they varied the number of the ones stopping the coaches to throw people off-track as to descriptions and numbers.

In the cantina at the table next to theirs sat a thin, wiry-looking man who could have been anywhere from thirty to fifty years old. He had a belligerent, mean look about him. His face was clean-shaven except for the bristly mustache beneath his curved beak of a nose. Garth and his men were drawn to the man like moths to a flame, thinking he might prove to be an interesting addition to their group. The dangerous man even impressed Big Bear. Since they were the only customers in the cantina that afternoon, it was inevitable they began conversing.

"Name's Buster," the man stated, regarding each man at Garth's table with steely, impassive eyes.

"What do you do?" Garth asked. He knew this topic was normally forbidden, but he couldn't help his curiosity, and he knew the others felt the same.

Buster shrugged. "I'm at loose ends right now. But I'm always on the lookout for something profitable to turn my hand to. And I'm not talking about work, neither," he said frankly.

Garth peered at the others. Their expression held curiosity, but their gestures said they would leave Buster to him. He could use one more man to make up the gang he needed.

When Garth got up to sit at Buster's table, he asked the only question he could come up with. "Ever break the law?" It was a chancy subject, but he had to start somewhere.

Buster laughed, the sound grating in the quiet room. "Do I look like I'd care about the law? Are you a lawman looking to get shot? In this place, they don't much care if you're law or not. You'll just be dead."

Garth took a deep breath and let out a hint of what his gang was up to. Buster's eyes lit up for the first time.

"Sounds entertaining. I believe I'll join you." He motioned to Garth, and they went to sit with the others at their table. Garth introduced everyone. He wasn't about to show their hideout to a stranger until he'd proven himself.

"I heard of a stage coming up. We only select special targets, and I make the decisions. It should come along around ten tonight. We plan to stop it a few miles outside of Contention. Meet us at the cottonwoods along the trail."

It was on this trip the gang realized their mistake in taking Buster on. He not only was experienced, but mean, sadistic, and completely lacking in conscience. His first time out with them, while Garth and the others were performing their usual duties, Buster climbed up on the stage and pistol-whipped the guard because he talked back to him. He started to order the passengers out.

Garth jerked him away; the others were clearly shocked. After the stage pulled away, Garth took Buster aside.

"We don't do violence. We'll have the Earps down on us if you start that sort of brutality. I think we'd better part company right now. I'll divide the take and —"

"I can tone it down. I don't like back talk, is all. It riles me up something bad. I can be a lot of help to you. You got an Indian as tall as a tree that you mostly have to hide so no one will recognize him. That old Mexican man might have come over on Noah's boat, a swishy fellow who might be of some experience, and that old English fellow who won't ride a horse. What in the hell have you got to lose by keeping *me* on?"

It didn't take Garth long to absorb the truth in Buster's words. Everything he said was dead right, except that together they worked as a team and so far their efforts *had* been profitable. But his plan was to needle their uncle until he did something drastic, or until they found evidence in letters proving what Uncle Millard had done back in St. Louis. The longer it took them, the more danger they ran of having a posse come after them. If it came to light their uncle was the only target, he would be on a stage headed out here in no time. They needed him to stay put in St. Louis.

Knowing somehow he would regret it, Garth told Buster he could stay. But there was no way to avoid taking him back to the hideout, since they all had to retreat there.

The next time Sam came to work with them, she and Buster locked horns immediately.

"I don't cotton to the idea of having a snotty nosed kid trailing along with us, even if he is your kid brother. He could get us caught if he can't keep up."

"I can keep up with the best of you," Sam shouted back, keeping her voice as low and deep as she could. "It's *you* we don't need."

On their next job, they set out to rob a mercantile belonging to Uncle Millard in Lodestar. It was late at night, and they hadn't counted on a guard sitting inside smoking a cigarette. Garth smelled the smoke the moment he coaxed open the back door. He held up a hand for his gang to wait until he could tiptoe around and reconnoiter. Before he moved, Buster sneaked past him, located the man dozing, and smacked him on the head with his pistol butt.

"Jesus, Mary, and Joseph, why did you do that?" Garth knelt beside the prone man and held his fingers to his neck for a pulse.

Relieved to feel it steady, he stood and hit his fist into Buster's shoulder. "We could have subdued him and tied him up, you jackass."

Buster swung on Garth, pistol raised, until he heard the *snick-snick* of two rifles cocking. The major and Elvin pointed the rifles at Buster.

He lowered his pistol. "Aw, hell. It was easier this way. He might have been able to finger one or all of us. You said we wouldn't need the masks on this job." He glared at Garth, his eyes cold with fury. "But don't ever touch me, man. I can't take that."

Garth was unable to open the big safe in the back room. While he was struggling with the tumbler on the lock, Buster found a cashbox under the counter the clerk must have thought was protected. He shot off the lock and took out the money, shoving it into his saddlebags. After that, he moved around trashing the store, even though Garth shouted at him to stop. They hurried out the back door with the idea that he wouldn't want to be left behind. No way could they leave him with the money in his saddlebags. He finally joined them, and they went back to the hideout. All the men were quiet, an uncommon thing after a successful raid. Usually they slapped each other on the back and laughed with relief that the job was over.

Not only did Garth not approve of violence, he worried that if there were too many needless assaults, the authorities would begin to watch for them. Right now they were actually a laughing matter with the law. If the Earps or a posse decided to hunt them down, there would be no way to continue. They would have to disband, throwing away any chance at getting even with their uncle or proving anything against him.

That would be Garth and Sam's worst nightmare, to have to set aside their revenge. It would be like trampling over their father's grave. While they were back in St. Louis, Garth had compiled a long list of Tremayne's holdings in Arizona from the letters and records he'd appropriated and they had barely started on that list.

One night, while Sam was in Powder, the gang sat around drinking at the hideout. Only Don Pancho and Big Bear abstained and had gone to sleep rolled up in the bedding in back of the cave.

Elvin, befuddled by liquor, accidentally kicked into Buster's bedroll. Knowing Elvin's choice of partners, Buster must have assumed he did it on purpose. In a blinding rage, he knocked Elvin to the ground and began stomping on him. Everyone rolled out of their blankets and Garth quickly lit a lantern. Big Bear and Garth pulled Buster off the huddled and sobbing Elvin, half dragging him toward the campfire.

"What you need to stomp him for?" Big Bear towered over Buster, who wasn't backing up an inch but held a pistol pointed toward them.

"Never mind him, let's tend to the kid." Garth silently blessed the fact that Sam wasn't there. When they could pry Elvin from his fetal position, they felt certain he had several broken ribs and a broken nose. After they made him as comfortable as possible, Garth turned to Buster, who leaned against the cave opening, a sneer on his face.

"That's it. Get the hell out of here and don't come back." Big Bear and the major stood next to Garth to back him up.

"The hell you say!" Buster snarled back at them. "Keep that Nancy-boy away from me. I ain't leaving. Send him away, why don't you?"

Garth's head pounded, his body stretched tight with the fury he barely held in check. He ignored the gun in Buster's hand, even while Big Bear nudged his shoulder to stop him.

Buster waved his pistol to emphasize his

184

words. "You're on to something. I don't know where you get your information or how, but I can see there's money to be made with you and this crazy gang of yours. So I'm sticking. Keep the fairy princess away from me and we can get along. If you try to force me out, I'll have to tell where you're hiding."

Over the next day as Elvin gradually grew stronger, nothing anyone said to Buster moved him to change his mind. References to the problem only made Buster surly and harder to get along with, so gradually they left him alone. He wasn't bothered in the least when everyone pointedly ignored his existence.

"I think I should leave the gang," Elvin told the men as they sat outside the cave soaking up the early morning sun. Buster had lit his usual cigarette and strolled away, as he did most every day now.

Garth shook his head while the others voiced their disapproval. "We can't let you go. For one thing, you were here before Buster. For another, your ribs aren't healed completely and your nose looks like you been in a stampede."

Elvin grinned. "Maybe that's a good thing. I was always too handsome and young-looking to suit myself. Hard to live the outlaw life looking like a theatrical star." He spoke without a trace of conceit, as if he were talking about someone else.

Don Pancho had been boiling some leaves and twigs he'd found in the nearby desert and made poultices for his chest and ribs. He shook a gnarled finger at Elvin. "No. You stay. Bad man go."

If the gang was surprised at his struggling English, they pretended not to be.

"Big Bear, try to tell him best you can why we can't get rid of Buster — for now."

In Spanish and a few words of Basque he must have learned from Don Pancho, Big Bear complied. The sheepherder's expression said he understood but wasn't happy. None of them were. Theirs had become a very uneasy camp.

For the first time, Garth feared leaving the men to go to the boardinghouse. But if he waited too long, Sam was sure to come out on her own. He'd caught Buster watching her when she placed letters and documents in their saddlebags after a job, but the man never asked questions. Garth was beginning to wonder if Buster had caught on to how they found out about jobs when Sam came to camp. It was only a matter of time before Buster saw through Sam's

186

disguise, and then someone was going to die.

The next time Big Bear went into Powder to find out information from Sam, she refused to tell him unless he brought her back to the cave. She had determined not to listen to any of his excuses, knowing in the long run he couldn't refuse her.

When she and Big Bear returned to the hideout, Garth took her aside, and she told him what she'd heard from rumor in town. Tremayne's personal stagecoach line was sending a coach with a payload.

The following day when they rode out to intercept the vehicle, both Garth and Sam were relieved they wore the black hoods. Buster complained the hoods were too hot, but he wore one today anyway. Deputy Wade sat next to the driver, big as life. His steel gray eyes blazed down on them, but with the gang's rifles and pistols all trained on him, he didn't move.

Sam felt as if a fist had plunged into her midsection. She kept her eyes away from the deputy while she helped Elvin and the major check the passengers for weapons. After that, they tied the doors shut. Garth had always drawn a line against molesting or robbing passengers, and the gang agreed since they usually received enough payback from the chests retrieved from under the guard's seat.

What was so important about this cargo that it needed a deputy to guard it? Sam felt smothered by a wave of fear she'd never experienced before. While she and Garth speculated about that, Buster caused a commotion. They turned and ran back to the front of the stage to see Wade lying on the ground, unconscious. Buster stood over him with menace in his posture that said he was about to shoot the prone man. Sam rushed forward and knelt in front of Wade.

"The bastard must have pulled it out of his boot." He gestured at a small derringer lying on the ground a few feet away. "I'm going to plug him right now." He raised his gun and looked up to see the major and Big Bear pointing rifles at him.

Garth shook his arm. "We have to get out of here. That's a deputy, in case you didn't know." He motioned for the driver and guard to haul the deputy up on the seat with them. It took both men, since Wade was not a lightweight, but they made it.

Buster shrugged Garth's hand away, but he yielded with a sulky curl to his lips.

Garth told the driver to head on to town, and the gang watched the dust rise when the driver urged the horses to a gallop.

"I'll talk to you later about putting yourself in danger by shielding the deputy," Garth said to Sam.

By then, everyone was keyed up and ready to return to the hideout, but Annabel wouldn't start. The gang members took off their hoods and circled around the machine, no one knowing how to help. Buster grabbed the strongbox lying forgotten on the ground and leaped on his horse to leave them behind, aiming toward the hideout.

"Big Bear, go with him. There may be papers in that box I need to keep private. We'll be there soon as we can."

The Indian looked hesitant. "You sure, Boss? You might need me here if the stage comes back."

"Hurry. No time to argue. I think that strongbox holds something special, and I don't want Buster going through it. See if you can keep him from it without having to shoot him."

Without another word, Big Bear wheeled his horse and followed Buster's trail toward their cave.

"Annabel, I'm ashamed of you. That blighter is making off with our money," the major fumed. He kicked his darling motorbike in agitation.

Garth put his hand on the major's shoulder. "Sorry, old man, but we need to abandon her for now. You'll have to ride with one of us. As soon as the stage hits town, we could be facing a posse." He tilted his hat to shade his eyes and pointed to a billowing dust cloud coming from the rise where the stage had disappeared.

The major shook his head in stubborn refusal. "I can't bloody well desert her." He knelt down and started to tinker with something underneath the frame.

"We don't have time for that," Sam protested. The major raised his head in surprise, for the lad seldom spoke. Sam was thinking how humiliating it would be for Wade to return and discover who they were. Never mind the trouble they would be in.

"Please, Major," she pleaded. "You'll get us all shot up, because we won't leave you."

"Well, lad, what would you have me do? Abandon the shameless hussy?" Elvin, Sam, and Garth looked at the major standing so protectively in front of Annabel. His toupee slid dangerously from under his ten gallon hat, and he pushed it up in agitation.

It was finally Elvin who broke the uneasy silence. "Tell you what, old sport. Just this once, if you climb up behind Sam, we'll hide Annabel where she won't be seen and come back for her later. I can help fix whatever ails her, but it might take a while for us to figure it out. I've worked on a lot of army equipment in my time."

The major shook his head, eyes filled with doubt.

The cloud of dust was coming closer. Garth and Elvin began clearing a place away from the dirt road. Reluctantly the major wheeled Annabel toward them. They laid her down and covered her with mesquite branches. Sam swept the trail they'd made with brush she'd cut from a nearby bush so no one would track the bike.

The major turned to the horses with misgivings clear in his expression. "I vowed I'd never touch one of the bloody beasts again, but I can't let you get caught because of me."

He reached for Sam's saddle, ready to swing up behind her.

"No!" Garth protested loudly. They all stopped in amazement and turned to stare at him. Garth seldom let his emotions get away even under duress. "What I mean is, Sam's mare has a swollen fetlock. It wouldn't do to double up on her. Hop up behind me."

Sam and Garth exchanged amused glances. That was a near one. Even as old as the major was, he would surely be able to feel the difference in Sam's body when he wrapped his arms around her waist to hold on. Or worse, held on to her hips. Both Garth and Sam had discussed it and felt the gang would not be insulted if her true identity became known, but they dared not take a chance with Buster.

They doubled back several times through a small rocky creek to eliminate their tracks. In spite of the ominous dust cloud coming closer, they made it to the hideout without being seen.

When they arrived, Buster had already shot the padlock off the cashbox. He had discarded papers and letters in a heap, dangerously near the campfire.

"We agreed not to open any safe boxes until we were all together." Garth kicked at Buster's feet where he sat on the dirt floor. Buster ignored him while Sam swept up the papers and letters and piled them together on Garth's bedroll.

"Don't worry none. Your Injun was here when I opened it. The cash and silver is all there. What do you need those papers for anyway? Are they valuable?" Buster lowered his brows suspiciously, his mustache quivering in irritation.

It wasn't easy, but Garth suppressed his anger. "That's my business. If you don't like it, go find yourself another gang."

"Look here! This is the most we've got in one haul," Elvin exclaimed. He flipped the currency back and forth in his hands after Garth made the split.

"Reckon that's why the deputy was riding shotgun. Must be a special payroll shipment." Garth said what was expected of him, and when he looked at Sam, she turned away to hide her grin. They both knew Garth wanted to get the gang's minds away from the documents. If it was a hefty payroll, then the papers might be very interesting.

It was time for Garth to take Sam back to Powder.

CHAPTER 18

Garth and Sam returned to the boarding-house. Everything was as usual, calm and dull after their escapades. This time it was Aunt Twila who repeated a valuable conversation she'd overhead at the mercantile store.

A train carrying special passengers was coming through Tombstone and the surrounding towns two days hence.

Garth shrugged the information off as nothing they needed to know. "Do you think we've gained enough experience to stop a train? Anyway, that wouldn't have anything to do with Millard Tremayne."

Sam's eyes lit up and she twirled around the kitchen excitedly.

"What on earth?" Aunt Twila looked aghast at her niece.

"Yeah, what's going on in that noggin of yours, sis?"

She beckoned him closer and their heads

194

bent together. As he listened, he moved back and stared at her uncomprehendingly for an instant, then light dawned behind his eyes.

"Sam! You're an absolute genius!" He hugged her.

Seeing their aunt's puzzled frown, Garth took pity on her. "We'll tell you all about it, love, but wait until it is over. The story will be that much more enjoyable."

When they calmed down, Sam held up her hand. "I'm going to be in on this one, so don't say no. Nothing will keep me away."

They agreed that the less they explained to the men, the better. If Buster ever uncovered their plans, no amount of broken bones or threatened prison time would defer him from exacting revenge.

As soon as Garth and Sam returned to camp and told the gang about the rich train filled with wealthy passengers coming through the area, Buster was the first to gloat about the haul they would make. The others seemed nervous about the notion of attacking a train, but it appeared they would follow Garth anywhere.

Garth had counted on Buster asserting his rights as the most experienced outlaw. Sam and Garth were not disappointed when he commanded the lead and assigned posts to everyone. The major, Elvin, and even Don Pancho looked to Garth in protest, but he shrugged and made no comment.

"The Mex can watch the horses as usual. Major, you keep a lookout up there on that rise. The rest of you take over the engineer and get the train stopped. I'll jump on and start with the passengers." Buster paced back and forth in front of the campfire they'd started away from the railroad tracks behind some mesquite bushes. His dark complexion, his hawk nose, and the long coat he wore flapping around his boots made him appear like some evil bird of prey in the flickering light. They all watched him as if hypnotized.

"Hey, hold on a minute," Garth pretended to protest at last. "What makes you think you give orders around here?" He struggled to sound offended.

"Hellfire!" Buster exploded. "I been waiting for a big break like this. None of your penny-ante stuff this time. I don't want you dudes messing it up. I got the experience, don't I?"

"Get off your high horse," Garth soothed. "No need to get riled up. I don't like the men thinking you're the boss. I don't think they'd go for that, either."

"Who gives a damn what these poor

196

excuses for men think?" Buster stared at each person ringing the campfire as if searching for any defiance from them.

Garth was proud that they in turn stared back at Buster without flinching. Buster finally had to look away. Buster was too mean to fear the devil, but if he even came close to any sort of respect for anyone, it was for Big Bear. He couldn't have missed the malevolent look in that one black eye glaring at him. Buster had to know that, gun pointed at him or not, the Indian would have jumped him when he beat up Elvin if Garth hadn't stopped him.

Bright and early the next morning, the gang put out their campfire and rode the horses through the high brush to await the train. They picked an excellent spot, at the bottom of a steep hill that would cause the train to slow down enough to allow them to board. The major and Elvin had tinkered with Annabel until she purred like a kitten.

On the way to their destination, Elvin rode up beside Sam and Garth. He looked around furtively to see if Buster was near. Satisfied, he turned in his saddle toward the two of them. His bent nose marred his handsome face somewhat, but he appeared little-boy likable.

"How come Buster is calling all the shots?

The others want to know too."

Garth looked at Sam and then back to Elvin. "Trust me on this. Have I ever steered you wrong? Let Buster have his time alone with the passengers."

"Yeah, but you know how sneaky that bastard is. He'll skim all the cream off and when we get back there, the passengers will be lucky to have their boots on," he argued.

Sam hid a grin behind her gloved hand while Garth coughed, smothering his laughter. Knowing he was not going to get any answers from them, Elvin turned back to ride with Big Bear and Don Pancho.

They didn't have long to wait before they saw the trail of black smoke preceding the train. It was dark, but the false dawn made the air crisply cold. With the full moon sinking behind a ridge of purple mountains, the desert seemed peopled with eerie shadows. When Buster leaped off his horse on to the slowed train, Don Pancho grabbed up the trailing reins and brought his horse back to where they all stood clustered together.

Garth felt a surge of energy. Everything was going according to plan.

"Pull up your bandanas, get ready," Garth said.

When the train slowed even more for the incline between two hills, the gang jumped aboard the engine. Big Bear had bragged about seeing it done in a Wild West Show once. He leaped off his galloping horse to land between the engine and the train and managed to disconnect the two. Garth hadn't confided in them as to his reasons for doing anything, but he insisted they follow his instruction to the letter.

When they climbed onto the engine, they thrust themselves into the circle of light from the lanterns hanging in the engine compartment. It was hard to know who was the most surprised. The engineer and his helper and three men in crisply neat army uniforms stood staring open mouthed at the intruders. While the major and Elvin held pistols trained on the men, they felt the engine picking up speed when it let loose from the rest of the train. The engine crested the hill and swooshed over it and down. Garth hoped Don Pancho and Sam would be able to bring the horses along in time.

"Brake the engine!" Garth shouted. "Where's the cashbox?" He snarled in what he hoped was a businesslike manner.

The engineer looked worried. "I don't have a cashbox up here, mister. Could be carrying an army payroll, but I don't know nothing about that. Have to ask one of these gents." He gestured at the three uniformed men, standing with their hands up in the air. One of them shot a venomous look at the engineer.

"We aren't carrying a payroll. That will follow on the next train." The one in charge looked at Garth, apparently recognizing him as the leader. "But I don't suppose you'll believe that."

"I don't like it much, but I reckon I believe you." Garth turned to his men. "Tie 'em up, and let's get out of here. This is just not our day."

"Hold on a minute, you ain't gonna give up that easy, are you? I think these fellows are lying through their teeth. Back there on the passenger train I saw shadows of what had to be guards walking back and forth down the aisles. They got to be toting something important." Elvin waved his pistol around for emphasis.

"Hell, man, this here's a troop train," one of the army men said, with a hint of amusement in his voice. "We aren't carrying anything more than a bunch of mean, ornery men who are mad as hornets at being sent out here to this hellhole in the first place."

"A troop train!" Both the major and Elvin exclaimed together. Garth spared a glance at Big Bear, who was probably thinking, "It's only natural."

"Come on, let's go. What are you waiting for?" Garth urged the gang toward the door. "Do we have to tie you men up, or will you behave until we leave this damn jinxed train?" Garth asked.

The men exchanged glances. The engineer spoke. "We don't want any trouble. Far as we're concerned, you haven't done much to get too excited about." The others nodded in agreement and turned away as Garth and his men jumped over the side. Don Pancho and Sam stood by with the horses, and they leaped on the saddles and took off.

They rode as far as the line of cottonwoods to hide and watch as the engine backed up the hill and descended toward the motionless train.

"I jolly well demand to know what is going on here," the major blustered.

Elvin grinned in the remaining moonlight, his teeth white in the gloom. "I'm beginning to smell a rat." He turned in the saddle to stare at Sam and Garth. "You knew it was a troop train all along, didn't you?" he accused.

For the first time since they'd known him, Garth saw Big Bear's wide smile.

Garth tugged at the mustache he was so

proud of. "Now what makes you think I would do a thing like that? Attack a troop train? Why, that would be plain suicide."

Before anyone could say more, the noisy engine had almost backed up to the train. In the dimness of the kerosene lamps within, they saw men rushing around, flailing arms and legs, and several shots sounded above the roar of the engine.

"Come on. Let's vamoose before they send out men to look for us." Garth whirled his horse around and headed for the hide-out. It would be a long ride, and he was already tired.

"You mean we aren't waiting for Buster?" Elvin said with a smirk on his face.

"I reckon not," Garth said. "I think he'll be tied up for a very long time."

That night, sitting around the campfire, they were mostly silent, contemplating the fate of Buster with satisfaction. Once in a while one of them burst into laughter and the others joined in or smiled in appreciation. Garth had explained the whole plan to them on the way back to the cave. Between Big Bear and Sam, they let Don Pancho in on it. They could tell he understood by the wide smile that lit his face and his dark eyes lost in crinkled laughter. He had hated and feared Buster more than any of them. He must have sensed the man's inborn cruelty and lust for giving pain.

Over and over, all the way back, they had speculated with glee about Buster's fate at the hands of the bitter, angry army men.

"What if Buster tells about our hiding place and what we do?" Elvin thought aloud.

Garth shook his head. "I'd stake my life that he won't. He would have no reason to suspect we set him up. He's been an outlaw long enough to know that squealers don't live long. He'll keep quiet. Hope he stays locked up long enough to forget about us."

Sam shivered inside her wrapped blanket. She could tell Garth was not convinced entirely that Buster wouldn't figure out they had tricked him. He was a mighty suspicious, paranoid character. If he did suspect them, he had two alternatives. He could tell the authorities about the gang and the hideout, or he could take his medicine and live for the day when the prison released him and come looking for them. It was hard to figure out which he would choose. She looked at Garth and realized those same thoughts had occurred to him. It would be something they would have to live with and always look over their shoulders.

Garth glanced at Sam. "Don't be such a

worrywart, little brother. Buster's gone, and let's forget we ever knew him."

And they very nearly did.

CHAPTER 19

The gang threw a gigantic celebration, deciding to take a vacation from work. Sam slipped back into her ordinary life at the boardinghouse. Her excuse for not being present at meals was that she suffered from migraines and at times was unable to leave her room. During the times Sam was with the gang, Aunt Twila dutifully brought trays of food upstairs to Sam's room and sneaked them back down untouched when no one was about. Since delicate single ladies were known to suffer frequently from the vapors, only an occasional question from the deputy or Blue Jay surfaced, and Aunt Twila was able to fend them off.

Big Bear had returned with Sam, and one morning they were in the stables talking. Big Bear was trimming the hooves of his horse, which he stubbornly refused to have shod. Sam currycombed her chestnut mare, totally unprepared for the unexpected. Her sleeves were rolled up, displaying her tanned arms. She had piled her hair carelessly on top of her head in what Aunt Twila might have described as an untidy mop, almost the same color as her horse. Her nose and the side of her square jaw were touched with grime.

Neither of them was prepared for Ernestine.

Both Big Bear and Sam stopped what they had been doing and stared at the intruder standing in the stable doorway.

Sam was the first to recover her voice. "Hullo. What brings you here?" Sam brushed aside the straggly curl that kept flopping across her forehead. This woman, Ernestine, was a vision in her crisp gabardine dress with crinolines underneath and her blond hair done up in what had to be the latest fashion, with small flowers tucked here and there into the curls.

The young woman smiled, her teeth pearly and white, as she said in a slight southern drawl, "My name is Ernestine Sommerfield, and I am looking for Mistress Brody. The gentleman on the porch swing mentioned you might be in here." Her delicate eyebrows turned into a frown when she studied Sam and Big Bear.

Sam fumed. Blue Jay was sitting on the

porch last time she looked. He knew she was knee-deep in horse, helping Big Bear. Not to mention looking the part of a stable hand. He could have sent this person to Aunt Twila. Sam brushed her dirty hands on her already wrinkled and dusty apron and brought her hands up to touch her hair in the event it hadn't completely lost its moorings.

"Follow me inside if you will," Sam said as politely as she could through clenched teeth. When they passed the smugly grinning Blue Jay on the porch, it was all she could do not to push the swing over backward. It could be done. Garth had caught her once with that trick.

The memory of the bygone days when she had resembled this young woman brought a wry smile to Sam's face. It seemed so long ago, and her life then had been aimless and empty. She tilted her nose in the air and sailed by the blue jay without speaking, even though she sensed the woman expected an introduction.

In the cool, dim parlor Sam motioned Ernestine to sit. Upon looking closer, Sam noticed the visitor was not so young as to be called a girl. She could be even a bit older than Sam, judging from the sharp, assessing look in her eyes she didn't bother to hide.

"I am Samantha Brody. What can I do for you?"

Ernestine's eyes widened in surprise and her mouth made an astonished O. "But I thought . . . that is, I was told . . ." She stopped in confusion, and then took a deep breath to begin again. "I'm an unmarried schoolteacher, and I was informed that this was the most respectable boardinghouse in Powder."

Sam bit back a retort in the face of Ernestine's obvious anxiety.

She turned to the doorway. "Aunt Twila, could you come to the parlor please?" She didn't have to raise her voice, knowing curiosity would have had her aunt glued by the edge of the door. Sure enough, with a moment's hesitation for appearance's sake, she pushed through the door, standing next to Sam as if to protect her.

"Aunt Twila, may I present . . ."

Before Sam could finish the introduction, Ernestine rose to her feet and held out her hands to both of them. "Oh, my. I got off on the wrong foot, didn't I? Mercy me. The gentleman outside gave me no indication that you were in the stables." She nodded toward Sam. "My name is Ernestine Sommerfield."

There should be a way to get even with the blue jay. Oh, to think of something fitting.

Ernestine projected a haughty demeanor even while supposedly apologizing. Her attitude didn't sit well with either Aunt Twila or Sam.

To Sam's delight, Aunt Twila hauled out her seldom-used lorgnette from her skirt pocket and perched it on the end of her nose to peer at Ernestine in a close inspection. There were telltale smudges of flour here and there on her aunt's shirtwaist. Ten to one she'd been elbow deep in bread making, but who would have guessed the lady had ever stepped into a kitchen?

"I was just telling Miss Brody that your boardinghouse came highly recommended. I am all alone in a strange town — actually, a strange land. One cannot be too careful of one's reputation and good name, don't you agree?" Ernestine spoke in a soft manner meant to placate.

Somehow Sam found the southern accent a trifle false and chided herself for being unkind to think so. Ernestine had come from the East, and certainly this would all be strange to her.

"Perhaps." Aunt Twila gave a ladylike snort with her patrician nose. "It so happens that my niece Samantha is also an unmarried lady, and I can assure you — Miss Somerton, is it? This is indeed a most respectable home."

"Sommerfield," Ernestine corrected. "Yes, I see that now, but you can probably understand my confusion upon meeting your niece in the stables."

"Where do you come from?" Sam asked, changing the subject abruptly.

For a moment Ernestine appeared hesitant. She covered it with a smile before answering. "I lived in Mississippi. With my parents. I decided to take a chance and answered an ad in our newspaper requiring a schoolteacher here in Powder."

Aunt Twila and Sam looked at each other. It was odd that Miss Sommerfield hesitated before answering as to her origins, and unusual for a newcomer to know the shortened version of the town's name. Who in Powder would place an ad for a teacher as far off as Mississippi?

It could be she was escaping a dreadful family situation, or perhaps she thought her future would be a bit brighter if she moved away. By now, both Sam and Aunt Twila knew never to pry.

If Sam thought she'd been uncomfortable before in Ernestine's presence, dinnertime proved she hadn't even touched the surface of uncomfortable. Ernestine captured the interest of all the men at the table, including crotchety old Jasper and Seth, who appeared completely smitten. She zeroed in on Blue Jay, who was plainly enchanted. Only Deputy Wade seemed impervious to her charm, which was odd. But then, he never spoke two words at the table except a polite thank you once in a while. For some odd reason she couldn't explain, Blue Jay's rapt attention to the new boarder irked Sam beyond words. Granted, every time she had the chance, she was rude to him. She told herself it was because he was so condescending and patronizing when they talked.

Yet Ernestine prattled on about nothing that could have interested him, and he clung to her every word as if she spewed pearls of wisdom. Sam caught him looking her way with an irritatingly amused twitch to his lips.

After that, Sam skipped breakfast and sat in tight-lipped silence through dinners with Deputy Wade sending searching looks her way and Blue Jay with a mischievous grin and a knowing look in his eyes. The two men and Ernestine made her long for the gang and the desert.

A week later Sam sat on the porch swing one evening. She worried about Garth, and had sent Big Bear out that afternoon to see if he was all right. She had nothing to report to him, and the town seemed almost too quiet.

To her dismay, Ernestine walked up and smiled.

"Do you mind if I join you, Samantha?" She sat quickly, not waiting for a reply. She adjusted her skirt daintily around her. She was so short, her feet barely touched the porch floor.

Usually short people gave Sam a secret air of superiority, but with Ernestine, Sam's height made her feel clumsy and awkward.

They sat for a while, Ernestine chatting about her charges in school and seemingly unperturbed by Sam's silence.

"Where did you say you come from?" Sam interrupted her monologue.

"What? Why, I believe I told you. You might have guessed by my accent. I was born and raised in Mis . . . Mississippi."

A frisson of alarm swept over Sam. Had the woman almost said Missouri? Surely not. No one from back home knew they were here; she was becoming too distrustful.

"You don't always sound like a southern belle. I suppose you were born on one of those plantations with slaves and all that."

"Goodness, no!" Ernestine retorted. "My papa is a poor preacher man. Anyway, all of us in the south don't necessarily speak in accents. My training as a teacher corrected my enunciation."

Much to Sam's disgust, she sounded like a teacher for the first time. But if the idle talk she'd heard was true, then Powder had a one-room school with only a handful of kids attending. Maybe she should sound out the school board, if there was one, and find out if they sent ads all over the country for a teacher. There was that mistrust again, she chided herself.

"For some reason, I can't see you as a schoolteacher," Sam persisted. "Have you taught for a long time?"

Ernestine shrugged, an evasive look coming into her blue eyes, which she turned away to hide. "No, actually not long. In fact that's why I've come to this godforsaken wilderness. I had to start some place and with no experience or references." She held up her hands and gazed out into the dusty street as if ending this conversation.

Before Sam could ask any more questions, Deputy Wade appeared with the blue jay close behind.

Sam looked at both men appraisingly while they talked mostly to Ernestine. The

213

deputy was solid male, broad of shoulders, narrow of hips, his face escaping handsomeness by his dark eyes that were close together and his lips that were too straight and tight looking. Sam blushed and turned her head to hide it. She had a thing for lips, she found them very telling in a person.

Blue Jay, on the other hand, had lips in spades. His mouth curved naturally in a smile, although mostly it came off as smug. His jaw was square and strong looking while his eyes were his best feature. Sharply blue, fringed with dark thick lashes, he could have been the best-looking man she'd ever seen if she wasn't put off by his superior airs and his penchant for being so immaculately dressed.

"Miss Samantha, what are you staring at?" Deputy Wade spoke to her in a most uncommon manner. He was usually tongue-tied around her. "I was asking a question."

"Me? Oh, I was thinking about something, please excuse me." She darted a glimpse at Blue Jay, who smirked as if he'd read her thoughts. Dratted man!

"Would you ladies care to go to the dance with me this Saturday?" Deputy Wade asked. "I suppose you've heard of it?" He leaned against the porch rail and looked down at the women, his cool gray eyes quietly studying them.

"But I was going to ask Miss Sommerfield!" the blue jay protested, rising from his seated position on the porch steps and brushing his perfectly creased dark blue trousers from invisible dust.

Ernestine darted a quick look at Sam and then smiled at the blue jay. "Oh, but don't you think it would be sooo much more fun to all go together?" she trilled.

Sam smiled in spite of the jab of unexpected hurt by Blue Jay's revealing speech. Ernestine could be a thoughtful person when she wanted to be.

The matter of the dance was quickly settled. If Sam had not been worried about Garth, she might have enjoyed the conversation among the four of them.

"You've been awfully busy lately, Deputy Wade. We haven't seen much of you at meals." Sam looked at the big man, pointedly ignoring the blue jay's existence. Sam admired the deputy, but for reasons she couldn't explain, she wasn't attracted to him.

"No, ma'am," Wade answered, a flush coloring his tanned face caused by their sudden attention. "Fact is, Mr. Earp gave me a job all my own. I'm supposed to find out about a new gang that's all of a sudden

215

cropped up out here. He didn't want me to spread it around, but I'm sure I can trust you not to repeat anything I tell you."

Ernestine held her hands to her mouth in a gasp of what could only be dismay. "Oh, really! How exciting! Is it a dreadfully dangerous gang? Will you be in peril?"

Sam was glad no one looked in her direction. She was certain her face turned pale and they could hear her heart beating loudly.

"Naw." Wade skidded a stone away from his boot toe. "Bunch of amateurs. Damned foolishness if you ask me. Pardon my language, ladies. Wyatt and his brother call them the desperados." He laughed at their combined expressions.

"Strangest bunch of outlaws you'd ever hope to see, and that's the truth. I saw them once with my own two eyes, and one of them knocked me to the ground." He looked embarrassed. "I barely caught a glimpse of an old codger's mustache under his hood, and a giant of a fellow, must be seven feet tall. They all wear head masks."

By now Sam was caught between laughter and indignation, and she wasn't sure which would win. Imagine those awful Earps calling their gang the same name they'd chosen

216

for themselves, but in such a demeaning fashion.

While the deputy basked in the attention from his audience, even Blue Jay looked intrigued, so the deputy continued.

"There's a fellow all duded up in a silk shirt and leather pants so tight I don't see how he can sit or ride a horse. Oh, and there's a scruffy runt, a punk kid who looks pretty ornery. There's some kind of a ghostly person holding the horses. No one has ever seen anything of him but his shadow."

"That's enough. Are you trying to frighten us?" Sam tried to change the conversation. But the deputy was not inclined to let go of the spotlight.

"Who is the leader? There must be someone in charge."

Leave it to the blue jay to keep the subject going. Sam wanted to clobber him.

Deputy Wade shrugged. "Hard to say. There's one of them that's mean and downright dangerous. He's the one who grabbed my rifle and knocked me off the stage. Reckon that's why the Earps are getting edgy about this gang. There is one fellow who looks about average — could be he's the leader. He pulled the mean one away from me."

"Do they rob stages? What do they do?"

The blue jay was persistent.

Was he thinking of Millard Tremayne's interests? Sam wondered. But surely they hadn't done enough robbing and pilfering to show they had chosen one victim. This was all getting too close for comfort.

Sam stood. "Enough of this talk. You'll have Ernestine and me staying up all night with nightmares," she chided them. She turned and sped through the screened door, hoping they would disband and go their separate ways. Ernestine hurried behind her, but as Sam looked back, to her dismay the blue jay and the deputy stayed on the porch in deep discussion. She hoped their conversation didn't center on their gang. She should have stayed and listened. She had bluffed, trying to get them apart, but she'd lost. Bidding Ernestine good night, Sam climbed the stairs to her room and closed the door.

CHAPTER 20

Sam both dreaded and looked forward to the dance coming up. When she stood before her mirror, she wrinkled her nose in disgust at her image. Her skirt was wren-brown, not her color at all. She closed her eyes and for a brief, hurting time recalled Jeffery's eyes when she had appeared dressed for a dance in her golden silk. That look couldn't have been pretend. He must have admired her — just not enough.

Aunt Twila knocked and entered, and sat on a chair near the window. "You need to wear brighter colors, child. I've been saying that since I arrived."

Before Sam turned to look at her, she swiped furtively at the moisture gathering in her eyes. "Maybe. But why?"

"It's enough that you dress up like a boy, traipsing all over the land doing the Lord knows what."

"Shh! You mustn't talk like that. Someone

219

might overhear."

"Oh, botheration. All this cloak-and-dagger thinking of yours. Who would be skulking around the hallway listening to our conversation? You are changing the subject as usual. You look like a mouse."

Sam flopped down on the bed and regarded her aunt. "I don't know why I want to be sort of invisible. Yes, I do know. I feel safer this way. Don't you see? I don't want to catch anyone's attention. That's why I enjoy Garth's men so much. They accept me, and I don't have to prove anything to them."

Aunt Twila shook her head. "Sam, you need to stop dwelling on Jeffery. He was a terrible human being. I warned you, but you didn't listen. I suppose love or imagined love is like that. Truth is, you let your father push you into that relationship. Bless his heart, he wanted security for you and thought Jeffery would provide it."

"I know. I am trying to forget that episode in my life. But I don't feel like taking any more chances right now. Not that there is any danger of that."

"You aren't fooling me, dear. Even if you think you're fooling yourself. I've seen you take quick looks at Clarence J. when you think he's not paying attention. What I don't understand is why you would be attracted to Lord Fauntleroy and not our big, strong deputy. The man you and Garth call the blue jay is handsome, I will concede that, but he is so sissified and arrogant at the same time. And he seems awfully attracted to Ernestine."

Her aunt would never know how her words crushed Sam. They left her speechless.

Aunt Twila stood and walked over to Sam's closet, rifling through her dresses. "Your trust has been badly bruised, but it was the best thing in the world when Jeffery showed his true colors before you actually married him. Now, about the dance. Don't you want to show that silly Ernestine what the Kirklands or Brodys are really like when they take the notion to dress up? You're a picture of your mother, you know. Your father and I . . . well . . . luckily, you didn't take after our side of the family," she admitted.

Sam hurried to hug her aunt. "You are beautiful in your own way, inside and out." And to Sam and Garth, she was. Tall, spare, almost shapeless — Sam didn't see any of those qualities when she looked at her aunt. She saw years of selfless devotion spent on another's children. She saw the years of care and thoughtfulness her aunt had invested in her and Garth. And she really had nothing to show for all that time and love.

As if Aunt Twila understood Sam's thoughts, she burst out, "Oh, how could I have survived when Stephen died if I hadn't had you and Garth to tuck under my wing?"

She motioned for Sam to sit while she removed the pins from her hair and let it fall down to the middle of her back. Aunt Twila brushed Sam's hair until it shone and tied it back with a ribbon at the nape of her neck. She went to the closet and held out the golden silk gown. "Take off that skirt and blouse and leave on your chemise," her aunt commanded.

"Oh, no, Aunt Twila. I couldn't wear that, not here in Powder." It was the only dressy gown she'd brought with her, and she couldn't have imagined why she did it. It was meant to be special, for her engagement ball.

"Fiddlesticks! This dress looks charming on you, and you've never worn it."

Silently yielding, Sam waited while Aunt Twila lifted the dress over her head, careful not to disturb her hair, and let it settle around her body. When she turned to the mirror, Sam swallowed nervously. The diaphanous layers of sheer golden fabric had never appeared so elegant. Her smooth tan reflected back the richness of the dress as her former pale rosiness never would have. She turned and made a curtsy to her aunt.

"That's more like it, Samantha. Get some of your spunk back. No need to let that mealy-mouthed schoolteacher take over all the menfolks."

Sam chuckled. "I don't really care, you know." She sputtered and then gave up. There was no use in arguing with her aunt when she made up her mind.

When Sam descended the stairway as the time of the dance neared, she couldn't stop worrying about Garth and the other gang members. At the same time, she wanted to enjoy the evening.

Both Blue Jay and Deputy Wade leaped to their feet when she entered the parlor. Sam smiled, noting out of the corner of her eye the suddenly neglected Ernestine sitting on the settee. Wade walked to her side and took her hand, carefully, as if she had been made of china and might break. His gray eyes held approval.

At first Sam thought she might ignore the blue jay, but she turned a smile in his direction. She didn't miss the fleeting look of surprised admiration in his eyes, and he appeared flustered. Good. For once she had *him* at a disadvantage. He removed his glasses and rubbed them absentmindedly, watching her sail toward him on Wade's arm.

Ernestine was looking daggers at her. Surely the woman couldn't be jealous of her and the deputy? The woman had always shown the blue jay all her attention and acted as if Wade was beneath her notice. Probably she was mistaken in Ernestine's glare and the reason for it. As if to prove Sam's reaction false, Ernestine ran forward and embraced her.

"Oh, my, Samantha! You are a sight. I do believe you purely outshine little ole me tonight." She lapsed into an exaggerated drawl, as if needing to draw some attention back to herself.

Sam shook her head. "That will never happen, Ernestine," she said generously, thinking about the odd look in Blue Jay's eyes. "Indeed, that is a charming untruth. You wear that shade of blue so well." It *was* the truth, Sam reflected. Ernestine wore a beautiful gown the color of her eyes. Her rounded white arms and peaches-and-cream complexion almost dazzled the senses. There was only that brief, telltale look around her eyes that had Sam wondering. Was Ernestine creating a frivolous image for some nefarious reason, or was that truly her? What did it matter?

Sam waved a kiss to Aunt Twila, and as they stepped out into the yard, intending to walk to the dance, they stopped in confusion. At least three of them did. The blue jay looked proudly toward the conveyance standing in front of the boardinghouse.

Sam's eyebrows rose at the sight of the gaudy, ornate coach. "What in the world?" she exclaimed when she could catch her breath. She noticed Ernestine took the coach in stride, as if she had the elegant ride coming to her.

The blue jay grinned sheepishly. "A bit overdone for my taste, but my generous employer said I could borrow anything he had. He sent this from Missouri to be ready when he planned to come out here." On the side of the vehicle, in lush gold leaf, could be seen the initials MLT.

Uncle Millard! Sam nearly lost her balance as Wade handed her into the coach. She had almost balked at entering. The smell of their uncle's hair pomade and shaving lotion overpowered her senses and caused her stomach to lurch. Oh no, she couldn't be sick right here in front of everyone in the immaculate coach. She looked around to see if anyone had noticed her hesitation but the blue jay concentrated on helping Ernestine settle her wide skirts so that he could sit next to her.

Was it just an odd coincidence that the blue jay, employed by her uncle, had come to Powder and found their boardinghouse to take his meals? Of course it could be easily explained. For one thing, Powder was the location of the most important of their uncle's holdings. The Peaches Mine was nearby. That and the saloon his paramour managed had to be his most principal properties. It made sense that Uncle might want to send the blue jay here first as an accountant, if not a spy.

Garth seldom misjudged a person. For someone his age he had a lot of common sense. Could he be wrong about Clarence J.? Could the man be innocent of spying?

Sam straightened her shoulders and gave an automatic answer to Deputy Wade's question, which she hadn't even heard. Let Garth dismiss the blue jay as some innocuous servant and toady of Uncle Millard if he wanted to, she decided, but there was more here than appeared on the surface. She would be wary and very careful around him.

All the way to the dance the blue jay and Ernestine chatted while she and the deputy sat silently across from them. Sam could not help but feel sorry for Wade, since the lovely Ernestine completely ignored him. But if her neglect bothered him at all, his bland expression didn't show it. Sam spent her time trying to recall if she had spoken out of turn in any way or let some small thing slip that the blue jay would have picked up on, in the event he *was* a spy for their uncle.

In the first place, she'd tried to avoid his company as much as possible, only speaking to him out of politeness at the dinner table. For some reason beyond his eternally raised eyebrow and sharp eyes behind his glasses, he made her edgy in other ways she didn't understand.

When they went through the wide open door of the newly refurbished barn, every head turned their way. Sam began to enjoy the attention. Before Aunt Twila came to Powder, she'd had to hide her femininity; and with Garth's gang she played the part of a boy, so now was her time to shine as herself. In her mind's eye she saw the picture the four of them presented to the crowd. Everyone knew and liked Deputy Wade. The blue jay was spectacular in his blue regalia. Ernestine and Sam were easily the most dazzling of the women gathered.

She danced dutifully with Wade. He was striking in a muscular, masculine way, but not exactly graceful on the dance floor. Several times when she looked away at the crowd, she caught the blue jay regarding her. She kept her smug satisfaction to herself as she watched the other couple. Ernestine looked like a child next to the blue jay; he was so much taller than she. Men shyly asked for dances, and Sam noticed Ernestine detached herself from the blue jay to accept dances from strangers who asked.

Removing herself from the dance floor, Sam stood behind a pillar, catching her breath and thinking about going outside to cool off. She changed her mind when she heard the raucous laughter of men standing outside beyond the door. A hand touched her arm, and an electric shock sped up and down her body. She turned, knowing she would see the smiling Blue Jay.

"Will you dance with me, princess?"

His question sent more shivers up her spine, and she hoped he hadn't noticed her pulse rate kicking up in the hollow of her throat. "Of course." She swept him a curtsy and held his arm while he led to the dance floor. Together they danced as if they'd always known each other. In spite of his height, he was light on his feet without the cumbersome bulk of the deputy. He held her closer than was necessary, but she didn't try to pull away. She finally relaxed and enjoyed the sensation of whirling around effortlessly.

"Charming." She thought he'd murmured that word close to her ear. A shot of pure joy sped through her until she remembered his entrancement with Ernestine and reduced her pleasure to pitiful.

"We don't communicate well, do we?" He leaned back to look into her face.

She shook her head. "Probably not. You seem to prefer company other than mine."

"Jealous? That's encouraging," he grinned down at her, but without his usual annoying condescension. She could see into his eyes so much better since he'd put aside his spectacles for the night.

"Not jealous." She disagreed. "Merely observant."

"Hmm. Interesting."

By then the fiddle had slowed, and then the music stopped. Sam and the blue jay didn't realize it for a moment and continued dancing until she pushed away gently.

"You are intriguing, Samantha. I don't know what to think about you." He whispered the words while escorting her off the dance floor.

She grinned and caught herself flirting with him. "Why must you label everyone? I suppose that's the accountant in you."

They stood alone for a moment, but Sam could see Ernestine heading their way. That shouldn't have bothered her, but it did.

The blue jay shook his head, and that tempting swath of dark hair fell across his forehead. Her fingers itched to touch it. He brushed the hair back impatiently. "Not everyone. I don't try to label everyone." A mischievous look came into his eyes as he studied her from the top of her head past her uncovered shoulders, and down her body so that she felt as if she stood in her chemise before him.

She blushed. "Thank you for the dance. Ernestine is coming to claim you." She moved away, his soft laughter following her.

Suddenly the hair on the back of her neck stirred, and her gaze swept toward the bar that had been hastily erected for the dance. There stood Garth, Elvin, and the major, big as life. What could her brother be thinking? He was at home in the boardinghouse, but the major could be recognized by his accent from one of their jobs. Hadn't Deputy Wade noticed a large mustache on one of the gang?

She gasped and covered her mouth with her hand when she saw the Earp brothers standing at the bar right next to the three gang members. They were even having a conversation. Her heart sank down into her shoes. She looked around for the deputy, but he had his back turned as he spoke to Aunt Twila and Ernestine. Sam stared long enough that Garth lifted his head and nodded to her. He followed with an impudent grin.

Sam headed for the back door, hoping Garth would follow. Sure enough, she wasn't outside two minutes before he showed up.

Before she could speak, he stood back, studied her, and whistled in appreciation.

"Never mind that." She held her voice steady and stayed her temper.

"Careful, sis. You'll come busting out of the dress if you take a deep breath."

"Don't be vulgar. And don't change the subject. What in the holy hell are you doing here and with the major and Elvin? And having a lovely conversation with the Earps! You could jeopardize everything."

"Aw, come on. You're no fun anymore." His voice dropped to a conspiratorial whisper. "We never pulled a job without wearing our masks. Who could recognize us? We needed a change from that raunchy old Dry Gulch saloon and heard about the barn dance here."

"Where are Big Bear and Don Pancho? Surely you wouldn't leave *them* out, as if anyone could possibly recognize the two of them."

If he noticed her sarcasm, he let it pass. He turned and beckoned to Elvin and the major. When they sauntered over, Garth took Samantha's hand. "I want you to meet my cousin, Samantha Brody." Both Elvin and the major doffed their Stetsons and swept them low. A most cavalier gesture, Sam decided.

"My pleasure, miss," Elvin said with a wide smile. The major regarded her with a speculative look that caused her unease.

"Something wrong, Major?" Sam asked in her most feminine voice.

He shook his head. His answer came slowly, as if he were thinking hard. "It is only that you resemble our boy here amazingly." He thumped Garth on the shoulder.

"I've read that everyone has a *doppelgänger* somewhere," Sam replied, trying to sound unruffled.

"A look-alike? That's refreshing, my dear. Who is that lovely vision I saw you talking to before your dance?" The major gestured toward the edge of the dance floor.

"Oh, you mean Ernestine? The little blonde?"

"No, no," the major said. "I was speaking of that slender lady with the gray hair tucked into a delightful knot at the back of her lovely neck."

Garth broke out into a loud guffaw, and Sam hid her amusement behind her palm.

"The older lady is my aunt," Sam said to the major. "Would you like to meet her?" Her aunt would trim the major's sails in no time flat, even if he fancied himself a ladies' man.

She wondered at Garth not being more interested in the lovely Ernestine. Did he have his eye on Peaches at the saloon? She hoped not; that couldn't turn out well.

Elvin swept his hat off again and glanced toward the bar. "I'm going over there and do some serious drinking. 'Scuse me."

"Thank you, my dear. I would love to meet your aunt later. For now I think I will join Elvin," the major said. "I've got some catching up to do."

Sam and Garth watched the major join Elvin at the bar. "Elvin's a handsome devil, isn't he?" Garth mused.

"Sure he is. Too bad . . ." They looked at each other and started laughing.

Garth touched her arm to get her attention. "I'm glad to see you've come out of hiding, Sam. You really look elegant. The loveliest girl at the dance."

Sam smiled, enjoying the compliment. She swayed gently to hear the light swish and the rustle sound of the silk moving with her body. "Aunt Twila is quite enough chaperone, not to mention Big Bear standing guard over my virtue. He frowns even when Deputy Wade or the blue jay talk to me."

Garth laughed. "But what about this Ernestine creature? She looks almost too good to be true. And you say she's a schoolteacher?"

Sam shrugged. "I thought so in the beginning, too, but she seems to be a really nice person. At least the blue jay seems to think so."

"Hmm. And does that bother you?"

"Of course not. She even has old Jasper and Seth under her thumb, so you might as well join her legion of admirers. Maybe it will keep you away from the Silver Buckle." The faraway look in her brother's eyes made her wonder what was going on with him.

Garth turned back to Sam, suddenly serious. He whispered in her ear, "I've got something I want you to see from our last raid, Sam. I'm not sure I'll be able to make it to the boardinghouse tonight. I may have to lead Elvin and the major back to the hideout if they can't find their way. Looks like they are tying one on."

"Did you see the major getting chummy with the Earp boys? I should think that would make you a tad uneasy."

Garth smirked. "He doesn't have a glimmer of who they are."

Sam stamped her foot with impatience. "That's what I'm telling you. He could be letting out all kinds of information. That's pure carelessness, and you should tow them in."

Garth looked across the room to see Deputy Wade regarding them, wariness in his eyes. He quickly hid his expression, but Garth was sure he caught it. "Does Wade have his cap set for you? Because he sure was looking daggers at me for whispering in your ear. No one knows we're brother and sister. And we never let out what kind of cousins we are."

Sam held still to avoid turning and looking at the deputy. "Why, no. Of course, Wade isn't interested in me. Actually he and Ernestine would be a good match, but they ignore each other. I've been polite to him; after all he is a paying guest at the boardinghouse. I believe him to be a very open and honest person."

Garth snorted. "Don't go forgetting that he's being mentored by the Earps. He came here after we did, but he's inserted himself into the thick of things pretty easy-like."

"He said his father is an old friend of the Earps and they are doing him a favor by giving him some law experience. I don't see anything sinister about it."

"Well, just so you don't start getting sweet on the blue jay too," Garth countered, laughing and ducking when she swung her drawstring purse at his head. As a parting shot he asked her, "Maybe we should introduce the major to Aunt Twila. I think he fancies himself a ladies' man." He turned away, chuckling, and Sam went back to the outer edge of the dance floor.

The blue jay must have been watching for her to return. He stalked up to her and bowed. "Might I have this dance, Miss Samantha?" He smiled, and the lamplight glanced off his glasses, which he'd put on again. She couldn't read the expression in his blue eyes. If indeed there was one. She nodded absentmindedly and moved into his arms, feeling oddly as if she belonged there. His arms were surprisingly strong and firm as he guided her into the graceful swaying of a waltz.

Her heart thudded in her chest. She hoped he didn't notice the throbbing of her pulse in her wrist when he took her hands. A slow warmth spread its way from her throat to her toes and hit everyplace in between. She closed her eyes to the rhythm of the dance rather than chance looking up into his probably arrogant expression. The blue jay danced well, but then why shouldn't he, since he did everything well. He would be the first to admit it.

"I saw you talking to that fellow. He stays at the boardinghouse sometimes, doesn't he?"

"Jealous?" She tossed back at him.

"Touché." He grinned. "Maybe a little."

Fortunately he didn't pursue the subject. For the time being they set aside their mutual animosity in the dips and gentle sways of the dance. From across the floor, Garth watched with a thoughtful look in his eyes. Sam's golden silk gown shimmered, bringing out the reddish-gold hints in her hair that Aunt Twila had piled up gracefully in a kind of a twist. Her décolletage was nothing compared to some of the ladies present, but men showed interest when they looked her way.

The cool, composed Blue Jay appeared even more dashing than usual. They danced well together, as if they'd known each other for years. This worried Garth. Was Sam falling for the man? What if he was the spy planted by their uncle? She could be hurt badly, considering the fiasco with Jeffery. Why hadn't she shown an interest in the deputy? He was big, strong, and decent looking. Of course Garth would have to admit Wade could make their plans more difficult.

The blue jay dipped his head to whisper in Sam's ear. Garth sighed. They looked so good together. Whatever he'd whispered caused Sam to draw back.

They had sailed past his position at the bar, and Garth heard him say, "The dance isn't finished yet, Samantha." He then purposefully danced her toward the open door and out into the night.

"What are you doing? We can't dance out here alone." Sam protested, dragging her feet.

"I wasn't thinking of dancing. I wanted to talk."

"About what?" She pulled away and glared up at him. "You always seem to be laughing at me. Why is that?"

He smiled. She took in the slight curve of his mouth and she wondered how it would be to press her lips against his, even as she struggled to deny the thought that had flashed through her. He'd put his glasses away, and she couldn't help think he was quite manly without the spectacles.

"Laughing at you? That's the most ridiculous accusation I've ever heard." His expression showed true amazement.

"Well, it seems like you are."

"You really are lovely, but a very spoiled young lady, aren't you?"

She stomped a foot, hoping to land it hard on top of his. "*Me* spoiled? Why, you arrogant, pompous, overinflated popinjay." Words failed her, and she shot daggers at him that might have withered a lesser man.

He regarded her outburst calmly. The pale light from the lamps inside the building shone on his dark hair.

What would it take to discombobulate him? she wondered. To her relief, she heard someone come up behind them and tap the blue jay lightly on the shoulder . . .

"Hey, dude, you've hogged the little lady long enough. It's my turn, if she'll do me the honor." A large, rawboned cowboy stood in front of them when they both turned. It was an unwritten rule at a dance that no one cut in. Sam uneasily expected Clarence J. to take offense. Instead, he surprised both her and the cowboy by smiling at the stranger.

"Certainly. Be my guest." He stepped away from Sam as if fearful the cowboy might think him unwilling to comply.

Sam shot him a look of pure disgust. She held out her hand to the cowboy and they both returned to the dance floor. She chanced a quick look back to see the blue jay had put his glasses on again, and was watching her with a thoughtful expression.

Before she had taken two steps in the dance, pandemonium broke out in the corner near the bar. The sound of hard fists plowing into softer flesh reverberated around the room. Fortunately everyone had been required to check his pistol or rifle at the door before entering.

Sam couldn't see over the dancers' craned heads, but she had the sinking feeling Garth, Elvin, and the major were somehow involved in the melee. The cowboy released her, indecision written on his homely face. He wanted to join the fight.

"You best go sit over there by the wall, miss," he said as he steered her firmly in that direction. The dance must have been much too quiet for most of the men, and they all now headed in the direction of the fight, leaving only the women and a few older men on the sidelines.

To Sam's disbelief, the blue jay stood next to Aunt Twila.

"Such ruffians. Barbarians." Clarence J. sniffed with disgust.

"If you weren't such an insufferable bore and teetotal coward, you wouldn't be standing here with a crowd of women. Do you need us to protect you?" Sam felt the same way he did about the fight, but she'd be darned if she would admit it. It was beyond her how men could enjoy a fight, not knowing how it started, whose side they were on, or what they were fighting for.

Ernestine visibly cuddled closer to the blue jay. "I think Mr. Westcott is right," she stated flatly. "Those men *are* ruffians and barbarians." She looked up at him and actually batted her long golden eyelashes at him.

Sam turned away in disgust and watched the fight for a moment. Out of the corner of her eye, she saw Garth standing off to the side and taking aim with a bottle. He let it fly toward the large kerosene lamp hanging over the bar. When Garth's bottle hit the lamp, the room was plunged into darkness. Only a few small lamps around the perimeter of the room feebly put out yellow lights. Apparently those in charge had been aiming for a romantic gloom.

Before the lights went out, Sam saw Wade,

standing at least a head above most of the others, shaking, knocking heads together and generally fighting a losing battle while trying to create order in the midst of bedlam. Sam saw with relief that the Earps were nowhere in sight. They'd probably left earlier.

"Will you please escort me to the carriage?" Ernestine asked Clarence J. tremulously. "I feel faint."

"Of course. What could I have been thinking, standing here gawking like some spectator at an arena. We are very near the door." He took Ernestine's elbow along with Aunt Twila's arm and nodded his head toward Sam, belatedly inviting her along.

She sniffed and turned away, needing to see if Garth and the others were all right.

The blue jay was only gone for a moment before he returned and, taking Sam's arm, practically dragged her to the buggy. She didn't protest, because his action came as such a surprise.

When they passed the edge of the building, she recognized the three horses tied to the rail. She hoped the gang would be able to leave soon, but since there was nothing she could do to help them, she reluctantly let the blue jay hand her into the carriage to join the others.

Silently they rode back into town and the boardinghouse.

CHAPTER 21

Three times during the night Sam peeped into Garth's room, but the bed was made and the room empty. Finally she gave up in resignation and slept soundly for what was left of the night.

The next morning she woke, disgusted for sleeping late. Downstairs Aunt Twila beamed at her, steam rising from the big iron kettle on the woodstove.

"You're always in the kitchen, Aunt Twila. You're not a servant, you know." Sam tried to keep the crossness from her voice.

Her aunt continued to stir the kettle, unperturbed by Sam's sometimes early morning mood. Especially if she slept later than usual, she became grumpy.

"I guess you should know by now this is my favorite place. Besides, do you imagine I would let anyone else touch my soup?"

Sam smiled and kissed her aunt's cheek. "I'm sorry. I didn't mean to be a grouch."

She poured out a cup of coffee and inhaled the aroma.

"Did you have a nice time last night? We came home early, but then there was that altercation at the bar."

"I had a wonderful time. But I'm worried about Garth. I thought he would come back to the boardinghouse after the dance."

"That is something else. I couldn't believe my eyes when Garth appeared at the dance."

"Why wouldn't he? Probably the townfolks have seen him come and go from here." Sam sat at the table and sliced off a thick piece of homemade bread.

"I saw him friendly-like with two men. Could they be from the gang? If so, they were all talking to some mighty dangerous-looking men."

"He did have two of our gang with him. That's why I'm worried. It could be that he had to take the major and Elvin back to the hideout if they imbibed too much. I think the major and Elvin had something to do with starting the fight. Seems like Garth was outside talking to me when we heard raised voices. Luckily the Earps had left earlier."

"You mean those rough-looking men were the Earps?" Aunt Twila's voice rose two decibels with shock.

"After Garth threw a bottle to knock out

245

the light over the bar, I think the battle kind of died down."

"He shattered the light? I didn't see that. My heavens. What was Deputy Wade doing when all this fighting was going on?"

"Oh, he was in the middle of it, knocking a few heads together."

"Do you suppose the boys are in jail?"

Sam shrugged. "It wouldn't hurt them a bit. Teach them to mind their manners at a civilized dance instead of acting like barbarians."

Aunt Twila plopped down on a chair, fanning herself with a dish towel. "What if someone recognized them?"

Sam took a big bite of bread after she had buttered it and spread a light sprinkling of sugar on the surface. That always brought her back to when she was a child, her favorite dessert, only with cinnamon added. "Impossible. In the first place, we don't work anywhere near here, and in the second place no one has seen any of our faces, thanks to the masks you made us. You know that Wade sees Garth all the time. If he recognized him from when he rode shotgun on Uncle Millard's stage, don't you suppose he would have questioned Garth by now? He seems to take his job pretty seriously."

Pausing in fanning herself, Aunt Twila looked at Sam in a manner that said she wanted the truth. "What about this major you two said joined you. Where did he come from?"

"Oh-ho, so you noticed him, did you? Hard to look away from that bounteous mustache, I bet. He's a retired British Calvary officer who suddenly became allergic to horses."

"Well, for heaven's sake! Now I've heard everything. How does he get around then, up to the hideout and all?"

Sam grinned. "You aren't going to believe this, but he has a steam-driven motorbike he calls Annabel." Sam suddenly wondered if the major had brought Annabel in town when he came to the dance.

"I think I'll walk to the jail to see if anyone's in there we know. How about cutting off some slices of bread and adding some of those beans warming at the back of the stove? I can use the excuse to take the food to the newest jailbirds."

Her aunt took the knife Sam was using and sliced the bread, wrapping it in a clean tea towel. "Good idea, child. And you come right back and tell me."

Sam smiled in spite of her worry. Garth would always be Aunt Twila's special boy, no matter how grown up he got or how much mischief he got into. Even though their aunt doted on Garth, having raised him from an infant, Sam never felt left out or unloved. The tall, spare old woman had an abundance of love in her heart, and she was never stingy with it.

Halfway down the block, Sam ran into Deputy Wade. She could see his head towering above the men walking past on the rough board sidewalk.

"Why, good morning, Miss Samantha. How are you this fine day?" He stood with his Stetson in his hand, the sun glinting down on the gold highlights of his straight brown hair. He glanced at her tray of food. By all rights, she should have been attracted to him, but she didn't have the feeling she got when she was near the blue jay, who probably wasn't worth the deputy's shiny badge.

She smiled up at him, deciding to ignore his pointed look. "I suppose you knocked a few heads together last night at the dance."

He grinned and tried to hide the enjoyment of this moment to tell Sam, "But more than that, I'm keeping a secret till the Earps get back. They headed east last night to the funeral of a family member." He paused as if considering his next words, but couldn't keep them inside.

"I'm right sure I caught a member of that crazy new gang that's been terrorizing the country." He roared with laughter and slapped his thigh as if he'd told the merriest of jokes.

Such an outburst was so uncharacteristic of the man that for a second, Sam didn't grasp what he'd said. When his words burst through her temporary blankness, she gasped.

"You what?" She hid her trembling hands beneath the tray she held. She only hoped she didn't drop the whole mess of food on the ground.

He was chortling when he looked at her. It was clear he didn't know whether to continue his story and trust Sam not to repeat it. But in the end, it was too good not to share.

"Would you believe it if I told you one of those desperados is at least sixty, if he's a day, and rides a bicycle with some kind of noisy engine attached to it?" Mistaking her horrified look for amazement, he laughed again until tears came into his eyes.

Oh Lordy, he captured the major. By the time the deputy had calmed down, Sam hoped she might have gained control of her voice enough to speak.

"How did you catch him? I mean, how do you know he is a part of that dreadful gang? And what does all this have to do with the dance?" They started walking slowly back toward the boardinghouse. She didn't want to go to the jail now. Her worst fears had been confirmed.

He clamped his hat back on his head and shoved his hands into his tight pants pocket as they walked. "Can you believe that cheeky bas— . Uh, 'scuse me, ma'am." He shot an embarrassed look at her and then rushed to finish his news. "That felon refuses to tell me his name but says I can call him Major. Major of what, I'd like to know? Anyway, he came to the dance and started the fight. I saw it all from across the room."

"But are you sure he's not some old codger who just felt like a fight coming on? I bet you've seen a lot of them."

"Sure have. But when that gang held up the stage I rode shotgun on, I recall this same man reaching up to scratch his mustache under the hood he wore. Who can forget such a bush like that? A handlebar mustache that went from one side of his cheek to the other? I'm paid to be observant, you know." He patted his flat stomach in smug satisfaction, and Sam wanted to kick him.

She hoped her face reflected a proper degree of admiration, which was what Wade seemed to require. But the thought of the major, barely reaching to the deputy's shoulder, loftily admonishing Wade to call him Major was almost more than she cared to hear. At any other time, it would have been hilarious.

"That seems fairly circumstantial. You couldn't have been that close to him." She stopped, aghast at what she'd said. To cover her hasty words, she asked. "Was he alone?" To her dismay, her voice came out as a squeak. She cleared her throat and asked the question again.

"I reckon his pals could have been with him at the dance, but I only recognized this varmint." The deputy sounded disgusted. "Maybe I might have grabbed the whole gang if I'd recognized him before I took him to jail." He looked pointedly at the tray in her hands.

She turned around to go back to the boardinghouse. "Excuse me, Deputy, but I was on an errand of mercy for an ailing friend, but think I'll ask my aunt to go in my stead."

He tipped his hat in farewell and they

went their separate ways.

Sam was certain by now everyone in the gang knew the major was missing. She didn't want Garth and the others coming into Powder. The deputy was sure to be watching and waiting. Garth had warned her time and again about coming to the hideout alone. But she would have to chance it. And it would have to be tonight.

CHAPTER 22

Sam chose the big stallion rather than her little mare, Gracie, remembering she'd taken Gracie out to the desert the last time. She rode the horse into a silent, moonless desert when she left the boardinghouse late that night. A few clouds scudded across the darkening sky. She felt the tense tautness of a thunderstorm in the air and sniffed to smell rain. Odd how you could always smell the distant odor of rain in the desert.

She needed to make her way to the cave before a thunderstorm broke. Wishing for moonlight to watch for the landmarks leading her to Garth, she also blessed the darkness and was glad her silhouette didn't show her to anyone wandering around in the desert. Maybe on such a murky night no one would be about.

The wind picked up, cool on her flushed cheeks. She tightened the string of her flat-brimmed hat more securely. It had been a hard job convincing Aunt Twila she had to warn Garth. It was then she finally realized her aunt loved them both equally. Twila begged Sam to stay and wait, even though it meant not warning Garth. Sam recalled the warmth of her aunt's embrace when she left. Luckily, their aunt knew nothing about the desert or any of its hazards. Aunt Twila refused to venture any farther than the mercantile store.

Sam's thoughts broke apart with the sound of galloping horses behind her. She glanced back in icy fear and heard a loud cry. At least five Indians headed straight toward her, yelling. With a sinking feeling, she realized there was nowhere for her to hide. She was *so* close to the cave. Desperately she kicked the sides of her mount and worried about prairie dog holes the horse might step into. With the steady pounding of hooves behind, her heart sank when she realized she would never make the outcropping of rocks and mesquite trees ahead that might hide her.

She tugged at the rifle tucked in its scabbard by the saddle. Why hadn't she ridden with it across her lap, as Garth had cautioned her to do so many times? Her horse's stumbling over rocks and jouncing gait prevented her from drawing out the rifle.

An arrow zinged close to her, landing almost in front of the now terrified stallion. Closing her eyes tight, Sam held on for dear life, but her mount was tiring, his sides heaving with the effort. Another mistake, not to have taken her fleet little mare. She would be lucky if an arrow struck her in the back and killed her outright. If the Indians caught her and discovered she was a woman . . . she shuddered and pounded the stirrups against the horse, urging him on mercilessly. A peal of thunder shot across the sky, followed by a jagged slash of lightning.

Simultaneously she thought she heard the crack of a rifle and then another followed by the wailing cry of a banshee. One part of her mind wondered why, if the Indians had rifles, they hadn't shot the horse from under her. The sky released its burden of rain in a punishing downpour so loud she couldn't hear anyone following her. She maneuvered the horse up through the brush toward the hidden cave. At one point she got off the horse and led the weary animal along the rocky trail. She didn't worry about the Indians following her to the hiding place. One of them must have accidentally shot his companion and they turned around. She was alone; she knew it.

Soaking, bone-tired, and frightened nearly out of her wits, Sam entered the cave and released her rolled-up bedding from the back of the saddle. Unmindful of her wet clothing, she took several deep breaths, striving to relax. When she finally recovered enough to look around, her heart sank. The cave was empty. Everyone was gone.

She moved to take the saddle and bridle off the horse, rub him down, and lead him toward the rear of the cave where there would be hay, grass, and water.

Tears of anger and frustration coursed down her cheeks. Had they figured out the major had been captured and were hell-bent to rescue him? Surely none of them could be that foolish. The deputy had set a trap to catch them all.

She struggled out of her wet clothing and donned a dry set of trousers, shirt, and jacket. Aunt Twila had helped wrap her breasts tight, but even that wasn't uncomfortable enough to take her mind off her predicament.

Sometime during the night Sam heard her horse snort in the darkness. She jumped up, instantly alert, running back to the horse to hold its nose to keep him from whinnying. The mountainside was honeycombed with caves, some natural, some old mining claims. Perhaps some wild animal had burrowed in a cave nearby and made the sound of rocks sliding. She heard it again, along with a light smattering of rain against the rocks outside. A clump of gnarled mesquite bushes partially hid the entrance to the cave. The cave would not be easy to see ordinarily, but if someone — an Indian — searched for it, he could find it easily enough.

Sam tied a handkerchief around the horse's nose to keep him quiet. After that she sat back down, leaning against the rear wall of the cave with her rifle trained toward the entrance. She was relieved she hadn't lit a fire, even though she would have enjoyed hot coffee. She was tempted when she saw coals glowing beneath the ashes.

During the long night, Sam fought sleep with every ounce of strength she possessed. A stone rattled down the slope of the mountainside from time to time, and she was aware of dozing off when the slight sound startled her awake. She finally gave in toward morning. The next thing she knew, someone was shaking her shoulder. She looked up, startled, and reached for her rifle lying at her side.

Relief flooded her when she recognized Garth, Big Bear, Don Pancho, and Elvin staring at her with amazement.

While the men made a fire and Elvin fixed coffee, she told them about her narrow escape. Briefly she'd forgotten the major in her fear of the Indians.

Garth's hand shook as he punched her lightly on the arm. "What the hell have I told you about coming out here alone? I thought the Indians around here were friendlies."

"Renegades," Big Bear muttered.

Sam could tell Garth was troubled and vexed with her at the same time.

"Did you shoot one of their horses out from under him?" Elvin asked, his admiration showing in his wide grin.

"No! I barely had time to escape, let alone try trick shooting from the back of a galloping horse."

Garth looked puzzled. "There's a dead Indian pony lying out there not far from where the rocks begin. If you didn't shoot it, who did? It had a very definite hole in its neck."

"I thought I imagined the sound of two rifle shots while I was trying to escape, but that didn't make sense. I had almost outdistanced them at one point, and they could have shot me anytime if they'd had a rifle. It was when they were almost on top of me and could have slashed out with a knife or let go another arrow that I heard the shots and the Indians turned away. I thought one of them must have wounded or killed a companion by mistake."

"Injuns make no mistake," Big Bear piped up. They all looked at him, startled, and then laughed, easing the tension that had built up in the cave.

"I'm sorry you had a close one, Sam, but what the hell are you doing out here alone?"

"Hey, yeah, little buddy. It ain't no place for a kid to be parading out there in that desert alone at night," Elvin added.

"I plumb forgot about the major!" She told them about the Englishman's capture and that the deputy was sure he recognized him as part of the gang.

They all fell silent after Sam finished explaining why she'd braved the desert alone to come find them. Don Pancho was especially stricken. For some odd reason, he and the major had become fast friends. Neither of them understood a word spoken between them, yet they had formed a bond. Most likely due to their being older than the others in the gang. Don Pancho made it clear he was all for going to Powder and breaking the major out of jail immediately.

Garth sat down wearily on a blanket and

shook his head. "No, Don Pancho, I'm afraid it's not quite that simple. Oh, we'll do something, don't you fret. Only I have to think about it some."

They sat around the cave dejectedly, staring into the fire. No one said a word, but the overwhelming absence of the major was uppermost in everyone's thoughts. Their worry was not that he would betray them, but how they could rescue him. The whole aspect of rescue would be more than dim, though, if the Earp brothers returned soon.

"There is something we might do to set their minds to thinking about the major's innocence," Garth mused. The others waited, ready to try almost anything to help.

"This is Thursday, isn't it, Sam?" At her nod, he continued. "Monday morning a stage is due from Benson. According to a report that I got, a very important shipment of mining equipment and possibly some of the payroll will be coming in at this time." He paused dramatically to let the news sink in. By their puzzled expressions, he could see they'd made no connection between the major's captivity and the stage arriving.

"Well, here's my idea. It's not so great, but it's the only one I have. We'll hold up the stage as we normally do. When word gets back to Deputy Wade, do you reckon

260

he'd suppose we wouldn't likely rob a stage with one of our own in jail? We'd be lying low, right? Holed up and scared for our lives, in fact. So that means Sam will have to hightail it back and somehow get word to the major that he should protest his innocence most vigorously. Pretend kinship with the king and queen or something. Claim to have bought that confounded machine from some shyster recently, and he didn't know how to run it. I'm sure the major will come up with something grand."

"You're thinking that when we do a robbery without the major, the authorities will believe he has nothing to do with us?" Sam's smile lit her face and Garth gulped, hoping the others hadn't noticed. At the moment she did not resemble a man.

"But this deputy feller claims to have seen the major in one of our stage robberies," Elvin said.

Garth pushed his hands through his unruly hair impatiently. "He claims to have seen him, but briefly. You said he only saw his mustache, Sam. We have to remember that and work around it somehow."

CHAPTER 23

Sam returned to the boardinghouse accompanied by Big Bear. The next days were hard to get through while she waited for Garth to pull his next robbery. She longed to visit the major, but they'd decided it would be best not to alert him that they knew where he was.

Ernestine was continually underfoot when she was not at the schoolhouse and, much to Sam's annoyance, Aunt Twila seemed to have taken a liking to the petite blonde. The blue jay stayed close, closer than Sam would have liked also. Just when she needed to be alone to organize her thoughts and figure the best way to visit the major. The one person she needed to be around, to glean any tidbits that might help Garth and the gang, was Wade, whom she seldom saw.

"Miss Samantha? Oh, bother. I'm not going to be formal. Samantha, mind if I sit down a minute?" The blue jay parked himself on the settee next to her. "I hope I'm not intruding upon your deep thoughts?" He leaned forward, light glinting off his spectacles.

Drat the man. She didn't have time for this. She glared at him. Something about him engaged her interest far more than she wished. All he had to do was touch his long fingers to her wrist, as he was doing now, and her pulse nearly zinged out of her skin.

"I heard about your mishap in front of the saloon today," she said. At his crestfallen look she was almost sorry to have mentioned it.

He cleared his throat, plainly unhappy. "Ahem, yes. That was most unfortunate and embarrassing. I suppose the men must permit steam to escape once in a while though."

"Really? How *could* you let those awful cowboys force you to dance? In the middle of the street, no less. I would have let them shoot me," she declared.

He removed his glasses and polished them with his ever-present handkerchief as he was wont to do when troubled. His hands shook, and Sam swallowed a lump in her throat at upsetting him. She'd never seen him anything but annoyingly calm and composed.

She was startled at the cold, implacable

fury in his eyes when he looked up from wiping his glasses. "How could I *let* them do it, did you say? You should have troubled to ascertain the entire story before you let your pretty little mouth get carried away. There were six of them, all with pistols, and all shooting at my feet at once. What would you really have done, I wonder?" He stood up and, with one last cold glare, he turned on his heel and stalked away.

Sam felt a scarlet wave wash over her face, and she sank back on the settee. Granted, he was pompous and arrogant, but she hated herself at that moment. In all her years, she'd never deliberately set out to hurt someone. She winced again at the thought of those steady blue eyes showing hurt for a moment before they turned cold. He had a streak of honed steel buried inside that was barely perceptible, but she saw it. He'd tried to make the best of a bad situation, one that he had no control over, and she had mocked him. She felt so ashamed.

Later that day, Aunt Twila finally figured out how best to visit the major. She insisted on taking the message that the gang was aware of his capture along with bread and soup as an excuse.

"That's ridiculous," Sam protested. "Garth would never permit you to become involved in our doings."

"Horsefeathers! It's about time I get to do something constructive, not to mention interesting for a change. You two are always leaving me out. Besides, this will be simpler. You've already shown the deputy you were heading in the direction of the jail. If he saw you twice, he might become suspicious. Not to mention that this Major person might recognize you."

Aunt Twila sat at the kitchen table after gathering writing materials, as if things were all settled. Sam could only raise an eyebrow. At that, her aunt laughed and said she looked like Garth when he tried not to pout.

"In the event someone is nearby to listen, we'll write a note as if it came from Garth and hide it in with the food. We'll explain that Garth stays at the boardinghouse when he's in town and asked me to deliver this message."

"Well, it might work." Sam looked unconvinced. "But Garth won't like it."

Her aunt drew up to her full height, almost as tall as Sam. "When will you two realize that *I* am the elder in this family and am not to be protected like some fragile china cup? Or maybe *because* I am older, you prefer to treat me as if I have one foot in the grave."

It was rare that Aunt Twila scolded, and Sam felt properly chastised. "Oh, dear, please don't say such a thing." She rushed forward to hug her aunt. "You are our only family, and we just want to protect you. We certainly don't look on you as old." Sam frowned. "You knew that argument would get me, didn't you, you rascal."

They both laughed.

Early the next morning, Aunt Twila sallied forth to deliver the note and food. Another deputy was at the desk and walked back to the cell with her.

"I don't know as I should leave you, ma'am. I've heard this desperado comes from a dangerous gang." He hid his chuckle politely behind his hand.

"Thank you for your concern, Deputy. It will be fine. It is my duty to bring Christianity to the fallen."

The deputy nodded, opened the jail door, and walked quickly away as if he didn't care to hear any preaching.

When she entered the darkened area, the major appeared to be the only customer. He rose from the cot and doffed his tall hat. "Good morning, ma'am. I remember seeing your loveliness at the dance." He smiled beneath his bristly mustache.

Aunt Twila might have felt an odd twinge

at his admiration, but she wouldn't have let him know it for anything. "I have brought you homemade bread and soup, sir." She placed them on the tray in the small opening of the jail door and motioned with her shoulder toward the open door to the office.

He nodded, took the bowl, and went back to set it on his cot. He took off the tea towel and immediately saw the note.

"I bid you good day, sir. I must be on my way."

The major made a deep, courtly bow. It was plain to see he didn't know whom he dared ask about, so he smiled and thanked her.

When Aunt Twila returned to the boardinghouse, she beckoned Sam to meet her in the bedroom where they wouldn't be overheard.

Her aunt's face flushed out of its usual pallor, and her eyes twinkled as she settled in her favorite chair.

"Did you see him? Was he well? Did you tell him not to worry? That Garth would figure how to get him out?"

"Tsk tsk, Samantha. Patience is virtue. He is quite the charming man. You didn't tell me you had a gentleman in your . . . your group. I thought they all were a pack of villains. He wasn't sure what he dared ask me about Garth, so I let it pass. He can read the note."

Sam grinned. Her aunt could never force herself to refer to them as a gang. "Aunt Twila, you know better than that. We've described every one of them to you in great detail. None of them would so much as harm a fly." She left out Buster, since he was long gone anyway. "But yes, I believe the major is a true gentleman. A rather unorthodox one, I admit, but a gentleman to the core."

"Deputy Wade wasn't there, thank goodness. The attending deputy didn't want to hear my sermon, so he left us alone but with the door open to the office. I didn't want to whisper to cause attention, so I left the note."

"I'm glad you didn't say anything that could be overheard," Sam said.

"Oh, dear me, no. I was very careful. I hope they let the poor man go free."

"Don't worry. If the major can't talk his way out, then Garth will think of something else." Sam wasn't as sure as she tried to make her aunt believe. "We've set the rendezvous in place. Now all there is to do is sit back and wait for something to happen. We should be hearing about Garth's last robbery any day now. Probably the next time we see the deputy, he will have a lot to talk about."

The next time Deputy Wade showed up at the dinner table, he dropped a bombshell in their laps.

"I think that Desperado gang is heading for the last roundup." He looked at Sam and her aunt for approval. "Caught two of the rascals all by myself last Monday. Guess that old duffer in jail isn't one of them after all." He sopped up his gravy with a stray biscuit and chewed thoughtfully for a moment. Then he slanted a quizzical look at Sam.

Her aunt gasped and covered it quickly with her napkin, as if she had coughed. Sam didn't dare look at her, but clasped her trembling hands together under the table and tried to breathe normally.

Ernestine spoke up, her lilting voice all aquiver. "Oh! I think that's marvelous. You caught that dreadful gang of cutthroats all alone?"

Sam gritted her teeth at Ernestine's simpering voice, and barely restrained herself from throwing the bowl of gravy at her. The thought of the contents dribbling down Ernestine's perfect hairdo and face almost made Sam laugh.

The deputy shook his head and waved denial with his now empty fork. "No, ma'am. Well, I mean, yes, I caught them alone, but no, they aren't exactly cut-throats."

Much to Sam's relief, he scraped back his chair, excused himself, and presumably hurried back to the jail. One glance at Aunt Twila's white face was enough, and Sam gently led her upstairs to her room while the other boarders departed.

"Who do you suppose he has captured?" Aunt Twila whispered hoarsely after Sam had shut the door firmly and they sat on the edge of the bed.

Sam shrugged, but the furrow between her eyes gave her away. She was worried.

"He looked at you funny, Samantha. You saw it. Do you think one of them talked, and maybe he put two and two together? Although that's unlikely. To tell the truth, I always thought him dumb as a rock."

Sam smiled. "What could they say if they did talk? No one but Big Bear knows about my dual identity, and he would die before he let that out. I know that much about him."

"Garth is in jail, I know it. Oh, dear God, why didn't I stop you children from this folly?" She wrung her hands. Sam was frightened to see the usually calm and matter-of-fact woman falling apart.

Sam patted her aunt on the shoulder. "I'll have to go and see inside that jail." So saying, she went to her room, fixed her hair up in a bun, and stuck a bonnet on her head. Back in her aunt's room she said, "I'll be back as soon as I can. Sit here and knit or something and don't go downstairs. You look like death warmed over." She smiled at her aunt to soften the sharpness in her voice. If her aunt went downstairs in this condition and if the blue jay or the deputy happened by, they would certainly have cause to wonder.

Out in the street, Sam breathed deeply of the evening air. At first she dragged her feet, dreading to see the people the deputy had captured inside that infernal jail.

When she reached the steps of the jail, she saw Deputy Wade tilted back in his chair, leaning against the wall of the rickety old slat building. She pasted a nonchalant smile on her face and entered the room.

"Why hello, Miss Samantha. What brings you here?" He dropped the chair legs and stood, doffing his hat politely.

"I thought . . . that is, if you wouldn't mind . . . or if it isn't against any rules, I would like to take a peek at that band of outlaws you captured. I've never seen any real desperados before." She held out her pad and pencil. "I sometimes report for our local newspaper and thought this might be of interest, that you were able to capture the desperados by yourself."

"You mean you want to go in there?" His cocky expression told Sam he'd heard her lavish praise. Saying the words out loud had almost choked her, but on the other hand, he was only doing his job. He frowned in perplexity and then a wide grin broke on his face. "Oh, I understand. Somehow you must have heard about that big ugly Indian who used to work around your place." He shook his head. "I can't believe how talk flies around this town."

"Indian?" Oh, horsefeathers, they'd caught Big Bear! This wouldn't go well for him, considering the town's prejudice. Sam glanced into the deputy's gray eyes and discovered he didn't look quite as uncomplicated and harmless as she and Garth had believed him to be.

She forced a smile. "No, I hadn't heard anything about that. You mean Big Bear? He used to help out at the boardinghouse, but I haven't seen him for weeks. Is he a part of that gang?"

"Looks that way. Caught them dead to rights robbing a stage, but two got away."

It had to be Garth who'd escaped, or the deputy would have named him as someone he knew from the boardinghouse.

Wade held the door to the back room open for her. "I reckon it's all right if you want to take a look at them. Charlie tells me some lady came by to feed that old English coot some home-baked goodies this week. I let him go. Wyatt may not like it, but I can't see him as part of the gang. If he had been, they wouldn't have dared pull this robbery, knowing we'd captured him."

Well, thank God, that was one problem she didn't have to worry about.

Deputy Wade touched her lightly on the arm. "We try to keep the jail clean, but it's mostly filled with weekend drunks and rowdies. Sometimes a traveling marshal uses it as a sort of stopover on his way to Tucson or Yuma." He followed her to the back.

Resolutely, she strode forward to face the cells. There were several men she didn't know in one cell, and she hurriedly looked away. One man stood up to glare at her with a sullen expression and then lay back down on his cot, staring at the ceiling.

"They look rough, but probably feel worse. Last night a bunch of cowboys from

273

a trail drive busted into town, tied on a drunk, and tried to tear things up. We'll hold them a few days to let them cool off and sober up, and then turn them loose."

She felt Wade's gaze on her, watching her, as if trying to fathom who or what she was looking for. A huge sigh of relief burgeoned up from her toes when she beheld no sandy-haired man among the group. At least Garth remained free. Her elation didn't last long when she gasped at the sight of Big Bear and Elvin sitting on cots near the rear of the cell. Big Bear pretended not to notice her. Finally Elvin took off his battered hat, thumping it against his leg and whistled. Plainly he thought people would expect such behavior from him. After that display, he turned his back to her, as Big Bear had done.

"Do you recognize either of them?" Deputy Wade asked.

Sam recovered and sniffed daintily. "I believe that is the Indian who used to work for us. I'm not exactly sure." If she didn't own up to knowing him, someone would remember her saving him in that street fight. She made a dismissive move toward the door, and the deputy followed her. When they were closing the door behind them, a loud raspberry sound emanated from the cells. She put her gloved hand up to hide her smile. That could have only been Elvin. She recognized his favorite sound of defiance. Deputy Wade frowned and turned as if to go back, but she took his arm and steered him inside the office.

"Satisfied your curiosity?" he asked politely.

She nodded. "I suppose so. But how did you capture both men by yourself? What will happen to them?"

For a moment he looked puzzled. "Oh, you mean the Injun and the fairy princess? Wyatt will be coming back from the funeral any day now. I'll leave that up to him. Probably it'll mean a necktie party for the Injun. They won't bother carting him back to Yuma. As to how I caught them? Let's say I knew where to look. Almost got a third one. In fact, I think I winged him."

Her pulse raced, and she instantly imagined Garth hurt and holed up in the hideout, unable to get back home. Maybe the deputy shot at Don Pancho, but usually he stayed out of sight holding the horses.

"I thought you said that particular gang wasn't to be taken seriously. They don't sound so terribly dangerous to me."

"I didn't think they were much to worry about either until . . ." His dark brows lowered over his eyes and he paused, as if considering. "I reckon there's no harm in telling you this, but some important cuss back East decided the robberies were interfering with his activities out here. I'm not at liberty to name names. Since Wyatt felt the gang beneath his dignity, he assigned the case to me. It's only a matter of time until we round up every last one of them, and then we can get back to serious threats like the Curly Bill crowd."

CHAPTER 24

Sam didn't know how she got out onto the street again without her legs buckling under her. A pack of rowdy cowboys almost ran her down, swerving at the last minute amidst catcalls and whistles as they passed. Two things had niggled at her memory during her conversation with Deputy Wade. The first was, he hinted that he knew when they planned to attack a stage. The second — and more telling — did he know the name of the man back East? Garth said Peaches wouldn't say who owned the Silver Buckle Saloon.

Was it natural that Wade accepted her nosiness without question? No doubt it was his nature to be stolid and incurious, but something nagged at her not to underestimate the big, friendly lawman. She was becoming unreasonably afraid with worry about the broken desperados.

As soon as the front door closed behind

her, she headed for her room. To her utter dismay, Ernestine sat in the parlor near the bottom of the stairs. The woman lifted her arms in a careless gesture of tiredness and stifled a yawn. Had she been waiting for Sam?

"Hello, Samantha. You look distressed. What's the matter?"

Sam raised a scornful eyebrow but held her impatience in check. "What are you doing home at this hour? Not stepping out tonight with Clarence J.?" Why did that idea irritate her? She brushed away the unwelcome emotion. Drat Ernestine, Sam wanted to see Aunt Twila right away, before her aunt heard her voice and came down the stairs.

"I am fine. Now if you will excuse me, I need to go to my room and freshen up. I've been outdoors and it's dusty out there, as you know." Well, maybe she didn't know. There wasn't a speck of dust near Ernestine and not a hair out of place. It was plain Garth remained unfazed by her charm, but then, he was attracted by Peaches, shameful as that was. The fact that the blue jay appeared to be under the blonde's spell didn't bother her a bit, she told herself. It was just so undignified to see the haughty, vain man slide under Ernestine's dainty thumb, just like any other conquest.

Sam pushed aside her thoughts and ran up the stairs, without another word to Ernestine. In answer to her knock, a quiet voice bade her enter. Apparently her aunt had been striving for control, waiting to hear what Sam had discovered at the jail.

"Has Garth been caught?" Twila's bony fingers grabbed Sam's arms with surprising strength.

"It's not Garth in jail, but it's bad. Sit down, please." Sam retraced her steps to the door, peered out into the hallway, and closed the door firmly. While she paced agitatedly back and forth in the small room, she whispered the discouraging news that Big Bear and Elvin were imprisoned. At least the deputy had let the major go. For a few moments after she had finished speaking there was complete silence, and then her aunt spoke.

"Garth will know what to do, Samantha. We will have to wait for him. Although what even he can do for those poor unfortunate boys languishing in jail, God only knows."

"But what if Garth doesn't realize Big Bear's life is in danger? When Wyatt Earp returns, Wade as much as admitted Big Bear would probably be hanged long before he reached prison." She took a deep breath before she continued. "There's something else. Something I haven't told you yet."

Wordlessly her aunt waited, her expression anxious.

But no, Sam couldn't tell her one of the men had been wounded.

"Deputy Wade *knew,* Aunt Twila. He let it slip that someone from back East had ordered the gang's capture. He had to mean Uncle Millard. He said he had expected the gang to be at a certain place at a certain time. That's how he caught them. Shh!" Sam tiptoed to the door and opened it with caution. She saw a flicker of petticoat before Ernestine's door closed. Why should she be near Aunt Twila's bedroom door? Or had she just come upstairs simply to enter her own room? Sam chastised herself for wasting time worrying about a frivolous, small-town schoolteacher whose only goal in life was probably waiting for a rich husband to turn up.

Sam returned to the room and closed the door again. She knelt in front of her aunt, leaning her forehead on the older woman's knees as she used to do as a child. Her aunt smoothed her hair, and they were silent, each thinking her own thoughts.

After a moment, Aunt Twila spoke. "Do you suspect someone in town or, heaven forbid, in our home of spying on us, Sam?" Her use of the pet name let Sam know how worried her aunt was. Her father had hated the nickname and had forbidden anyone to use it. Of course Garth refused to be intimidated, and had always called her Sam.

Sam looked up at her. "I suppose I have to suspect someone close. I hate the thought of it, but how else could Deputy Wade know when the gang was supposed to attack that stage?"

"Is it likely one of the boys spoke out of turn, my dear? One of them might have mentioned it if he'd had too much to drink. Isn't that possible?"

Sam shook her head. "Possible, but I don't think so. I know those men, and none of them drink excessively. Anyway, Garth is like an old mother hen. He seldom lets them out of his sight for fear they'll come to harm. Don't you think the deputy would have been bragging about how he got the information if it had come from one of Garth's own men? No, he was very secretive about that. In fact, I surmised he was sorry he even mentioned he knew their whereabouts in advance. If anyone's a spy it has to be the blue jay. He admitted he works for Uncle Millard, for goodness sakes."

Her aunt leaned back in the chair and

rubbed her hands over her face. "I knew I should have put a stop to this the first time you two told me what you had planned. I couldn't have stopped *you,* but Garth might have listened to me."

Sam winced at the implied criticism. "We were having our revenge on that bastard and getting back some of our own money," she said in her own defense.

"Yes, I know. But at what price? Is revenge so sweet that you two risked your lives and the lives of others? If so, your uncle will have the last laugh." She patted Sam's head as if to take some of the sting from her words.

Sam offered a placating smile. She had to get to Garth. He could be wounded. No need to worry her aunt further until she made sure what had happened. It would be a relief to share her anxiety about Elvin and Big Bear's future. She regretted the notion of the blue jay being a spy for their uncle, but what else could she think? The idea intruded that he had never tried to make his relationship with Uncle Millard a secret. But then, that could have been a stratagem to throw them off-track.

"I've got to go to Garth, Auntie." Sam looked down at the older woman's face. To her consternation, she seemed even more lined and old than Sam had noticed before.

Had Twila guessed Garth was in trouble? "Don't worry so. Everything will turn out all right." Her words sounded hollow to Sam's own ears, and she knew her aunt discounted them straightaway. What she, Garth, and the others were doing wasn't a lark or a game any longer. Even Garth should realize that by now. Sam closed her eyes and turned away so her aunt couldn't see the frustrated anger in her expression. Their antics were no longer a nonviolent, harmless vendetta between their uncle and them. It had mushroomed and involved others now. Not that they were responsible for everything that had happened. The men who rode with them were like lost souls and had joined their cause freely.

Abruptly, Sam realized that, somehow, their uncle might have discovered he and his property had been singled out for raids. If he discovered she and Garth were behind the raids, his fury would know no bounds. He was capable of the most malicious actions against them. Kinship would mean nothing.

But who was the viper in their bosoms? Who had listened carefully to scraps of conversation and pieced it all together — or nearly all of it? That left Clarence J. the likeliest candidate. Yet she thought they had been cautious in their conversations, especially around him. There was the lovely Ernestine in the mix, too. Granted, there had been no connection between Ernestine and Uncle Millard, as far as any of them had seen. But Sam was certain there was something cloudy about a cultured, beautiful woman choosing to hide herself away in a backwater town like Powder. Why had she come here all of a sudden?

Sam's thoughts swirled with the backwash and currents eddying around her mind. What sort of monster had she and Garth created with their bittersweet idea of revenge?

CHAPTER 25

Sam waited impatiently for darkness. She had donned her grimy, sweat-stained boy's outfit and slid a threadbare Mexican poncho over her shoulders to keep out the night air. She hoped her aunt would stay in her own room until she left. They had already said their goodbyes, her aunt with an uncharacteristic flow of tears. Sam was hard put to keep up her courage. She recalled the last time she'd ventured out alone, and only the thoughts of Garth in danger and Big Bear's calamity could force her into the desert by herself. But even her aunt agreed that she had no alternative. To keep her aunt from learning someone was hurt, Sam had to secretly raid their store of medical supplies, taking what she thought she might need.

Out on the desert, looking up, she beheld the stars scattered across the sky like diamonds on black velvet. This truly was a remarkable place. She had no desire to return East. But Aunt Twila and Garth might have other ideas. The thought was distressing, and Sam set it aside for now. When she looked back at the receding town, the desert lay silent around her. Sam fought the urge to gallop. She needed to be able to hear if anyone followed her, and she might need to save her horse's strength. The notion of outlaws or Indians made her shudder. Clip-clop, clip-clop, a lonely godforsaken sound in the dark.

If only they had quit sooner and let everyone go their own way. Garth admitted they might have enough evidence against Millard Tremayne to keep him in misery for the rest of his scheming life. Maybe they could even blackmail him to get their inheritance back before he spent it all. But now even this had turned to ashes when she realized her ruthless uncle would never succumb to them holding anything over his head. He couldn't afford to. He would have to dispose of them when he discovered their game, as if they were ants he could casually step on.

Her heart leaped into her throat when she suddenly noticed an echoing clip-clop coming from behind. The beating of her heart almost silenced the sound, but it came through, loud and clear. She reined in her horse to listen. The sound behind her stopped too. Someone was following her. She searched the eerie desert with the moon rising from behind a nearby mountain, but every mesquite bush, every cactus, appeared ominous and threatening.

Sam turned and urged the horse forward. It wasn't Indians behind her. They would have known she was alone and run her down by now. She heard metal striking rocks — shod hooves. That told her the follower wasn't hostile Indians. But someone was definitely stalking her.

The knife in her belt eased her fears a bit, but could she stick the blade into another human being? She could if it meant her life. The need to get to Garth was uppermost in her mind. Cursing her foolish pride in not bringing a pistol or rifle, as Big Bear and Garth always urged her to do, she thought she could handle most any situation without violence. It tormented her that she might have cause to regret her overconfidence.

She *had* to get to Garth. She kicked her boot heels into the horse's side and he leaped forward in surprise, starting to trot at first and then broke into a gallop. She flew through the night, the wind whipping the loose flapping poncho, praying her horse wouldn't step into a hole or that a snake or rabbit wouldn't jump out in front of her.

Glancing back over her shoulder, she saw a shadowy figure on horseback. Desperately, she looked toward the outcropping of rocks leading to their hideout. For some reason, her shadowy pursuer did not try to overtake her.

There was no way she dared lead her pursuer to the cave. If Garth was injured and helpless, if they were not on guard, that could be fatal for all of them. She had to evade her pursuer before she climbed the rocks.

Sam slapped the reins, not looking back again. Once in a while a cloud drifted across the three-quarter moon, and she hoped the night would remain dark, but in a moment the clouds shifted and the moon came out bright and shiny, throwing its light across the desert floor. She spied the break in the rocks leading to the box canyon ahead. Going at an angle away from the hideout, she remembered this area well — or hoped she did. She was taking a calculated risk and it could prove her undoing. If it was the box canyon she and Garth took shortcuts through, it would be all right. But there were many true box canyons with no outlets. She would be in trouble if she went into one of those. When she broke from the rocks and headed down into the green meadow below, she heard rocks falling behind her. She hadn't dodged her shadow at all. He was sticking like a burr.

She pounded into the canyon and reined the horse up sharply. It was the wrong canyon. Heart thudding in her throat, matching the sound of the horse's hooves on the solid desert floor, she wheeled around, but it was too late. The intruder was almost on her. She peered up at the sky. If only the clouds would pass over the moon, she might pull over to the side and hide until he raced past.

There was no alternative now but to mask her fear and try to bluff her way out. She pulled her hat down low to cover her forehead and squared her shoulders. Trying to steady her breathing proved hard to do, but she didn't have long to wait.

The lone rider pulled up in front of her with a cloud of dust rising between them. His laugh frightened her even more than the sight of his face when Buster removed his hat to stare at her.

"That you, Sam?" He came closer with a grunt of satisfaction. "I figured it was you when I followed you out of town. You scrawny little misfit."

She remained still, mesmerized by his hard, shiny eyes.

He sidled his horse up next to hers and bumped her leg rudely. "You don't strike me as having a friendly attitude. 'Course you always was a snotty little bastard. If it hadn't been for your big brother and that damn Injun, I might have knocked some respect into you." He glared at her, cold hatred in his eyes.

Looking around, he smacked his thin lips with arrogant appreciation.

Did he know she was not a boy? The thought sent chills through her body, and she struggled to hide her fear.

"Box canyon, huh? Couldn't be better. Figger on learning you a lesson and then, by God, I'm gonna get every one of them other sons-o'-bitches, one at a time."

"But why?" Sam no longer dared keep silent. Her silence made him furious; she sensed it building up inside him. "What did we ever do to you?" She had to bluff as long as possible so she could think about how to escape.

"Oh, yeah," Buster said with a sneer. "You crazy loonies thought you'd get away with it, didn't you? I suffered in the hands of that army bunch on the train. They beat me up good, broke a few ribs. But on the way to prison, I escaped. I knew you was trying to get rid of me all along, but I didn't give you enough credit for being so slick." He peered at her from under shaggy brows that crashed together with his frown. "Did you know I got me some busted ribs and was hiding in a shack in Mexico for a month after them soldier boys worked me over?"

Sam couldn't control the shudder that swept through her. She was in for a beating — or worse. The man in front of her was lean as a whip and powerful. She felt rage rolling off him in waves. She pulled the knife from her belt and held it in front of her. "You might beat me, kill me even, but you won't get away unhurt." She forced her voice to stay firm in spite of the chill that had settled deep in her chest.

He snickered. "It'll be even better than I expected. I like a fight when I'm beating up on someone. It don't rightly seem fair to beat up a coward."

"Fair! You don't even know that word. When did you ever do anything fair?"

Buster stared at her in honest amazement. "Being an outlaw ain't got nothing to do with being fair. I'm talking about being square with your gang. That's the onliest way. You fellers weren't square with me, no how. That's why ever last one of you is going to pay. You got to be taught a lesson."

With that, he leaped off the horse and

reached to grab her. She slashed down with the knife, heard him yell, and urged her horse away. He would kill her now for sure.

Her horse obeyed, galloping down the trail, out of the box canyon. She tried to block the sound of the thundering hooves behind her and saw the rock spilt ahead, leading at last to the open desert. Too far, too far.

Sam glanced back and saw Buster riding, spurring the horse's sides and beating it with the reins, his fierce hawklike face scowling, his teeth clenched in rage. She turned to look in front and heard the hissing noise as a lariat fell over her shoulders and jerked tight. She felt the searing burn of the heavy rope and flew off her horse to land on the hard-packed ground. As she hit, she saw bursts of light and then blackness when her breath leaped from her body. She expected Buster to drag her behind his horse, and she prayed for unconsciousness. Before she had time to catch her breath, she'd stopped rolling on the ground and he jumped astride her, grinning down at her. She saw where her knife had penetrated his sleeve and saw some blood there. But not enough.

"I got you. No one to help you now." With that, he reached down to slap her hard, rattling her. "Don't want to do this too fast. You need to feel it." He kicked her, and she felt her ribs hurt down to her toes.

Thankfully she still had the heavy poncho covering her. She clasped her hands tightly to the front of her shirt and glared up at him. *I won't beg.* "I'm Garth's brother, and if you hurt me you will pay with your life." She cursed her tongue, knowing that was the worst sort of challenge she could fling in Buster's face. His exultant expression made her close her eyes for a moment.

She opened her eyes and shrugged, then grimaced in pain. Her back and shoulders were solid aches from her fall. She knew by the night air sifting over her that her clothing was torn, and she bore some deep scratches. She felt the warm trickle of blood in several places.

Before she could prepare herself for his intentions, he reached a hard, calloused hand toward her to rip her shirt front. He licked his lips, fury in his expression.

"Don't!" She tried to turn away but his hands held her in place. "You bastard! Garth will kill you for this."

"He won't know. When I'm through with you, I'll bury you in the desert so no one will ever find you. Then I'll go get each o' them boys one at a time."

Tears sprang to her eyes, and she willed them away. She kept her eyes closed to avoid looking up into his twisted face. He slapped her hard again and a scream of desperation and terror tore from her throat. Her heart pounded with fear and she felt vomit rise in her mouth. Blessedly, she succumbed to total blankness.

Sam came to slowly, giving an involuntary animal cry and huddled in a fetal position as if for protection when she spied Buster's back turned to her as he stirred a campfire. At least he hadn't killed her yet. If she hadn't made a noise, he might think she was asleep and leave her alone. She saw him glance her way through the mist of her tears. It was hard to make out his face in the darkness. For a moment the steady, relentless pain in her body turned aside her fear, but what would he do to her next?

The last thing she remembered was the slap against the side of her face and the horror of thinking he might discover who she really was. It surprised her now to see that he'd laid her on a blanket and covered her, the blanket smelling of horse and tobacco. She hadn't vomited before, but it wouldn't be long before she did. She clenched her teeth to prevent another outcry.

As if he had heard or felt her fear, the man turned from the fire and walked slowly toward her. She wanted to fight, to hurt him back, but realized it was no use. She closed her eyes again, waiting, tears seeping down her cheeks.

He knelt at her side. Gentle fingers thumbed the tears from her cheek. "Samantha, sweet woman. Are you awake?" The familiar voice slammed into her, and she opened her eyes with surprise and relief.

"Blue Jay!" she exclaimed before thinking. "But how . . . where is . . ." She could not force his hated name from her mouth. The man staring at her looked so different without his glasses. She saw his eyes so clearly, and they contained nothing but pity and sorrow.

Clarence J. reached over carefully to push the matted hair away from her dirt-streaked face. She cringed from his touch and he let out a groan. His blue eyes flickered with stony anger that surprised her.

"He'll never harm you again, Samantha. Can you sit up and drink some hot coffee?"

She nodded and pulled the blanket up around her torn shirt. She struggled to sit, and a cry of anguish escaped her lips. In a second, Blue Jay was at her side, kneeling over her. Before she realized what had happened, she found herself on his lap within the protective circle of his arms, and she was sobbing and trembling uncontrollably. He patted her blanketed back softly, soothing her and murmuring soft words, as if she were a wounded child.

Exhaustion finally overtook her and she relaxed, tilting her tear-streaked face back to look up at him. "He . . . he hurt me. He slapped and kicked me and said he was going to kill me and put me where no one would ever find me."

"Hush, dear one. It's all over. Don't think about it."

"But you don't understand," she cried out in her shame. "I've never been so completely helpless. And when he finished with me, he was going after the others." She shivered and ground her fists into her eyes as though to shut out the sight of Buster's face.

The blue jay leaned back, putting a finger gently against her lips. "Hush, sweetheart." He looked uncomfortable but doggedly continued. "I was searching for you. When I heard your scream, I came upon this man attacking you. I shot him. In the back — and I'm not ashamed of it. Where did he kick you?" He reached for a cloth he'd soaked in water and touched it to her face to wipe away the blood and encrusted dirt.

She flinched as he began to pull away the blanket. "He kicked me in the ribs, but I don't feel too much pain there. The poncho saved them from being broken, I think."

"Let's have a look at your back." He ran his hands over her back carefully, as if to smooth away the rope burns. "That monster cut you with his lariat. I wish I could have killed him twice. At least he didn't get the chance to find out you are a woman. His clothing was intact, as was yours." He spoke grimly through his teeth as she turned her back to him and allowed him full access. He rubbed something into her skin that felt cold and soothing.

"Horse liniment," he chuckled. "I'll get you a shirt from my bedroll." When he returned with the shirt, he stopped in front of her and offered a hand to help her to her feet. The dirt from the desert floor had mixed with her tears and blood from a cut lip, but he had wiped much of that away. He looked at her as if she were made of the finest porcelain. She and Garth had made fun of him behind his back and considered him a pompous ass. Was that ages ago? Was this the same man?

Wordlessly he handed her the shirt. When she dropped the blanket, he turned away to stir the fire.

"I'm decent," she said, forcing her voice to remain steady. She sank into the blanket, and Clarence J. turned back to bring her coffee. He squatted on his heels and helped her wrap the blanket around her shoulders. The night was chilly before dawn. Her trousers were torn in many places; she'd felt the cold draft until she covered up with the blanket. But the shirt covered her down to her knees.

While she sipped the strong, hot coffee, she watched Clarence J. over the rim of her cup. "You didn't look surprised when I called you Blue Jay." She needed to fill the silence that surrounded them to take her mind away from what had happened.

A taut smile lit his face, softening the hard lines of his jaw, and he regarded her thoughtfully. As if to give her time to collect herself, he spoke. "You don't like me much, do you? Can't say I blame you. But you really never gave me a chance. Anyway, unless you are fond of calling me Blue Jay, you can call me Jay. I've never used the name Clarence."

She didn't know what to say.

"But what are you doing out here alone? I saw you leave the boardinghouse and decided I'd better follow you." At the stubborn set of her jaw, he continued, "This isn't the first time I've tracked you. I never bothered when the one you call Big Bear accompanied you. I felt you were safe then. You nearly lost me this time, and I didn't find you until I heard your scream."

"You were the one who shot at those Indians when they were after me."

He nodded. "That was me. I noticed you slipping out of the house dressed up like a boy and wondered what you were up to, so I followed. Damned good thing I did, too. Those renegades meant business and would have soon run you down."

"I almost wish they had. Then I wouldn't be here." Her voice cracked with bitterness.

"Hey, enough of that talk. The important thing is you're alive. You hear that, Samantha? You're alive, and any other concerns are merely incidental."

She would have shaken her head in denial but knew if she moved, her whole body would feel it, and her headache would return in full force. She stared down into her coffee cup as if it held the answers. He had spied on her, followed her. That meant he could be the undercover agent for their uncle and probably knew their hiding place and all about their gang.

She looked up, eye to eye. "I'm grateful. Don't think I'm not, but that proves you are working secretly for *him.* And not just as an accountant."

"For whom? For God's sake, woman, you aren't making any sense. Whom do you suspect me of spying for?" He looked truly incredulous.

Sam leaned back against a rock. "Don't play games with me. It's too late for that."

He reached over and, taking her shoulders, shook her lightly. At her grimace of pain, he dropped his hands, his expression contrite.

"I didn't mean to hurt you, but I need an explanation. What the hell are you babbling about?"

"Why, you are a spy for Millard Tremayne, your boss. Garth and I suspected you from the first, even though you never denied working for him. As an accountant you say. I bet." She watched as his puzzlement changed to anger. Speaking of Garth made her remember why she had left Powder in the first place. He was in trouble. Their whole gang was in trouble.

"I came out here to find Garth. He might be hurt, and there's something important he needs to know."

Jay groaned and brushed the loop of straight black hair out of his eyes. "So it's true. You and Garth. I suspected all along, but you were both so damned sneaky. Were

300

you afraid your aunt would disapprove?"

"Leave Aunt Twila out of this. She didn't condone our actions, but she knew she couldn't stop us, so she let us alone. But she's not a part of it in any way."

"Well, I should hope not," he shot back. "Is this cad married? Is that why you have to slip away to meet him and sneak into his room every time he comes to town?" His eyes narrowed at her stunned look. "Oh, I haven't spied on you a lot, but I don't miss much. The boardinghouse isn't that big."

"What are you saying?" Sam sputtered. "Are we talking about the same thing?"

His smile didn't reach his eyes. "I was speaking of you and your lover, Garth. Isn't that what you were talking about?"

"My *what*?" Her eyes widened, and her voice rose a notch. "You mean you think Garth is my lover?"

He had the grace to look uncomfortable. "I am not judging you, of course. I'm merely an observant bystander, as it were."

"Now you are getting pompous again." For an instant she was tempted to let him believe his misinterpretation, but she needed his help to get to Garth. If he hadn't realized she and Garth were brother and sister, then he wouldn't consider their connection with Millard Tremayne suspicious.

301

Yet. She flushed, humiliated by his thinking she could be capable of such flagrant moral turpitude. In front of her aunt, no less.

She couldn't help but see that he was pleased at her temper. How odd. Could it be he wanted to take her mind off what had happened to her?

His next words confirmed this idea, and she wanted to hug him.

"That's my girl, Samantha. You've got fire in your eyes again. I don't ever want to see it dimmed."

"The truth is, Garth is my brother."

For a long moment he stared at her as if he didn't believe her. The odd look bordered on relief he tried to hide, and it gave her pause. Why would he care?

"You do look a lot like one another, now that I think about it, except for your hair and eyes. If you think he's in danger, can you ride to him? I wish you would lie back down and get a few hours of sleep before you get on a horse again. At least wait until dawn. When I looked at your back, it was solid bruises and scratches."

She must have dozed off in spite of not wanting to. In the morning she awoke to shuddering sobs, thinking about Big Bear hanging, Garth possibly gun-shot, and not being able to get home to tell Aunt Twila. Her ordeal with Buster kicked into her thoughts as much as she tried to delay it. Jay rushed to her side at once, picking her up and holding her close on his lap, soothing her. At first she pushed against him, not wanting anyone to touch her. Gradually she subsided with hiccups, and her trembling stopped. He kissed the tears on her cheeks.

"I've admired you since I first saw you kneeling, digging in that godforsaken garden. Actually 'admired' does not even come close to my feelings." The words seemed wrenched from him as if against his will, but his eyes said even more.

Her heart lurched at his expression of affection. She'd tried to deny, it but her feeling for him had gradually blossomed also.

"I wanted to keep my distance, thinking you and Garth were involved."

"And I thought Ernestine was your intended target."

He grinned. "Jealous?" He leaned in and pressed his mouth to hers, at first tentatively, as if to see if she would push him away. She only clung closer and reached up to push her hands through his hair. He groaned, and his tongue lingered on the seams of her lips for a moment. When she opened her mouth in surprise, he put his tongue inside, wanting to taste her. At last he pushed gently away from her and sat her back on the blanket. He stood, and his smile told her everything.

"I think you'd better trust me enough to let me go with you to see Garth. The fact that I work for Millard Tremayne bothers you. Has always bothered you. Why is that? I can see contempt in your eyes when you speak of him, although you've tried to hide it. I think you'd better explain."

"Not yet. I owe you my life, but I have reservations. You'll have to wait and talk to Garth."

If her bluntness startled him, he hid it well. Having put on his spectacles again, he was almost back to being the man she thought she knew.

For all the tenderness and care Blue Jay'd given her after he rescued her from Buster, it only showed he was different from the irksome, foppish person he'd always shown himself to be. It was like a disguise. How could she and Garth dare to trust him? And yet she knew he would never permit her to leave alone to go to Garth, and that gave her a warm feeling.

Sam let him help her up onto her horse. Before they left, she turned to him. "Where is he?"

He knew exactly whom she meant. He pointed behind a large mesquite tree, where she saw a pile of rocks that could hide a body.

"So, you did kill him?"

"I had no choice. I saw the knife he held to your throat and hoped my back shot would stop his hand in time. If I'd accosted him, there would be no reasoning with a man like that. He would have slit your throat before I could have stopped him." A shudder ran through his body.

Sam nodded. "I am in your debt. As vile a man as Buster was, I'm sure you wouldn't want his death on your conscience."

He looked at her with speculation, giving her a twisted smile. "Thank you for your consideration, Samantha, but I ask you not to worry about my immortal soul. That Buster character was like a cockroach to be stepped upon. He hurt you, and I couldn't stand for that."

He urged her ahead, and for a long time they rode silently across the early morning desert. She felt every step her horse took and wondered if she bled in places where Jay hadn't seen or asked to look at. Her muscles ached, her bones hurt, and her head pounded. When the sun came up, it felt as though it burned through her hat and into her skull. She closed her eyes and let her horse continue.

Jay put his hands on her reins to stop her. "Are you all right? You're swaying in the saddle. I knew we should have waited one more day."

She turned to look at him, and the agony reached her neck. She hadn't realized how maniacally Buster had slung her around and twisted to take her down to the ground. "I'm fine, considering. Just sore in places."

After some time passed, Jay insisted they rest beneath the shade of a large palo verde tree.

"You look right at home here on the desert," she said in an accusing tone. "Yet in town you gave the impression you were the greenest dude ever to come West. I wonder which one is really you."

He took off his hat and reached to rake fingers though his thick dark hair, considering her question for a moment.

"It's really no big mystery. I came out here six years ago in search of my brother. The darned fool kid joined up with a wagon train and took off without saying a word." Jay raised both arms up in the air to get the kinks out of them.

"Did you find him?" Sam could never abide a slow storyteller.

"Not at first. You see, we let him go. He was always impatient, wanting to jump into life with both feet. My father was a strict disciplinarian. He raised my brother and me after our mother died. When he had a stroke, he wanted to see Isaac one more time and asked me to go look for him. I found the wagon master who had returned for another trip, and he told me the general direction Isaac had headed when he left the train." Jay stopped talking and looked off toward the closest mountain, his eyes cloudy with remembrance.

For once Sam kept silent, knowing he didn't want his thoughts interrupted and he would finish the story in his own time.

He finally spoke, his voice low, his mouth set in a grim line. "After a year of following leads, trailing men and listening, I found his grave. I never did learn how he died. When I got back home, my father had passed too, so I had no reason to stay. I came back out here." He grinned in an apologetic way. "I didn't mean to inundate you with my life history." He motioned with a jerk of his head, and they started across the desert again.

"So you see," he continued as if he'd never stopped talking, "I *am* a greenhorn. There are a lot of things I don't know about this country and, for that matter, have no need to know. I did learn about trailing someone and, out of self-preservation, learned to shoot a rifle and a pistol. But as an accountant, I tried to stay away from violence, so I decided to act accordingly. Men usually don't pick fights with a duded-up fellow. I can hold my own if I have to, but it's just easier this way. Although I admit it hurts a little to know you all called me Blue Jay behind my back."

"Well, you sure had us all fooled," Sam said. "But that doesn't explain how you came to be working for Millard Tremayne."

"Oh, no you don't. You want to learn all of my dark and sinister secrets, but you haven't shared anything with me about the tornado you are in the middle of. I suppose I should count myself lucky you shared the information about your brother."

Not caring for his teasing tone, she clucked her horse forward. A feeling of relief soared over her when she spied the telltale outcropping of rocks ahead that led to the hideout.

CHAPTER 26

"Garth! Don Pancho! Hello the camp!" Sam shouted upward, not wanting anyone taking potshots in their direction if they wondered who approached.

The major stuck his head out of the cave opening cautiously. His toupee tilted, and looked quite ferocious. Sam had forgotten that he might not recognize her. She wore her trousers and one of Jay's too-big white shirts. But her long chestnut hair flowed loosely around her shoulders.

"Major! It's me. Sam." She sensed he had trained a rifle on them as they progressed. She swallowed against a tight throat. He was an unpredictable shooter at best.

"Sam?" He looked aghast and automatically raised his hand to straighten his toupee. "Sam did you say? By Jove, I think you really are."

She patted his shoulder, gently pushing the astonished Major aside to enter the cave, squinting at the sudden change of light.

"Garth? Are you here?" She heard a rustling noise in a corner,

"Sam?" Garth called to her. She rushed to kneel near his bedroll, bending over to kiss his forehead. "I was sick with worry about you. Are you hurt?"

He shook his head, his sandy eyebrows raised in a questioning way. "Did you come from home?" His eyes lit on Jay standing near the entrance, and he took a sudden breath.

"Before you say anything, I haven't told him about us. Except that we are brother and sister. Things became very inconvenient, and I had to tell him that much. Besides, I think we were wrong about him, at least partly. He said he would help us."

Sam looked around the cave and noticed Don Pancho wrapped up in his old serape and watching everything with his sad black eyes. She smiled at him. He returned the smile and said with a bit of pride in his voice that he knew she was a female from the first; she hadn't fooled him. But he liked her very much. She blew a kiss in his direction.

The major, on the other hand, was for once dumbfounded and speechless. He plopped down on his bedroll and turned his head back and forth, following everyone who spoke.

"Are you hurt badly?" Jay inquired, since Garth hadn't answered his sister.

This time the major could not be silent another moment. "He's had a nasty go of it, poor blighter. He's on the mend now, thanks to that fellow over there." He pointed to Don Pancho. "He knows magic herbs and plants out there in that barren, forsaken land and doctored our boy."

"So go on, Sam. Tell me about the blue . . . tell me how you come to be with him."

Jay smiled reassuringly. "Don't worry. I know what you and Samantha called me. Perhaps still do. But your sister is right. I don't know what sort of trouble you two are mixed up in. I said I'll help all I can."

Garth and Sam looked at each other. *Hold off, I want to talk to you alone first,* her eyes signaled. Garth understood immediately.

Sam and Jay sat side by side in front of Garth, who sat up too. She thought he didn't miss the flush that seared her face when Jay touched her hand.

Don Pancho had made a good-sized pot of beans, cornbread, and cowboy coffee. They suspended all talk while they ate. Sam worried how to tell Garth about Big Bear

311

and Elvin being locked up in jail and Buster being dead. She smashed the cornbread into her beans and then forgot to eat.

Garth noticed her preoccupation at once. He cleared his throat and frowned at them. His bandaged shoulder was plainly not very comfortable.

"There's something more here than meets the eye." Garth's voice sounded loud in the stillness of the small cave. "You need to tell me more, Sam. Did you bring him here from town? Oh, my God. Now I see you have a gash on your cheek and bruises on your wrists. What the hell happened?" He cast a suspicious glance at Jay.

Jay opened his mouth as if to speak, but plainly didn't know where to begin.

"Buster came back, Garth." Sam's voice was soft and hesitant. "He followed me. He figured out how we tricked him and planned to take care of each of us in turn in his own way."

Garth tore himself from his bedroll and crawled forward to put his arms around Sam. "Oh, no!" His eyes widened in horror as he stared into her face. "Did he hurt you?" His eyes begged her to deny it.

Sam knew what he meant, but before she could say anything, Jay spoke up, his voice steady and sure.

"No, it wasn't what you might be thinking. But it was a close thing. He slapped her around and kicked her, she told me." He grimaced and tried to smile at Sam reassuringly. "Anyway, you don't have to worry about Buster. He's planted safely under some rocks out there somewhere."

Garth sucked in his breath and looked at Sam and Jay with speculation.

The major could be silent no longer. He asked Jay if he knew anything about steam-driven motorbikes. When he saw he had an interested audience, he pulled Jay outside to show him Annabel. Don Pancho had wrapped himself up in his blanket again, and they heard him gently snoring.

As soon as they were alone, Sam quickly filled Garth in about Big Bear and Elvin. She assured him Jay knew nothing about their connection with Millard Tremayne. However, they both conceded he must realize they were lawbreakers, hiding out in a cave and Garth with a bullet hole in his shoulder.

"I reckon it's time we pulled out of this game of ours, as Aunt Twila always calls it. If that old buzzard puts all the pieces together, he could be dangerous. His fury won't be contained, and even Aunt Twila won't be safe from him."

"Do you think we can trust Clarence J.?" She asked the question not wanting to hear a negative response from Garth.

He regarded her thoughtfully for a long moment. "You know him better than I do."

Sam recoiled at his barbed remark.

"Ah, Sam, I didn't mean it like that. I suppose we will have to trust him up to a point. Did he say how he and Uncle Millard got together?"

"No. He didn't answer that when I asked him. But if he can help us get Big Bear and Elvin out of jail, we need him."

When the major and Jay returned and Don Pancho woke up, Garth and Sam told them about the men in jail. They all had suggestions ranging from the outrageous to the grand.

"I will take Annabel and break down the doors," the major threatened when he learned the possible fate of Big Bear. "Damnably unfair of you Yanks!"

Garth finally calmed him down and Sam spoke. "The deputy did mention that the Earps are in New Mexico and aren't expected back this week. That gives us an edge."

Don Pancho sat wrapped in his blanket. His black eyes shone as he uttered one word. "Fuego!"

Everyone started at the sound of his voice.

"Fire?" Sam repeated. "I guess he wants us to burn the jailhouse down." She looked at Don Pancho, who nodded in agreement.

"My, but you have a bloodthirsty gang," Jay drawled. He had been silent during most of the conversation, letting the others do the talking, but now he spoke up slowly and with quiet determination.

"The way I see it, if you will permit me a suggestion, is for Samantha and me to return to town separately. You fellows come on in when you can and sneak into the boardinghouse. Your aunt can hide all of you, since we can't be certain if the deputy or his helpers can identify any of you as part of this so-called gang. You might be safe walking down the middle of Main Street, but we don't know yet. I presume your aunt will not object?"

Garth laughed. "Yes and no. She is aware of some of what we do in our spare time, but she sure as heck doesn't approve."

Sam realized Garth wanted to keep Aunt Twila out of trouble as much as he could. She admired him for that. None of their problems were their aunt's doing.

"I shan't go without my darlin' Annabel," the major warned.

Jay laughed. "I'll gladly leave that problem

315

up to Garth. If you think you can sneak the old gal into town, more power to you. You should remember though, someone might be watching and waiting for such a move."

"But they let the major go," Sam protested. "Surely they can't suspect him of wrongdoing."

Jay shrugged. "I don't know. There's something fishy about that. They should have held the major at least until the Earps returned, to make certain it was all right to let him go."

Garth looked at Jay with admiration. "Say, I never thought of that. Then we'd best be on our toes. Could be a trap."

Sam hit her palm against her forehead and winced at the pain, "Oh, how stupid of me. In all the drama, I forgot one important thing to tell you. There could well be a spy in our midst. The deputy as much as told me that he *knew* when you were going to hit that last stage." She threw an apologetic look toward Jay. "And all the time we thought *you* were the one."

Garth regarded Jay thoughtfully. "Well, we're *fairly* sure it isn't him." He grinned to take some of the bite from his words. "So who would it be?" His sweeping gaze touched everyone in the cave.

Jay stood up abruptly. "Now see here, I

don't understand this at all. Why should I have suspected you of being outlaws, and why should I spy on you? And why are you incensed that I work for Millard Tremayne? These things don't add up to anything. Apparently you are leaving out a big chunk of the story."

"What would we be holding back?" Garth asked. "You heard Sam. Someone obviously is spying, else how would Deputy Wade know exactly where to nail us when we robbed that last stage?"

"So you admit to being outlaws with a gang? Someone must have overheard one of you bragging about your shenanigans in some cantina or saloon."

Garth shook his head stubbornly. "Not on your life. I never tell the men where we are going until we're on our way. That way there's less for them to tell if they get caught."

"What about the deputy?" Sam interrupted, as if sensing an argument looming. "You know we were so sure it was Jay that we didn't even watch anyone else." She smiled at them. "Oh, and then there's dear sweet Ernestine."

"Be serious, for gosh sakes," Garth scolded. "What could she possibly have to do with spying? You're mad at that gal

317

'cause you figured Jay might have his eye on her."

Sam flushed. "Indeed not." Jay had been listening to their conversation with a lazy, amused twist to his lips that made her want to smack it off his face.

"I don't think Ernestine has anything to do with us," Garth said.

"Well, I have a feeling there's something wrong with her story. She doesn't fit as an out-of-work schoolteacher ready to sink into a small town like this," Sam insisted.

"I agree, Garth. Her story doesn't hold water," Jay spoke up.

Sam turned to stare at Jay, wondering if he was teasing or being his usual sarcastic self. His piercing blue eyes appeared serious.

"What makes you say that?" Garth demanded.

"Nothing factual, but I agree with Samantha. It's a strange coincidence that she should pop up in Powder now. Though why in the world she would be interested in spying on your gang beats me."

He said "your gang" as disdainfully as only he could. Both Sam and Garth flushed with annoyance, but said nothing. As far as they knew, he still didn't connect them with Tremayne.

"The woman is obviously up to something. She is by far overeducated for her job, sophisticated and well-traveled, used to comfortable surroundings. Her story doesn't fit."

"My, aren't we a great detective." Sam glared at Jay. The words he used to describe Ernestine made her feel insignificant in his eyes. He'd certainly made quite a study of the woman.

"I guess we'll have to watch both Ernestine and the deputy." A worried frown crept into Garth's face. "But that doesn't solve our problem with Elvin and Big Bear."

"I said I would help in any way I could. Legally, of course. That is, if you are certain your days of highway robbery are over." Jay raised an eyebrow, showing skepticism.

Garth and Sam exchanged looks. Maybe the word *legal* was overused.

"I said we were giving that up, didn't I? The best way you can help is by keeping your mouth shut about us until we figure how to get our men out of the lockup."

Sam knew Garth's usually easygoing temperament was nearing the breaking point. She started to try and smooth the waters, but Jay interrupted.

"Has it occurred to you that when you do that, you aren't exactly giving up your outlawing hobby?" Jay reminded him.

"Hellfire, I knew it was too good to last!" Sam exploded. "You are a pompous know-it-all. How could I have ever thought differently even for a minute. We have no choice, don't you see? We can't let those two take the blame for all of us. Besides, I did tell you what would likely happen to Big Bear on the way to Yuma. Do you think that's righteous?"

Jay studied Sam as he considered her words, his usual smirk missing from his lips. "I think you either misunderstood Wade, or he was exaggerating. Hanging the Indian would be too barbaric even for this place."

Garth pushed forward to end the conversation. "Sam and I are grateful to you for saving her from Buster and getting rid of him once and for all. We'd take it kindly if you let us sort this out ourselves. All we are asking from you is your silence."

When they parted, Sam and Garth shared reservations about whether or not they could trust Jay.

CHAPTER 27

Garth walked down the dusty street, his thoughts in an uproar. The desperados, or what was left of them, were hiding out in the boardinghouse, much to Aunt Twila's dismay. He was reasonably certain none of them had been recognized or identified, but he was not sure about the major. Did the deputy suspect the major of being involved in the gang and deliberately turned him loose to try to entrap the rest of them? He rubbed his fingers across the bristle on his chin and decided to shave in the morning.

He stepped onto a board porch and looked up at the sign hanging over the entrance reading the "Silver Buckle Saloon and Gambling Emporium." Uncle Millard picked out a mighty fancy name. Garth came to see if his uncle had been doing any serious investigating, but he admitted to enjoying Peaches's company too. He wished he could talk about Peaches. She was really a sweet person, and he figured only her life's circumstances had placed her in their uncle's web.

When he pushed the swinging door open to enter the large room, it was almost empty in the midafternoon. He knew this was due to Peaches and her sense of orderliness. The smells were only from spilled beer and tobacco smoke and included none of the usual urine and disinfectant smells he had encountered in other bars.

Peaches sat at a corner table with Dan, the telegraph man, as the townfolks called him. Garth thought naming him Gabby Dan would be a better nickname, since he loved to spread gossip.

Peaches said, "Good afternoon, Mr. Garth. Dan came in to visit before he went back to work. Sit and have a cold one."

Garth took off his hat, nodded, and sat in a chair next to her, putting his hat on the table. "I have asked you to call me Garth." He grinned at Peaches, ignoring Dan.

She was a sight for sore eyes. She had arranged her honey-blond hair in a loose knot at the base of her neck. When on duty, she wore it swept up in a cascade of curls but he liked it better this way. It gave her a classic look, like a picture on a cameo. There were tiny lines around her mouth and at the corners of her eyes, even though she was probably only a year or so older than he. But she'd obviously not had an easy life. Even so, she kept an optimistic outlook and appeared mild-tempered. He tried to keep a lid on his admiration for her, but it grew stronger every time he saw her.

Dan scraped back his chair and stood. "I was fixing to tell Miss Peaches something, but I reckon it kin wait." His look was petulant, his voice thin, and he was obviously annoyed by Garth's arrival.

"Oh, come on, Dan. For goodness sakes, you can tell me what you came in to say," Peaches soothed.

"Yeah. Tell me too." Garth grinned at the tall, skinny man and poured him another beer from the pitcher on the table.

"I don't know." He glanced at Peaches. "Concerns your boss. Might be I'd get in trouble."

Both Garth and Peaches sat and waited, knowing Dan couldn't keep the information to himself even if he should have. Sam said he had diarrhea of the mouth, not a very ladylike expression, but that was Sam for you.

Dan sat back and picked up his beer to swig with thirsty gusto, his Adam's apple bobbing up and down in his scrawny neck.

"This here town's gonna bust wide open, unless I miss my guess." He watched Garth and Peaches, but they looked politely disinterested to egg him on.

Peaches spoke into the sudden quiet. "I don't think it would hurt for Garth to hear what you have to say. He's new to town and knows hardly anyone. I doubt very much if he knows my boss, Mr. Tremayne. Besides, we promise not to repeat anything you say, don't we, Garth?"

They looked at each other for a long moment, and then Garth said, "You got it. Lips sealed." He made the motion. What was the old coot getting at?

"You know that high-stepping dude that stays here and takes meals at Miss Samantha's boardinghouse? Well, you should know him, too, since you rent a room there, don't cha?" He stared at Garth.

Garth shrugged. "Yeah, when I'm in town, but I do a lot of business in Benson and am gone a lot. Salesmen don't stay put, and I like to keep a home base." Had he explained too much?

Dan glanced behind him toward the swinging door. "I just wouldn't want that dude mad at me. He has mean-looking eyes, the color of bullets."

"I assume you are speaking of Mr. Clarence J. Westcott? Do you have a point to this conversation?" Peaches sounded exasperated. "I've got to go to work to get those lazy girls up and dressed."

"I dunno exactly." Dan scratched his thinning hair as if pondering whether he should continue to speak or not.

"Forget it." Peaches started to rise. "We don't want you to get into trouble. Keep your story to yourself."

Garth figured she had begun to think it might not be in Millard Tremayne's best interest for Dan to continue speaking. As his loyal employee and "letter-writer lady friend." it was only right she would try to protect him. He didn't like that notion. Maybe if she ever came face to face with the old coot, she'd change her mind. But if she was an out and out gold-digger? He shied away from that idea. His feelings for Peaches were becoming too complicated.

Garth held his breath, baiting Dan. "You don't know anything the whole town doesn't know about anyway, old man. You're always trying to be important by letting out secrets that aren't even secrets."

"That ain't so, you young punk. What do you know about our town anyways? You ain't one of us. A certain person told Mr. Tremayne . . ." Dan tilted back in his chair and squinted his eyes half shut, as if seeing the telegram in front of him. "Yep. This fellow said he's got information to tell Mr. T that will blow the town wide open. And for him to wait in St. Louis till he gits there." Dan brought the chair back down with a bang, smacking his thin lips in satisfaction, taking a big sip of his beer. "Now ain't that remarkable that someone we don't hardly know could bust open this town with some kind of information? Reckon Mr. Tremayne is planning to come out here to Powder? I sure would be pleased to see that man. He's a legend. Owns half of Powder, Dry Gulch, and Woebegone, I hear, and we never set eyes on him."

"You keep saying *someone,* but at first you mentioned Mr. Clarence J. Westcott," Peaches reminded him.

Dan shook his head with vigor. "No, I never mentioned names. I was recalling what I thought of that fellow, but it had nothing to do with the telegram. I'm not saying who sent it. Fact is, a boy delivered it with the money to pay. I can't say 'zactly who sent it."

Garth was relieved that Peaches and Dan started arguing, since his mind was swirling with anger at what could be the blue jay's treachery. The telegram must have come from him. And Sam had that moonstruck look every time she even thought about Clarence J. She would be hurt all over again. Maybe some women had a natural bent for picking the wrong man. She might have become interested in Deputy Wade if Blue Jay hadn't shown up.

"That's real interesting, Dan. But I'd suggest you keep that under your belt," Peaches said in a firm, no-nonsense voice that surprised Garth. "If Mr. Tremayne owns half the town, as you say, both of us could find ourselves out of jobs if he has to come out here when it inconveniences him."

"Say there, I reckon you're right." Dan stood and touched his sweating forehead with his arm, forgetting about the celluloid wrapper he affected to protect his sleeves from ink. "I'd best get back to work. Excuse me, Miss Peaches."

Garth and Peaches sat quietly for many minutes, both lost in their own thoughts.

Finally Garth spoke. "What do you suppose he meant by saying the telegram said for him to wait for me in St. Louis? Is it possible this Tremayne fellow was planning to come out here to Powder?"

If Peaches thought Garth was fishing for information, she didn't show it in her expression.

He gulped through a dry throat when she shrugged her soft white shoulders, the silky low-cut dress moving against her well-endowed bosom. Apparently she wasn't cinched up tight with a corset the likes of which Aunt Twila and sometimes Sam were. Something he wasn't supposed to notice.

"I don't suppose it matters, since you aren't from around here, but Mr. Tremayne owns this saloon and I owe him a lot." Her eyes softened in a way that sent a jolt of jealousy down Garth's spine all the way to his boots. "We do correspond."

"And you've never met him?"

"No. That's what is so wonderful about the man. I've never set eyes on him, but he did send me a likeness. Would you care to see it?" She retrieved a golden locket that nestled in her cleavage and opened it proudly to show to Garth.

A snort of derision escaped Garth's lips, but he quickly suppressed it with a cough. That picture of Uncle Millard had to be twenty years old. What was he trying to prove? For sure, he had never intended to venture out West. Or maybe he figured by the time he got around to showing himself, Peaches would be so indebted to him for his many generosities, it wouldn't matter how old and ugly he was.

"But if you never met the man, how did you come by all this?" Garth looked around at the splendid furnishings of the saloon and at Peaches's obviously expensive clothing.

She candidly explained. "I came out here with a husband — a drunk, if you must know. He got in a gunfight, and he's buried out there with the rest of the losers in Boot Hill." Her voice was bitter, her full lips compressed with the painful memory. "Then I met Mr. Tremayne's lawyer. He said Mr. Tremayne was looking for someone honest and respectable to help run this gambling emporium."

At Garth's skeptical look, she sighed and continued.

"He didn't want someone with experience. He wanted a 'lady,' was the way the lawyer put it. I warned him at the time I would put up with no hanky-panky, that it would be strictly a business deal. He assured me Mr. Tremayne wouldn't have it any other way. I think I've done my share toward making the business successful. I knew friends from back east who had lost their husbands or never married, and they gladly came out here to dance with the men and serve drinks. A lot of them have left to become wives. When word got out that I was keeping a decent place, girls kept coming to work."

She took a deep breath, which Garth thought a wonder to behold.

"But what about this Tremayne fellow. You sound impressed with him."

"Not exactly, but he does write the sweetest, most adorable letters." She fingered the gold locket absentmindedly. "I hope he comes out here. I want to thank him personally for his generosity."

Garth patted her hand. "You're probably better off if he stays where he is. Sometimes the real thing can be disappointing."

Peaches looked at him thoughtfully. "I know. I've thought about that too. It doesn't look as if he will be coming anyway, if Westcott or someone else stops him."

"That's a puzzle. Why should anyone warn him to wait in St. Louis?"

Peaches sighed. "A crazy gang of cutthroats is loose. Deputy Wade told me, in strict confidence, of course, that it appeared the gang was concentrating on harassing Mr. Tremayne. Can you imagine? That terrible bunch of killers is tormenting and robbing a good, fine man. It might not be safe for him to be here now."

"Oh, my, that's hard to believe," Garth said.

She stood and brushed her palms against each other in a dismissing gesture. "That's soon to be over. They have two of the miscreants in jail now, and as soon as Marshal Earp returns, he will force them to tell everything they know about the others." She looked around. "Excuse me, Garth, but I have to get the girls together. We usually go for a buggy ride in the afternoon to air out. Good for the complexion."

Garth slid away from the table, stood, and tipped his hat. He watched her pleasantly round hips sashaying toward the stairs when he let himself out the door. He should have concentrated his efforts on Peaches before this. He might have learned a lot, and sooner. It was almost too late now. He realized that he had been allowing his emotions to rule his head. He'd admired Peaches from the first, even when he had incorrectly suspected she and his uncle had been lovers back in St. Louis. It was a stunning relief to know that wasn't true. He'd been avoiding her for nothing. and the whole gang might suffer because of it.

As soon as he returned to the boardinghouse he called Aunt Twila, Sam, and the major to his room for a meeting. He told them about the telegram and said they suspected the blue jay to be the one who sent it. He tried to avoid Sam's eyes when he related that, but he didn't miss the pain she quickly hid.

"We don't know for sure how much he knows about us, do we Garth?" Sam asked.

"You mean about our relationship with Uncle Millard? You can bet he knows the whole thing, or he wouldn't presume to order the old gopher to wait in St. Louis for him."

"But what if it isn't him who sent the telegram? Are you sure?" Sam wanted it not to be Jay, and Garth kept pity from his expression.

Aunt Twila voiced her sour opinion in no uncertain words. "I warned you two you were playing with fire, but you thought it all a great adventure. A game."

"Now darling girl, you mustn't talk like that. What is done is done," the major put in.

"Oh, you old goat, leave me be. I am not a girl, and I'll talk as I please. I always have," Aunt Twila sputtered. She looked pleadingly at Sam and Garth. "Can't you do something about this man? He follows me around continually, even thinks he knows more about cooking than I do. He's always underfoot like some puppy dog." She spoke as if the major was not in the room.

Instead of taking offense, the major beamed with pleasure. "I've never met a woman like your dear auntie," he exclaimed. "If only my darling mum could meet her."

Sam and Garth looked at each other, barely refraining from laughing out loud. The major stood at least a half-head shorter than their aunt and, though both were slender, she outweighed him by at least fifteen pounds. It was plain to see he regarded her as a veritable Amazon, and he admired every towering inch of her.

Then they got down to the business of rescuing Big Bear and Elvin. They wouldn't have a chance once the Earp brothers showed up.

CHAPTER 28

That night, as agreed upon, Sam and Aunt Twila kept Deputy Wade occupied at the dinner table in the boardinghouse. He was in an unusual hurry, but between them, they drew him into a conversation.

Sam didn't like the idea of flirting with the man; and Ernestine, who sat across the table from them, took offense. Her usually round eyes narrowed, and her lips tightened when she watched Sam and Deputy Wade, but she didn't speak. This notion of Ernestine being jealous because Sam coaxed Wade into talking goaded Sam on to more outrageous flirting, until Aunt Twila stepped in and brought dessert, plunking it down on the table. For some reason she refused to discuss, Sam's aunt hadn't taken a liking to Wade, yet the obnoxious Blue Jay took her fancy.

"I think this is my cue to leave," Ernestine said, standing up. "I have some shopping to

334

do before the mercantile closes. If you will excuse me." Her frosty tone had Deputy Wade's forehead in a wrinkly frown, which made Sam want to laugh. When had the haughty miss begun to notice the deputy? Sam hadn't seen that reaction coming. Or was the woman envious of anyone Sam spoke to?

Wade looked inclined to leave with Ernestine, but Sam and Twila couldn't allow him to leave yet.

Meanwhile Garth, the major, and Don Pancho mounted their horses and took two more with them as they hurried into the alley behind the jail.

"Big Bear! Elvin! Can you hear me?" Garth called to Big Bear and Elvin in as loud a whisper as he dared use.

"Garth, be damned. Your voice sounds like music to my ears. I thought you forgot about me and the Injun here," Elvin answered.

"Take these matches I'm throwing through the bars. Start a fire in your mattresses," Garth whispered back.

Elvin's plaintive voice raised a notch. "What if we burn up? That Deputy Wade's a mean *hombre.* He wouldn't piss on the best part of me if I was on fire."

"Gosh darn it, Elvin!" Garth almost forgot

to whisper in his irritation. "Did you try your shenanigans on *him*? No dang wonder he's so down on you fellows. Of all the dumbest ideas in the world. Why couldn't you let well enough alone?" He could almost see Elvin shrug his skinny shoulders.

"Hell, man. He was really nice and polite to me at the dance. I figured nothing tried, nothing gained. I was hoping to get us out that way."

Behind Garth, the major let out a snort. "Bloody hell. They will probably hang him alongside the Indian."

"Never mind that now. The deputy is at the boardinghouse, and Sam is trying to stall him. Do as I said. Big Bear, you do it if Elvin's too chicken. You want out, don't you?"

Garth heard the Indian grunt, and knew he would light the fire. Now he and the major had to casually walk back out of the alley to the front of the jail. They stepped up on the wooden sidewalk. Don Pancho stayed with the horses in back.

"Don't hurry," Garth cautioned the major. They lingered on the boardwalk until they smelled smoke. Before the deputy inside the building could react, both Garth and the major ran through the front door.

"Deputy! Do I smell smoke? Is your jail

burning up?" Garth shouted.

The deputy looked stunned, his eyes wide, his mouth open.

"Look! The blighter is standing there lollygagging whilst his entire jailhouse is in flames!" the major shouted, pointing to the cell room where smoke billowed out.

Coming to his senses, the deputy rushed back to the cells while Garth quietly closed the front door and slipped the catch. Then he followed the deputy.

In the cells, pandemonium reigned. Big Bear huddled in a corner, moaning one moment and, in the next, breaking into what must have been a loud war dance. Elvin banged on the bars with an empty tin cup, yelling his head off. It was plain to see he wasn't pretending; his panic was real. The other cells were empty.

The deputy stood in the middle of the hallway in front of the cell, his expression almost comical. He wanted to be anywhere else.

"Here, give me your gun," Garth said. "I'll keep you covered while you put out the fire. I'll get that blanket over in the empty cell. You can throw that on the fire."

"Hell, no! I ain't going in that cell with them two varmints. Deputy Wade warned me they was dangerous. That Indian is a bon-i-fide cannibal and the other one . . . well, he's even worse than that!"

"Would it look any better if they burned to death on your watch, Deputy?" Garth began to panic when he saw the flames building up and smoke rolling toward them in a huge black cloud. The smell of urine rose in the air when the long and well-used mattresses burned. *Damn it, did Big Bear have to do everything so thoroughly?*

"Look." Garth tried to keep his voice level and reasonable. "I'm a civilian, trying to help. It's not my place to go in there. Those men are in your charge, their safety your responsibility. They don't look dangerous. I want to help you, but if you don't need me, I'll leave." He made as if to turn back toward the front, hoping his bluff would work. If it didn't, he would have to over-power the lawman, and then they would all be doomed when the deputy later described them to Wade. The deputy jerked out his gun and handed it to Garth. "Watch 'em close. I don't much care if they burn up or not, but reckon I got to do my duty."

With that, he opened the cell door. Rush-ing across the room with the blanket, he began beating on the cot. Garth signaled Big Bear, who slipped up behind the deputy and gave him a quick chop to his neck with the side of his huge hand. The lawman went down like lightning had struck him. The gang members put out the fire and hurriedly closed the cell door on the peacefully sleeping deputy.

"Horses here?" Big Bear asked when they ran into the alley.

Garth nodded. "I think it's best you come on back with me to the boardinghouse until the hullabaloo dies down. Then we can split up. Guess it means the end of our gang." Regret tinged his voice, and he swallowed behind a lump in his throat.

"Just when you fellows were startin' to learn how to outlaw," Elvin complained. He peered at Garth. The daylight was beginning to turn to dusk, and the alley was completely in shadow. "Do you have any idea of the indignity we suffered at the lawman's hands?" Elvin's voice raised in resentment. "They called us the desperados and laughed at us. I never been so humiliated in my life. How can I face my buddies back in Yuma? What if they heard about it?" His voice rose in a squeak of outrage, and he cleared his throat and coughed to cover the sound.

"I know. But we *were* learning and, face it, we didn't have a whole lot of nasty outlaws to join us, did we? Only Buster."

"Move on," Big Bear suggested.

"Yes, we can't stand here jawing. Someone might come along and smell smoke. Need to get to the boardinghouse before Deputy Wade gets here."

"What will you tell the deputy? The one we left behind will describe us," the major said.

"You two stay hidden at the boarding-house, and when I'm questioned, I'll say Big Bear and Elvin overpowered us, kid-napped us, and took us out of town before they let us go. Think that will work?" He turned and started down the alley toward the horses.

"Maybe," Big Bear said, not moving.

Garth, the major, and Elvin turned to look back at him.

"They search for two men. I go alone. I know desert, mountains. Go to Mexico. Take two horses, they think we leave to-gether." He shrugged. "It's only natural," he couldn't resist adding. He permitted his usual stern features to relax into what he clearly meant to be a smile.

The three other men stared at Big Bear in amazement. Only Garth knew his "Indian talk" was directed at Elvin and the major.

"Tell Samantha . . . tell her . . ." Unable to finish, Big Bear leaped on his horse and grabbed the reins of the spare, causing the horses to walk in circles, churning the ground in the dusty alley.

What the devil was he up to, Garth wondered. Then he realized the wily Indian had provided proof of a struggle in the alley.

He watched as Big Bear trotted off down the now dark alley, on his way out of town.

"Will we see you again?" Garth called out.

Big Bear twisted in the saddle and shook his head. When he turned around, he never looked back again.

Garth mounted his horse and motioned to the others to follow. His shoulders sagged, and a heaviness coursed through him. A good friend had exited his life. He feared how Sam would take Big Bear's departure. He looked back to watch the major hesitatingly step into a stirrup, his mouth set under his quivering mustache. Maybe at long last this would remedy his aversion to horses.

Sam heard the upstairs door close on squeaky hinges and knew Garth had come back. She closed her eyes, praying he had the others with him. They must have sneaked through the alley and entered the back door.

Deputy Wade rose to his feet and excused

himself. "It has been fine talking to you lovely ladies, but duty calls. I must get back to the jail."

Sam nodded.

"I'll be sending over some biscuits and gravy for the fellows in your jail," Aunt Twila said to his retreating back.

"That would be fine, Miss Twila. The Earp brothers should be back any day and, after that — well, it won't matter none. The prisoners'll be gone from here."

Sam and Aunt Twila watched out the kitchen window until the deputy disappeared down the street. It didn't take long for them to lock the front door and pull the curtains together. Aunt Twila hurried to the kitchen to bring out coffee and cups, along with her berry pie and plates, and set the table fresh.

"Come on down, everybody. The coast is clear, and the door is locked," Sam called up the stairs. She closed her eyes, waiting to see who would emerge and prayed it would be all of their gang, safe and sound. When she backed into the dining room, Garth, the major, and Elvin came down the stairs, grins on their faces.

Sam noticed at once that Big Bear and Don Pancho were missing.

Garth held up his hand for her to wait,

and ushered the men into the dining room.

"Ah, Lovey. I knew you would be waiting with food and coffee." The major made as if to go toward Aunt Twila.

She raised an eyebrow, which usually stopped everyone in his tracks, and stood firm. "Sit down, you little wheezer. Eat." Her voice was stern, but her eyes showed humor and something else Sam couldn't put a name to.

When they had all settled at the table, Sam looked at Garth. "Where are Big Bear and Don Pancho?"

"Don Pancho elected to bed down in the stables and take care of the horses. I think the excitement overwhelmed him. We can take a tray out to the stables in a minute. How about letting me start at the beginning of our adventure in the jail and I'll get to everything?" Garth said.

Sam knew he was stalling and had bad news, but she sat back and waited along with Aunt Twila.

Garth told how Big Bear set fire inside the jail and how they escaped. He got up from his chair and went to Sam, putting his hands on her shoulders. "Big Bear knew there was no way to hide here anymore. He took the extra horse, so the trackers would think he and Elvin escaped together, and headed toward the border. He'll make it fine. The lawmen haven't had time to get a posse together, thanks to you and Aunt Twila."

"But what will Big Bear do in Mexico?" Tears ran down Sam's cheeks, and she brushed them away with her napkin.

Garth gave her shoulders a squeeze and went back to his chair to sit. "I think he will wait a while until things die down here, and then head out in the desert to find his people."

Sam sighed. "That would be my fervent hope."

"He wanted me to thank you for all you did for him and to tell you that he couldn't say goodbye to you."

Sam nodded. "I understand. That would have been hard for both of us. He's a good man."

"But how are you going to explain yourself and the major, Garth?" Aunt Twila asked, her forehead creased with worry lines. "The deputy saw you both and will tell Deputy Wade."

Garth grinned, a look of understanding in his eyes. "Big Bear solved that problem. At the time, I couldn't figure it out. He messed up the alley so it looked like a fight had taken place there. The major and I can claim Big Bear and Elvin kidnapped us and then let us go at the edge of town."

"Perfect!" Elvin chortled behind a big forkful of pie. "Soon as the coast is clear, I'm heading for Yuma."

"But no one will know what you've been up to. You aren't wanted there. You can't just waltz up to the prison and say let me in," Sam protested.

Elvin stared at her. "I'll think of something. You haven't introduced me to this lovely lady," he admonished Garth. "Did we meet at the dance?"

Garth's grin was mischievous. "You did meet at the dance. Let me introduce my sister, Samantha. You probably know her better as Sam."

Elvin's eyes widened in his baby face. "*Our* Sam? As in our gang? Why, sure, I see it now." His face flushed. "Sure hope I didn't say or do anything ungentlemanly whilst you were with us."

Sam laughed. "I don't think so, Elvin. And if you did, it was excusable under the circumstances. After all, it was I who played the game."

Elvin turned away, and they could see he was embarrassed, trying to recall anything embarrassing he might have said or done in front of Sam. After all, ladies were not supposed to be aware of differences in people.

"Never mind all that soul-searching, Elvin. We have more serious things on our minds now. I feel rotten that our gang had to disintegrate before we caused Tremayne any real damage."

"So do I," Sam mourned. "It was exciting, fun, but at the same time, I do think we hurt him in his pockets. At least some."

Aunt Twila snorted. "Fun. Time you two grew up. You could have been hurt and caused these men to live the rest of their lives in prison."

"Oh, sweetheart, don't take on so. It was a bloody amazing adventure in the Wild West, and one day Sam might write a story about it to send back to England. They would eat it up." The major nodded to Sam. "I've never seen you without paper and pencil, my dear." He reached over to pat Aunt Twila's hand, and she waved him away — but not too strenuously, Sam noticed.

"We have more serious issues here," Garth said with a catch in his throat. "We decided to bust up the gang. Hellfire, we didn't exactly decide. Elvin, you and the major are welcome to stay here until you figure out what you want to do next. We need to wait for the blue jay to bring back information about Uncle Millard, I reckon."

"We must find Don Pancho a family. Wouldn't do to put an advertisement in the *Tombstone Epitaph.* 'One Andalusian sheep-herder. Needs a good home,' " Aunt Twila blurted.

They all had a good laugh at that one.

Garth leaped toward the door. "Come on, Major, we have to get back to the jail and tell Wade about our kidnapping and fortunate release. Mess up your clothes a little." Garth proceeded to rub his fingers through his hair and tear buttons off the front of his shirt. He looked apologetically at Aunt Twila when she reached to pick up the buttons from the worn carpet.

When the two returned from the jail, both were subdued. Even the major didn't want to talk. Garth spoke into the silence. "The posse's already headed out, but I left a note on the desk telling them what happened to us. Deputy Wade will expect me to join the posse, and I should in case I have to use delaying tactics if they get close to finding Big Bear. I'll handle Deputy Wade's questions if and when he comes to supper. I may not get back until night."

The corners of his lips notched up a bit, but he hid a grin.

Sam wanted to shake him. He looked on this as a gigantic lark, an adventure. Yet she supposed he had that right.

Later she sat on the porch with Ernestine. They had assumed an uneasy truce, but even Ernestine was disinclined to talk. She seemed unusually edgy. Hearing an odd commotion from the upstairs window of the major's room, Sam excused herself and ran up the stairs.

He didn't hear her knock. When she gingerly pushed the door open, she couldn't believe her eyes. The major sat on the floor, a bed sheet beneath his beloved Annabel, tears streaming from his eyes and running into his bristly mustache.

"What in the world?" Sam came closer, closing the door behind her.

"It's a bloody shame, but have to dismantle the old girl. At least for now. Folks have heard of some kind of weird locomotion in the desert. I cannot bear to have her confiscated." He looked up at Sam.

"Never you mind. I have taken her apart and put her together till I can do it with my eyes closed. I've removed all the parts that might soil your aunt's carpet, and left the wheels buried under hay in the stables. I'll tuck what's left of her under the bed here, and she'll be fine."

They both came downstairs. Sam repressed a grin as she leaned back in her chair at the kitchen table to hear her aunt and the major argue.

"You wouldn't be so horrid to look at if you'd leave off that awful toupee and try to speak English so a body could understand you."

The major sidled closer to Aunt Twila and tugged mischievously on her apron strings. "Ah, my gentle dove, your words are music to my heart."

Sam delighted in watching the major treat her crusty aunt like a dainty flower. About the only thing they agreed on was her appreciation for Annabel and their mutual distaste for horses. Aunt Twila would never venture near the stables, either back in St. Louis or here.

Sam chewed on a dry biscuit, listening to the continued bickering of the couple until finally the major gave up and, blowing Twila a kiss, he let himself out the kitchen door.

"Aren't you being too hard on him, Aunt Twila?" Sam regarded her aunt fondly.

"Oh, that penniless bum. Can't even speak English properly." Belying her stern tone, her eyes twinkled. "Still and all, he really isn't such a bad fellow once you get to know him, is he, Samantha?"

"True, so true. Garth and I both like him."

Her aunt subsided with a sigh and began

349

to gather ingredients for the next meal while Sam slipped out the door and sat near Ernestine, who had never moved from her seat on the front porch.

CHAPTER 29

They watched as a buggy pulled up in front of the gate and a tastefully dressed woman emerged to walk toward them. She looked almost regal in her long, navy-blue skirt with the hint of black boots showing. Her crisp white blouse had long sleeves with caps at the end that brushed around the middles of her hands.

Sam knew the woman was Peaches. She felt certain Garth entertained a definite liking for her. She had expected to see a frowsy, blond creature with a large bosom and wide, swinging hips. It came almost as a disappointment to see that she didn't even wear face powder. She had no need to. She was a handsome woman about Sam's age, a few years older than Garth.

Surprisingly enough, Aunt Twila must not have heard the screech from the front gate. Otherwise her curiosity would have prompted her to come out on the porch.

"Miss Brody?" Peaches looked hesitantly between Ernestine and Sam.

"I am Samantha Brody." Sam strode toward Peaches, holding out her hand.

The relief on Peaches's face was apparent. She obviously hadn't wanted Miss Brody to be Ernestine.

"Please take a seat. This is Ernestine Sommerfield, our town schoolteacher." Sam motioned toward the swing. "Miss Peaches is manager of the Silver Buckle," she added mischievously. For a moment Ernestine looked horrified that a saloon person might sit next to her. She recovered her usual aplomb and scooted way over to the corner of the seat.

Peaches shook her head at the idea of sitting. "Thank you, but I won't be long."

"I'm afraid you have me at a disadvantage," Sam said. "I only know you by the name of Peaches."

The woman blushed, tilting her chin up. "Peaches is good enough. Everyone calls me that."

"Then, please call me Sam. My bro—cousin, Garth, speaks very highly of you."

Ernestine tilted her pug nose in the air disdainfully. Every line of her expression and body language spelled out furious disapproval.

Peaches couldn't have missed the message emanating from Ernestine, but she chose to ignore it, which made Sam smile.

"I know Garth. He's a fine person and we have many interesting conversations. But I didn't exactly come here to chat, although it does please me to visit you, Sam. I shouldn't be standing here on your front porch with Mr. Tremayne's buggy outside the fence. You will be the talk of the town tomorrow."

Sam didn't miss the regret in Peaches's eyes as she spoke. Before she could respond, Ernestine leaped to her feet, hands on her hips.

"You are right there, missy. You are compromising both of us by your uninvited presence."

"Lordy, Ernestine! Peaches is a guest, and if the townspeople don't like it, who cares? Garth assured me that Peaches is a very moral person with as much integrity as you or I."

"Oh, Garth! What does that immature young man know about anything?"

For a moment Ernestine's words about Garth sidetracked Sam. It was true, sometimes his enthusiasm and sense of humor might come off as immature to some people. Especially narrow-minded ones like Ernestine. She decided to let the insult go for now, waiting to see if Peaches would respond.

It didn't take long. The woman's eyes narrowed and she chewed on her bottom lip but refused to be ruffled, turning away from Ernestine to talk to Sam.

"I really came here to see if Deputy Wade had returned with the posse. I went to the jailhouse, but the door was locked. I need to talk to that man."

"Why would *you* want to talk to Wade?" Ernestine demanded, her voice shrill.

Before Sam could step in to diffuse the situation, one look at Peaches told her to back off and let the chips fall where they may.

Apparently Peaches had reached the limit of politeness. "That's none of your damned business," she snapped back.

"Maybe it *is* my business. Maybe I wish to make it mine." Ernestine had sat down but now leaped to her feet again, her eyes flashing fire.

"I found out from Mr. Tremayne's lawyer that someone was sent to watch us. Mr. Wilder and me." Peaches's full figure trembled with indignation. "Mr. Tremayne suspected his own lawyer, and perhaps even I, had something to do with the dreadful robberies and invasions of his property. Can you imagine that?" The anger fled, and her eyes filled with tears.

"Why wouldn't you be a suspect, since you are in the thick of things? But what's that got to do with Wade?" Ernestine demanded.

"Everything, that's all." By now Peaches was yelling in a very unladylike voice, and Ernestine responded in kind.

Sam saw Aunt Twila emerge on the porch and close the screen door quietly behind her. Would she put a stop to this situation? Judging from her amused expression, Sam guessed she would wait it out to see what happened next.

Peaches continued speaking louder than she needed to. "Mr. Wilder and I suspected someone was spying out the town, but we blamed Clarence J., since he was a newcomer. Now we find out it is the deputy who is the sneaky, double-dealing viper in our bosom."

Ernestine could control herself no longer, lunging forward and sinking a fist into Peaches's midsection. Peaches doubled over, clutching her stomach. Then she gathered a second wind and grabbed Ernestine's hair. That carried both women off the porch and onto the meager grass of the sparse lawn. They rolled over and over, the dust flying in the air while they kicked and squealed.

For a brief instant Sam and Aunt Twila stood watching, stunned and unbelieving. What held Sam enthralled was the statement that Peaches thought Deputy Wade was a spy and not the blue jay. Coming to her senses, Sam leaped off the porch to join the fray, working to separate the combatants. Ernestine gave Sam a left hook to the eye. Since Sam didn't like Ernestine anyway, it gave her great pleasure to pull Ernestine's neat hairdo down around her ears. Dresses ripped, and the air filled with grunts, groans, and shrieks.

The major opened the door. Once out on the porch, he doubled over laughing and patting his knees in glee at the tumbling mass of females. But Aunt Twila wasn't pleased at his reaction. She went inside, came back with a pitcher of water, and flung its contents right on top of the fighting women. Immediately they parted and sat up with shocked bewilderment in their faces. Their once-tidy hair straggled wetly down their cheeks, and their ripped bodices soaked in the water with sodden greed.

Peaches collected herself first. She stood and dusted her wet and torn skirt with as much dignity as she could muster. Then, not speaking a word to anyone, she sailed majestically through the gate and marched down the street, forgetting her buggy parked near the fence.

Sam brushed water out of her eyes and struggled to sit up. She watched with satisfaction as Ernestine pushed away the long, straggly blond locks that had come undone from the usual neat knot at the top of her head. Sam felt certain she looked twice as funny as her foe, but at this point, she didn't care. Aunt Twila dragged the still-laughing Major inside, Sam supposed to give Sam and Ernestine an opportunity to salvage what dignity they could hope for. She blessed her aunt's thoughtfulness, unable to take any more of the major's cheerfully helpful comments.

"You hit me first," Sam challenged Ernestine before she could speak first. She almost felt sorry for the schoolteacher, who resembled a sadly treated doll. It looked as if she had received the worst of the brawl.

Ernestine held her tattered gown close to her body, but did not reply.

"Why did you carry on so with Peaches about Deputy Wade?" Sam persisted. "I didn't even know you liked him. You seldom speak to him at the dinner table. Actually

I've always thought you treated him like a country bumpkin well beneath you. It seems as if you are jealous."

Ernestine brushed the wet hair from her face wearily. "I can't tell you. Perhaps later, but certain things are coming to a head, and just let me say you aren't involved in any way, so why should you care?"

Sam stayed silent, knowing that, indeed, she *was* involved. Apparently Ernestine wasn't aware of that yet. But to what extent was Ernestine mixed up in the complicated Tremayne-Brody mess? What exactly was her connection with Wade? Did the woman have a secret crush on the big deputy? And if Wade was a spy for Millard Tremayne, although Sam was not entirely ready to believe Peaches's distraught story, then who or what was the blue jay? Garth had relayed the information of Dan gossiping about the telegram.

Without a word to each other, both women crossed the porch, entered the house, and made for their own rooms.

Sam would be so relieved when Garth returned from the posse.

CHAPTER 30

Garth wasn't back, but Sam heard of the posse returning empty-handed and supposed her brother had decided to hole up in the hideaway a few days.

She stood waiting her turn in the post office one afternoon to send her monthly letter to her friend in New York. It might be a waste of time, since either Deputy Wade or the blue jay appeared to be filling Millard Tremayne in on all the happenings of late. She shrugged and turned in the letter for her friend to forward to their uncle.

The musty, dusty post office was the center for local gossip from a group of old codgers who lounged around outside and likely never mailed a letter in their lives.

"I say we ought to run them Mexican sheepherders out of that valley. Those damn sheep will clean out all the grass down to the roots in no time," one of the men said, his voice laced with righteous anger.

"Aw, come on, Josh. Ain't no call to get excited. Barney and Luke took a ride out there to palaver with them yestiddy, and they swear they're on their way to California."

"Yep. That's government land they're on. We don't own it," sounded a voice of reason.

An idea came to Sam, and she hurried back to the boardinghouse to look for Don Pancho. He didn't care to be inside because he was afraid of Aunt Twila, so he hung around the stables most of the time.

Once she had changed to her masculine clothing, she persuaded the sheepherder to take one of the extra horses in the stable and come with her.

The day was brilliant and hot as they rode out toward the valley. When they rested once against the shade of a mesquite tree, Sam told Don Pancho of her plans.

"If what you believe is true, *Señorita,* tonight I will be with my kinsmen again." He spoke in a slow mixture of Spanish and the few words of English he had picked up from the gang. Garth laughingly called it Spanglish.

"I hope so, Don Pancho." Sam certainly didn't see any kind of a future in Powder for him.

When they topped the rise before the valley, they saw a huge herd of sheep scattered around, with dogs running here and there, circling them. A rickety old wagon covered with tattered canvas perched at the edge of the green field.

Even though Sam didn't think they'd made any sound approaching the camp, five swarthy young men walked out of the shade of the wagon to face them.

When Don Pancho saw the men, he burst into a voluble speech, which the men answered with waves and flashing smiles.

They spoke in rapid excitement, but Sam caught a few words now and again that sounded Spanish. Since they all talked at once and used extravagant gestures, it didn't matter if she understood them or not.

Suddenly they remembered their manners.

Don Pancho held up his hand for silence and introduced Sam to the men in an odd mixture of English and, mostly, Spanish. She saw no reason for subterfuge, so she removed her hat, letting the long braid fall against her back. Their mouths opened in amazement, and Don Pancho let loose with another barrage of speech. He and Sam dismounted, and she shook each man's calloused hand. She accepted their invitation to sit and drink coffee with them over their campfire. Don Pancho's face was cracked with what looked to be a permanent smile while they drank their coffee liberally laced with what appeared to be tequila. Sam shook her head at that addition. She had never tasted tequila and decided now was not the time to try it.

"Lo siento, Señorita. Estoy muy triste," Don Pancho said when the men quietly waited, not speaking.

"Why should you be sorry or sad, Don Pancho?" Sam smiled encouragingly. "Aren't you happy to find kinsmen again?"

"Sí, Señorita, sí. Pero . . ." He looked around at the somber men sitting at the campfire. He shrugged, words failing him.

"Oh, I understand." She reached to take his weathered hand in hers. "You are afraid of disappointing my brother and me. But no, that won't happen. You need to be with your kinsmen, heading safely toward California. We have been very worried about you."

"*Señor* Garth will not be disappointed in me? We have not finished that which he wanted to do."

Sam laughed. "You weren't cut out to be a *bandito.* Matter of fact, none of us were, actually."

He shook his head and smiled, but sadness lurked deep in his eyes.

Sam knew he thought back to the first time Garth came upon him amidst his dead flock and took him in. He'd tried to repay Garth the only way he knew how: to be part of the gang.

"Any debt you think you owe us is clear, *mi amigo*. Paid in full." Sam stood and looked up at the sky. "Clouds are coming up fast, and soon it will be dark. I must go back to town. And you should get ready for a storm." She shook hands all around, with Don Pancho trying to insist that someone accompany her.

"No. That won't be necessary. It is too dangerous for any of you to come to town right now." She embraced Don Pancho and settled on her horse, taking the reins of the extra one. She waved back at the group of men once when she topped the canyon wall and then headed out. The wind whipped through hair loosened from the long braid, and off in the distance Sam heard thunder.

Looking straight ahead when she crossed the narrow range of hills, she caught a great puff of dust coming straight toward her. Indians!

Without overthinking, she quirted her horse on the rump and looked back at the valley she'd just left. Too far away, and she didn't want to bring the riders down on the peaceful sheepherders. She turned to the hills and galloped toward them. It was awkward, holding the reins of the extra horse, although he loped along at their side fairly well. At least this time she had her rifle.

Looking over her shoulder, the puff of dust seemed to be coming closer, but it didn't appear as large as she first thought it to be. It could be only a half-dozen renegades, but that wasn't much of a consolation. "They'll never take me alive," she gritted out loud. She slowed enough to reach back and wrest the rifle from the case on the saddle. She finally had to give up and let the reins of the extra horse drop. It was hard enough to keep hold of her own galloping horse's reins, the rifle, and her seat as they leaped over rocks and sagebrush. Terror was on her side, and she clung to the horse like a burr.

The sky continued to darken; she didn't have to look up to know that. It didn't look like a rainstorm was coming, in spite of the thunder she'd heard before. The sky gradually turned to a light brown, which told her to expect a dust storm. A dust storm could be a blessing, making it easier to elude her pursuers, but she might be unable to find her way out of the woods.

The desert had become eerily still, waiting for the onset of the dust storm. The lack of sound penetrated above the pounding hooves of her lathering, heaving horse.

Sam should have let someone in Don Pancho's group accompany her home. Surely they had rifles among them. Both her father and aunt had warned her that her independent streak would do her in one day. This might be the day. In a rush, almost taking her breath away, she thought of everything she would miss if she died. Garth, Aunt Twila, the thrill of getting even with their uncle, so many new people she'd met. Gooseflesh rose on her arms, and the hairs on the back of her neck lifted when the sandstorm finally hit and a rush of stinging sand overtook her and the horse.

She heard a horse close behind her and hoped it was the extra horse catching up, but she had no time to ponder the notion. Sand struck her in the face, grains of it lodging in her nose and eyes, and even though she kept her mouth tightly clenched, she tasted grit. Attempting to guide the horse proved useless, since they couldn't see in front of them. She turned the horse against the wind, bent her head, and clutched the rifle in one hand, but feared she might drop it at any time.

Out of the murky depths, someone leaped on her horse behind her saddle, holding her against him with almost rib-cracking strength. She twisted and saw a riderless horse plunging through the storm close by. Sam tried to wrest herself from the stranger holding her, but arms like steel held her firmly in place. The man put a handkerchief gently over her face, and she wriggled harder in terror.

"Be still, you little devil. You'll suffocate if you don't cover your face."

Her relief was palpable when she recognized Jay's voice. "You don't have to break my ribs holding so tight," she said, trying to recover her heartbeat.

"Nonsense," he murmured into her ear, holding her even tighter. "Hold on, and I'll get us out of here if I can find the place."

In spite of her fears mixed with relief, a frisson of awareness sped through her body, feeling his hard-muscled thighs gripped tight against hers. She didn't know if she could trust him at this point, but she knew he would never harm her.

Without warning, the wind died away, and quiet took over. The siren banshee wail of the wind had ceased, leaving a vacuum that hurt her ears for a moment. When she opened her gritty eyelids to look around, she saw they had ridden into a half-cave away from the wind. The walls of the towering curve of rock were soot blackened, telling her the cave must be a stopover for outlaws on the run or traveling Indians.

Jay leaped off the horse and reached for her, letting her slide down the length of his body. She looked up at him and caught a smile on his lips. "Thank you for rescuing me. Again. Are you making a habit of it? I was certain Indians were following me."

He reached with gentle hands to brush her hair back from her cheeks. "I did see Indian tracks, but they headed in the opposite direction when the dust storm came up."

"But what made you follow me?" She noticed his horse and the extra one had gathered nearby.

He brought the horses closer and poured water from a canteen into his hat for them to drink. She noticed another canteen hanging from his saddle. Seeing her look, he set his hat down on the ground, reached for his canteen, and handed it to her. She nodded and drank, sparingly, in case they had to stay awhile.

When he threw down the bedroll he'd stored on the back of his saddle, he motioned for her to be seated. He sat next to her. Their legs nearly touched.

"I have followed you every time you took out alone," he admitted. "If I hadn't tracked you that first time with Buster . . ." He took her hand in his and raised it to press his lips to her palm.

She shivered but didn't pull away. "We thought you'd gone East." She didn't bring up her uncle.

Jay smiled, reaching to brush a stray strand of long hair from her shoulder. "I did go for a short time, but I wasn't ready to stay long. That turned out lucky."

Sam thought they must look ghostly, with the sifted dust covering their clothes, turning them into monotonous beige.

"I thought you'd have been more interested in Ernestine's doings than in keeping track of me."

He laughed. "Jealous? Oh, my. Actually, I had no interest in the schoolteacher, since I figured her attention had been captured already."

Sam must have looked surprised.

"The deputy and she were somehow together. I figured that out early on."

"Really? None of the rest of us thought that. They didn't even appear friendly," Sam scoffed.

"Ah, but that was the tip-off. They protested too much."

"You certainly are observant."

"I have to be. It's my job —" He broke off as if he'd said too much and looked down at his boots.

"What do you mean, your job? You're an accountant, aren't you? This is all so mixed up, and no one is who they are supposed to be. Garth and I still think you might be a spy." She moved away from him, annoyance in her expression.

His eyes widened, his dark brows curved in surprise.

"Oh, don't bother to give me that boyish look of innocence. It won't work. You are a spy for our uncle Millard. Admit it."

He leaped to his feet and pulled her up close. His eyes narrowed, and the blue turned glacial. "Continue. This is very interesting. You were saying?"

Sam could hardly think straight with him holding her. Underneath the dust, she smelled his shaving tonic along with horse and leather. She tried in vain to steady her heartbeat.

"Come. Let's sit on the blanket again. I don't dare start a campfire with the wind so fierce, but I doubt we need fear any coyotes or wolves are out in the midst of this."

In a daze, Sam let him lead her back to the bedroll he'd spread on the ground next to the large rock. He held her hand while she settled down and then sat gracefully beside her.

He turned to her and tilted her chin gently with his hand. "You finally let the cat out of the bag, when you said Uncle Millard. You don't have to say anything until you're ready. As soon as I found out you and Garth were brother and sister, I put two and two together."

"That's why you went back to St. Louis? You guessed about our family ties and wanted to warn him about us? Did he offer you a nice, juicy reward?" She brushed his hand away in exasperation.

He sighed and leaned back against the wall of stone. "I guess I don't blame you for thinking that. I admit this isn't something I'm proud of, but I peeked into your aunt's desk in the corner of the parlor. I didn't know what I was looking for or what made me do it." He added sheepishly at the outraged look in her eyes, "I found a minia-ture of two children and their father. You and Garth haven't changed that much."

"You sneaked around for Uncle Millard?" Sam said, striving to hold her temper.

"Think for a minute, woman. Why

shouldn't I work for Millard Tremayne? I lived and worked in New York, mainly. He knew mutual friends who recommended me, so he hired me to take care of his Arizona business. It was supposed to be a surprise for his wife later. You haven't told me about this spy-persecution complex you have."

She brushed away his pointing finger. "I'll just bet it will surprise the heck out of Aunt Grace. *If* she ever finds out. Supposing you're not a spy, then why did you send that telegram and leave town so suddenly?"

"Oh, so *that's* it. I should have known Dan, that old gossip, would spill the beans the minute I turned my back. But I had no choice. You wouldn't believe me or trust me. I promise, Samantha, I am only an investigative accountant — nothing more, nothing less." He paused and then went on. "I could see, after all my checking, that there was nothing going on either accidentally or intended with Mr. Tremayne's books. Unless he keeps a second set. Everything was in perfect order. But he sure as hell was losing money, as well as depositors and clients. Actually, Wade accidentally let me in on the business. I overheard him talking to someone at the Silver Buckle. He thought this mixed-up group of misfits, as he called them, was only out to get Millard Tremayne."

Sam shook her head, not knowing how to reply. She and Garth had thought they were so clever. Yet they had come close to spoiling their uncle's ambitions, and that gave her a thread of satisfaction.

"Peaches told me Tremayne planned to come to Powder and check it out, but that was to be in strict secrecy. I couldn't allow that. He would have discovered you two were behind all of his troubles. What you and Garth did was wrong, and I don't have a clue what's behind your mischief, but you must have had good reasons. In the end, I couldn't stop him from coming. He's headed for Powder now."

Sam stared at Clarence J., not missing the regret in his eyes.

"Do you think I care about that? We are ready to face him. We've saved up enough evidence." She stopped and darted a look at him, wanting to explain everything.

"You still don't trust me, do you?" he growled. "Well, I have a bit more information for you, but first you owe me an explanation."

"You won't believe me."

"Try me," he said quietly.

So Sam told him their story from the

beginning: about their father and the partnership and how things went wrong, and that they had the proof of it, then and now.

They sat in silence for a few minutes after she finished speaking. The sandstorm raged outside their cave, but it had lessened, she could tell by the sounds.

"That's hard to swallow." Jay held up a palm to her to stop her arguments. "But I believe you, Samantha. I surely do. You poor innocents, trying to take the world on your shoulders. Didn't you know you couldn't win against a man like your uncle? He'll step on you like bugs under his shiny leather shoes."

"He wouldn't dare harm Garth or me," Sam exclaimed. She didn't feel as certain of that as she had at the beginning of their conversation. Garth believed Uncle Millard would try to get rid of them.

"You really think so? While I was in his office, he received a call. When he finished, he looked like the proverbial cat who'd swallowed a canary. A lady, a female from around here I assumed, wired him about you two."

"A female. Peaches, no doubt," Sam said sourly.

"No, it was definitely not Peaches. I saw the name he wrote on a paper on his desk.

Ernestine."

"Ernestine!" Sam echoed in disbelief.

"Haven't you guessed by now that she and Wade are married?" He ignored Sam's sharp intake of breath and continued. "They are a Pinkerton team from New York your uncle hired to 'infiltrate the enemy,' as he put it. Actually, at first he mistakenly thought his enemies were Peaches and Mr. Wilder. He knew someone on the inside had to be getting close to his business dealings in Powder. It was a lucky accident for her that Ernestine chose your boardinghouse to stay. Also, she and Wade could meet once in a while on the sly that way."

"Somehow Ernestine found out about Garth and me?"

He nodded. "Probably by poking around like I did."

"Suppose I do believe all this," she said, disregarding the angry look in his eyes and the tightening of his lips. Just looking at his mouth did things to her midsection she tried to ignore.

He interrupted her with an icy glare. "You mean after all this, you still doubt me?"

"Even if I did believe you, I don't under-stand your part in the mess. Have you come out here to Powder to find and deliver us to my uncle?" Sam felt outwardly calm, but inside, her body trembled with a bundle of live nerve ends. Wade and Ernestine. Whom could she really trust? Was everybody the exact opposite of who they pretended to be? What a crazy world.

Jay groaned. "Let me get this straight. You and your brother think I came out here expressly to spy on you under Tremayne's orders?" His voice was cold, his eyes icy blue.

Sam swallowed past a lump in her throat. No, she didn't want to believe that at all. A jolt of warmth flashed through her when she remembered Jay's kiss, and she wanted to experience that again. "I know, it sounds odd, but what else could we think at the time? Someone was spying on us, someone close. Someone who knew when the stage would be robbed."

"Certainly. Wade and Ernestine. You can believe me or not, but the only reason I'm involved in this aspect of Tremayne's concerns is that I wanted to extricate you and Garth from the mess you've gotten yourselves into. I figured you both needed all the help you could get. Maybe if you'd been able to see beyond Wade's big, broad shoulders, you might have suspected him earlier," he teased. His eyes crinkled at the corners when he smiled at her, but she could see a flash of what might have been jealousy before he turned away.

Sam felt it was beneath her dignity to respond to that jibe. Truthfully she had been intrigued by the deputy's virile masculinity for a time, but there had been no spark there. Darned if she would admit it. Yet she should have guessed the truth about that sneaky Ernestine. She recalled the brawl among Ernestine, Peaches, and her and welcomed the sense of satisfaction when she recalled how Ernestine had received the worst in that fight. But worry chased any humor away when she wondered if Tremayne's people knew about the hideout and the gang that lived in broad daylight inside the boardinghouse. Had the two detectives come across hidden papers of Garth's that could prove incriminating to them, or perhaps destroy? She never asked Garth exactly what he'd brought home in that clasped leather bag the last time he went out.

"If we can't clear our father's name, at least I'm praying we can get some of our inheritance back. Before he knew Millard Tremayne's true character, Father named him as our guardian, and we are his wards. He retains control of our resources and may be spending it to make a new life out here."

"Perhaps I can help with that, but I can't tell you yet." Jay stood and pulled her up to hold her close.

In spite of not wanting to, Sam trembled with a sudden longing she didn't understand. Parts of her tingled, and she wanted to get as close to this man as she could.

"You do realize that after staying out here alone all this time with me, you are compromised? We have to marry." Jay nuzzled into her hair and kissed her ear.

Sam tried to pull away but he held her fast. "What a romantic proposal! How can I resist?" It was hard to see his expression in the gloom. Was he laughing at her again, or was he serious? "I'm not marrying anyone," she protested. "I'm a confirmed spinster and intend to stay that way."

"If you say so. I'll let the matter of marriage go for now. Let's turn in and get some shut-eye." He lowered her gently to the bedroll. "Don't worry your sweet head about my intentions." He touched her cheek. "You've been through too much and I won't intrude, at least for now."

He nestled her back to his body and pushed up his legs to make a spoon to keep them both warm. The action cost him a few hours of sleep until he could calm down.

CHAPTER 31

The next morning Sam and Jay awoke to bright sunlight. When they looked out of the mouth of the cave, dust covered the trees and nearby rocks. They fed and watered the horses, then packed up and set out for Powder. As soon as they neared the town, Sam held back. Jay turned to question her.

"I can't go into town looking like this." She ran her hands over her messed-up hair, which was spread out over her shoulders, minus the usual braid. "We've lost our hats."

"What do you suggest? I said I'd marry you, make an honest woman out of you." Jay laughed at her outrage.

"It's early morning and folks will be out. We could go up the alley to the boardinghouse, but someone might see us. Uncle Millard would love to hear of my besmirched reputation."

"I didn't think of that, love. I sure don't

want my intended's reputation besmirched. No, siree."

"Oh, can you ever be serious? When you should have a sense of humor, you don't; and when it is inappropriate, you're all laughs. What happened to the pompous, stuffy blue jay we knew and despised?"

Jay laughed.

"Something like this could work in my uncle's favor if he comes to Powder. He would blacken my name, and that would discredit anything I say about him. Garth would kill him for that. And then where would we be?"

"I never thought of that. If you will wait here, I'll go into town and bring back your buggy. No one would see you inside that."

Sam narrowed her eyes, watching him suspiciously. "You planned on this, didn't you? We could have waited out the storm and come back last night in the dark."

Jay shrugged. "No, you give me too much credit. But if that's what it would take to marry you, I'm all for it."

"Not happening."

Rather than go to get the buggy, they decided to enter the town separately, waiting at least a half hour between entries. Sam would sneak into the alley.

On the way into town, Jay laid out a tentative plan that might get them out of their dilemma.

"I sure hope Garth hasn't taken Deputy Wade into his confidence while they are on that posse," Sam said worriedly.

Jay frowned. "I wonder how Garth will take it to learn the Pinkerton couple has tricked everyone. So far, those two have to be in the dark about the gang members hiding in plain sight, unless Ernestine has found a clue in Garth's room. I presume the rooms have no locks."

Sam shook her head. "No. Crazy Kate, the former owner, probably needed access to everyone's room to clean and whatnot."

When they reached the main and only street of Powder, as Sam had thought, there were cowboys riding toward the saloon and café and a few early-shopping women on the wooden sidewalk. They parted nearer to town, and Sam turned off into the alley going behind the boardinghouse.

When she tried to sneak inside, it didn't work. Aunt Twila and the major spotted her right away. She was speechless to see the major meekly sitting in the living room holding her aunt's bundle of yarn while she knitted.

"My lands!" When her aunt could finally speak after rising to her feet and hugging

Sam, she said, "Where in the world have you been, and why are you dressed like that? Ugh, you're full of dust."

"You are back to your old high jinks, eh?" The major touched her sleeve.

"No, not really. I'll explain after I get out of these clothes and wash up. Not a moment sooner." Sam held up her hand to stay their questions.

"I'll wait if I have to," her aunt said. "The major and I will carry up some warm water to your room. It's been sitting at the back of the stove and should be about right."

When the door closed behind her aunt and the major after they'd brought water for her bath, Sam shucked out of her dusty clothes, hoping this was the last time she'd have to wear her disguise. The air felt cold on her body. This was the first time she'd ever been completely naked in the daylight. She self-consciously glanced in the mirror but could only see her top half. After she looked askance at the mess of hair, she took a peek at her bosom. She wasn't as large as Peaches in that area, but she was bigger than Ernestine. She blushed at her wayward thoughts and wondered if men liked to look at or touch that part of a woman.

What had gotten into her? She moved quickly away from the mirror and slipped on her chemise and pantalets. She would do without the corset until she had to leave the house. She avoided the mirror when she brushed out her hair and braided it in its one long braid. It was as if the mirror held naughty secrets someone might come upon and shame her.

By the time Sam came down the stairs, everyone had gathered in the kitchen around the big oak table. Garth had returned from riding with the posse looking dirty and bedraggled, as Sam had only a few minutes earlier.

Garth told his story first. The posse didn't catch up with Big Bear, and they couldn't even find his tracks after a while. The big dust storm had hit that area, too, which helped rid the desert of any trail Big Bear might have left behind. "He got away slick as a whistle. He'll make an Indian yet."

They all laughed.

When it was Sam's turn to talk, she knew she'd better leave out most of her adventure, or Aunt Twila would have her married to the blue jay instantly. She began telling about reuniting Don Pancho with his people. Then she had to assure them the blue jay was not the spy in their midst. She watched their stunned expressions when she told them about Wade and Ernestine being married and about their jobs as Pinkerton agents.

"Jay does work for Uncle Millard, but I told him what we are doing here, and I believe he listened and is on our side."

"Jay, is it now?" Aunt Twila frowned.

Sam touched her aunt on the shoulder. "He saved my life. When I left Don Pancho and the other sheepherders, the dust storm came up, and I didn't know where to go. He said he followed me from town because he didn't think Don Pancho was a safe escort and he was curious as to where we were headed."

Aunt Twila looked stunned by Sam's revelations and, for a time, speechless. Not so the major and Garth, who both walked up to slap her on the back and congratulate her for her courage.

"But Jay thinks Uncle Millard is coming out here to see to his property." Sam took up the cup of coffee Aunt Twila had poured for her.

"Peaches might be able to help us with that if he does. She's aggravated with him about now."

"Why is that?" Sam asked.

Garth looked embarrassed. "I guess you know by now that Peaches and I have become friends —"

"And you'd like your relationship to be more than that," Sam interrupted.

"Maybe," Garth admitted. "But what I'm getting at is that one day I couldn't resist when she was going on about how generous he had been. I showed her the likeness of Aunt Grace and him at their wedding. The photograph was taken years ago, but he didn't look like the person in the picture he'd sent her from when he was still in college, for gosh sakes. She hadn't known he was married either."

"You scoundrel." Aunt Twila smirked. "I was impressed with Peaches the other day when she came to call. That was until she, Ernestine, and Sam started fighting, pulling hair and rolling on the ground like common pugilists."

"What?" Garth exploded from his chair, his face contorted in disbelief. "No one told me about that."

" 'Course not. You are never here to tell anything to. Stay home more, and you'll learn a lot." Sam laughed at his shocked expression.

That's when the major plunged into the conversation and told the whole story about the fight, or as much of it as he had witnessed safely behind the screened door. "The three of them looked like a bunch of drowned kittens after my lovely here threw a pitcher of water on them."

Garth slapped his denim-clad leg in glee, and dust flew up in the air. "I sure would have given a lot to have seen that fight."

Sam looked around. "Where is Elvin? He's the only one missing from our gang."

Aunt Twila looked puzzled. "Now that you mention it, I haven't seen him since Garth left with the posse and Sam disappeared with Don Pancho."

They all trooped up the stairs to make a beeline to his room. Garth knocked and, when he didn't get an answer, he threw open the door to an empty room. That is, it was empty of any of Elvin's belongings.

"Where in the world? He seemed at home here but I think he was put off by Sam's true identity and fearful of Aunt Twila," Garth said.

"There's a paper on the bed," the major said, reaching for it and handing it to Garth.

Thanks for letting me into your gang. I never had so much fun. I appreciate your kind hospitality, but I'm getting on back to Yuma before the posse returns. E

"For heaven's sake. I hope the boy will be safe out there all alone." Aunt Twila looked worried.

"He's probably already in Yuma by now. Don't you worry about him. I think he's like a cat that always lands on his feet, no matter what." Sam peered around at the concerned faces in the room.

"She's right. Elvin can take care of himself. I'm glad he hightailed out of here in case someone recognized him. I reckon that takes care of the desperados." Garth grinned ruefully.

"Thank heavens for that," Aunt Twila breathed. "I've never been so worried about you two in all my life."

Later that day, after everything had calmed down and Aunt Twila settled in for her usual nap, Garth and Sam sat on the porch swing.

"I wonder where the blue jay is," Garth said.

"Who knows? He said he had some ideas about how to help us with Uncle Millard, but he didn't say where he was going." She felt hurt, as if he'd abandoned her after their closeness. Even though she was sure his teasing about marriage wasn't for real. That didn't bother her in the least, she told herself firmly. She wasn't interested.

Garth chuckled. "I think the major has it bad for Aunt Twila."

"I think so too. He's wearing his heart on his sleeve, and she goads him unmercifully. It's charming to see he absolutely adores it. But the poor old duffer hasn't anything to offer her. I think he was on the stage for California when he decided to join us."

"Too true, but wouldn't they be an amazing match?" Garth grinned at the thought. "Anyhow, she has enough in the finance department to take care of them both. Uncle Stephen left her well off. I guess that's why I always appreciated her. As a woman of independent means, she didn't have to stay around and take care of us, but she did it anyway."

"That brings us to Ernestine and Wade. I'd never have thought them a couple, the way they ignored each other. In fact, I imagined you had kind of a crush on her." Sam looked at Garth inquiringly.

"Heck no. I never thought of her as my type. Too immature."

Sam had a good laugh at that. It was Peaches who held Garth's interest, even though he wasn't going to admit it yet. How would that sit with their uncle? And would Peaches respond to Garth?

"What do you suppose the blue jay has in mind? He certainly is an irritating person."

Sam wanted to deny this, but held back.

"Oh, he's not exactly how we think of him. Looks can be deceiving, and actions more so. Anyway, he advised us to hide any incriminating evidence we'd collected really well and if our uncle comes to Powder, we should try to be welcoming. There really isn't anything to tie us to his problems. Also, you might find out more from Peaches. I don't think she's so taken with our uncle anymore, thanks to you showing her that picture."

Garth made a face. "Do you suppose we can pretend a fondness for the old goat when we never did before? I bet he'll put two and two together and realize we're behind all his troubles."

"I suppose he will eventually figure things out. Meanwhile, we could try to act friendly, although I'm not so sure about Aunt Twila. She isn't able to hide strong feelings very well. But I think the key to our squeaking by resides with Peaches. On the other hand, why should she bite the hand that feeds her? She might have been annoyed with him at one time, but she probably got over it in a hurry."

"Aw, sis, she's nothing like that," Garth protested. "If she thought something was wrong, she'd stand up to it, no matter what."

Sam raised an eyebrow. "You know a lot about her. You must have been sneaking into town more often than either Aunt Twila or I imagined."

Garth looked uncomfortable. "All I'm saying is that she is really a good person, and I wish you knew her like I do."

His admission stopped Sam from saying anything else. She turned and hugged him for a brief instant before he wiggled away. "I believe you. She showed a lot of spunk talking back to Ernestine, and yet she is a lady. When Uncle Millard had her and his attorney watched, I thought she would quit him then."

"You bring up a point. I think I'll mosey on over there and see what's up."

Sam smiled. Garth tried so hard to fit in this country, and she supposed she'd been really trying too. The idea of returning to St. Louis seemed further and further away from reality. She watched Garth step off the porch, heading for town.

It dawned on her while talking to her brother that he was truly smitten with Peaches. That would be Millard's crowning humiliation. It served him right, but it could be the calamity that might push him over the edge, wreaking punishment on them, even if he didn't learn all the particulars of what they'd done. His ego wouldn't be able to tolerate Peaches's defection, and from that, he would figure something was fishy with them all being here in Powder.

They still had Ernestine and Wade to deal with. How much information had they been able to gather? Sam wanted to hate them, but couldn't. They had a job to do and were doing it. She hoped the couple would never return to the boardinghouse now that they'd done whatever job they'd set out to do for Uncle Millard. Actually, she wasn't one hundred percent convinced Jay was trustworthy yet.

But when could trust be built up again? First there was Jeffery, then Uncle Millard and Ernestine and Wade. What if Clarence J. was a traitor? Yet something inside her wanted him to be on the up-and-up. She definitely had to admit she had strong feelings for the man. He'd saved her life twice.

That night at the dinner table, the missing duo of Ernestine and Wade created quite a void in the conversation. Garth returned, silent and morose. When Aunt Twila asked innocently where half her boarders had disappeared to, Sam knew it was time to tell her everything.

When the dishes were done and the two

codgers went upstairs to bed, Sam and Garth sat their aunt and the major down in the parlor to talk. They told them everything, and that Millard Tremayne was on his way to Powder.

Aunt Twila turned pale, looking anxiously from Garth to Sam as if wondering how to protect them.

Garth shook his head and reached out to pat her hand. "He's not here yet."

It was then Sam realized Garth had been to see Peaches, and she must have told him she'd wait and talk to their uncle. She intended to give Millard a chance to explain himself. Then she would decide if she wanted to work for him. But her decision would be not personal, she'd probably assured Garth. That explained her brother's dark mood, since he had to know there weren't many ways a good woman could make a living if she was alone in the world.

"Don't you worry your pretty little head about that nefarious bloke," the major said. "I'll protect you." He'd evidently mistaken Aunt Twila's expression as fear for herself.

"Oh, you!" Aunt Twila retorted. "You don't even know the man or what he's capable of. Anyway, I can take care of myself. Have for ages. It's Sam and Garth I fear for."

"Ah, don't worry, Auntie. We'll go on like everything is normal and see what happens," Sam said quietly. Her voice, however, didn't hold much conviction. To Millard, it might seem too much of a coincidence that Sam, Garth, and Twila would come out West to the very town he had chosen as his sanctuary. He knew they hated him and suspected him of terrible things. Plus, they knew about his wife. No, things would not be great when they all met.

CHAPTER 32

For two days after that, Garth disappeared, telling everyone he wanted to be alone. He aimed to go to his hidden valley, as he liked to call it. The townspeople referred to the area as Iron Springs. Garth sat astride his horse on the rise leading down to the valley and gazed in wonder. The Mustang Mountains on one side, and the Whetstones on the other, surrounded a peaceful scene. The grassy meadow formed a sort of a bowl in the middle. Garth knew water ran freely there, even in the dry season. Cottonwood and willow trees edged the center where the creek ran. It always amazed him that no one had laid claim to this valley yet.

He wondered if Peaches could be content living on a ranch in so isolated a place. And yet it wasn't that far from town. Would Sam and Aunt Twila come too, if he built a ranch? For a while he'd imagined Sam had her eye fixed on Wade, but when they realized he was a traitor, his villainy only annoyed her. His defection hadn't hurt her as Jeffery's faithlessness had. But someone or something had definitely brought a bloom to her cheeks. Who? The only other man they'd met out here was the blue jay.

Garth closed his eyes and saw a sprawling ranch house nestled in the valley. Not something that could happen as long as their uncle was involved in their lives.

The man was a cold, calculating monster. He might not have killed their father outright, but he had caused his suicide, and he also held their purse strings as guardian.

The fact that Sam had turned twenty-eight before they left Missouri might be important if they could get their hands on their father's will, but the will had been missing since his death. Their father might have made some changes in his will at the last minute, but the crooked lawyer their uncle had hired claimed the will had been misplaced, and he would try and find it.

Some of the papers they'd confiscated could be used against their uncle, but Millard held most of the cards, what with his expensive attorney and his reputation as a circumspect and impeccable gentleman. If Aunt Grace found out about his planned double life, what would she do? Why would he have yoked himself to a dried-up, prune face like her, if not for her money? It was her fortune that started him in business until he partnered with their father. But by now, he probably had complete control of her money as well as theirs.

Garth surveyed the land in front of him as if he'd already lost it.

Sam felt edgy in Powder. She hoped and prayed Big Bear and Elvin had made it to their destinations without trouble, but she would never know for certain. Aunt Twila and the major existed in a world of their own, bickering and arguing cheerfully, so Sam left them alone.

Before Garth returned, one late afternoon, she met Peaches on the sidewalk in town. Peaches lowered her delicate, lacy umbrella to tentatively touch Sam's arm and say, "I'm worried about your brother."

"He's fine. He's out on the desert, hiding away in his favorite place until he gets his thoughts together. He's always been like that."

"I mustn't be seen speaking with you in the middle of town," Peaches said. She started to move away.

Sam put her hand on Peaches's arm. "Stop thinking like that. If Garth accepts you for the woman he believes you to be, so do my aunt and I. Nor do we care what anyone else might have to say about it."

Peaches laughed. "Thank you. That gives me so much pleasure to hear. Did you know your uncle came in last night?"

"Oh, Lordy, no. I didn't know that, but we were expecting him. Are you all right?"

Peaches flushed, her expression unhappy. "I know what you are trying to say, Samantha, and I will just have to be all right. I guess I can defend my honor. Lord knows, I've had to do it often enough in my lifetime. Being married to a no-good gambling man helped teach me a thing or two. Which means I have a general idea of what men are thinking before they can translate their thoughts into action."

Both women nodded at the truth to Peaches's statement.

"I've got to see my uncle. Is it possible? I'm so afraid he's planning something awful. As soon as Garth finds out he's here, all his fine talk about waiting for Uncle Millard to take the initiative will float away in the wind. Garth is not the soul of patience."

"I'm well aware of that," Peaches said. "However I'm afraid seeing him would be impossible. He's brought a whole battalion of plug-uglies as bodyguards. They won't let anyone get close to him, not even me, unless I answer the summons of the great man himself. Then he allows me an audience of a moment or two before he waves me away. I believe he has been using me to keep the saloon in shape until he could come to Powder."

"What is your impression of him now that you meet him face-to-face? Garth thought you were angry after he showed you the picture of Uncle Millard and Aunt Grace."

"Good gracious, it's no wonder your uncle wasn't ready to come here." She touched the gold locket around her neck. "He sent this to me when I first came to work for him. It supposedly has his likeness. He demanded that I keep it on for appearances' sake, since I'd told everyone he sent it to me. I certainly do not want him to suspect that I care for Garth." Her expression reflected fear.

Sam was appalled. Peaches had only just met their uncle, yet she already feared him. "I have an idea. Please don't say no until you hear me out. I've been very successful with disguises since I've come out West. Honestly, it's been fun. So far. You take your girls out every day for a buggy ride, don't you?"

Peaches nodded cautiously.

"I was thinking: why don't you leave one girl behind and bring along a change of clothes. I'll meet you down at the cottonwoods at the edge of town. I'll change and pretend to be one of your girls so that I can work my way into seeing my uncle. I believe I could calm him down, talk some sense into him before Garth storms his fortress and gets into trouble. If I can get past Uncle's bodyguards, I'm almost certain he would see me, if only out of curiosity."

Peaches seemed shocked, but only for a moment. "Absolutely not! You don't understand the danger. Garth would be furious if I participated in such a crazy scheme. And are you forgetting you are a lady and your reputation would be shot to hell — pardon me — if word got out that you even entered the saloon?"

"I don't fear my uncle physically," Sam persisted. "Garth and Uncle Millard have always had a tumultuous relationship, but in the past, he admired me and my work with horses. He even wanted to adopt me when our mother died, but our father wouldn't hear of it. Once I get near him, I know he won't harm me."

"I'm not worried about *him* harming you. It's those frightening bodyguards he surrounds himself with." Peaches shuddered.

"You would only be fair game to them. The reason they leave me alone is because of your uncle. The other night one of the girls had a terrible experience."

"Shush. You are trying to dissuade me. Don't you see I have to see Uncle Millard before Garth gets back? Maybe if I can talk to him, I can make him understand why we did what we did. If he doesn't back down, then we will have to bring out our big guns: proof of his evildoing."

"You can do that?"

Samantha nodded, showing more certainty than she felt.

"Then I suppose we can try it." Peaches shrugged in reluctant agreement. "Tomorrow morning?"

Sam smiled grimly. "I'll be ready."

Sam's next step was to confide her plan to Aunt Twila. It would be hard to convince her, but Twila couldn't be kept in the dark in case something bad actually did happen to Sam.

"I forbid it!" Her aunt pounded the kitchen table in a rare outburst.

"But don't you see? It's the only way to keep Garth from meeting Uncle Millard head-on. With all his bodyguards, a confrontation would be suicide for Garth. He'd never last long enough to talk to him."

Sam saw from her aunt's expression that Twila struggled between worry about Sam weighed against her concern for Garth.

"You say Peaches can protect you?"

Ah, a waver in her stubbornness. Sam grasped her aunt's hands. "I promise to take care of myself. It's the only way. Uncle Millard has always liked me. You know that."

"I don't worry so much about your safety with the villain, but posing as a saloon girl? What if anyone found out? Your reputation would be in shreds."

Sam laughed. "Who do we know here who might care? And probably no one will recognize me anyway. Don't forget, we're going back to civilization when this is all over."

With her aunt's half-hearted blessing, Sam insisted the major drive the buggy.

When Sam rode into the coolness of the clump of cottonwood trees, Peaches emerged from her waiting carriage. The sound of giggles intruded into the quiet desert.

"You didn't change your mind. I figured you wouldn't."

Sam opened the buggy door and took the package Peaches held out to her. "You brought some of the girls. Will they tell anyone what we're up to?"

"I had to bring them so you would blend in. They are *my* girls, loyal to the last."

"I'll go behind these trees and change clothes."

The girls sat in the coach, comfortable in the shade of a huge cottonwood tree, talking and laughing on their day off. The major waited to accompany them back to town.

Sam let out a gasp from behind the trees and ventured out, holding her hands up against her front to hide her nearly exposed bosom.

Peaches grinned, and the ladies peered out the windows of the coach. "It's the most modest of all our dresses that would fit you. Don't forget, you are much taller than most of us."

The major's raised eyebrows and between-the-teeth whistle told Sam she wasn't imagining her charms. She looked down at her chest swelling like creamy waves out of the low-cut dress. The corset that went with the dress cinched her small waist even smaller.

Peaches reached out to bestow a blond wig on Sam's head and began tucking Sam's dark locks inside. Several of the girls left the coach and came to help, straightening the long curls hanging over her shoulder and down her back. They applied dabs of rouge to Sam's pale cheeks and a touch of powder to her eyebrows to lighten them. Finally, someone placed a beauty mark at the side of her mouth.

Then they all stood back to look at their handiwork. Sam could tell the result impressed them. Peaches reached into her reticule and pulled out a large hand mirror.

Sam peered into it and stared, dumbfounded. She didn't recognize herself. "Do you suppose I resemble our dear sweet Ernestine just a bit?" She teased.

Peaches laughed, thinking of the prissy Ernestine dressed as a saloon girl.

"The only real problem we will have is hiding your tanned skin, but if you keep gloves on and stay out from under the chandeliers, I think we can pull it off. I certainly wouldn't have recognized you. What do you say, Major?" Peaches looked up at the man standing near the carriage.

For once, the major was speechless. He stared at Sam as if she had two heads.

Going back to town, the major drove behind the women's coach, veering off at the boardinghouse while they continued to the saloon, where a man came out to take the coach when the ladies unloaded.

By now, Sam's stomach was tied in knots, and she wondered how she'd ever pull off this masquerade.

"Are you sure you can trust the ladies not to talk about this?" Sam worried.

"Definitely, especially after what one of the men did to poor Thelma the other night."

Peaches's words raised goose bumps on Sam's arms, which went along with her roiling stomach, but she took a deep breath and straightened her shoulders. This act would be worth it if she could bring Garth and Uncle Millard together to reach some agreement. They would never have the satisfaction of Uncle Millard admitting to causing their father's death. But he needed to know he was no longer in charge of their lives and money, and that he would be punished if the truth of his shady dealings were made public.

Sam wondered how Peaches was coping with Millard on a personal basis, but knowing her uncle, she doubted he would presume a relationship until he was certain of a returned response. He had to realize his persona didn't resemble the picture he'd sent to Peaches.

"We'll go in now. It's not likely that we'll have too many customers at this hour, and the men are used to seeing us come in from our daily outing around this time. Stay close to me," Peaches admonished.

"How do I start?" Sam asked.

"Smile and flirt just a bit. The afternoon crowd is a bunch of pussycats, but later they can get rowdy. You won't get any guff from our regulars. It's the men your uncle brought in who are a tough bunch."

"I'm sure I can take care of myself," Sam assured her.

"Like with the one who beat Thelma within an inch of her life?"

Sam looked at Peaches, shocked to the core. "My uncle permitted this?"

"I don't know if he is aware of it. He keeps an office upstairs and stays there most of the day. Some days he takes a carriage and rides out to other places where he owns businesses, I suppose. He's not here all the time. But I take partial blame for what happened to Thelma. I've told the girls their job is to add to the customer's *visual* enjoyment. Cadging drinks, flirting, some dancing and singing on stage."

"And that's all?" This wasn't exactly what Sam had heard about saloons.

"I don't tolerate men upstairs. If a girl wants to meet a man, they go elsewhere and that's her business. But I'm afraid Thelma teased that awful man too much, and when she didn't want to go through with whatever he wanted, he went berserk." Her daintily arched eyebrows drew into a frown as she regarded Sam in her borrowed finery.

"I don't think my uncle would meet with me any way other than by trickery," Sam soothed.

The girls filed through the door of the saloon, chattering like a flock of birds, as if looking forward to the coming evening. They all grew quiet when passing a line of men standing at the bar. Sam knew right away these were her uncle's hired guns. For a fleeting moment, Sam worried if any one of them had counted the number of girls who'd left the saloon earlier. But surely Peaches would have taken care of that. Luck was with Sam, as the men had only arrived two days earlier and hadn't had time to familiarize themselves with the ladies.

Sam stayed in the center of the group as they entered the elegant room. She tried to hide her amazement while she stared at the luxurious furnishings. Chandeliers hung from ceilings with scores of candles nestling in the glass. The walls were covered in soft velvety material, while the bar shone with polished brilliance. She'd always imagined a saloon as a dark, smelly place with brass spittoons all around. She did see shiny brass spittoons, but that was only natural where men who chewed tobacco gathered. Sam struggled for nonchalance, leaning against the piano, trying to blend in. The girls ambled around the room, talking first to this customer and then the next one. Only about fifteen men sat at tables, drinking. From where Sam stood, she could see into the two rooms off to the side, which appeared to be the serious gambling areas. In one room she saw a roulette table and in the other an additional small bar. Toward the back of the place came the sounds of dishes and pots and pans clattering, which indicated the kitchen.

The sensation of eyes burning into the gauzy material covering her back jerked her attention to the main room. She whirled around to encounter a questioning stare from the most cold-blooded face she'd ever seen. The man reminded her instantly of Buster. His thick, dark brows crashed together in a frown, and his lips turned up in a malicious smile that made her shudder. Was he just a customer? Maybe an important customer?

Peaches sidled up to her and whispered, "Don't make eye contact with him. That's Davy."

When she didn't explain further, Sam nodded.

"You're not on duty yet. The customers haven't come in for the evening. You don't play piano, do you?" Peaches's voice was hopeful.

"Some," Sam admitted.

"Great. Then sit here and plunk, as if you're practicing. They don't expect much. It will keep you busy until your uncle decides to show up."

"I should go up there and knock on his door," Sam protested.

"Oh, heavens no! You can't do that. Not even *I* am allowed. He won't permit anyone near his door. We all live on the other end of the building and use a back staircase. You could retire to one of the girls' rooms temporarily if you are fearful."

"Oh, no, I'm not scared," Sam lied.

"Perhaps your uncle has changed since you last saw him," Peaches suggested gently. "I never knew him before, of course, but I would consider him fearful in the extreme. He doesn't trust his own shadow."

"Sounds like he's deteriorated since I left St. Louis. I'd have to talk to him to see what's going on. That ugly man who stared at me, you say his name is Davy?"

Peaches slid a glance his way. "He's the chief bodyguard and the man who beat up Thelma. The only one of the lot of them your uncle trusts."

Sam sat at the piano while Peaches moved away. Sam's dress swished sensuously as she moved her legs beneath the piano bench. She wished for a wrap to cover her bare shoulders when she dared glance in Davy's direction, only to see his continued stare. She shivered and turned to the piano keys. Had she made an error in judgment?

The family regarded her as the cool head in the family, compared to Garth. Peaches hadn't been able to stop Thelma's confrontation, and her uncle apparently didn't concern himself with such matters. Sam had to plan what to say to him when he came down those stairs. Peaches might intercede for her, as he wouldn't recognize his niece dressed in such a manner.

The afternoon passed without incident. No one paid any attention to her sitting at the piano plunking keys aimlessly. Once in a while, a cowboy passed by and winked or stopped to ask her name, but most of them stayed with the regular girls. She thought she recognized the owner of the mercantile entering the saloon, and a thrill sped through her at the notion he would never recognize her as the priggish young woman from the boardinghouse.

Later, when she glanced up to see the

saloon door open, she almost gasped aloud when she saw Deputy Wade standing at the front of the saloon, his eyes searching the room. How humiliating it would be if he recognized her. He would probably call her out in front of everyone, and that would put an end to her chances of talking to her uncle. But Wade sauntered past while her fingers trembled on the keys. He only spared a cursory glance in her direction as he continued on toward the bar. The bodyguards parted at the bar and respectfully gave him room. She watched as he tossed back a drink and turned to head straight up the stairs. That was almost the final proof Sam needed to prove he was a spy.

She had a clear conscience though, since she'd never given more than a fleeting thought to any alliance with him. The blue jay flashed into her thoughts and she smiled, feeling her face warm under the thick makeup.

Across the room the man named Davy drew her attention. He had apparently noticed her flush and smile, and his eyes narrowed with interest. Sam looked quickly down at her hands lingering on the keys.

"Play a tune for us, girlie," a shout came from one of the tables in the big room. Sam looked up in dismay to see a ring of men standing, looking her way. She started to rise, searching for Peaches, but didn't see her in the room. A hard hand reached her shoulder and pushed her back down.

Sam swallowed her angry response when she looked up to see the hand belonged to Davy.

"Didn't you hear the gents, little lady? They want to hear some music."

"You can't tell me what to do," she flared. "I work for Peaches."

Davy grinned at her, but his eyes stayed dead cold. "That may be. But Peaches works for Mr. Tremayne, and he made me a partner in this here saloon last night. Won it fair and square in a poker game." He nodded toward Peaches who had just come in from the kitchen. "She don't know it yet, either, but she works for me now." He frowned, staring at her. "I don't think I've seen you around. Are you new?"

"You have only been here a few days yourself. I'm sure there is a lot you aren't aware of yet." Sam didn't want to anger him, but it wouldn't do her any good to show fear.

"Play!" He commanded.

She played the liveliest tune she could think of while trying to steady her nerves. Peaches couldn't know about this latest wrinkle with Davy either. Maybe she had shown revulsion toward her uncle when she first met him unexpectedly, and her uncle had retaliated by putting Davy in charge. If so, both Peaches and Sam were in deep trouble. But then again, why couldn't she just walk out through the front door if she chose to do so? If Uncle Millard didn't come down by dinnertime, that was exactly what Sam would do. There was the deputy to contend with, so she'd better not call too much attention to herself.

Sam continued to play automatically amidst the rowdy laughter and talk. She watched the girls circulating around the room, encouraging men at the tables to play cards and buy drinks. It was a boon that she was able to play the piano, because she had no idea how to maintain a flirtatious demeanor, and the very idea collided against her straightforward way of thinking. For all their practiced coquettishness, the girls stayed far away from Davy. Glancing at the stairs but trying to be nonchalant about it, Sam saw the deputy descend the staircase and leave in a hurry, without a backward glance. A wave of relief washed over her and she sighed.

Davy moved up and sat on the piano bench next to her.

"Whatcha watching the stairs for?" he asked.

"I was expecting to see Mr. Tremayne come downstairs to join the crowd." She tried to scoot away when she felt his thigh touch hers, but he moved against her again.

He laughed, the sound grating on her last nerve. "You *must* be new here. The boss don't look at no one but Miss Peaches, so you needn't set your cap for him. Anyways, he ain't here tonight. Took a trip out to his mine, and that means I'm in charge." He put a rough hand under her chin and turned her to face him. One look into his flat, dead eyes and she barely kept from crying out, but she held herself firm until he dropped the stare first and stood, moving away without another word.

This was beyond her worst imaginings. Everything was going wrong. She had to talk to Peaches, but the woman was nowhere in sight. Her only option was to head toward the kitchen and maybe sneak out the back door. Millard's hired guns stationed themselves around the room and especially at the front door. Before she could think of leaving, Peaches needed to know about the latest news making Davy part owner of the saloon. The thought made chills run up and down her arms and she rubbed them vigorously, looking around the room. Finally she spotted Peaches and lifted her chin to let the woman know they needed to talk.

"What's the matter, Samantha? You look like a ghost walked over your gravesite."

What an image. "Sit next to me. You need to know something, and I don't want anyone else overhearing."

Peaches sat and patted Sam's hand resting lightly on the keys.

Sam told her about Millard making Davy a partner, and how he was in charge when her uncle was out of the building. Peaches gasped and then covered her mouth.

"Oh, it's worse than I'd imagined." Peaches paled under her makeup. "Your uncle as much as promised me a part interest in this saloon. Not that I'd accept it now. I'm sure I showed some shock, to put it mildly, the first time I met Millard. He looked nothing like the portrait he sent me, but then, Garth had warned me about that."

They sat, not speaking for a long moment. "You've got to get out of here, pronto," Peaches whispered. "I couldn't help notice Davy's got his eye on you."

"Deputy Wade was just here, but he left already. I feared he'd recognize me, and then I was almost afraid he wouldn't. That would have been an easy way out, to leave with him, but it would take too much explaining. Anyway, we're pretty sure he's the spy."

Peaches nodded. "I saw him enter and wondered if he'd come close enough to recognize you." She looked toward the kitchen. "You should be able to sneak out the back door. I don't see his hoodlums watching there. If only Garth were here, he'd know what to do."

"That's what I'm trying to avoid. He would try to take on Uncle Millard's whole army, and we can't let him do that. I got myself in this mess, and it's up to me to figure it out."

"What about that Clarence J. fellow? Garth calls him Blue Jay. He stays here sometimes. Millard reserved a suite for him since he was working as an accountant. He could help if he comes in tonight."

"That would be even worse than the deputy discovering me. In the first place, I don't really know whose side he's on for sure. Secondly, I'd be completely humiliated if he saw me like this."

"Well, dear lady, you'll be far worse than humiliated if someone doesn't help you."

Sam shook her head with stubborn determination. "If Davy bothers me before I can escape, I'll tell him the truth, that I'm Millard Tremayne's niece. He wouldn't dare harm me."

As if conjured up by their conversation, Clarence J. entered the saloon.

"Don't you dare say a word to him about me," Sam said, grabbing Peaches's arm. "If you want to help, go over there and steer him away from me."

Sam lowered her head and applied herself to the music, although the ruckus inside the saloon almost covered the sound of the tinkling piano. It was hard to imagine how the men heard anything from her corner, but apparently some of them did, for when she stopped to rest, she heard applause.

Once she dared glance in the direction of Blue Jay and Peaches, deep in conversation. Her heart thudded against her chest when a beefy hand clamped heavily on her shoulder. The hand moved up and she felt calloused fingers caress her neck and under her tied-back hair. She didn't need to look up to know it was Davy.

"Don't touch me!" Sam cried out between clenched teeth.

"Why? Does it excite, sweetie?" He sneered. "Don't put on airs with me. You ain't nothing but a party girl like all the rest of them here. I sort of took a liking to you."

She wriggled away from his hand as if it

burned her. "I may work here, but I don't do a damned thing I don't want to do. And I don't want anything to do with the likes of you."

He laughed, a soft menacing sound that rolled over her like a tidal wave. "That's what I like about you. Fire and ice all mixed up in one package. I promise you won't do anything you don't want to do. I can see to it you'll want what I want. All you need is some help in that direction and a good teacher," he bragged.

Sam caught a whiff of sour whiskey on his breath when he leaned closer, and she struggled to hide her sudden fear. She darted a look to where she'd last seen Peaches, but the blue jay stood alone. He looked straight into her eyes, shocking her, his dark brows drawn into a frown. Did he suspect her identity? But no, he turned away.

She realized she was on her own. She'd gotten herself into this mess, and it was up to her to get out of it. Jay couldn't help her, being no match for the bodyguards. Anyway, he still worked for Uncle Millard and his priority would be with his employer.

By twos and threes the girls headed into the kitchen for their dinner. Peaches came to get Sam.

Davy slid off the piano bench with a look that promised he'd see Sam later.

"Thank you. I was beginning to think that man would attack me here in public." Sam stood to go with Peaches.

"Why don't you let me tell Clarence J.?" Peaches scolded, taking Sam's arm and leading her toward the kitchen. She sounded exasperated, but Sam felt the underlying fear in her voice.

"If you tell him, everyone in town will know about it. No. I have to get myself out of this on my own." It showed how scared she was that she'd forgotten to retrieve the small notebook and pencil that she'd hidden inside the piano bench.

"You know, if I didn't like you so much, I'd be offended. You care so much about people thinking you a dance-hall girl for one night that you'd sacrifice your safety? It's incredible. You're a snob, Samantha."

Was it true? Peaches's words hurt Sam, and she didn't know how to answer. She wasn't ashamed of the occupation the women had chosen; it just wasn't her choice.

They had reached the kitchen, and the cook ladled up a bowl of soup for her along with slices of roast beef. She should be starving, but her stomach rebelled at eating.

Sam and Peaches sat at the long kitchen

table, alone in the room, except for the cook.

"No, I'm not ashamed to be here." Sam put her hand on Peaches's arm. "It's the combination of this dress, with my bosom sticking out for all and sundry to gawk at, this rouge on my face and the wig. Oh, I'm making things worse. But I know Clarence J. He would never let me live this escapade down. And I don't want him hurt. He's kind of helpless in that department, I'm afraid."

Peaches regarded Sam with narrowed eyes. "There's something going on between you two. You can't fool me about love. I can spot it a mile away. At first I thought the gleam in your eyes might be for the deputy, but I'm glad I was wrong on that count."

"Don't be ridiculous. There's not a thing between the blue jay and me." Sam worried that she'd protested too much.

Peaches finished her coffee and stood to leave. She nodded at the back door. "I think Davy's stationed someone out there, too. We'll come up with something, but honey, it had better be before we close these doors. That's promptly at two in the morning."

Sam noticed her hand holding the cup of coffee tremble. "When the girls finish their shift, don't they go up to their rooms?" she asked.

"Sometimes. One or two might leave to

418

meet someone. That's what happened to Thelma. She was found beaten in the alley behind the saloon, and we all knew she was meeting Davy, but what can we prove? Anyway, this is a man's world, and his say-so will always be believed before ours."

"Which room is Davy's? Maybe he left some kind of evidence."

"I doubt that. He's in the room next to Millard's. In fact they have adjoining rooms, because it was the only suite in the house, and your uncle insisted on it. In truth, I was supposed to have Davy's room, but after I met Millard, I couldn't go through with what he'd proposed. In anger, he put Davy there and shoved me over to the other side with the girls. Which I didn't mind in the least."

Sam nodded. "I understand."

"But what do you care about Davy's room? I pray you never see the inside of it. Got to go now. You can stay here awhile to gather your thoughts if you like." Peaches bent to brush her cheek against Sam's.

"No, we'll go back together." Sam followed Peaches into the main room, and the din of laughing and talking men struck her. The kitchen had been quiet behind the heavy doors.

Davy lurked nearby, hands folded across

419

his chest as if he'd been waiting. Sam hoped he hadn't heard any of their conversation. She went back to the piano and played for the dancing girls on the stage. After a while the room quieted, and Sam figured it was near closing time. Her heart leaped into her throat when she noticed Davy going out the front door. He must have an assignation with one of the girls. She pushed back from the piano and headed toward the stairs.

"Say, missy, where you going?" One of Millard's guards stopped her when she set foot on the bottom step.

"Why, to Davy's room, of course," she said. "You'd better let me pass if you know what's good for you."

The man sniggered, and Sam's stomach roiled from the leer he turned on her. He nodded for her to go on.

"She's okay, Pete. Show her to Davy's room," he called up to the man standing on the landing in front of her.

When she reached the top of the stairs, she caught what could have been a look of pity in the man's eyes before he turned and beckoned for her to follow. Near the end of the hallway, he threw open a door and waved her inside.

"Sure you want to do this, miss?"

She nodded. "Close the door, please." Her

420

mouth was dry and, belatedly, she was having second and third thoughts about what she was doing. She held her breath when she heard the key turn in the lock. The sound of the man's boots walking away seemed loud.

Sam's plan was to enter her uncle's room through the adjoining door, lock it behind her, and wait for her uncle to return. He'd have to talk to her. She hurried over to turn the doorknob between the rooms.

CHAPTER 33

Her heart hammered in her chest. The door was locked. Of course, she should have realized her uncle wouldn't trust anyone, not even his so-called partner.

She moved back to sit heavily on the bed, then leaped to her feet as if it had burned her. This could be even worse than her experience with Buster. She was sure Peaches had no idea where she had disappeared to, and might even think she'd made it out the door and was already back at the boardinghouse. *If only.* Sam allowed her thoughts to center on the blue jay. She should have confided in him. Looking down at her watch pin, she knew there wasn't much time left. She expected no help or mercy, having set herself up as a trollop waiting for Davy's return.

Thick draperies at the window made the room dark and virtually soundproof. What a terrifying thought. She pushed aside the curtain fabric and looked out. Balconies spread along the front, where the women sometimes stood waving and calling to passersby, but her hopes sighed away in a hurry. Thick Spanish-type bars covered Davy's window and that of her uncle's next door. Peering between the bars, she saw the street was empty. The only sounds on the silent street were the mules and horses tied out front of the saloon. Even if she could break a pane of glass, who would hear her so far above the ground?

Sam swallowed against a dry throat, hearing boot steps coming down the hall toward her. She recognized Davy's whiskey rasp. If only she'd brought her derringer, but then, where would she have concealed it? The gown she wore didn't even have pockets. Her first thought was to hide under the bed. She looked around frantically for any kind of a weapon. Horror almost overcame her when she heard a rustling sound come from her uncle's room. When the door swung open, she feared to turn around to see who would emerge. When she did, the blue jay stood in the doorway, his expression cold, his eyes like a stormy sea.

She stared in shock. Was she imagining this? Before she could speak, he grabbed her arm.

"Come with me and don't say a word, or they'll hear us." By now the voices came from right outside Davy's door.

Sam felt the pounding of Jay's heart when he pulled her to him and shut the door behind them, shoving the key into the lock. When he brushed against her bottom to fix the lock, she took a deep breath. Even under the multitude of petticoats she felt the warmth of his hand.

He pulled her away from the door and held her out to look into her eyes, shaking her by the shoulders. "Damn, Samantha, what if I hadn't come in time? Do you even have a *notion* of what might have happened to you?" His lips crushed hers, giving no quarter, and in spite of what she'd been through in the past moments, she let herself answer, parting her lips to allow him access. She felt his intake of breath, and she grew braver, reaching up to entwine her fingers in his hair.

Millard's bedroom was semidark, the draperies partially open. A light from the street shone weakly into the room. Davy's cursing and throwing objects around in the next room didn't faze the blue jay. He grinned and nodded toward the big bed, his eyebrows moving up and down.

"You must be out of your mind!" Sam

struggled to stay the laughter along with a blush.

"It was only a brief thought, sweetheart," he whispered. "But when we marry, don't lose the dress. Let's get out of here first, and we'll have plenty of time for that later." He laughed softly at her outrage and ran his hand across her bare shoulders.

"In a pig's eye that will ever happen." She had a hard time whispering in her indignation.

He took her hand and headed toward the closet.

"Wait! What are you doing?" Davy rattled the door to Millard's room, sending a shudder through her so strong, she could barely think. Davy wouldn't dare harm her if she told him who she was, but Clarence J. would surely die.

"Hurry! He might have a key." He turned and touched her cheek gently. "You will have to trust me."

She gulped and nodded, following him into the closet. He pushed away the hanging clothing, smelling strongly of her uncle's cologne. She felt like gagging, and her lips tightened in disgust.

"Pull the door shut behind you," he whispered.

He pushed past the clothes, pulling her

along, and moments later she smelled fresh air. A doorway opened to freedom. She stopped.

He turned to her in puzzlement. "What now?"

"Peaches. Do you think she will be blamed for my disappearance?"

He shook his head. "She's under your uncle's protection. Davy wouldn't dare lay a finger on her. Besides, why would he assume she had anything to do with your escape?"

Sam saw the logic in his answer and motioned toward the door at the bottom of the staircase. He held her hand as they made it, single file, down the long narrow stairs. She admired Jay's protectiveness. He was always ready to take care of her.

Once in the alley, Jay took off his jacket. She wondered if he was going to lecture her about her clothing, but he merely placed the jacket around her shoulders. He tweaked a blond curl. "I suggest you take off that wig in case some of the thugs are watching from the balcony."

Gladly, she pulled off the wig, and her braid of chestnut hair fell over her shoulder.

"That's better. Now you are beginning to look like my old Samantha."

She snorted. "Old, indeed. Didn't you like

the new Samantha even a little bit?" she teased, surprising herself, not realizing she could flirt.

"Oh, yes," he murmured in a hoarse voice that sent chills through her body. "But I want to be the only man who ever sees that much of you."

She hid her smile in the darkness, pleased that she had so much power over this man. When they neared the entrance to the alley, a light penetrated a bit, and she slanted a look at him. No more of the dithering demeanor he had affected in the past. He stood straight and tall, his lean build hiding his quiet strength. His face, minus the spectacles, was an uncompromising handsomeness relieved by his sensuous mouth. She wanted him to kiss her again.

"How did you know where to find me? Moreover, how did you know about that secret passageway?" The idea of him in that bedroom with one of the girls caused her steps to falter. He brought her up short when they emerged onto the street.

In the dimness of the moon that had appeared, she saw him smile. They were close to the boardinghouse now and pursuit was unlikely.

"Did you imagine I wouldn't recognize you in that absurd disguise? I'd know you anywhere under any circumstances. I hated to see Davy lurking over you, but thought you should be safe with a room filled with people. Then you disappeared. If you wanted to talk to your uncle so badly, I could have helped."

She kicked a stone out of her path. "I didn't want your help. Frankly, I don't know for sure if we can trust you."

"Wh-a-at?" He took her elbow and turned her to face him. "After all we've been through together? You can stand there and say you still don't trust me? That's out and out pitiful."

She could tell by the coldness in his eyes and the grim set to his mouth that he was deeply offended. For once he left off joking, which made her uneasy.

"I'm sorry if I hurt your feelings. You've saved my life more than I'd like to admit, and I'm most grateful."

"You ninny. I don't want your gratitude," he interrupted. He pulled her close and murmured something into her hair that she didn't quite hear, but it sent gooseflesh along her neck where his lips moved.

She pressed closer and he groaned, moving away. "When your aunt didn't want to tell me what you were up to, I really became worried. I finally got it out of her — and don't fuss at her. She was worried about you, too. Then Peaches wouldn't tell me where you were at first. That frustrated me, because I could *feel* you nearby until I looked across the room and saw you. She finally realized I was your only hope to get out of there. She told me about the hidden door and gave me Davy's key. He's probably still looking for you."

Sam smiled at the idea of nasty Davy searching all over for her hiding place.

Before they reached the front porch Jay took her hand and looked down into her eyes. "Don't ever do that to me again, Samantha. I can't stand the thought of what might have happened to you if I hadn't been there. Davy's an animal, and if he'd wanted to harm you, he could have taken you away where no one would have found you." He bent his head, and their lips met. His kiss wasn't the gentle, questioning ones of before, but passionate and demanding. She melted into his arms, her mouth opening in wonder while his tongue took quick advantage. She tentatively ventured her own tongue and he groaned, pulling her even closer.

Emitting a huge sigh, he released her, enabling her to ask a sensible question after she'd caught her breath.

"What will we do about Uncle Millard? If we leave things hanging like this, we may as well return to St. Louis. Even if he can never prove we were behind the harassment, he will know for certain when he sees Garth and me." The thought of going back to St. Louis hung like a shroud over her thoughts. She was amazed that she had immersed herself in Arizona, but she knew Garth felt the same way. Yet it was Garth who was in danger. Their uncle had never liked his nephew, had blamed him for the death of their mother when he was born. He would have no compunction about getting rid of Garth as he would a pesky fly.

"Millard Tremayne is a powerful man," Jay agreed. "I'll have to think about the problem." They had stopped on the side of the street leading to the boardinghouse, beneath the protection of trees. The sky was getting light.

"Garth won't want to leave, that's for certain. He's already found a place he wants to build a ranch, and I believe he and Peaches will eventually be together." Sam stopped talking at his surprised expression.

"Are you saying you'd stay out here? In this wilderness?" he asked incredulously.

"I presume that gives you the perfect out for your ridiculous marriage notion. Actually, I love it out here. Freedom from so many restrictions, especially for a woman. The sunrises and sunsets . . . why, it's an amazing place."

A brief moment of silence followed Sam's words. The crickets in the nearby brush dinned loudly in her ears above the sound of her beating heart.

Sam saw a sudden flash of white teeth as Jay smiled and looked down at her in his arms. "You mean you'd give up your life back in civilization? I heard you lived in a mansion. I'm shocked. I believe there is a way to blackmail your uncle into giving you back your home if you want it."

She stared intently into Jay's blue eyes. "If you think you know everything about us, you should also know I don't give a tinker's dam about that mansion in St. Louis, and neither does Garth. It only holds sad memories for us. We've brought our hearts out here with us, and here they'll stay." A dark sadness settled over her, as she realized this was the end of things between her and Jay. They'd had a beginning and now they were having an ending. He would certainly return East.

Jay and Sam had reached the boarding-house steps, where Aunt Twila stood on the porch. At first she didn't recognize Sam,

431

but after peering closer, she rushed down the porch steps. Jerking off her apron, Twila flung it over Sam's shoulders. Sam had forgotten she still wore the saloon dress and that she'd given Jay back his jacket. Jay chuckled, tipped his hat, and walked up on the porch to sit. He showed he was in no hurry to go anywhere.

"Samantha Kirkland! Get yourself upstairs immediately. Imagine traipsing all over town looking like a . . . never mind. Just go." She pushed her niece toward the stairway.

"By Jove, young fellow, I see why you've acquired an interest in our Samantha." The major chuckled, causing Sam to blush and Aunt Twila to smile, in spite of her indignation.

Sam tried to hide her embarrassment while Jay watched from his lazy position on the porch swing. Dang the man! She ran upstairs to her bedroom, and slammed the door behind her.

The new maid had filled a tub of warm water while they had been talking on the porch. Sam shucked her finery and settled into the steamy warmth. She needed the water to wash away the harshness of Davy's hands on her arms. She closed her eyes and leaned back, thinking how much she owed Jay. She found it difficult to connect his former persona as a simpering, pernickety fop from the past, to the person who had emerged as her strong, honorable champion. She swallowed past a dry throat when she realized that she cared for him. A lot. She enjoyed his company, he made her laugh — even at herself — and he was handsome as the dickens now that she saw past his disguise. But she feared to engage her heart. Jay would soon be gone from her life.

When she descended the stairway in her nicest blue day gown, Jay ran to take her hand. "Delightful, love. Your dress is the same color as my eyes."

"Shush, you ninny." His assumed lack of manliness no longer put her off. She knew better.

"Doesn't she make a better saloon singer than a boardinghouse manager?" He teased the major.

Sam and the major laughed, while Aunt Twila stifled a groan. Reaching for Jay's hand, Sam led him outside to the swing.

"Oh, so now you expect a full courtship with a porch swing, flowers, dances, and the whole shebang?" Jay clasped both of her hands and leaned forward to kiss her as they sat down.

"I'm not sure your words carry any weight," she replied. "You already expressed your preferences when I mention Garth's dream of having a family ranch nearby."

"I admit I might have spoken too soon. The idea grows on me." Jay brought his hand under her hair and pulled her forward for a kiss, making waves of desire flood her body. She leaned even closer, pressing her breasts against his chest.

When the kiss was over and they both leaned back for air, he continued. "I'm not letting you go, no matter what devilment you find yourself in. You need a full-time keeper. I admit I never gave a thought to living out here permanently. But I'm open to change."

"You mean you would give up your accounting business?" Her voice did not hide her skepticism. Not more than a few weeks ago, she had overheard a conversation between Jay and Ernestine. He had been extolling the virtues of his work and how much he enjoyed every mathematical moment. His words had made Ernestine yawn with boredom. Sam remembered the stab of envy she'd felt when she believed he didn't take her seriously enough to confide his ambitions with her.

"To tell the truth, I do have ability with figures — always have had. It came easy to me and frankly, my existence has been predictable and ordinary. Until I met you. I had my life neatly planned, but now all that planning has gone up in a puff of smoke. I'm not sure of what I want to do next. Except to be close to you always."

She loved looking into his eyes. It was like diving into a blue lake on a sunshiny day. Would he tell her he loved her? Could she admit the truth — that she'd come to realize her love for him, and she'd known for some time?

"Like I said, before I met you, I thought investigating accounting was the most exciting, challenging work I could ever do. Actually investigating accounting is practically my invention."

"My, how dreadfully modest. How so?" she asked.

"Mostly in my work, I'm hired to uncover plots of elaborate embezzlement, so I strip away veneers of sophisticated pseudo-corporate ethics and shift through the layers."

"Hold on! Stop right there," Sam laughed. "You make it sound like something Ernestine and Wade are doing with the Pinkertons."

His expression was serious. "Just about. That's what has always made it so interesting. If I'd been working for your father, perhaps we could have come up with some concrete facts. He might still be alive, and all this wouldn't be happening to you now."

Sam took a deep breath, thinking of the possibilities. "Still, you have given me no idea what you see in your future."

Jay pulled her to her feet and hugged her close, kissing the side of her cheek and moving slowly down her neck with light, moist kisses.

Sam's legs turned to putty, and she would have fallen had she not been pressed up close to him. She reached to touch his hair, so soft, above his collar.

He held her away to look at her intently, his blue eyes warm and tender. "I'm not a pauper, Samantha. I've made a good living, and with careful investments, we won't go hungry, even if I do turn out to be the world's worst rancher."

Sam leaned her head against Jay's shoulder, marveling at the solidness there. She didn't know if she wanted to be a rancher's wife either. The ranch was Garth's dream, not hers. Anyway, would any of them survive to carry out future plans?

CHAPTER 34

Garth returned the next day. He scolded Sam roundly for taking the chances she'd taken when Aunt Twila told him what she'd been up to. Yet Sam saw hidden admiration deep in his eyes. Would her brother ever grow up? Maybe with Peaches's help he would, eventually. They had gathered in Garth's room: Aunt Twila, Sam, Jay, Garth, and the major. Jay made them all laugh when he imitated Davy's puzzlement at losing Sam, as if she'd dropped off the face of the earth.

Sam felt her pride well up when he naturally took charge.

"The best way I see is to bring matters to a close before any more time is wasted. We need to get ahead of them," Jay said into the waiting silence.

"But how?" Aunt Twila sat across from the major, and Sam noticed with a surge of amusement mixed with pleasure that her aunt was dressing more stylishly and wore her hair in a most becoming French twist instead of the usual tight ball at the nape of her neck. A glance in Garth's direction showed that he must have noticed the change in Aunt Twila too. He kept alternating between staring at their aunt and sneaking looks in the major's direction. Not long after he had moved into the boardinghouse, Aunt Twila had coaxed the major into abandoning his beloved toupee. Even though his hair was a silvery gray, thick around the edges and bald on top, he looked ten years younger without the rug. He refused any suggestions about shaving his mustache though.

"We don't know what Ernestine and Wade discovered or what they reported to your uncle, first off," Jay said. "That's a definite disadvantage to our side. She stayed here long enough that she might have snooped in Garth's room and learned who you are. We have to act before Tremayne marshals his thought and ideas. We need to catch him long enough to talk to him. The saloon is off limits. Too dangerous. There are his banks, but we would have a hard time finding which one he's visiting. You three need to stay away from banks, anyway." He looked pointedly at Sam, Garth, and the major.

Garth looked embarrassed, Sam refused to meet Jay's eyes and the major chuckled.

"The way I see it," Jay continued, "is to meet him at the Peaches Mine. He's sure to check on the mine when he goes out again."

"But what about the hired guns he'll have at his disposal? I'm sure the miners themselves will be on his side, won't they?" Garth wondered for the umpteenth time where Elvin had gone. They could use his help right about now.

"The miners are sure to be on Tremayne's side, since he's paying them, but they aren't working now. We'll have to catch him after he leaves the mine and heads back to Powder. He'll be relaxed by then, and so will his guards. I hope. We'll have surprise on our side, anyway."

"So, after we've surprised them, what then?" Sam asked.

"We will force him to sit down and have a serious talk."

"And his guards?" Three voices popped up in unison.

Jay grinned. "If Samantha and Garth stand up so he can see them, I doubt even a corrupt person like him would dare harm his family in front of so many witnesses."

He pointed to Garth and Sam. "I presume you've collected some incriminating evidence on him by now. And when I went back to St. Louis this last time, I discovered his second set of accounting books he was so sure were hidden from me."

"Sounds like you plan a bit of blackmail on the rotter," the major observed.

Jay nodded. "Exactly. If we offer to leave him alone, he'll have to forget how you've harassed him. Maybe he doesn't yet know the extent."

"But that's no solution!" Sam protested. "We can't let him get away with all he's done to our family. He's in charge of our inheritance as our guardian. Are you forgetting that?"

Jay regarded Sam and Garth for a long moment before speaking. "He isn't getting off scot-free. From what you've told me and showed me, he's lost upward of a million dollars on bonds and bearer notes, credit vouchers, and stock certificates, not to mention papers you've destroyed. By now he'll realize he's lost face with his stockholders back in St. Louis, and they'll be jumping ship. And the topping on the cake is Peaches. I believe he counted on her to start a new life with him out here and leave his past behind."

"She knows what a ruthless person he is by now. She's not buying that anymore," Garth blurted.

"Exactly." Jay took a deep breath. Sam tried to digest how they had managed to get to their uncle, but was it enough? Enough to satisfy what had started out as their thirst for vengeance? She and Garth could get by on the money their mother had left them, and the boardinghouse was finally making a small profit. Eventually they would divest Uncle Millard of his guardianship. But if Garth wanted to fulfill his dream of owning a ranch in the valley, they would need their full inheritance.

Jay walked up to Sam and sat down beside her on the bed. "I know you two blame him for your father's death, and in a way you are right. But you might be wrong, too. From what you've told me, and from what I've gained from talking to your aunt, your father's life was over when your mother died. He never truly recovered, did he? He lost the will to live but hung on to see you two grown enough to take care of yourselves. Is that the way you see it?" He looked up at Aunt Twila.

She glanced at Garth and then Sam and nodded. "Yes. That's how it truly was. But you see it so clearly, young man, and you don't even know our family." She turned to Jay with a puzzled expression.

"It was actually a process of deduction," he admitted. "Sam told me about some of her life before she came out here, and you told me more. And then all I had to do was realize what a bastard Millard Tremayne is, and it came together." He smiled at Aunt Twila.

"I don't see how Uncle Millard can connect us to his problems. But there are those letters I had my friend send from New York. If he gave any thought to how I managed that, he'd have to wonder."

"It's settled then." Jay looked around at the group. "If you all agree, let's get on with it. Tremayne could be heading back to Powder from his mine as we speak, but even with his bodyguards around him, I don't think he'll want to travel across the desert at night. He'll wait until morning. Major, do you want to get mixed up in this last caper?"

"By Jove, try and stop me, laddie." He glanced at Aunt Twila, who nodded in approval. "We could use Elvin's help, I imagine."

"I reckon he's in Yuma by now. Least I hope so." Garth didn't sound certain.

"I'm in on this, too," Aunt Twila blurted

442

into the hush that followed the mention of Elvin.

"Oh, no!" A chorus of three erupted together. They looked at each other and laughed before turning to Aunt Twila.

Hands on hips, a fierce look in her eye, she faced them all down. "Ever since I came here, you've left me out of everything, except to take care of this place. I want to help tying up Millard Tremayne until he won't ever harm anyone again, if that's what you have in mind."

Garth looked at Sam. No use arguing with Aunt Twila when she got *that* look in her eyes.

Later, in the back alley, the desperados gathered for what could be the last time. Their bedrolls ready, they saddled up the horses.

"I never thought to ask, Aunt Twila. Do you ride?"

The major stepped up, holding on to Twila's arm. "I've a headache, something I get now and again. We'll be along later. You three go ahead."

Garth suspected the major wasn't up to riding a horse and needed to put Annabel together. Would their aunt cooperate and ride on the strange vehicle? He almost insisted on Aunt Twila coming with them, but clearly something had come up between her and the major, and Garth hesitated to interrupt. Since he had drawn a map of where they were headed, Aunt Twila and the major would catch up. They would need an extra gun, and Garth knew Aunt Twila could shoot with the best of them. But either way, he decided to trust the major and let the matter go.

Halfway to the trail where Garth had planned to waylay their uncle, they came across a wide stream. It was shallow enough, so they crossed it without trouble.

They made camp that night beyond the mountain pass, a narrow-necked place that barely allowed a buggy to pass through. Garth had taken the chance that their uncle would have to come this way to avoid a longer trek across the desert. They settled down near a crop of mesquite trees for cover, to hide them from the trail. When they spread out their bedrolls, Garth felt a shock of surprise to see the blue jay and Sam sitting side by side, shoulders touching, talking quietly. When had this happened? They looked serious. Like they were in love. He didn't say anything at first. He longed for a cup of hot coffee, but they didn't dare build a fire. Even if it was out by the time their uncle came their way, any outriders would smell the smoke.

Garth leaned back against a tree trunk and regarded Sam and Jay. "When did this happen, Sam? You never mentioned being so close to the blue jay." The foppish prig had disappeared. He no longer even wore those spectacles. What was going on?

Jay reached for Sam's hand and held it to his lips. "You may call me Jay," he suggested.

"It was quick," Sam admitted. "One day I despised this man, or thought I did, and the next day, it became clear to me what a special person he is. By the way, his name *is* Jay, so I'd like you to call him that, please."

"Actually, I thought she had eyes for Wade," Jay said.

Sam punched his shoulder. "You're ridiculous. You never thought that for a minute."

He smoothed a lock of hair from her cheek. "Well, maybe not. But who could have suspected that Wade and Ernestine would be a Pinkerton couple? There's an unlikely pair if I ever saw one."

"Not really," Sam answered. "They are both devious and sneaky. We should have seen that quality in them from the start."

"That's going a bit far, sis. They guarded their relationship so well, not even Aunt

Twila guessed." Garth realized Sam and Jay had steered the conversation away from themselves. When they were ready to talk, he'd listen. He lay back on his blanket and regarded the stars, leaving the lovebirds to their privacy. He was happy for Sam. She'd finally found someone who would stand up to her, yet side with her when something was important. It took a strong man to do that, and he believed Jay equal to the task.

He leaned up from his position to say one last thing. "By the way, watch out for Sam if she gets her pencil and pad out. She'll write about you, and you won't like it. Not one bit."

"Oh, you!" Sam picked up a small rock nearby and tossed it at her brother, who pulled the blanket up over his head, laughing.

"What's this about a pencil and paper? I've noticed you with a pad of paper once in a while, but you always hid it away when anyone came near," Jay said.

Sam couldn't help but admire the lean planes of his cheekbones, and especially his blue eyes. She swallowed nervously. "I am writing a novel. About the West," she declared, chin in the air.

"Splendid! I'm sure you'll do well, with your vivid imagination."

She poked him in the ribs with her elbow. "I have always wanted to write, but truly never had anything special to write about that moved me. Since coming out here, things began to settle into place and I knew I was onto something. Only men can write westerns, and hope to be published it seems. I'll sign my name as Sam and no one will guess."

"Not unless they ever meet up with you." Jay laughed when she swatted at him.

As day was breaking, the last of the desperados heard the jingle of a harness and the clip-clops of many horses coming their way.

"I might have known he'd be sitting in a buggy. I've never heard of him riding a horse," Garth grumbled.

"The major hasn't shown up, and we might need him," Jay said. "Want to stay hidden and call the whole thing off for now?"

Both Garth and Sam shook their heads. "We've come too far," Sam protested in a whisper. "We have surprise in our favor, and I don't believe our uncle would shoot us down in cold blood, no matter what he thinks when he sees us."

Garth wasn't so certain, but he didn't comment.

While the buggy thundered closer, the three took their positions. They had tied a rope from tree to tree across the trail. Sam wouldn't allow them to tie it low to trip the horses so they conceded and tied it chest high to stop the oncomers.

When the horses came in contact with the rope, they reared and stopped suddenly, throwing the coach sideways, almost tipping it over. The guards raised their rifles but didn't see any target to shoot at.

Tremayne shouted, "Open the damn door! It's stuck."

Several of the riders dismounted and rushed to do his bidding. When Tremayne stepped out of the buggy, he stood in the middle of the trail surrounded by mounted men, all holding rifles trained on the road ahead.

Sam, Garth, and Jay stepped out of the trees, aiming their own rifles at Tremayne.

"Go ahead. Shoot us, but he dies, too," Jay growled.

"You! The Pinkertons warned me, but I didn't believe them. I should have known my own family was behind my problems out here. You have caused a great nuisance, not to mention inconvenience."

"We don't consider you part of our family anymore," Sam replied. "You stole our inheritance, our home, and probably killed our father. I only hope we *did* inconvenience you."

Tremayne shook his head. "I didn't expect this of you, Samantha. I have always cherished you since you were a child. Not so, Garth. I blame you for the death of my sister, but of course, you must have known that."

Garth shrugged. "I never knew my mother, and I expect I mourned her more than you did. How could I have been blamed because she died at my birth?"

"The same way you both blame me for your father's death. I had nothing to do with that. He was a weak man."

"Yes. Weak enough to allow you to seize everything that belonged to us," Garth said.

"Enough! They aren't going to shoot me." He spoke low to the men surrounding him, and without another word, they rushed forward, instantly knocking over Garth and Sam with their horses while one shot sang. Jay dropped to the ground.

Sam turned to run toward him, crying out his name. Before she could move, one of the men grabbed her arms and tied her hands behind her. They had to subdue Garth by slamming a pistol butt on his head.

"I warned you not to hurt my niece and

449

nephew," Tremayne said, walking up to them and looking down at Garth.

"We didn't hit him hard, boss. But he wouldn't cooperate."

"You've killed Jay," Sam cried out, struggling to be free.

"Good riddance. He's a traitor. I paid him well to keep my accounts. I trusted him."

"At least let me see if he's alive. There's so much blood," she pleaded.

Without another word, Tremayne motioned for the men to pick Garth up and bring him and Sam back to the buggy.

"You are going to kill us, aren't you? You monster!" Sam kicked out at him, and he stepped back.

"Yeah, boss. What's next? We ain't aiming to shoot the young'uns for you, if that's what you want," one of the guards said, and the others nodded.

Tremayne drew a cigar from his jacket pocket, and one of the men rushed up to light it for him. He leaned back and let the smoke slowly rise.

Sam glared at him, wishing she could smash that cigar into his fat face. "We only wanted to talk to you. Your guards wouldn't let us come to your room in the saloon."

"I never knew you tried that until Davy told me, and I made Peaches tell me the truth. But you certainly didn't show good faith by pulling rifles on me, did you, girl? I'm going to have to set you both aside until I think this over. If there's a way I can prove you two were swindling me, I can have you put in prison for a long time. The circuit judge is on my payroll, so to speak." He leaned back and regarded Sam calmly through the haze of cigar smoke.

Sam looked at Jay's prone body and gritted her teeth to keep her tears inside. He had no quarrel with their uncle and had died for nothing. She realized how much she had come to love him and how empty she felt. At least he didn't suffer, if he'd died instantly.

"Take them to the shed next to the mine, where we store the dynamite," Tremayne told the men. "Let them do without food and water for a while. Maybe they'll be ready to confess."

"And go to prison. That will never happen. You can't prove a thing against us." Sam felt sure she was right. Their gang had dispersed, except for the major, and no one had ever identified any of them. They'd never physically harmed anyone in their forays. Well, maybe with the exception of Buster.

"Get this buggy turned around. I'm going

back across the desert. Too much chance for an ambush on this narrow trail, although I doubt there's anyone left of their gang." Tremayne frowned at Sam, his bushy eyebrows nearly hiding his squinty eyes. "I may not even remember you two are there. No great loss."

One of the men hoisted Sam up onto his horse in front of him, while another draped Garth's unconscious body behind his saddle. The other men turned the carriage around.

Sam watched while dust engulfed the vehicle as it headed away. She gave one last lingering look back at Jay, until the man holding her jerked her forward. Since she was wearing trousers, he set her astride, for which she was glad. She felt the heat radiating from his body and leaned forward as far as she could. He only snorted at her.

When they arrived at the mine, he pulled her from the horse and pushed her forward, while the other man slung Garth over his shoulder and shoved them both into the shed. Before they slammed the heavy door, one of them threw in a small flask. They not only turned a key, but slammed down what sounded like a heavy bar across the door.

Sam rushed to Garth and knelt beside him. A knot had formed on the side of his head and bled a little, but his breathing sounded normal, which gave her relief. Now what would they do? Was their uncle merely threatening when he said he might forget them?

A long death of starvation, especially without water, made her heart thud until she thought it might jump out of her chest. He could never be accused of killing them outright. He could return in a month when their bodies were dried up, bury them in the mine, and probably most folks would assume she and Garth went back to St. Louis. The major and Aunt Twila would never think to look here.

Sam thought of Jay lying on the desert. She bent over with sorrow, holding her middle as if she might break in two. When she straightened, she waited for Garth to wake up.

CHAPTER 35

Sam looked around the shed. It was a long, narrow building with sturdy log sides. The chinks in between the logs let in air and some light, for which she was grateful. In the corner lay a wilted canvas tarp. When she kicked it, a scorpion ran out and zipped through a small opening at the bottom of the shed. Sam held her breath and feared moving the tarp again. She had faced rattlers and other desert critters since they had come West, but spiders and scorpions gave her the shudders.

When she'd caught her breath, she continued to move the tarp from the corner. Her heart sped up and she cried out when she saw two sticks of dynamite underneath. She didn't see how she and Garth might use them, but they were something to hold onto.

Garth finally woke up, rubbing his forehead. "What a headache. Was I out for long? What happened? Where are Uncle Millard and his men?"

Sam knelt at his side. "Shh. Stay calm. Untie me. They're gone, but they locked us in here. It's an old storage shed that stores dynamite they used to open the mine."

Garth sat up and released Sam, then stood, wobbling on his feet, to look around. "Is he going to leave us here? I'm so thirsty."

Sam shook her head, trying to keep pity from her eyes. "Here's a canteen of water one of them threw in before they shut the door. But it's half empty and all we have. No more water or food. He said he may forget us. Unless we agree to sign a confession, and then he will see that we have a quick trial with his bought judge and go to prison for a long time."

"Well, thanks for laying it on me all at once." Garth's grin was weak. He shook the water container to see how much it contained, but refrained from taking a drink. They paced the floor from one end of the shed to the other, touching the tarp briefly.

"One good thing I found," Sam said. "They forgot two sticks of dynamite. I left them under the tarp in case someone comes back."

"Don't know how we'll use them, but it's something." They could tell darkness had settled since they no longer saw light from the chinks in the walls.

"It's going to get cold tonight. Bad enough sleeping on the dirt floor, but we can cover up some." Garth brought the folded tarp to spread out.

"Does your head hurt?" Sam asked. "I don't understand why he cautioned the men not to harm us, yet may leave us here to die."

"I'll bet he didn't want any witnesses or to leave marks on us if we die and someone finds our bodies, when they begin working the mine again. Do you think they killed Jay?"

Sam tried to speak, but her throat tightened and a deep sadness with a crushing sense of loss settled over her, and she had to wait until it passed. "I'm sure of it. There was a lot of blood, and no one would help him." Tears fell from her eyes and she wiped them away with her sleeve.

"Ah, sis, I'm so sorry." He enfolded her in a warm hug.

"We didn't have time to speak of it, but I know he loved me, and I've loved him even when he was at his most despicable." She smiled to think of his disguise. "I've been a spinster this long. It's my destiny. But I'll always regret not spending more time with him."

If Garth knew what she actually meant, that she wanted one night of making love with him, so the memory would last the rest of her life, he didn't comment.

They tried to smooth part of the tarp under them when they sat and leaned against a wall. Then they pulled the rest of the tarp across their bodies to keep in some warmth. The canvas felt rough, even through their clothing, and smelled old and fusty.

By the third day of sleepless nights, their throats so dry their tongues had swollen and they could no longer talk, they decided they had to come up with a plan. It had been thundering for two nights, with no sign of rain, but lightning flashes lit up the room from time to time.

Sam had a sheaf of notepaper in her back pocket. They shredded the paper at the front end of the building and gathered some granite rocks they'd found on the floor. Both of them took turns trying to strike the rocks together to start a spark. It took a long time, and by then both Sam and Garth's fingers were blistered so badly, they could barely hold the rocks. But a spark finally kindled, and a small fire started. The papers were in limited supply, so they had to work quickly.

Garth said, "Go to the back of the shed

and hunker into a corner. Pull the tarp over your head and wait for me to join you. I only dare use one of the sticks. Two might blow up the whole building, with us in it."

"We might blow ourselves up with one stick, mightn't we?" Sam asked. Her mouth was so dry, she could barely get the words out. Her hands were bleeding, but so were Garth's.

"We might die, but isn't that better than slowly perishing from thirst and starvation?" Garth hugged her to him briefly, and then motioned for her to get in place.

He lowered the dynamite to the flame, laid it down next to the door, and ran back to join Sam under the canvas. They huddled close together, heads down, and made themselves as small as possible. It only took a moment before a great blast sounded. They saw the flash of explosion even under the cover of the tarp. Pieces of wood flew past their hiding place and one came near to striking them, but when things calmed down, they threw the canvas aside to look.

The front of the building had blown completely away, fortunately mostly out-ward. One edge of the tarp caught fire, but they stomped it out quickly. Remnants of a fire burned on the dry grass outside. It had started to rain, which would extinguish the flames.

"Come on, let's get out of here." Garth took Sam's hand and pulled her outside. They would have liked to take the tarp, but it was heavy and too stiff to fold. Neither of them had enough strength to carry it. Garth motioned for Sam to go ahead. Then knelt, touched the last dynamite stick to the fire, and threw it into the mine entrance. He and Sam ran behind the bushes that surrounded the mine and hunkered down. They didn't have long to wait before the front of the mine collapsed in a giant cloud of dust and tremendous noise.

"That won't stop them for long, but it will sure as hell annoy the old bastard," Garth muttered. "Let's see if there's anything of use in the landfill behind the mine. Then we'd better look for water."

There wasn't much trash except empty tins of beans, but they did find a thick rope that had frayed in places. The rain fell faster now and they put their faces up, mouths open to receive the life-giving water. Sam had her hat and held it upside down to catch what water they could.

"Not too much at once, Garth," Sam cautioned him. "It will make you sick." She ripped off a piece of her shirttail and wiped the blood from Garth's forehead.

"Come on, we have to get moving. We'll head down the trail again."

Oh, no, Sam thought. *We'll have to pass Jay's body.* "If we come across Jay, we must try to bury him," she blurted. They started walking down the trail leading from the mine.

Garth paused to turn back and look at her. "I don't know. We're so weak, we can barely walk. We'll tackle that problem when it comes up."

They had picked up the pace as their legs grew more used to walking, but both of their stomachs growled so loudly, it would have been comical under better circumstances. The rain hadn't let up, and the road beneath their feet turned the desert sand to slush, making it even harder to walk. They passed the spot where they could see where the struggle had taken place. Blood still clung to bushes and rocks, but they saw no sign of Jay.

"They must have taken his body to town. They'll come up with some cock-and-bull story, but at least he'll be buried," Garth said.

Sam swallowed a lump in her throat, but her tears had dried up inside her.

After a while, when darkness descended,

the wind howled around them, almost pushing them backward. They heard a terrible sound. When they turned at a bend in the road, Sam wanted to perish right on the spot.

The creek had swollen enormously, the rushing water roaring as it tumbled down the widened creek bed.

Garth took her hand. "We have time, Sam. I don't see the boulders where we crossed before, which means the flash flood hasn't come down from the mountain yet. We can make it."

Sam looked doubtful, as neither she nor Garth had ever learned to swim. But what choice did they have?

Garth unwound the rope from where he had carried it on his shoulder and motioned for Sam to grab one end. "We'll tie the ends around our waists. That way we can hold on if one of us slips."

Sam wasn't sure of this idea, but she kept still, grateful that Garth had reverted to his old take-charge self again.

They walked up the bank, looking for a likely place to try to cross the raging stream. It had become so wide. The water tossed and frothed, but they finally decided it was do or die, and they began to make their way across, Garth in front, holding the rope in case it came loose from the tie on his waist. Sam followed, but her feet sometimes couldn't find purchase, she was so cold and weak. While Garth made the shore and crawled to safety, a mighty roar came from the mountain and, to their horror, a wall of water two stories high and filled with huge boulders and uprooted trees came rushing toward them.

"Sam! Hurry!" Garth sprawled on the sand of the opposite shoreline, trying to catch his breath. He rolled over and sat up, pulling frantically on the rope holding his sister.

When Sam heard the roar, she knew what was happening. In sheer panic, she forced her legs to move, tugging her boots from the sucking sand and almost springing out of the water near where Garth sat pulling her rope. Without a word between them, they crawled frantically on their hands and knees, trying to reach the bluff in front of them. If they got that far, they would be safe from the flood and boulders that roared down the creek.

"Thank God," Sam whispered when they climbed upward and sat safely watching the rocks, uprooted trees, and debris rushing past. They held each other close for a moment, in awe that they had escaped.

The storm finally passed, but with the clouds disappearing, there was light enough to travel down the path. The light wouldn't last long. Sam shuddered to think of the scorpions, tarantulas, and snakes that came out in the coolness of the night. Their boots were soaked, and their feet squished inside them. Blisters would form while their boots dried.

"Bet you regret using your paper on the fire. I noticed you have your pencil tucked in your back pocket."

Sam knew Garth was trying to lighten their situation. "You're right, but actually what happened to us will be forever emblazoned in my mind, so I don't need paper. Anyway, paper would have been waterlogged, like me."

"Sam, do you hear that?" Garth stopped abruptly, turning to look at her.

She'd been plodding along with her head down, barely moving and trying not to think too much. Deep down, she knew they had little chance of making it all the way back to town. In the morning when the blistering sun came up, the desert afforded no shade to speak of. They had refilled their flask with creek water, but that was not going to help a lot. When their boots started cracking from the dry and heat, their feet would

463

swell. Yet they couldn't walk barefoot across the desert.

She stopped and tilted her head to listen. Was Garth beginning to hallucinate? But no, she heard it too. The sound of an engine. Could that be . . . ?

CHAPTER 36

They waited for a moment and then saw the major barreling down the trail on Annabel, raising dust high in the air. Behind him came a small buggy with Aunt Twila holding the reins of the one horse. As soon as the major stopped his motorcycle and their aunt descended in a flounce of fabric from the buggy, Sam and Garth staggered up to hug them.

"Oh, my goodness, you both look a sight, but you're both so wonderful to these old eyes," Aunt Twila said. She removed her glasses to rub them with her sleeve, as if to give her time to compose her emotions.

"Water?" Garth croaked out. The creek water they last drew out had been half mud.

The major retrieved a bottle from his saddlebags on the motor bike and handed it to them. They drank thirstily, and then waited to hear how they'd been found.

"You can tell me all about it on the buggy

ride home," Aunt Twila said, herding Garth and Sam toward the buggy. The major had already mounted Annabel, and was ready to turn around.

"Jay?" came the first question from Sam's mouth as they headed back toward town.

"Oh, child, he's doing well. We rescued him, but he was unconscious for almost three days after we took him back to the boardinghouse. He'd lost a lot of blood from a gunshot to the shoulder, and a bullet skimmed his temple. We had no idea where you were, but as soon as he came to, he told us what Millard had planned for you, and we hurried right back here. If only we'd continued when we found Jay, we might have found you at the mine."

"But then Jay might have bled to death," Sam protested.

"Jay wanted to come with us in the worst way, but the doctor prevailed. With a jigger of laudanum, he stayed put."

Sam felt as if the weight of the world had vanished from her shoulders. Jay was alive. "Now we have to figure out our next move with Millard Tremayne." Darned if she could think of him as *uncle* ever again.

Garth took a deep breath, and his anger colored his next words. "He has to be brought to some kind of justice. We need our inheritance back, and we need to be free from his so-called guardianship."

"Oh, he'll pay, all right." Aunt Twila giggled.

Both Sam and Garth turned to her in surprise. A giggle? From Aunt Twila?

"I sent for Grace. She should be here any time and set Millard straight. Wait till he sees her. *She'll* take the wind from his sails. We can't let him know. Her arrival will be a delightful surprise."

Sam and Garth laughed so hard, tears came to their eyes. Then they sobered, thinking about his threat to put them in prison.

Aunt Twila pulled out some sliced beef and cheese from the carpetbag she had set on the floor of the buggy. "I had an idea you two would be hungry, and I heard one of your stomachs growling. Don't eat too fast," she cautioned them.

Nothing had ever tasted so good to Sam and Garth.

As soon as the buggy pulled into the yard, Garth began to unhitch the horse. The major roared up with Annabel, and Aunt Twila and Sam headed for the front door. Sam ran inside and up the stairs, rushing into the bedroom her aunt pointed out as Jay's. She sat on the side of the bed, and touched him gently on the shoulder to wake him.

"Oh God, is that really you, Samantha?" He reached shaky hands to bring her down for a kiss. "I've never felt so helpless in my life, worrying about what that monster would do to you and Garth." He lay back and held her hand to his lips, kissing each finger. "Is Garth here too?"

Sam stared into blue eyes fringed by impossibly thick black lashes. He was so dear to her, it made her throat dry. His kiss had been soft and searching, but she knew he wanted more. Was what she felt for him love? It had to be. It was so strong and made funny tingly feelings from the top of her head down to her toes. Did he feel the same? His eyes told her he might.

"Yes, we both are fine, no thanks to Millard Tremayne." She told him about their imprisonment and what Tremayne had intended to happen to them. When she told about getting through the flash flood, his face paled and he groaned. "When you get well, maybe you can help us figure out what to do next. He threatened us with prison, and he might have some proof of what we've been up to. But I believe we have enough incriminating evidence to show he was double-dealing some of his investors."

"Don't you worry about that. I've gathered enough proof of his larcenous dealings that he could go to prison for a long time. He was certain I was too gullible to dig deeper and discover he had two sets of books, but I found them. He only hired me as a front, to let his investors think he was keeping track of their money." Jay's hand tightened on hers, and a muscle flicked in his jaw. "I want to hurt him bad for what he did to you and Garth. If your aunt and the major hadn't found you in time, I don't want to think about what might have happened to you both."

They heard a ruckus downstairs: a door slamming and loud voices.

"Go see what's up, Samantha, and come back and tell me. Or I'll have to get out of this bed from curiosity." Jay grinned and pushed her shoulder lightly.

Where he touched her felt as if lightning had zapped her, and Sam wondered if he had felt it, but he had closed his eyes as if he were tired from talking.

She ran downstairs and skidded to a stop to see Peaches in the foyer, with the major, Garth and Aunt Twila gathered around her, all talking at the same time.

"What's happening?" Sam asked.

The four began talking and Sam held up

469

her hand to stop them.

"I know I shouldn't be here," Peaches said. She wrung her hands, and tears slid down her cheeks as she looked at Garth. "I sneaked away because I knew you were in danger. I overheard Tremayne bragging to Davy that you two were no longer a threat. I'm so pleased to see you are safe."

Garth walked up and held her shoulders with gentle hands. "I'm fine, thanks to Aunt Twila and the major. But can you get away from him?"

She shook her head. "Not yet. I have to stay and try to protect my girls from the likes of Davy. He won't bother me as long as he knows I'm under Millard's protection."

Garth scowled and his lips thinned. "I don't want you there." The thought of his uncle putting his hands on Peaches made him see red. She'd already told him Millard hadn't tried anything with her yet because he was too consumed by his own problems. She was a good woman; out of her depth in what she must have assumed would be a peaceful running of a decent saloon. He took her hand and walked her outside to the porch, settling her in the swing.

"It's dangerous with Davy there," Garth admonished. He leaned forward and touched his lips to hers. He felt elated that she didn't back away. "When this is all over, we have to talk."

"Yes. Of course." Her eyes told him everything he needed to know. She had grown to care for him, too.

"I must go now, Garth." They stood and embraced. Her body felt so right, close to his. Her soft breasts pressed into his chest, and he pulled her even closer. Her tripping heartbeat melded into his own.

"I need to walk you back to the saloon."

"No! I'll go through the back alley into the kitchen entrance. It would be too dangerous if someone should see us together."

Garth didn't care, but he didn't want to make matters worse for her. He reluctantly watched her walk away.

"I was beginning to realize you cared for her, Garth," Sam said. After her long hot bath and clean clothes, she was beginning to relax a little. She stepped out onto the porch when Peaches left.

"You're damned right I do. It bothers me that she has to go back there, but she's worried about the girls and Davy."

Aunt Twila joined Sam and Garth on the porch.

"You're friendly with Aunt Grace, aren't you?" Garth asked his aunt.

"Of course. I used to go over to play cards with her on the nights Millard had to go out of town. But I never liked him. He knew it and avoided me." She rubbed her hands together in glee. "Oh, this will be rich. Wish we could be there when he sees her. I like her, but she is wicked cantankerous and has always wielded an invisible rolling pin over Millard's head. It was her money that got him where he is. Probably the only reason he married her. I'm sure she won't approve of his being out here. Chances are, he might have to dissolve all his holdings and skedaddle back to St. Louis."

"If we can get our inheritance back and throw out his guardianship, I'd be willing to call it even. How about you, Sam?"

She nodded. "Certainly. I'd like to see the last of him with his round bottom heading East."

The next week passed quickly, and was the most peaceful week any of them had ever had while in Powder.

Sam and Jay sat out on the glider one balmy afternoon. He was up and about but hadn't left the boardinghouse yet. He would have a thin scar on the side of his face, but Sam thought it only gave him character. He was much too handsome otherwise, now

472

that he had shed his "disguise" and his popinjay ways.

"Samantha, there's something I have to tell you, and it's difficult for me to begin."

Sam tried not to show her dismay. Sooner or later, she knew, he would go back East.

He reached to take her hand in his, absent-mindedly rubbing the calluses on her palm from her days of training horses.

"You're under no obligation to stay here," Sam assured him, struggling to keep the hurt from her voice. "Your work is done, and you're free to do as you want."

"But what do *you* want, Samantha?"

She was looking out at the street, and Jay gently put his hand under her chin to turn her his way.

Blast it! Her eyes felt teary, but she would not cry! "What do you mean?"

"I have to go back to wrap up a few loose ends, but I needn't be gone long. If there's a reason to hurry back."

Sam sniffed. "Stay as long as you need to."

He leaned forward and pressed his lips to hers in a soft kiss. When she didn't pull back, he put his hand at the nape of her neck and held her closer while he moved his mouth over the fullness of her lips. She opened in surprise, and his tongue explored her mouth in a way that sent shivers of delight down to her toes. She shyly touched her tongue to his in answer and trembled at his low groan.

Jay pulled away only to nuzzle into her neck. "Oh, God, you smell so good," he murmured. They sat close together for a time, neither speaking.

"What is it you want, Samantha, truly?"

She took a deep breath to get her emotions under control. "I suppose a home, children, and a husband. Sort of in that order."

"Cheeky woman," he admonished. "I want you beside me the rest of my life. I want to wake up with you next to me, and I want us to give each other gray hairs through the years. Is that too much to ask?" He spoke the words lightly, but she felt as if her answer was very important to him.

A shiver ran up her spine. She feared her heart might be beating so loudly, he was sure to hear it. This wasn't the time to admit she loved him though; he might not intend to return in spite of his warm words. "That sounds good to me. I have feelings, too, but we'll wait until you get back." Her unsaid words hung in the air: *If* you get back. If he didn't come back, he was taking her heart with him, but she wouldn't let him know that.

Jay took Sam's hand and put her palm against his cheek, moving it down enough to bestow a kiss in the middle. His eyes had never looked bluer, a bit darker than the clear skies over Powder. How could she have ever thought him ordinary?

After Jay took the next stage out of Powder, Garth begged Sam, Aunt Twila, and the major to come see the dream place where he wanted to build a ranch. Sam and Garth rode horses while the major and Aunt Twila rode in the buggy.

Garth inhaled the fresh desert air and looked to the mountains that lay as a backdrop to *his place.* While they traveled across the desert, Sam looked pensive, as if recalling events here that both dismayed and pleased her. Someday Garth hoped she would tell him all about it.

They stopped in the shade of a giant palo verde to rest the horses.

"It's a vast desert, Garth. Is this what you wish to show us?" Aunt Twila brushed the major's helping hand away while she alighted from the buggy to stretch her legs. The major only smiled, apparently not put off by her impatience.

"Actually no, this isn't it. It will only be a

few miles more. We are gradually going higher in elevation. I'm happy it's far enough off the trail so no one comes this way." He couldn't help but wonder if Peaches would be content this far from town if he built a ranch. As a widow, she had been wife to a rancher before. He thought of having someone he loved along with a bunch of kids running around the ranch and sighed. He wanted a son, especially, to name after their father. Would that ever happen?

After they rested and began traveling again, it wasn't long before Garth held up a hand to stop them. They looked out over a lush valley dotted here and there with huge cottonwoods and willows. A creek meandered gracefully through the middle. Wildflowers bloomed in riotous profusion. They dismounted to stand and look over the valley.

"Oh, my lands, this is breathtaking. How did you discover it, Garth?" Aunt Twila stood in the buggy looking outward, her bonnet screening her from the sun rays.

Garth couldn't help the raw elation rushing through him as he remembered the day he first saw the place. He beckoned for them to come down into the valley.

In spite of the dry heat of the desert, in

the valley buttercups and wild pink flowers bloomed along the edge of the creek, while puffs of cotton from the trees flittered in the air like thistledown. They headed toward the shade of a tree with a trunk as large as two men standing together.

"It's like day and night, coming into this valley," Sam exclaimed in delight. "Oh, I hope when this is all over, you can build your ranch, Garth. If we get our inheritance back from Tremayne and can sell the mansion in St. Louis, you would have plenty of money."

"It's what I'm hoping for, too, Sis. I fell in love with this place the first time I laid eyes on it. I hope you will come with me."

Sam shook her head. "That's sweet, Garth. But this is your dream, not mine. I might have something else in mind." She wanted to pursue the idea of the newspaper — and then there was Jay. Somehow, she couldn't see Jay as a rancher.

"How about you, Aunt Twila? And the major?" Garth persisted.

"By Jove, I envy you, Son. It's a beauty," the major enthused.

Aunt Twila's brow wrinkled while she carefully considered her words. "Like the major said, Garth, it is truly a lovely place. I can easily see your dream manifesting itself here. But no, I'm getting too old and set in my ways for such a drastic change." She shifted a bony hip to stand straighter. Obviously, the movement pained her. "I came out here because you two needed me. But now Samantha has Clarence J., and I would feel better if I knew you had someone, Garth."

He grinned, his face handsome in the sunlight. "I might have found someone special. But you are worrying me. You sound as if you're ready to take off on the next stage out of here." Garth and Sam looked at their aunt, concern in their expressions.

"Not on the next stage, certainly. I will stay to see this Millard thing through, I promise you that. But it's been a long time since I've done so much cooking and house-work. Not that I'm complaining, mind you." She held up her hand to stop their protests.

"Oh, my, we have put a lot of work on your shoulders, haven't we?" Sam went to her aunt and hugged her. Garth did the same. She laughed at them and pulled away gently.

"I'd like to get back to civilization. I like to be waited on, and I have two loyal servants waiting for me back home. I can see you both have found your places here, but it's far too raw and uncouth for me. It

478

isn't my cup of tea." She looked in dismay at their crestfallen faces.

"I say, don't I have a voice in this conversation?" the major sputtered.

Aunt Twila turned, giving him her best withering glare, which rolled off him without making a dent.

"You! What in the world do you have to say about what concerns me?"

Sam rolled her eyes. *Here we go again.* She almost felt sorry for the major, but he kept putting the wrong foot forward with her aunt.

"But Lovey, I thought we had an understanding," the major protested, a pained look on his face.

"Understanding!" Aunt Twila's voice rose several decibels, and the horse standing next to her reared in surprise. They all smothered their laughs, and some of the hostility in the air faded away.

"Do you want Garth and me to go on ahead?" Sam asked.

"Nonsense," Aunt Twila flared. "We have no secrets, I assure you."

The major scratched his head in puzzlement. "You seemed taken with Annabel," he offered weakly.

"So what?" Her anger frittered away slowly.

"What if I told you I planned to make more like her? We might be rich someday. Everyone who sees the old gal wants one just like her."

"Pish. Pipe dreams. Anyway, I don't care about being rich. I told you, I like my comforts, and I can provide my own, thank you."

He cocked his head, looking like the earnest young man he used to be. "And at night? Don't you get lonely for companionship?" He took her hand, and she didn't pull away.

Sam and Garth had gradually backed away from the two older folk.

"Isn't it awful, the major acting so hurt? Do you think he's spreading it on too thick?" Sam asked.

Garth chuckled. "I don't know. If he is, he's darned good at it. Had me feeling sorry for him, the old rascal."

"But he's an itinerant, unemployed bum if you get right down to it. Granted, he's lovable and has a certain air of good breeding, but how does he support himself, and what could he provide for Aunt Twila?" Sam thought she sounded very logical and reasonable.

"True. Everything you say is true, Sam. But she has enough to take care of them both, and somehow I don't think he would be too proud to share it with her. Not at the prospect of losing her. Can't you tell he worships her?"

Garth motioned for them to get back on their horses. They descended into the valley and pulled up beside a cottonwood tree to spread out their lunch. Fried chicken and biscuits spread with honey butter tasted good, Sam thought. From the buggy she retrieved the keg with lemonade, kept cool by wrapping with a blanket that had been soaked in water before they left. Aunt Twila had baked peach turnovers for dessert. They lay back on the sweet-smelling grass when they'd finished eating. Cloud shadows flitted through the leafy tree, drifting across Sam's closed eyelids. The major and Aunt Twila talked softly, in case anyone wanted to doze.

When the clouds began to gather closer together and the wind picked up, Sam stood and stirred the others. She didn't want to travel through the desert in another sandstorm, although she didn't smell wind or rain.

By the time they reached the boardinghouse, they'd barely got the buggy stashed inside the stable and the horses unharnessed before rain started pelting down. They ran inside in a hurry.

"Oh, Lordy, we should have left someone home to watch out for things." Sam had gone upstairs and stared at her ransacked bedroom. She ran out into the hallway to Garth. He stood in the middle of a chaotically destroyed room, hands on hips, mouth open in shock. He hurried to his desk and pulled open the drawer, turning to Sam with dismay written all over his face.

"I'm missing some valuable papers. Why didn't I hide them?"

By now, all of the other boarders had left to find other lodgings. No one had been home when the intruders saw their opportunity.

"Ernestine and Wade!" Sam and Garth said at once. No one else would saunter in without someone noticing, and know which rooms to plunder. The other rooms were untouched.

Sam felt keen disappointment when she imagined the big, overgrown deputy engaged in such an underhanded trick. They needed to find the pair of Pinkertons if they hadn't gone to their uncle yet.

As luck would have it, Garth and Sam met Wade and Ernestine approaching them on main street. To Wade's credit, he didn't hesitate when he saw them coming.

"Hello, Samantha. Garth."

Ernestine didn't speak. She just stared at them unblinkingly.

"Haven't seen you two around lately," Sam began, not wanting to tip them off that they were number-one suspects in the recent pilferage of the boardinghouse.

Wade's broad shoulders moved in a shrug beneath his leather vest. Ernestine was uncharacteristically quiet. "I've missed your aunt's cooking, that's for sure," Wade said.

"We've missed your company too, Wade. But that's not exactly our fault is it?" Sam ignored Ernestine.

"Yeah, we had the two of you figured wrong. Must have amused the hell out of you," Garth snarled. He couldn't be polite any longer.

Wade and Ernestine knew immediately what he was referring to and apparently decided not to deny anything. Wade had the grace to appear embarrassed, but Ernestine tilted her nose in the air.

"We were doing our job, and you two broke the law. We have nothing, absolutely nothing, to be ashamed of," Ernestine declared haughtily.

"Did it occur to you to wonder why we did what we did?" Sam asked.

"Not really. And we don't care, either,"

Ernestine flared.

"Now hold on a minute," Wade frowned down at his wife. "I can speak for myself, and I wouldn't mind hearing their side." The group had gradually moved into the shade of a nearby corral.

Garth and Sam took turns telling the couple how their trouble had started and what had brought them to Powder. They told the story baldly, without frills or emotions. When they had finished, Wade looked off into space thoughtfully, but it was clear Ernestine was not impressed.

"Surely you don't believe that drivel, do you, Wade?" she asked.

He stared at her as if seeing her for the first time. "Why would they lie? We informed Mr. Tremayne who was behind his problems, and he agreed to set them aside as family business. Our work here is done."

Ernestine stamped her booted foot in exasperation. "Oh! You are so stupid. They want to impress us, of course. These two may well be going to jail for stealing documents."

"How would you know about any documents we might have stolen?" Garth asked.

Ernestine's mouth worked, but no words came out.

"What's going on here? What have you

been up to, Ernestine?" Wade took hold of her arm and shook her slightly.

When she didn't answer, Garth spoke. "Oh, nothing much. She broke into our home, ransacked our rooms, and rummaged through everything we own." He didn't mind exaggerating when he saw the look of outrage begin to spread on Wade's face.

"She took some valuable papers, and Lord only knows what else while we were all away," Sam added.

"*You* did that?" Wade stared down at Ernestine in horrified disbelief. "Why? Why would you do such a thing? We did what we were paid to do and were getting ready to leave."

Tears sprang into Ernestine's eyes, and she put her hand on Wade's arm. "Mr. Tremayne offered me . . . us . . . another five hundred dollars if I could come up with some proof of these people interfering in his affairs. I didn't see anything wrong in that. *They* are the crooks, not us." In spite of her words, her voice didn't hold the conviction it usually did.

Wade shook her arm again, causing her carefully piled-up hair to sag down around her shoulders in disarray. Her eyes expressed disbelief. Sam almost felt sorry for her. She had lost control of Wade and might never get it back again.

"What did you take from my room?" Garth demanded.

Ernestine appeared anxious. Wade had apparently never been out from under her thumb since they married. "It was only some old clippings from the newspapers, the *Tombstone Epitaph,* and this rag here in Powder, about a motley crew of desperados robbing stagecoaches and banks. Missing stock certificates and property deeds might have been mentioned." She buried her face in her hands and sobbed.

Garth and Sam looked at each other in dismay. They should have been leery of their uncle giving up so easily. They had figured that, no matter what he suspected, he had nothing actually connecting them to the robberies. But now, even with the evidence Jay claimed to hold against their uncle, they had lost their leverage. He held the winning hand of cards now. With his money and influence in town, he could do anything he wanted to them.

Sam wished Clarence J. were here, with his calm steadiness. "Don't worry, Garth. Even if he has these things to hold over us, he can't *prove* where he got them. It's her word against ours." Sam turned to Ernestine, but the look on the woman's face stunned her.

"It won't be that simple, I'm afraid," Ernestine stammered. "Y-you see, he made me sign an affidavit that I removed the papers from Garth's room."

"Oh, no!" Wade slapped the side of his head. "What else did my conniving wife do for her thirty pieces of silver?" He glared down at the hapless Ernestine and stepped away from her as if she contaminated him.

Sam had never seen the big, easygoing man so riled.

"I should turn you over my knee and whale the daylights out of you in front of everyone. Would serve you right," said Wade.

By now townsfolk were passing by, glancing their way curiously.

Ernestine looked up at Wade in shock, but gave no reply.

"Well, it's too bad, but none of this will get us anywhere," Sam said, looking at Garth for confirmation.

She could tell neither of them had a clue what to do next. They would have to wait for Millard Tremayne to act.

CHAPTER 37

It didn't take long. The next morning Tremayne's fancy carriage, with his crest prominently displayed on the side, pulled up in front of the boardinghouse. He sat, magnificently splendid, in the midst of scarlet velvet cushions, waiting impatiently for everyone to pour out the front door.

All four of his victims lined up beside his buggy, staring at him: Aunt Twila, the major, Sam, and Garth. He glared at them, his eyes slits in his pudgy cheeks. Peaches sat next to him, eyes downcast. Bright spots of shame dotted her cheeks.

Sam noticed Tremayne was so sure of himself, he hadn't brought a bodyguard. Probably didn't want any witnesses to what happened between them. Tremayne's jowls trembled with suppressed laughter when he noticed Garth staring at Peaches. Sam longed for her slingshot to give him one in the middle of his stomach and let some air

488

out. Especially when he reached a ringed hand over to rest possessively on Peaches's arm. Sam held her breath, not daring to look at Garth, but she heard his hissed intake of breath and saw his clenched fist. He must assume Peaches sat there by choice, but Sam was certain that wasn't true.

"I have come by to inform the lot of you that you are in for a real treat. I've sent to St. Louis for two of the most distinguished attorneys in the state who have never lost a case. I'm prepared to spend a hundred thousand dollars, if necessary, just to see justice done. My own family. Trying to ruin me."

"You can't prove a thing against us." Sam strove for dignity, but she wanted to shout at him. "You have stolen our inheritance and our home. And killed our father."

"Oh, God, not that again. I had nothing to do with that weakling's demise. And you will never see your inheritance again or your home. I've put the house up for sale. It's my right, and you owe me."

Peaches pushed his big hand away, steadfastly refusing to look at any of them. Tremayne pulled her closer to his side.

Sam was certain she spied the glint of tears beneath Peaches's lowered eyelashes.

As if the woman had told her, Sam knew she was submitting to her boss because of Garth. Davy must have threatened to hurt Garth if Peaches didn't behave.

Smiling in triumph, Tremayne flicked his reins over the horses, preparing to leave. Maddened beyond control, Garth leaped up into the carriage and smashed his fist into the fat man's face. Peaches screamed, and the major and Sam ran to pull Garth out of the carriage, while Aunt Twila hurried to hold the reins at the horses' heads so they wouldn't bolt. Later, the three of them would wonder how she'd found the courage to do this, as she wasn't fond of horses and feared them.

Sam and the major, along with two passing cowhands, pulled Garth away from Tremayne. Tremayne slumped on the seat with a bloodied nose, while Peaches reached across his girth, grabbed the reins, and turned the horses back toward the saloon.

In spite of the worry about her uncle's threats, seeing his bloody nose and the immaculately expensive shirt and jacket ripped in fury by Garth, gave Sam a shiver of satisfaction.

They didn't have long to wait for Millard Tremayne's reprisal. Wade came by the boardinghouse later in the day to warn them. Tremayne had sworn out a warrant for Garth's arrest on assault and battery charges and, as soon as the papers were served, Garth was headed for jail.

"Thanks for the warning, Wade. That's good of you, considering, but I'm not running." Garth sat on the porch swing, his mouth narrowed with a stubborn twist.

"But dear, don't you think it would be wise to leave for a few days. Perhaps Millard will rethink his fury." Aunt Twila sat at Garth's side and patted his hand distractedly. The strained look in her eyes told Sam she didn't really believe what she'd said.

"She's jolly well right," the major piped up. "Show the blighter he can't lead you off to the jail like some bloody beast to slaughter. I should have planted him a facer, too."

His unfortunate choice of words caused both Sam and Aunt Twila to flinch.

Only Sam knew what motivated Garth to appear nonchalant about his fate. Early that morning, he received a note from Peaches. Garth showed it to them, his eyes filled with despair. Peaches apologized for any false impression she might have given him about her feelings for him. She had decided to accept Mr. Tremayne's generous offer of partnership in the saloon. She ended by saying that she hoped he would understand she wanted no further contact with him.

"Garth, can't you see something is wrong here? I am sure she was beginning to care deeply for you. Davy's behind this. I know it." Sam slammed her fist into her palm in frustration when she saw she wasn't getting through to her brother.

"I have to accept her decision, Sam. Why shouldn't she go for that bastard's deal? What do I have to offer her? If Millard takes our inheritance, as he threatens, we have only this boardinghouse and the money from Mother's will."

Sam gazed at him, sadness filling her heart. He was seeing the finish of his dream ranch and Peaches. A hard pill to swallow.

"Did you say the warrant was for assault and battery?" Sam asked Garth. "How come he didn't include breaking and entering, robbery, and all the other things he accused us of?"

Garth paced the wooden floor restlessly. "Hellfire, Sam. He doesn't want to jeopardize an open-and-shut case. He wants me put away safely for now, until his high-priced lawyers get to Powder. As if I'd run from the likes of that treacherous bastard."

Aunt Twila shuddered. "Ugh! He reminds me of a fat spider spinning his sticky web around us." Her thin lips twisted in a grimace. "I warned you both, but would you listen? Now we are all lost. If Garth goes into that jail, there's no telling what will happen to him, if Sam has described that Davy person accurately."

Sam looked at Garth, seeing the devastation in his eyes he tried to hide. He had to be thinking of Peaches, alone with his uncle, maybe submitting to his touch. He closed his eyes to shut Sam out, knowing she could see into his soul.

"And you, Wade? What are your plans? I suppose you'll have to remain here to testify." Sam struggled to keep the resentment from her voice. It was Ernestine who had proven their greatest enemy.

Wade put his hand on Garth's shoulder. "I'm taking Ernestine back East. We'll get lost for a few months. No need to testify. We owe you that much."

When Garth didn't answer, Sam spoke into the silence. "That's very generous of you, but do you think she'll go along with the idea?"

Wade grunted. "She'd better. I've suspected for some time now that she's had her own agenda without telling me, knowing I'd not approve. Sometimes our bank account increases more than it has reason to, but I've no head for figures and have always left that part of our marriage up to her. I reckon I move too slow to satisfy her ambitions. But she'll change. I know she will."

Sam wasn't so sure, but she kept her thoughts to herself. "Here they come." She turned toward the street, and they all watched the new deputy and his helper riding down the street toward them. When the two dismounted in front of the gathering, they tipped their hats politely to the women.

"Excuse me, ma'am." The man spoke directly to Aunt Twila, avoiding Sam and Garth. "I got a warrant for his arrest." He nodded at Garth. He sounded apologetic when he addressed Garth. "I recollect you helped me put out the fire in the jail and went along on the posse ride to find the Injun, young feller, but I got my orders."

"I understand and am ready to go." Garth stepped forward, holding his hands out. "I hope you don't have to handcuff me. I don't have any weapons."

The man standing beside the deputy looked disappointed. "You ain't gonna give us no trouble? We was told you needed close watching. Yore supposed to be a mighty tricky customer."

"I don't know who started that rumor, but it isn't true." Aunt Twila looked as if she wanted to take her umbrella to the man who'd just spoken, but refrained.

The four stood and watched Garth walk between the two mounted men, heading toward the jail. When Garth entered the jail and his eyes became accustomed to the dingy, dark interior, he gasped in surprise to hear a familiar voice coming from the corner of the cell.

"Hey, ole buddy. What brings you here?"

The deputy opened the cell door, and when Garth entered, the door clanged shut behind him. He walked closer to the bunk and, sure enough, there sat Elvin.

The deputy spoke from outside the cell door. "This here character claims to be the leader of that gang of desperados that's been plaguing Mr. Tremayne." As Garth's raised an eyebrow, the man continued. "It's real hard to take them serious, if the rumors about the members of that gang are true. This one sure fits the bill, all right." The deputy laughed loudly, slapping his hat against his thigh, and walked away.

When they were alone, Garth looked around cautiously. Two more men occupied the cell. One was sleeping off a drunk with the odor of sour mash billowing from his lips with each snore. The other man, a Mexican, turned his back and ignored them.

"You didn't answer me. What are you doing here?" Elvin asked.

"Nothing much," Garth said with a chuckle. "Punched an old geezer in the snoot. He was annoying my girl. But never mind that, you idiot. You won't get away with taking the blame for our gang. I'll never let you. How'd they catch you?"

"Catch me!" Elvin exploded off his bunk to face Garth, his voice raised in indignation. "I had the world's worst time getting in here. No one would believe me when I told them I was head of the desperados."

"But why? I don't get it." Garth took off his hat to scratch his head.

"I had to get back to Yuma. I lost my horse in a card game, trying to ante up enough to get grub and leave. I ran into Hard Rock Charlie, who just got out of Yuma Prison, and he told me the old gang was still there. They won't wait for me forever, you know. I been out a long time, although I don't reckon any of them will be up for a pardon any time soon."

Garth snorted. "You are certifiably crazy. I heard the summers there are deadly and the guards are brutal in Yuma."

"Say, didn't you hear a word I said? They are all there, waiting. My *friends.*" Elvin laughed in pure joy, as if his buddies had succeeded against all odds to outsmart the law and stay in prison.

"Besides," Elvin continued. "Most of what you said is rumor. Oh, it's hotter than the hinges of Hades in the summer. But you can't beat the winters in Yuma. And the guards, they take care of us. The warden and his missus even have picnics for us in the yard overlooking the Colorado River. 'Course we have to be in chains, but that's expected."

Garth sat down on a cot. "I guess we'll go together then, Elvin. My uncle's out for my blood, and it looks like he's finally scrounged up enough proof to get it."

"And Sam? Is she involved?"

"Thank goodness, no. So far, there's been no way for him to connect her, and I doubt he'd want to do that. He's always had a warm spot for Sam, if you can imagine him with a heart big enough to hold warmth for anyone. She'll be safe. I'm not letting you take all the blame for this crazy idea of mine though."

Elvin grinned and shook a stockinged foot at him playfully.

Garth smiled at the sight of his big toe sticking through a hole in the stocking. Aunt Twila would have darned that up promptly.

"Nothing you can do about it," Elvin said.

"Remember those papers you told me to burn after that bank job? Well, old buddy" — his voice echoed smug satisfaction — "I didn't do it. The papers was proof enough that I stole them from the bank."

Garth wanted to belt Elvin one in the mouth, and Elvin moved away.

Elvin held up his hand in an effort to make peace again. "It isn't that I intended any double-cross, Garth. I don't know why the hell I stuffed those papers in my saddle-bags, excepting they looked too pretty to burn. I decided I needed to hold on to them for a while. But when I tried to turn myself in, no one would believe I was the gang leader. They just laughed. So I got the papers out and showed them. After that, they were right obliging."

Garth groaned and stared up at the ceiling. "Why me, Lord? Why me?"

After a brief silence between them, Elvin spoke again. "Anyways, Garth, what will it hurt to keep your mouth shut for once? You don't have to admit to nothing, hear? Except maybe laying into that old scalawag you call uncle."

Garth closed his eyes in weary resignation. "If that's what you truly want, we'll try it for a time, but what if they want to hang you? Or both of us."

■ ■ ■ ■

Back at the boardinghouse, Sam, Twila, and the major sat in the kitchen drinking coffee and trying not to worry. Surely there was a way out of this mess. Jay had even hinted that when he returned, he could make everything all right. *If* he returned. Sam wasn't all that sure he would, and she felt heaviness in her heart to think she might never see him again.

While they sat despondently in silence, a boy came to the door announcing he was delivering a telegram for Lord Chauncey Claybourne. Sam and Twila watched the major in shock as he opened it.

When he finished reading the telegram, he turned to face Sam and Aunt Twila. "Beastly thing. My brother passed on. With no family, I'm the only one left to the manor." He spoke sadly, as if that explained everything.

"What are you yammering about? What manor? Sorry about your brother. What does this lord thing mean? Are you trying to impress me?" Aunt Twila fired off her questions like bullets aimed at the major.

"Yes, I'm sorry about your brother pass- ing," Sam said. "And it's so sad you weren't there for him."

"Brother Cecil has been ill with a lung condition since childhood, so his death was not unexpected. Although I would have liked to have been there with him in his last days. But we've never been close. I joined the British Calvary to escape the idea of the lordship duties. But they finally caught up with me, since there is no more family."

"But what does it mean? Will you leave soon?" For once Aunt Twila spoke to him with a surprising softness in her voice.

Sam was stunned to see tears that she tried to hold back lurking in her aunt's eyes. It was true what she and Garth had suspected all along. Her aunt and the major's bickering hid a deeper feeling between them. Now her aunt might lose her only chance to be with someone she really cared for.

"Ah, lassie, I'd not even think of leaving you. I should have told you sooner about this lord thing, but I wanted you to love me for my own sweet self."

"Why, you old goat. Now I've heard everything! Love you? That will be the day."

Sam started to get up and ease herself out of the room. Since they paid her no mind, she sat back, deciding to watch the fireworks.

The major only grinned at Aunt Twila's salvo, as if they'd been the sweetest love words ever spoken. "Hold up there, Lovey. Don't carry on so, bless you." He turned to regard Sam.

"My family founded a village generations ago. Ever since then, we've been obliged to run it for the blokes who live in it. We started a school and a church, and they pay us a portion of the profit from the fields and sheep they tend."

"In England?" Sam asked and felt foolish as soon as the words left her mouth.

"Of course, my dear. My brother loved the title and everything that went with it, while I jolly well avoided it. That is why I went to India, as far away from Old Blighty as I could get. But the title and land is entailed, and I've no choice now." He turned to Aunt Twila, who sat perched on the edge of her chair as if she wanted to dart away.

"Come back with me, pet. I see it all now. You would be a perfect Lady Claybourne. My, how you'd make those lazy servants jump about. You would love the home. It's perfect for you. I'll have another steam-powered bicycle just like Annabel made, and we can carouse about the countryside creating a great scandal. Put the blighters to shame with their fancy carriages."

"Hmph! You must be daft to imagine I'd go sashaying over to some foreign country where decent people don't even talk English properly." Aunt Twila's glare wasn't as telling as it usually was. She might be weakening.

Then she said, "I couldn't go if I wanted to. There's Garth to be seen to." Aunt Twila's voice softened. "Besides, you never said you cared for me."

"Oh, my precious one." The major knelt in front of Twila, grimacing when his knees creaked and didn't bend smoothly. "I've adored you since the first time I saw you. And I know you have strong feelings for me. You couldn't fuss and carry on so if you didn't." He took her roughened hand and rubbed it against his cheek. "I realize Garth is like a son to you, and we'll have to figure this all out, eh, Sam?" He turned to look at Sam, his eyes glinting with happiness. As if he'd already won Aunt Twila.

"I can take care of myself, Major," Sam said as if she'd read his unspoken question. "We'll see this through. I have faith that Clarence J. can bring back something to help us." But did she really have that much faith in him?

CHAPTER 38

Jay's telegram arrived before Sam, Twila, and the major set out to visit Garth. Sam gritted her teeth at Jay's brevity, but there it was. *Everyone to arrive in the morning on the stage from Benson.*

Everyone? Was he accompanying the expensive St. Louis attorneys? She longed to see Jay again, at least one more time. But everyone?

The stage was due any minute, so they had to postpone their visit to Garth in jail. They sat waiting outside the stage office on the hard wooden bench. Nearby, but not too close, stood the magnificent carriage of Millard Tremayne. Inside they saw the fat man and Peaches by his side. She kept her face averted from Sam and the others. It was hard to see her expression, especially with the bonnet she wore, but Tremayne cast venomous glares their way from time to time.

"I wonder why he's here." Sam said the words out loud, but didn't expect either the major or Aunt Twila to respond. Sam prayed hard that Jay hadn't brought the attorneys with him. She was almost grateful Garth wasn't present to witness Peaches sitting beside their uncle. As usual, the stage was late, but soon they saw the dust rising from its wheels that heralded the running horses.

Sam, the major, and Aunt Twila watched with apprehension as two well-dressed, confident-looking men stepped down from the coach and brushed themselves off. They glanced around briefly; both of their noses went into the air simultaneously, as if they smelled something bad, and they headed directly for Tremayne's buggy. The attorneys.

Sam held her breath, her heart thumping hard in her chest, when Jay stepped down from the coach. His sharp blue eyes searched the group on the porch until he located her. His broad smile melted her to her toes. He turned back to the stage and held out his hand to someone.

"Grace Tremayne!" Aunt Twila's voice split the air in a most uncharacteristic screech.

The lady in question glanced in their direction and nodded. It was as if the temperature in Powder suddenly lowered by ten degrees. Sam followed Aunt Grace's gaze to her uncle, who no longer lounged on the carriage cushions with one arm slung over Peaches's shoulder. His already-buggy eyes bugged more, and his usually florid complexion turned waxy pale. He moved to push Peaches away, but she must have had a notion about what was taking place. She clung to his arm possessively and leaned against his shoulder. Peaches's quick wink at Sam spoke volumes.

Jay bowed to Sam, the major, and Aunt Twila, and turned to escort Grace to the buggy. By now Tremayne had pushed Peaches away, and his driver had leaped down to open the buggy door. For a moment it seemed as if Tremayne wasn't going to step foot outside the carriage.

"Millard Tremayne!" Grace's voice shrilled into the sudden quiet. It must have been like chalk on a blackboard, because all the watchers cringed. By now Tremayne had shifted his bulk out of the buggy to face his wife.

Less than half his size, skinny as a toothpick, Grace shifted the rimless glasses perched on the end of her nose and glared. "Get that hussy away from my sight!" She pointed in the direction of Peaches, who had crept out of the buggy and now headed toward Sam.

"Now, now, dearest. I am delighted and surprised to see you." Tremayne's voice trembled as he walked toward her. "There is no need to air our linen in public, my sweet."

"Public, indeed." Grace glared at the surrounding audience made up of townsfolk who stopped and stared out of curiosity. "No doubt they all know about your philandering and wicked ways." She grabbed hold of his neckpiece and held on like a bulldog.

"I've put up with your pompous, arrogant bullying long enough. The money you squandered belonged to me, bequeathed to me by my sainted papa. *My* money gave you your power, and I'm taking it away. These two nice young men you hired as lawyers are now in my employ." She turned and gazed fondly at Jay.

"If this young man had not come to my home and told me the whole sordid story of what you've done, I would never have believed the telegram Twila sent asking me to come out here."

Tremayne turned his head as much as he was able to glare at Jay and Twila and the rest of them standing by. A step or two away from the buggy and Grace, Davy stood, picking his teeth with a straw and grinning.

"As of this minute, you are out of the company and you will be out unless and until I hear a lot of explaining. You might never get back in. Then let's see if your hussies want you or not." She hadn't lowered her voice in spite of being almost in his face.

Even though her voice gradually came down an octave or two, it was plain to see her regular manner of speaking was high and shrill — something Tremayne must have had a hard time living with on a daily basis. Sam and Garth had never been close to Aunt Grace. She was not a warm person. But they had visited from time to time when they thought they should.

"Let me back in the company?" Tremayne asked. "What do you mean?"

It might have been a smile that crossed Grace's face, but if it was, it fooled everyone watching. "I mean what I said. Mr. Clarence J. Westcott has shown me evidence of your culpability. You have defrauded people and failed to repay bonds of your investors. But your most grievous offense was your ridiculous idea of starting up a life out here unbeknownst to me. These nice young men who journeyed out here with me say I have an iron-clad case that will allow me to take back everything. Leave you out here with your floozies, and then what?"

"But . . . but honeykins. Those are *my* lawyers. You can't threaten me. You're a female. My wife. You have no power on your own." Tremayne blustered but didn't look at all sure of himself.

"The hell she hasn't any power." Jay left Sam's side and walked up to the battling Tremaynes. "In the time it took us to get here, we talked it all out. Mrs. Tremayne has the power to reclaim the money her father left her, or what's left of it. If necessary, trustees will be appointed to help her decide how to proceed."

"You!" Tremayne exploded in fury, his face turning bright red, his eyes bulging. "I should have had Davy make sure you were dead when he shot you. You have been a viper in my breast from the first. You and Garth. At least he has been taken care of."

Davy and some of the boys had edged forward when Jay stepped close to Tremayne, but Tremayne waved them away. "Never mind, it's too late." He gritted his teeth and pointed at the saloon. "Go collect your wages from the barkeep and be gone." His face, no longer pale but florid, beaded with perspiration.

"You win," Tremayne said, his voice composed and drained. "What do you want

508

from me?" He looked at his wife, who had finally released his neckpiece so he could catch his breath.

"That is more like it." Grace took off her glasses and polished them with the handkerchief she jerked from his vest pocket. "I want you to stop this outlandish notion of moving out here to this godforsaken place. No insult intended." She turned to look at her audience, and centered her attention on Sam, Aunt Twila, the major, and Jay.

"Your attorneys will help me get rid of your holdings, profitably if possible, and you'll be coming home with me. Where you belong. If I ever so much as *suspect* you are straying again, there will be no more warnings. You will be out on your arse." She blushed at her outspokenness, but stood straight and stared into his eyes.

Tremayne relaxed for a moment, now that the worst seemed to be over. Until he caught a smile between Jay and Sam. Then he burst out in rage, "What about my thieving nephew? I put him in jail, and there he will stay until the circuit judge comes this way. May take months." His lips curled in a vindictive smile.

This time Sam stepped forward. "He was only trying to stop you from plundering our inheritance, and we wanted justice for our father." She longed to jerk his neckpiece, as her aunt did, but refrained, not wanting to get that close to him.

Tremayne shook his head. All his anger had leaked out of him, and he deflated before their eyes. "I always thought the world of you, Samantha. You were such a charming little girl. I didn't have anything directly to do with your father's death. I've told you that."

"Then what about Garth?" Aunt Twila moved to Sam's side. "He can't get away with destroying his own nephew," she said to Grace. "You won't let him, will you?"

Grace shook her head. "The boy will be out by this evening, or I'll know the reason why. I owe you a debt of gratitude for sending me that letter about this scoundrel, even though I refused to believe its contents at the time. Some of the proceeds of the sale of property here and other places he might own will go to reimburse Sam and Garth for what he has stolen from them. I will be happy to see you three ensconced back in St. Louis where you belong."

Sam and Jay held hands. "We aren't going back to St. Louis, Aunt Grace. Garth and I have found a place we can call our own here in this 'godforsaken' place, as you called it." She turned to smile at Jay. "When our in-

510

heritance is restored, I plan to buy a half-interest in the *Powder Keg,* our local newspaper, and Jay wants to start an accounting office here."

"I don't object to marrying a beauty with an armful of money." Jay laughed and kissed her upturned lips.

"You haven't asked me yet," Sam protested.

"Must I get down on one knee in this dust?" He pretended to brush his pants leg.

Sam laughed. "Oh, no. Forget about acting like the old blue jay. I won't fall for that again, ever."

"And Garth?" Aunt Grace prompted.

Sam grinned. "He has staked a claim on what is to be his ranch, and I believe he knows who will share it with him." She looked directly at Peaches, who turned a bright red.

"Do you think he will forgive me if I explained why I went back with Millard?" she asked.

Sam patted her shoulder. "You bet. He knew you were only trying to protect him against Davy and his men. We know you are blameless."

The major moved to the front, dragging a reluctant Aunt Twila. "And I shall return to England with my lovely bride. If she will have us. That is, Annabel and me."

For once, Aunt Twila remained speechless, but Sam could see she was pleased and not against the idea. Sam would miss her aunt dreadfully but she would love to have a chance to visit her in England.

"Maybe we could have a double wedding, if Garth is agreeable. What do you think about that, Samantha?" Jay asked.

"Double wedding, my foot!" Aunt Twila shook her umbrella at Peaches and Sam. "What is wrong with a triple wedding before this blighter hauls himself off to England without me?"

And that's exactly what they did.

ABOUT THE AUTHOR

Pinkie Paranya is an established author with eighteen published novels of varied genres. She has also written more than fifty poems, multiple gardening and Op-Ed newspaper articles, a book of short stories, and a memoir.

Born and raised in Phoenix, Arizona, she and her late husband traveled extensively from Alaska to Mexico, where she experienced different cultures that played important roles in her books. The desert has always been her favorite place to live, so she settled in Yuma, Arizona, with her cats, family, and friends.

Visit her website at www.pinkieparanya .com.